THE PLAYBOY OF ROME

BY
JENNIFER FAYE

Published in Great Britain 2015
by Mills & Boon, an imprint of Harlequin (UK) Limited,
Eton House, 18-24 Paradise Road, Richmond, Surrey, TW9 1SR

ISBN: 978-0-263-25118-0

23-0315

Harlequin (UK) Limited's policy is to use papers that are natural, renewable and recyclable products and made from wood grown in sustainable forests. The logging and manufacturing processes conform to the legal environmental regulations of the country of origin.

Printed and bound in Spain
by CPI, Barcelona

Award-winning author **Jennifer Faye** pens fun, heart-warming romances. Jennifer has won the RT Reviewers' Choice Award, is a TOP PICK author, and has been nominated for numerous awards. Now living her dream, she resides with her patient husband, one amazing daughter (the other remarkable daughter is off chasing her own dreams) and two spoiled cats. She'd love to hear from you via her website: JenniferFaye.com.

For Ami.
To a wonderful friend who has kept me company
as we've walked a similar path.
Thank you for your friendship
and unwavering encouragement.

CHAPTER ONE

"*Scusa*."

Dante DeFiore stepped into the path of a young woman trying to skirt around the line at Ristorante Massimo. Her long blond hair swished over her shoulder as she turned to him. Her icy blue gaze met his. The impact of her piercing stare rocked him. He couldn't turn away. Thick black eye-liner and sky-blue eye shadow that shimmered succeeded in making her stunning eyes even more extraordinary.

Dante cleared his throat. "Signorina, are you meeting someone?"

"No, I'm not."

"Really?" He truly was surprised. "Someone as beautiful as you shouldn't be alone."

Her fine brows rose and a smile tugged at her tempting lips.

He smiled back. Any other time, he'd have been happy to ask her to be his personal guest but not tonight. Inwardly he groaned. Why did he have to have his hands full juggling both positions of maître d' and head chef when the most delicious creature was standing in front of him?

He choked down his regret. It just wasn't meant to be. Tonight there was no time for flirting—not even with this stunning woman who could easily turn heads on the runways of Milan.

He glanced away from her in order to clear his thoughts. Expectant looks from the people waiting to be seated reminded him of his duties. He turned back to those amazing blue eyes. "I hate to say this, but you'll have to take your place at the end of the line."

"It's okay." Her pink glossy lips lifted into a knowing smile. "You don't have to worry. I work here."

"Here?" Impossible. He'd certainly remember her. By the sounds of her speech, she was American.

"This is Mr. Bianco's restaurant, isn't it?"

"Yes, it is."

"Then I'm in the right place."

Suddenly the pieces fell into place. His staff had been cut in half because of a nasty virus running rampant throughout Rome. He'd called around to see if any business associates could loan him an employee or two. Apparently when Luigi said he might be able to track down a friend of one of his daughters, he'd gotten lucky.

Relief flooded through Dante. Help was here at last and by the looks of her, she'd certainly be able to draw in the crowds. Not so long ago, they hadn't needed anyone to draw in customers; his grandfather's cooking was renowned throughout Rome. But in recent months all of that had changed.

"And I'd be the luckiest man in the world to have such a beauty working here. You'll have the men lined up down the street. Just give me a moment." Dante turned and signaled to the waiter.

When Michael approached Dante, the man's forehead was creased in confusion. "What do you need?"

In that moment, Dante's mind drew a blank. All he could envision were those mesmerizing blue eyes. This was ridiculous. He had a business to run.

When he glanced over at the line of customers at the door, the anxious stares struck a chord in his mind. "Michael, could you seat that couple over there?" He pointed to an older couple. "Give them the corner table. It's their fortieth anniversary, so make sure their meal is on us."

"No *problema*."

Lines of exhaustion bracketed Michael's mouth. Dante couldn't blame the guy. Being shorthanded and having to see to the dining room himself was a lot of work.

Dante turned his attention back to his unexpected employee. She had her arms crossed and her slender hip hitched to the side. A slight smile pulled at the corners of her lush lips as though she knew she'd caught him off guard—something that rarely happened to him.

He started to smile back when a patron entered the door and called out a greeting, reminding Dante that work came first. Since his grandfather was no longer around to help shoulder the burden of running this place, Dante's social life had been reduced to interaction with the guests of Ristorante Massimo.

After a brief *ciao* to a regular patron, Dante turned back to his temporary employee. "Thanks for coming. If you give me your coat, I can hang it up for you."

"I've got it." She clutched the lapels but made no attempt to take it off.

"You can hang it over there." He pointed to the small cloakroom. "We can work out everything later."

"You want me to start right now?"

That was the plan, but perhaps Luigi had failed to make that part clear. "Didn't he tell you that you'd be starting right away?"

"Yes, but I thought I'd have a chance to look around. And I didn't think I'd be a hostess."

"Consider this an emergency. I promise you it's not hard. I'm certain you'll be fantastic…uh…" Did she give him her name? If she had, he couldn't recall it. "What did you say your name is?"

"Lizzie. Lizzie Addler."

"Well, Lizzie, it's a pleasure to meet you. I'm Dante. And I really appreciate you pitching in during this stressful time."

"Are you sure you want me out here? I'd be a lot more help in the kitchen."

The kitchen? With her looks, who would hide such a gem behind closed doors? Perhaps she was just shy. Not that anything about her stunning appearance said that she was an introvert.

"I'd really appreciate it if you could help these people find a table."

She nodded.

An assistant rushed out of the kitchen. "We need you."

By the harried look on the young man's face, Dante knew it couldn't be good. He turned to his new employee. There would be time for introductions and formalities later. Right now, he just needed to keep the kitchen from falling behind and giving the patrons an excuse to look for food elsewhere.

"Sorry for this rush but I am very shorthanded." When the girl sent him a puzzled look, he realized that Luigi might not have filled her in on the details of her duties. "If you could just get everyone seated and get their drinks, Michael can take their orders. Can you do that?"

She nodded before slipping off her long black coat to reveal a frilly white blouse that hinted at her willowy figure, a short black skirt that showed off her long legs and a pair of knee-high sleek black boots. He stifled a whistle. Definitely not the reaction a boss should give an employee, even if she was gorgeous enough to create a whirlwind of excitement on the cover of a fashion magazine.

He strode to the kitchen, hoping that nothing had caught fire and that no one had been injured. When was this evening going to end? And had his grandfather's friend Luigi been trying to help by sending Lizzie? Or trying to drive him to distraction?

Once the kitchen was again humming along, he retraced his steps just far enough to catch a glimpse of the blonde bombshell. She moved about on those high-heeled boots as if they were a natural extension of her long legs. He swallowed hard as his eyes followed her around the dining room. He assured himself that he was just doing his duty by checking up on her.

When she smiled and chatted with a couple of older gentlemen, Dante's gut tightened. She sure seemed far more at ease with those men than when he'd been talking with her. How strange. Usually he didn't have a problem making conversation with the female gender. Lizzie was certainly different. Too bad she wouldn't be around long enough to learn more about her. She intrigued him.

Obviously there was a misunderstanding.

Lizzie Addler frowned as she locked the front door of Ristorante Massimo. She hadn't flown from New York to Italy to be a hostess. She was here to work in the kitchen—to learn from the legendary chef, Massimo Bianco. And to film a television segment to air on the culinary channel's number-one-rated show. It was a dream come true.

The strange thing was she'd flown in two days early, hoping to get her bearings in this new country. How in the world did this Dante know she was going to show up this evening?

It was impossible. But then again, this smooth-talking man seemed to know who she was. So why put her on hostess duty when he knew that her true talents lay in the kitchen?

Her cheeks ached from smiling so much, but all it took was recalling Dante's flattering words and the corners of her lips lifted once again. She'd heard rumors that Italian men were known to be charmers and now that she knew that it was true—at least in Dante's case—she'd have to be careful around him. She couldn't lose focus on her mission here.

She leaned her back against the door and sighed. She couldn't remember the last time her feet ached this much.

Why in the world had she decided to wear her new boots today of all days?

Oh, yes, to make a good impression. And technically the boots weren't new—just new to her. They were second-hand, like all of Lizzie's things. But in her defense, some of her things still had the tags on them when she'd found them at the gently used upscale boutique. And boy, was she thankful she'd splurged on the stylish clothes.

Her gaze strayed to the wall full of framed pictures of celebrities. There were black and whites as well as color photos through the years. Massimo was in a lot of them alongside movie stars, singers and politicians from around the world. As Lizzie scanned the many snapshots, she found Dante's handsome face. In each photo of him, he was smiling broadly with his arm around a beautiful woman.

"Pretty impressive?"

She knew without looking that it'd be Dante. "Very impressive." She forced her gaze to linger on the army of photos instead of rushing to ogle the tall, dark and undeniably handsome man at her side. "Have all of these people eaten here?"

"Yes. And there are more photos back in the office. We ran out of space out here." His voice was distinguishable with its heavy Italian accent. The rich tones flowed through her as seductively as crème brûlée. "We should add your photo."

"Me." She pressed a hand to her chest. "But I'm a nobody."

"You, my dear, are definitely not a nobody." His gaze met hers and heat rushed to her cheeks. "Is everything wrapped up out here?"

Her mouth went dry and she struggled to swallow. "Yes…yes, the last customer just left."

Lines of exhaustion etched the tanned skin around his dark eyes. His lips were lifted in a friendly smile, but something told her that it was all for her benefit and that he didn't feel like doing anything but calling it a night.

"I can't thank you enough for your help this evening." His gaze connected with hers, making her pulse spike. "I suppose you'll be wanting your pay so that you can be on your way. If you would just wait a moment."

Before she could formulate words, he turned and headed to the back of the restaurant. Pay her? For what? Playing hostess for the evening? She supposed that was above and beyond her contract negotiations with the television network.

Dante quickly returned and placed some euros in her hand. His fingers were warm as the backs of his fingers brushed over her palm, causing her stomach to quiver. She quickly pulled her hand away.

"Thank you so much. You truly were a lifesaver." He moved to the door to let her out.

She didn't follow him. She wasn't done here. Not by a long shot. "I'm not leaving. Not yet."

Dante shot her a puzzled look. "If this is about the money, this is the amount I told Luigi I was willing to pay—"

Lizzie shook her head. "It's not that. I came here to meet with Chef Massimo."

"You did? You mean Luigi didn't send you?"

"I don't know any Luigi."

Dante reached in his pocket and pulled out his smartphone. A few keystrokes later, he glanced up. "My mistake. Luigi wasn't able to find anyone to help out. Thank goodness you showed up."

"And I was happy to help. Now if you could introduce me to Chef Massimo."

Dante's forehead creased. "That's not going to happen." His tone was firm and unbendable. "He's not here. You'll have to deal with me."

"I don't think so. I'll wait for him."

Dante rubbed the back of his neck and sighed. "You'll be waiting a long time. Chef Massimo is out of town."

"Listen, I know I'm here a couple of days ahead of time, but we do have an agreement to meet."

"That's impossible." Dante's shoulders straightened and his expression grew serious. "I would have known. I know about everything that has to do with this place."

"Obviously not in this case." Lizzie pressed her lips together, immediately regretting her outburst. She was tired after her long flight and then having to work all evening as a hostess.

"You're obviously mixed up. You should be going." He pulled open the front door, letting a cool evening breeze sweep inside and wrap around her.

She couldn't leave. Her whole future was riding on this internship, and the money from participating in the upcoming cooking show would pay for her sister's grad school. She couldn't let her down. She'd promised Jules that if she got accepted to graduate school she'd make sure there was money for the tuition. Jules had already had so many setbacks in her life that Lizzie refused to fail her.

She stepped up to Dante, and even though she was wearing heeled boots, she still had to tilt her chin upward to look him in the eyes. "I did you a big favor tonight. The least you can do is hear me out."

Dante let the door swing shut and led her back to the dining room, where he pulled out a chair for her before he took a seat across the table. "I'm listening."

Lizzie wished it wasn't so late in the evening. Dante looked wiped out, not exactly the optimal position to gain his understanding. Still, she didn't have any other place to go.

Her elbows pressed down on the white linen tablecloth as she folded her hands together. "Chef Massimo has agreed to mentor me."

Dante's gaze narrowed in on her. "Why is this the first I'm hearing of it?"

"Why should you know about it? My agreement isn't with you."

"Massimo Bianco is my maternal grandfather. And with him away, I'm running this place."

This man wasn't about to give an inch, at least not easily. "When will he return so we can straighten things out?"

Dante leaned back in his chair and folded his arms. His dark eyes studied her. She'd love to know what he was thinking. Then again, maybe not. The past couple of days had been nothing but a blur. She'd rushed to wrap up her affairs in New York City before catching a transatlantic flight. The last thing she'd wanted to do was play hostess, but she figured she'd be a good sport. After all, Dante seemed to be in a really tight spot. But now she didn't understand why he was being so closemouthed about Massimo.

"All you need to know is that my grandfather won't be returning. So any business you have with him, you'll have to deal with me. Tell me about this agreement."

Uneasiness crept down her spine. This man had disbelief written all over his handsome features. But what choice did she have but to deal with him since she had absolutely no idea how to contact Chef Massimo? The only phone number she had was for this restaurant. And the email had also been for the restaurant.

"The agreement is for him to mentor me for the next two months."

Dante shook his head. "It isn't going to happen. I'm sorry you traveled all of this way for nothing. But you'll have to leave now."

Lizzie hadn't flown halfway around the globe just to be turned away—she'd been rejected too many times in her life. Her reasons for being here ran deeper than appearing on the television show. She truly wanted to learn from the best and Massimo Bianco was a renowned chef, whose name on her résumé would carry a lot of weight in the culinary world.

"Surely you could use the extra help." After what she'd witnessed this evening, she had no doubt about it.

"If not for this virus going around, Massimo's would be fully staffed. We don't have room for someone else in the kitchen."

"Obviously Chef Bianco doesn't agree with your assessment. He assured me there would be a spot for me."

Dante's eyes darkened. "He was mistaken. And now that I've heard you out, I must insist that you leave."

These days she proceeded cautiously and was always prepared. She reached in her oversize purse and pulled out the signed document. "You can't turn me away."

When she held out a copy of the contract, Dante's dark brows rose. Suddenly he didn't look as in charge as he had just a few seconds ago. Funny how a binding legal document could change things so quickly.

When he reached for the papers, their fingers brushed. His skin was warm and surprisingly smooth. Their gazes met and held. His eyes were dark and mysterious. Instead of being intimidated by him, she was drawn to him.

Not that she was in Italy to have a summer romance. She had a job to do and this man was standing between her and her future. He may be stubborn, but he'd just met his match.

CHAPTER TWO

WHAT WAS IT about this woman that had him feeling off-kilter?

Could it be the way her touch sent currents of awareness up his arm? Realizing they were still touching, Dante jerked his hand away. He clenched his fingers, creasing the hefty document.

Or maybe it was those cool blue eyes of hers that seemed to study his every move. It was as though she could see more of him than he cared for anyone to observe. Not that he had any secrets to hide—well, other than his plans to sell the *ristorante*.

His gaze scrolled over the first lines of the document, pausing when he saw his grandfather's name followed by Ristorante Massimo. He continued skimming over the legalese until his gaze screeched to a halt at the mention of a television show. His gut twisted into a knot. This was much more involved than he'd ever imagined.

"You said this was for an internship. You didn't mention anything about a television show."

Her lips moved but nothing came out. It was as though she wasn't sure exactly how to proceed. If she thought he was going to make this easy for her, she'd have to think again. She'd tried to get him to agree to let her work here under false pretenses when in fact she had much bigger plans.

When she didn't respond fast enough, he added, "How

long were you planning to keep that little bit of information a secret?"

Her forehead wrinkled. "Obviously I wasn't keeping it a secret or I wouldn't have handed you the contract."

She had a valid point, but it didn't ease his agitation. He once again rubbed at his stiff neck. It'd been an extremely long day. Not only was he short-staffed but also the meeting with the potential buyers for the *ristorante* hadn't gone well. They didn't just want the building. They also wanted the name and the secret recipes that put his grandfather's name up there with the finest chefs.

Dante didn't have the right to sell those recipes—recipes that went back to his grandmother's time. They were special to his grandfather. Still, selling them would keep them alive for others to enjoy instead of them being forgotten in a drawer. But could he actually approach his grandfather and ask for the right to sell them? Those recipes were his grandfather's pride and joy. In fact, employees signed a nondisclosure agreement to maintain the secrecy of Massimo's signature dishes. The thought of selling out left a sour taste in Dante's mouth.

"As you can see in the contract, the television crew will be here on Tuesday." Her words brought Dante back to his latest problem.

"I also see that you've arrived a couple of days early." He wasn't sure what he meant by that statement. He was stalling. Thinking.

"I like to be prepared. I don't like surprises. So I thought I'd get settled in and maybe see some of the sights in Rome. I've heard it's a lovely city."

"Well, since my grandfather isn't going to be able to mentor you, perhaps you can have an extended holiday before heading back to—"

"New York. And I didn't come here for a vacation. I came here to work and to learn." She got to her feet. "Maybe I should just speak with one of the people in the kitchen. Perhaps they can point me in the direction of your grandfather."

"That won't be necessary."

His grandfather didn't need to be bothered with this—he had more important issues to deal with at the moment. Dante could and would handle this woman. After all, there had to be a way out of this. Without reading the rest of the lengthy details, he flipped to the last page.

"It's all signed and legal, if that's what you're worried about." Her voice held a note of confidence, and she sat back down.

She was right. Right there in black and white was his grandfather's distinguished signature. There was no denying the slope of the *M* or the scroll of *Bianco*. Dante resisted the urge to ball up the document and toss it into the stone fireplace across the room from them. Not that it would help since the fire had been long ago extinguished.

He refused to let the sale of the *ristorante*—the deal he'd been negotiating for weeks—go up in smoke because of some promotional deal his grandfather had signed. There had to be a way around it. Dante wondered how much it'd take to convince Lizzie to quietly return to New York.

"I'm sure we can reach some sort of agreement." He was, after all, a DeFiore. He had access to a sizable fortune. "What will it take for you to forget about your arrangement with my grandfather?"

She sat up straighter. "Nothing."

"What do you mean nothing?"

"I mean that I'm not leaving." She leaned forward, pressing her elbows down on the tabletop. "I don't think you understand how serious I am. I've cut out months of my life for this internship. I've said goodbye to my family and friends in order to be here. I had to quit my job. Are you getting the picture? Everything is riding on this agreement—my entire future. I have a signed agreement and I intend to film a television segment in that kitchen." She pointed over her shoulder.

She'd quit her job!

Who did something like that? Obviously someone very trusting or very desperate. Which type was she? Her beautiful face showed lines of stress and the darkness below her eyes hinted at her exhaustion. He was leaning toward the desperate scenario.

Perhaps he'd been too rough on her. He really hadn't meant to upset her. He knew how frustrating it could be to be so close to getting what you wanted and yet having a barricade thrown in the way.

"Listen, I know this isn't what you want to hear, but I'm sure you'll be able to land another job somewhere else—"

"And what are you planning to do about the film crew when they arrive?"

Dante's lips pressed together. Yes, what was he going to do? This situation was getting ever so complicated. He eyed up the woman. Was she on the level? Was she truly after the work experience? The opportunity to learn? Or was she an opportunist playing on his sympathies?

He certainly didn't want to spend his time inflating her ego in front of the camera crew for the next two months—two very long months. But he was getting the very unsettling feeling that there was no way over, around or under the arrangement without a lengthy, messy lawsuit, which would hold up the sale of the *ristorante*.

This was not how things were supposed to go.

Lizzie resisted the urge to get up and start pacing. It was what she usually did when she was stuck in a tough spot. While growing up in the foster care system, she'd found herself in plenty of tough spots. But the one thing she'd learned through it all was not to give up—if it was important enough, there had to be a solution. It'd worked to keep

Jules, her foster sister, with her through the years. She just had to take a deep breath and not panic.

Dante appeared to be a businessman. Surely he'd listen to logic. It was her last alternative. She sucked in a steadying breath, willing her mind to calm. "If you'll read over the contract, you'll see that your grandfather has agreed not only to mentor me but also to host a television crew. We're doing a reality spot for one of the cooking shows. It's been in the works for months now. Your grandfather was very excited about the project and how it'd give this place—" she waved her hand around at the restaurant that had a very distinct air about it "—international recognition. Just think of all the people that would know the name Ristorante Massimo."

Dante's eyes lit up with interest. "Do you have some numbers to back up your claims?"

She would have brought them, if she'd known she'd need them. "Your grandfather is confident in the value of these television segments. He has made numerous appearances on the culinary channel and has made quite a name for himself."

"I know. I was here for every one of those appearances."

She studied Dante's face for some recollection of him. His tanned skin. His dark eyes. His strong jaw. And those lips… Oh, they looked good enough to kiss into submission… She jerked her attention back to the conversation. "Why don't I recall seeing you in any of them?"

"Because I took a very small role in them. I didn't understand why my grandfather would sign up for those television appearances."

Her gaze narrowed in on him. "Do you have something against people on television?"

"No." He crossed his arms and leaned back, rocking his chair on the rear two legs. "I just think in a lot of cases they misrepresent life. They give people false hope that they'll be overnight successes. Most of the time life doesn't work that way. Life is a lot harder."

There was a glimmer of something in his eyes. Was it regret? Or pain? In a blink, his feelings were once again hidden. She was locked out. And for some reason that bothered her. Not that it should—it wasn't as though they were friends. She didn't even know him.

Not about to waste her time debating the positive and negative points of television, she decided to turn the conversation back around to her reason for being here. "Surely your grandfather will be back soon. After all, he has a restaurant to run."

"I'm afraid that he won't be returning."

"He won't?" This was news to her. Surely he couldn't be right. "But we have an agreement. And he was so eager for us to begin."

Dante rubbed his jaw as though trying to decide if he should say more. His dark gaze studied her intently. It made her want to squirm in her seat but she resisted.

"Whatever you're thinking, just say it. I need to know what's going on."

Dante sighed. "My grandfather recently experienced a stroke. He has since moved to the country."

"Oh, no." She pressed a hand to her chest. This was so much worse than she'd imagined. "Is he going to be all right?"

Dante's brows lifted as though he was surprised by her concern. "Yes, it wasn't as bad as it could have been. He's getting therapy."

"Thank goodness. Your grandfather seemed so lively and active. I just can't imagine that happening to him."

She thought back to their lively emails and chatty phone conversations. Massimo's voice had been rich and robust like a dark roast espresso. He was what she thought of when she imagined having a grandfather of her own. "He was so full of life."

"How exactly did you get to know him?"

Perhaps she'd said too much. It wasn't as if she and Massimo were *that* close. "At first, the production group put us in touch. We emailed back and forth. Then we started talking on the phone, discussing how we wanted to handle the time slots. After all, they are short, so we couldn't get too elaborate. But then again, we didn't want to skimp and do just the basics."

"Sounds like you two talked quite a bit."

She shrugged. "It wasn't like we talked every day. More like when one of us had a good idea. But that was hampered by the time difference. And then recently the calls stopped. When I phoned here I was merely told that he wasn't available and that they'd give him a message."

Dante's eyes opened wide as though a thought had come to him. "I remember seeing those messages. I had no idea who you were or what you wanted. I was beginning to wonder if my grandfather had a girlfriend on the side."

"Nope, it was me. And now that you know the whole story, what's yours?"

"My what?"

"Story. I take it you run this place for your grandfather."

His brows furrowed together as though he knew where this conversation was leading. "Yes, I do."

"Have you worked here long?" She wanted as much information as possible so she could plot out a backup plan.

He hesitantly nodded.

"That must be wonderful to learn from such a talented chef." There had to be a way to salvage this deal. But she needed to know more. "When did you start working with your grandfather?"

"When I was a kid, I would come and visit. But it wasn't until later that I worked here full-time."

She noticed that his answers were vague at best, giving her no clue as to his family life or why he came here to work. Perhaps he needed the money. Still, as she stared across the table at him, his whole demeanor spoke of money and culture. She also couldn't dismiss the fact that most women would find him alarmingly handsome. In fact, he'd make some real eye candy for the television spot. And if that was what it took to draw in an audience, who was she to argue.

She'd been earning money cooking since she was fourteen. Of course, being so young, she'd been paid under the table. Over the years, she'd gained more and more experience, but never thinking she'd ever have a shot at owning a restaurant of her own, she'd taken the safe route and gone to college. She'd needed a way to make decent money to keep herself and Jules afloat.

But then Jules entered her application for a reality TV cooking show. Jules had insisted that she needed to take a risk and follow her dream of being a chef in her own five-star restaurant.

Winning that reality show had been a huge steppingstone. It gave her a television contract and a plane ticket to Rome, where she'd learn from the best in the business. Jules was right. Maybe her dream would come true.

All she needed was to make sure this deal was a success. One way or the other. And if Chef Massimo couldn't participate then perhaps his grandson would do.

She eyed him up. "Your grandfather must have taught you all of his secrets in the kitchen."

His body noticeably stiffened. "Yes, he did. How else would I keep the place running in his absence?"

She knew it was akin to poking a sleeping bear with a stick, but she had to confirm her suspicions before she altered her plans ever so slightly. "But do your dishes taste like your grandfather's?"

"The customers don't know the difference." The indignity in his voice rumbled through the room. "Who do you think took the time to learn every tiny detail of my grandfather's recipes? My grandfather insisted that if you were going to do something, you should learn to do it right. And there were no shortcuts in his kitchen."

From the little she'd known of Massimo, she could easily believe this was true. During their phone conversations, he'd made it clear that he didn't take shortcuts with his recipes or with training people. She'd have to start from the beginning. Normally, she'd have taken it as an insult, but coming from Massimo, she had the feeling that he only wanted the best for both of them and the television spotlight.

"Will you continue to run the restaurant alone?"

Dante ran a hand over his jaw. "Are you always this curious about strangers?"

She wasn't about to back off. This information was important and she had learned almost everything she needed. "I'm just trying to make a little conversation. Is that so wrong?"

There was a look in his eyes that said he didn't believe her. Still, he didn't press the subject. Instead he surprised her by answering. "For the foreseeable future I will continue to run Massimo's. I can't predict the future."

"I still wonder if you're as good as your grandfather in the kitchen."

"Wait here." He jumped to his feet and strode out of the room.

Where in the world had he gone? She was tempted to follow, but she thought better of it. She'd already pushed her luck as far as she dared. But her new plan was definitely taking shape.

The only problem she envisioned was trying to keep her mind on the art of cooking and not on the hottie mentoring her. She knew jet lag was to blame for her distorted worries. A little uninterrupted sleep would have her thinking clearly.

This arrangement was far too important to ruin due to some sort of crush. She pursed her lips together. No matter how good he looked, she knew better than to let her heart rule her mind. She knew too well the agonizing pain of rejection and abandonment. She wouldn't subject herself to that again. Not for anyone.

She pulled her shoulders back and clasped her hands in her lap. Time to put her plan in motion.

One way or the other.

CHAPTER THREE

How dare she question his prowess in the kitchen?

Dante stared down at a plate of *pasta alla gricia*, one of his favorite dishes. The fine balance of cured pork and *pecorino romano* gave the pasta a unique, tangy flavor. It was a dish he never grew tired of eating.

He proceeded to divvy the food between two plates. After all, he didn't need that much to eat at this late hour. As he arranged the plates, he wondered why he was going to such bother. What was so special about this golden-haired beauty? And why did he feel a compulsion to prove himself where she was concerned?

It wasn't as if he was ever going to see Lizzie again. Without his grandfather around to hold up his end of the agreement, she'd be catching the next plane back to New York. Still, before she left, he needed to prove his point. He'd taken some of his grandfather's recipes and put his own twist on them. And the patrons loved them. This meal was sure not to disappoint the most discerning palate.

He strode back into the dining room and placed a plate in front of Lizzie. She gazed up at him with a wide-eyed blue gaze. Her mouth gaped as though she were about to say something, but no words came out.

He stared at her lush lips, painted with a shimmery pink frost. They looked perfectly ripe for a kiss. The urge grew stronger with each passing second. The breath hitched in his throat.

"This looks delicious." She was staring at him, not the food. And she was smiling.

"It's an old family recipe." He nearly tripped over his own feet as he moved to the other side of the table. "The secret to the dish is to keep it simple and not be tempted to add extras. You don't want to detract from the flavor of the meat and cheese."

He couldn't believe he was letting her good looks and charms get to him. It wasn't as if she was the first beautiful woman he'd entertained. But she was the first that he truly wanted to impress. Safely in his seat, he noticed the smallness of the table. If he wasn't careful, his legs would brush against hers. If this were a casual date, he'd take advantage of the coziness, but Lizzie was different from the usual women he dated. She was more serious. More intent. And she seemed to have only one thing on her mind—business.

"Aren't you going to try it?" Dante motioned to the food. Just because he wasn't interested in helping her with her dreams of stardom didn't mean he couldn't prove his point—he could create magic in the kitchen.

He watched as she spun the pasta on her fork and slipped it in her mouth. He sat there captivated, waiting for her reaction. When she moaned her approval, his blood pressure spiked and his grip tightened on the fork.

"This is very good. Did you make it?"

Her question didn't fool him. He knew what she was digging at—she wanted him to step up and fill in for his grandfather. Him on television—never. That was his grandfather's dream—not his.

"It's delicious." She flashed him a big smile, seemingly unfazed by his tight-lipped expression.

Her smile gave him a strange feeling in his chest that shoved him off center. And that wasn't good. He didn't want to be vulnerable to a woman. He knew for a fact that romance would ultimately lead to disaster—one way or the other.

He forced himself to eat because he hadn't had time to since that morning and his body must be starved. But he didn't really have an appetite. In fact, the food tasted like cardboard. Thankfully Lizzie seemed impressed with it.

When she'd cleaned her plate, she pushed it aside. "Thank you. I can't wait for you to teach me how to make it."

Dante still had a couple of bites left on his plate when he set his fork down and moved the plate aside. "That isn't going to happen."

"Maybe you should at least consider it."

Her gaze strayed to the contract that was still sitting in the middle of the table and then back to him. What was she implying? That she'd drag him through the courts?

That was the last thing he needed. He already had enough important issues on his mind, including fixing his relationship with his family. And the closer it got to putting his signature on the sale papers, the more unsettled he'd become about his decision.

"You can't expect me to fulfill my grandfather's agreement."

"Why not?" She smiled as though it would melt his resistance. Maybe under different circumstances it would have worked, but not now.

"Because I don't want to be on television. I didn't like it when those camera people were here before. All they did was get in the way and create a circus of onlookers wanting to get their faces on television."

He didn't bother to mention that he was just days away from closing a deal to sell Ristorante Massimo. But it all hinged on those family recipes. And somehow parting with those felt treasonous. His grandfather had signed the entire business over to him to do as he pleased, but still he couldn't make this caliber of decision on his own.

But how did he approach his grandfather? How did he tell him that he felt restless again and without Massimo in the kitchen, it just wasn't the same? It was time he moved on to find something that pacified the uneasiness in him.

He'd been toying with the thought of returning to the vineyard and working alongside his father and brother. After all of this time, perhaps he and his father could call a truce—perhaps Dante could in some small way try to make up for the loss and unhappiness his father had endured in the years since Dante's mother had died. But was that even possible considering their strained relationship?

"It isn't me you have to worry about." Lizzie's voice drew him back to the here and now. She toyed with the cloth napkin. "The television people will want to enforce the contract. They're already advertising the segment on their station. I saw it before I left New York. Granted, we won't have a show of our own. But we will have a daily spot on the most popular show on their station."

He'd forgotten that there was a third party to this agreement. A television conglomerate would not be easily deterred from enforcing their rights. "But what makes you think that they would want me instead of my grandfather?"

"I take it your grandfather truly didn't mention any of this to you?"

Dante shook his head. A sick feeling churned in the pit of his stomach.

"That's strange. When he brought your name up to the television people, I thought for sure he'd discussed it with you." She shrugged. "Anyway, they are eager to have you included in the segments. They think you'll appeal to the younger viewers."

Dante leaned his head back and expelled a weary sigh. Why hadn't his grandfather mentioned any of this to him? Maybe Massimo just never got the chance. Regardless, this situation was going from bad to worse. What was next?

When Dante didn't say anything, Lizzie continued, "I'm sure when I explain to them about your grandfather no longer being able to fulfill his role, they will welcome a young, handsome replacement."

She thought he was handsome? He sat up a little straighter. "And if I don't agree—"

"From what I read, there are monetary penalties for not fulfilling the contract. I'm not an attorney but you might want to have someone take a look at it."

A court battle would only extend the time it would take to sell the *ristorante*. Not to mention scare off his potential buyer—the one with deep pockets and an interest in keeping Ristorante Massimo as is.

Dante's gaze moved to the document. "Do you mind if I keep these papers for a little while?"

"That's fine. It's a copy."

"I'll get back to you on this." He got to his feet. He had a lot to think over. It was time to call it a night.

"You'll have to decide soon, as the film crew will be here in a couple of days."

His back teeth ground together. Talk about finding everything out at the last minute. No matter his decision, resolving this issue would take some time. Agreeing to the filming would be much quicker than a court suit. And in the end, would he win the lawsuit?

But then again, could he work with Lizzie for two months and ignore the way her smile made his pulse race? Or the way her eyes drew him in? What could he say? He was a red-hot Italian man who appreciated women. But nothing about Lizzie hinted at her being open to a casual, gratifying experience. And he was not about to get tangled up in something that involved his heart. Nothing could convince him to risk it—not after the carnage he'd witnessed. No way.

He was attracted to her.

Lizzie secretly reveled in the knowledge. Not that either of them would act on it. She'd noticed how he kept his distance, but his eyes betrayed him. She wondered if his demeanor had cooled because of the television show. Or was there something more? Her gaze slipped to his hands, not spying any rings. Still, that didn't mean there wasn't a significant other.

Realizing the implication of what she was doing, she jerked her gaze upward. But that wasn't any better as she ended up staring into his bottomless eyes. Her heart thudded against her ribs. This was not good. Not good at all.

She glanced down at the gleaming black-and-white floor tiles. She could still feel him staring at her. With great effort, she ignored him. Her trip to Rome was meant to be a learning experience, not to partake in a holiday romance.

Putting herself out there and getting involved with Dante was foolish. She had the scars on her heart to prove that romance could come with a high price tag. Besides, she was certain she wouldn't live up to his expectations—she never did.

It was much easier to wear a smile and keep people at arm's length. It was safer. And that was exactly how she planned to handle this situation.

Dante cleared his throat. "Well, since you're a couple of days early, I'm sure you'll want to tour the city. There's lots to see and experience." He led her to the front door. "Make sure you visit the Colosseum and the catacombs."

"I'm looking forward to sightseeing. This is my first trip to Italy. Actually, it's my first trip anywhere." She pressed her lips together to keep from spilling details of her pitiful life. She didn't want his sympathy. She was just so excited about this once-in-a-lifetime experience. Years ago in those foster homes, she never would have imagined that a trip like this would be a possibility—let alone a reality.

"I'd start with the Vatican Museums."

"Thanks. I will."

He smiled as he pulled open the door. The tired lines on his face smoothed and his eyes warmed. She was struck by how truly handsome he was when he let his guard down. She'd have to be careful and not fall for this mysterious Italian.

She glanced out into the dark night. "Is this the way to the apartment?"

His brow puckered. "Excuse me."

"The apartment. Massimo told me that he had a place for me to stay?"

"He did?" Dante uttered the words as though they were part of his thought process and not a question for her.

She nodded and reached into her purse. She fumbled around until her fingers stumbled across some folded papers. Her fingers clasped them and pulled them out.

"I have the email correspondence." She held out the evidence. "It's all right here."

Dante waved away the pages. "Are you this prepared for everything?"

She nodded. She'd learned a long time ago that people rarely keep their word. Just like her mother, who'd promised she'd do whatever it took to get Lizzie back from social services. In the beginning, Lizzie had gone to bed each night crying for the only parent she'd ever known—the mother who was big on neglect and sparing on kindness. At the time, Lizzie hadn't known any other way. In the end, that mother-daughter reunion was not to be. Her mother had been all talk and no follow-through, unable to move past the drugs and alcohol. Lizzie languished in the system.

She'd grown up knowing one simple truth: people rarely lived up to their word. There was only one person to count on—herself.

However, in Massimo's case, breaking his word was totally understandable. It was beyond his control. Her heart squeezed when she thought of that outgoing man being forced into retirement. She truly hoped while she was here that she'd get the opportunity to meet him and thank him for having such faith in her. It was as though he could see through her brave front to her quivering insides. During moments of doubt, he'd calmed her and assured her that all would be fine with the television segments.

She glanced at Dante. He definitely wasn't a calming force like his grandfather. If anything, Dante's presence filled her with nervous energy.

He leaned against the door. "There's no apartment available."

Her eyes narrowed on him. "Does everything with you have to be a struggle?"

"I'm not trying to be difficult. I simply don't have any place for you to stay."

"Why is it your grandfather seemed confident that I would be comfortable here?"

"Probably because there was a remodeled apartment available, but since I wasn't privy to your arrangement with my grandfather, I just leased it. But I'm sure you won't have a problem finding a hotel room nearby."

Oh, yes, there would be a big problem. She didn't have money to rent a hotel room. She could only imagine how expensive that would be and she needed every penny to pay down her debts and to pay tuition for Jules's grad school. Every penny from the contract was already accounted for. There was nothing to spare.

"It was agreed that I would have free room and board." Pride dictated that she keep it to herself that she didn't have the money to get a hotel room.

He crossed his arms and stared at her as though debating his options. "What do you want me to do? Give you my bed?"

The words sparked a rush of tempting images to dance through her mind. Dante leaning in and pressing his very tempting lips to hers. His long, lean fingers grazing her cheek before resting against the beating pulse in her throat. Her leaning into him as he swept her up in his arms.

"Lizzie, are you okay?" Dante's eyes filled with concern.

She swallowed hard, realizing that she'd let her imagination get the best of her. "Umm, yes. I'm just a little jet-lagged. And things were busy tonight, keeping me on my toes."

His eyes probed her. "Are you sure that's all it is?"

She nodded.

Where in the world had those distracting images of Dante come from? It wasn't as though she was looking for a boyfriend. The last man in her life had believed they should each have their own space until one day he dropped by to let her know that he was moving to California to chase his dream of acting. No *I'll miss you.* Or *Will you come with me?*

He'd tossed her aside like the old worn-out couch and the back issues of his rocker magazines. He hadn't wanted her except for a little fun here and there. She'd foolishly let herself believe that they were building something special. In the end, she hadn't been enough for him—she always came up lacking.

"I'd really like to get some rest." And some distance from Dante so she could think clearly. "It's been a long evening and my feet are killing me."

Was that a hint of color rising in his cheeks? Did he feel bad about putting her to work? Maybe he should, but she honestly didn't mind. She liked meeting some of the people she'd hopefully be cooking for in the near future. That was if she ever convinced Dante that this arrangement could work.

"Putting you to work was a total mix-up. My apologies." He glanced down at the floor. "I owe you."

"Apology accepted." She loved that he had manners. "Now, does this mean you'll find me a bed?"

CHAPTER FOUR

THE QUESTION CONJURED up all sorts of scintillating scenarios.

Dante squelched his overactive, overeager imagination. Something told him that there was a whole lot more to this beautiful woman than her desire to be on television and to brush up on her skills in the kitchen. He saw in her eyes a guardedness. He recognized the look because it was something he'd witnessed with his older brother after his young wife had tragically died. It was a look one got when life had double-crossed them.

Lizzie had traveled to the other side of the globe from her home without knowing a single soul, and from the determined set of her mouth, she wasn't about to turn tail and run. She was willing to stand her ground. And he couldn't help but admire her strength.

He just hoped his gut feeling about this woman wasn't off target. What he had in mind was a bold move. But his grandfather, who'd always been a good judge of character, liked her. He surely wouldn't have gone out of his way for her if he hadn't. But that didn't mean Dante should trust her completely, especially when it came to his grandfather.

Nonno had enough on his plate. Since he'd been struck down by a stroke, he'd been lost in a sea of self-pity. Dante was getting desperate to snap his grandfather back into the world of the living. And plying the man with problems when Nonno was already down wouldn't help anyone.

"Have you told me everything now? About your agreement with my grandfather."

She nodded.

"You promise? No more surprises?"

"Cross my heart." Her finger slowly crossed her chest.

Dante cleared his throat as he forced his gaze upward to meet her eyes. "I suppose I do have a place for you to stay."

"Lead the way."

With the main doors locked, he moved next to her on the sidewalk. "It's right over here."

He led the way to a plain red door alongside the restaurant. With a key card, the door buzzed and he pulled it open for her. Inside was a small but lush lobby with an elevator and a door leading to steps. He'd made sure to give the building a face-lift when his grandfather handed over the reins to him. That was all it took to draw in eager candidates to rent the one available unit that he'd been occupying until he'd moved into his grandfather's much larger apartment.

"Where are we going?" She glanced around at the new furnishings adorning the lobby.

"There are apartments over the *ristorante*."

A look of dawning glinted in her eyes. "Your grandfather mentioned those. It's where he intended for me to stay while I am here. Are they nice?"

"Quite nice." In fact the renovations on his apartment had just been completed.

As the elevator doors slid open, she paused and turned to him. "But I thought you said that you leased the last one."

"Do you want to see what I have in mind or not?"

She nodded before stepping inside the elevator.

Good. Because he certainly wasn't going to bend over backward to make her happy. In fact, if she walked away now of her own accord, so much the better. As it was, this arrangement would be only temporary. He'd pacify her until he spoke to his solicitor.

In the cozy confines of the elevator, the faint scent of her floral perfume wrapped around him and teased his senses. If she were anyone else, he'd comment on its intoxicating scent. It was so tempting to lean closer and draw the perfume deeper into his lungs. But he resisted. Something about her led him to believe that she'd want more than one night—more than he was capable of offering her.

The thought of letting go and falling in love made his gut tighten and his palms grow damp. He'd witnessed firsthand the power of love and it wasn't all sappy ballads and roses. Love had the strength to crush a person, leaving them broken and angry at the world.

He placed a key in the pad, turned it and pressed the penthouse button. The hum of the elevator was the only sound. In no time at all the door swished open, revealing a red-carpeted hallway. He led her to his door, adorned with gold emblems that read PH-1.

Dante unlocked the door and waved for her to go ahead of him. He couldn't help but watch her face. She definitely wouldn't make much of a poker player as her emotions filtered across her face. Her blue eyes opened wide as she took in the pillar posts that supported the open floor plan for the living room and kitchen area.

He'd had walls torn down in order to create this spacious area. He may enjoy city life but the country boy in him didn't like to feel completely hemmed in. He'd paid the men bonuses to turn the renovations around quickly. Though it didn't come close in size to his family's home at the vineyard, the apartment was still large—large enough for two people to coexist without stepping on each other's toes. At least for one night.

She walked farther into the room. She paused next to the black leather couch and turned to him. "Do you live here alone?"

"I do. My grandfather used to live here. When he got

sick, he turned it over to me. I made some changes and had everything updated."

"It certainly is spacious. I think I'd get lost in a place this size." Her stiff posture said that she was as uncomfortable as he felt.

He wasn't used to having company. He'd been so busy since his grandfather's sudden exit from the *ristorante*—from his life—that he didn't have time for a social life. In fact, now that he thought about it, Lizzie was the first woman he'd had in here. He wasn't sure how he felt about that fact.

"Can I get you anything?" he asked, trying to ease the mounting discomfort.

"Yes—you can tell me what I'm doing here."

Oh, yes. He thought it was obvious but apparently it wasn't to her. "You can stay here tonight until we can get this whole situation cleared up."

"You mean when you consent to the contents of this contract."

His jaw tightened, holding back a string of heated words.

"Don't look like it's the end of the world." Lizzie stepped up to him. "With your good looks, the camera is going to love you. And that's not to mention the thousands of women watching the segment. Who knows, maybe you'll become a star."

Dante laughed. Him a star. Never. Her lush lips lifted. The simple expression made her eyes sparkle like blue topaz. Her pale face filled with color. And her lips, they were plump and just right to lean in and snag a sweet taste. His head started to lower when she pulled back as though reading his errant thoughts.

He cleared his throat and moved to the kitchenette to retrieve a glass. "Are you sure you don't want anything to drink?"

"I'm fine. Have you lived here long?"

He ran the water until it was cold—real cold. What he

really needed to do was dump it over his head and shock some sense back into himself.

"I've lived in this building since I moved to Rome. I had a smaller apartment on another floor before moving to this one. You're my first guest here." He turned, waiting to hear more about what she thought of the place. "What do you think of it?"

He was genuinely curious about her take on the place. It was modeled in black-and-white decor. With the two colors, it made decorating easier for him. He sensed that it still needed something, but he couldn't put his finger on what exactly was missing.

"It's…it's nice." Her tone was hesitant.

Nice? The muscles in his neck tightened. Who said "nice"? Someone who was trying to be polite when they really didn't like something but they didn't want to hurt the other person's feelings.

She leaned back on the couch and straightened her legs. She lifted her arms over her head and stretched. He tried to ignore how her blouse rode up and exposed a hint of her creamy skin. But it was too late. His thoughts strayed in the wrong direction again. At this rate, he'd need a very cold shower.

He turned his attention back to the apartment and glanced around, trying to see it from her perspective. Everything was new. There wasn't a speck of dust—his cleaning lady had just been there. And he made sure to always pick up after himself. There wasn't a stray sock to be had anywhere.

"Is it the black-and-white decor you don't like?" He really wanted to know. Maybe her answer would shed some light on why he felt something was off about the place.

"I told you, I like it."

"But describing it as *nice* is what people say to be polite. I want to know what's missing." There, he'd said it.

There was something missing and it was going to drive him crazy until he figured it out.

He looked around at the white walls. The modern artwork. The two pieces of sculpture. One of a stallion rearing up. The other of a gentle mare. They reminded him of home. When he turned around, he noticed Lizzie unzipping her boots and easing them off. Her pink-painted toes stretched and then pointed as though she were a ballerina as she worked out all of the muscles. When she murmured her pleasure at being free of the boots, he thought he was going to lose it. It took every bit of willpower to remain in his spot and not go to her.

He turned his back. He tried to think of something to do. Something to keep him from going to her. But there was nothing that needed straightening up. No dirty dishes in the sink. In fact, he spent very little time here. For the most part, he slept here and that was it. The rest of his time was spent either downstairs in the *ristorante* or at the vineyard, checking on his grandfather.

"You know what's missing?" Her voice drew his attention.

He turned around and tried to ignore the way her short black skirt had ridden even higher on her thighs. "What would that be?"

"There are no pictures. I thought there'd be one of you with your grandfather."

Dante glanced around, realizing she was right. He didn't have a single picture of anyone. "I'm sorry. I don't have any pictures here. They are all at my family's home."

"Do they live far from here?"

He shrugged. "It's a bit of a drive. But not that far. I like to go home on the weekends."

"But isn't the restaurant open?"

"It's open Saturday. But then we're closed Sunday and Monday. So my weekend is not the traditional weekend."

"I see. And your grandfather, is he with your family?"

Dante nodded. "He lives with my father and older brother."

Her brows drew together but she didn't say anything. He couldn't help but be curious about her thoughts. Everything about this woman poked at his curiosity.

"What are you wondering?"

She shook her head. "Nothing."

"Go ahead. Say what's on your mind."

"You mentioned a lot of men. Are there no women?"

"Afraid not. Unless you count my aunts, but they don't live there even though they are around so much that it feels like they do." He didn't want to offer a detailed explanation of why there were no women living at the vineyard. He tried to avoid that subject at all costs. He took it for granted that the DeFiore men were to grow old alone. But that was a subject best left for another day.

"Sounds like you have a big family."

"That's the understatement of the century." Anxious to end this line of conversation, he said, "We should get some sleep. Tomorrow will be here before we know it."

"You're sure you want me to stay here?" She stared directly at him.

Their gazes connected and held. Beyond the beauty of her eyes, there was something more that drew him to her—a vulnerability. In that moment, he longed to ride to her rescue and sweep her into his arms. He'd hold her close and kiss away her worries.

Lizzie glanced away, breaking the special moment.

Was she thinking the same thing as him? Did she feel the pull of attraction, too? Not that he was going to act on his thoughts. It wasn't as though he couldn't keep himself in check. He could and would be a gentleman.

"I'll deal with it. After all, you said this is what my grandfather agreed to. There are a couple of guest rooms down the hallway." He pointed to the right. And then for good measure he added, "And the master suite is in that direction." His hand gestured to the left. "Plenty of room for both of us."

"My luggage hasn't arrived yet. I have nothing to sleep in."

"I can loan you something."

Just as he said that, there was a buzz from the intercom. He went to answer it. In seconds, he returned to her. "Well, you don't have to worry. Your luggage has arrived."

She smiled. "That's great."

A moment of disappointment coursed through him. What in the world was the matter with him? Why should he care one way or the other if she slept in one of his shirts or not? Obviously he was more tired than he'd thought.

CHAPTER FIVE

LIZZIE GRINNED AND STRETCHED, like a cat that had spent the afternoon napping in the sunshine. She glanced around the unfamiliar surroundings, noticing the sun's rays creeping past the white sheers over the window. She rubbed her eyes and then fumbled for her cell phone. She was shocked to find that she'd slept away half of the morning. It was going to take her a bit to get her internal alarm clock reset.

Last night, she'd been so tired that she'd barely gotten off a text message to Jules to assure her that she'd arrived safely before sleep claimed her. This was the first time in their lives that they'd been separated for an extended period and Lizzie already missed her foster sister, who was also her best friend. She had promised to call today to fill her in on her trip. But after converting the time, Lizzie realized it was too early in New York to call.

She glanced around, not surprised to find the room done up in black and white. The man may be drop-dead gorgeous but when it came to decorating, he definitely lacked imaginative skills. What this place needed was some warmth—a woman's touch.

She thought back to his comment about her being his first guest here. She found that surprising. For some reason, she imagined someone as sexy and charming as him having a woman on each arm. Perhaps there was more to this man than his smooth talk and devastating smile. What was the real Dante like? Laid-back and flirtatious? Serious and a workaholic?

She paused and listened for any sounds from him. But then again, with an apartment this big, she doubted she'd hear him in the kitchen. She'd be willing to bet that her entire New York apartment could fit in this bedroom. She'd never been in such a spacious home before. Not that she'd have time to get used to it. She was pretty certain that Dante was only mollifying her. Today he would have a plan to get her out of his life and his restaurant.

With that thought in mind, Lizzie sprang out of bed and rushed into the glass block shower enclosure with more water jets than she'd ever imagined were possible. But instead of enjoying the shower, she wondered what Dante's next move would be concerning the agreement.

Almost thirty minutes later, her straight blond hair was smoothed back into the normal ponytail that she wore due to its ease at pinning it up in the kitchen. She slipped on a dark pair of designer jeans. Lizzie didn't recognize the name, but the lady at the secondhand store had assured her that they were the in thing right now.

Lizzie pulled on a white tiny tee with sparkly silver bling on the front in the shape of a smiley face. It was fun, and today she figured she just might need something uplifting. There were decisions to be made.

After she stepped into a pair of black cotton shoes, she soundlessly made her way to the living room, finding it deserted. Where could Dante be? She recalled their conversation last night and she was certain that he'd said the restaurant was closed today.

"Dante?" Nothing. "Dante?" she called out, louder this time.

Suddenly he was standing in the hallway that led to the master suite. "Sorry, I didn't hear you. Have you been up long?"

She shook her head. "I'm afraid that my body is still on New York time."

"I've spoken to my grandfather."

Lizzie's chest tightened. "What did he say?"

Dante paused, making her anxiety even worse. She wanted to yell at him to spit it out. Did Massimo say something that was going to change how this whole scenario played out?

"He didn't say much. I'm getting ready to go see him."

She waited, hoping Dante would extend an invitation. When he didn't, she added, "How far did you say the vineyard is from here?"

He shrugged. "An hour or so out of the city."

She glanced toward the elongated window. "It's a beautiful day for a drive."

He said nothing.

Why wasn't he taking the hint? If she laid it on any thicker, she'd have to invite herself along. She resisted the urge to stamp her feet in frustration. Why wouldn't he give in and offer her a ride? She'd already mentioned how much she enjoyed talking to his grandfather on the phone.

Maybe Dante just wasn't good with hints, no matter how bold they were. Perhaps she should try another approach—a direct one.

"I'd like to meet your grandfather."

Dante shook his head. "That isn't going to happen."

Oh, no. She wasn't giving up that easily. "Why not? When we talked on the phone, he was very excited about my arrival."

"Things have changed since then." Dante walked over and grabbed his keys from the edge of the kitchen counter. "It just wouldn't be a good idea."

"Did you even tell him that I was here?"

Dante's gaze lowered. "In passing."

He was leaving something out but what? "And did you discuss the contract?"

"No. He had a bad night and he was agitated this morning. I didn't think him hearing about what has transpired since your arrival would help things." He cursed under his breath and strode over to the door and grabbed his overnight bag.

He was leaving without her.

Disappointment washed over her. She just couldn't shake her desire to meet the man who reminded her of what she imagined her grandfathers would have been like, if she'd ever met either of her own. But she couldn't tell Dante that. He'd think she was a sentimental dreamer—and she couldn't blame him.

How could she ever explain to someone who grew up in a big, caring family with parents and grandparents about the gaping hole in her heart? She'd forever been on the outside looking in. She knew all too well that families weren't perfect. Her friends in school had dealt with a whole host of family dynamics, but they had a common element—love to bind them together, no matter what. And to have her very own family was what Lizzie had prayed for each night. And at Christmastime it had been the only thing she had ever asked for from Santa.

Instead of a mom and dad and grandparents, she was given Jules—her foster sister. And she loved her with all of her heart. She would do anything for her, including keeping her promise to help Jules reach for her dreams—no matter the price. Because of their dismal finances, Jules had to put off college for a couple of years until Lizzie got her degree. Jules always talked of helping other kids like them. This was Jules's chance to become a social worker and make a difference, but in order to do that she had to get through grad school first.

Massimo had been insistent that her plan would work. He'd been so certain. And she couldn't shake her desire to meet him and thank him for his encouragement. "Take me with you. I promise I won't say or do anything to upset your grandfather."

Dante eyed her up as though attempting to gauge her sincerity. She sent him a pleading look. Under the intensity of his stare, her insides quivered. But she refused to turn away.

"Even though he insists on meeting you, I will leave you behind if I feel I can't trust you."

"So he does want to meet me." This time she did smile.

"Don't go getting all excited. I still haven't made up my mind about taking you with me. You know it's a bit of a ride."

Meaning Dante didn't like the thought of spending yet more time alone with her. To be honest, she couldn't blame him. She'd basically dropped into his life out of nowhere with absolutely no warning. How could she possibly expect him to react any different?

But then again, she had noticed the way he'd looked at her last night. As if she were an ice cream cone on a sweltering hot day and he couldn't wait to lick her up. To be fair, she'd had similar thoughts about him. No one had ever turned her on with just a look.

She halted her thoughts. It wasn't worth it to go down this path. It'd only lead to heartbreak—her heartbreak. In her experience, men only wanted an uncomplicated good time. And she couldn't separate her heart and her mind. It was so much easier to remain detached. If she was smart, she'd turn and leave now. But she couldn't. Not yet.

"You can trust me," she pleaded. "I won't upset Massimo."

"I don't know—"

"If you won't take me to him, then give me his address. I'll find my own way there."

Not that she had any clue how she'd get from point A to point B without a vehicle, but she was certain that Italy had public transportation. That was one of the things she'd discovered when she'd researched coming here. So now Dante wouldn't stand between her and meeting Massimo.

Dante hated being put in this position.

All he wanted to do was protect his grandfather—well, that wasn't quite the whole truth. He didn't relish the car ride with Lizzie. He was certain she'd keep at him, trying to convince him to change his mind about the television spot. His jaw tightened. He had other priorities with the sale of the *ristorante* to negotiate.

Then this morning when he'd phoned his grandfather to verify that he'd agreed to this television segment, his grandfather had come to life at the mention of Lizzie's name. After weeks of Nonno being in a black mood, this was the first time he'd sounded even remotely like himself. Dante made every excuse to get out of taking Lizzie to meet him. His grandfather would have none of it.

Unwilling to disappoint his grandfather, he said, "You can come with me on one stipulation."

Hope glinted in her eyes. "Name it."

"There will be no talking about the contract or the cooking show this weekend."

"But the camera crew will be here Tuesday morning expecting to begin filming before the restaurant opens. What will we do? We haven't even decided how to proceed."

"Let me deal with them." He'd already called his solicitor that morning. Even though it was the weekend, this couldn't wait. He'd pay the exorbitant fees. Whatever it took to find a way out of this mess.

She narrowed her gaze. "You're going to break the contract, aren't you?"

"Why wouldn't I? I never agreed to give up two months of my life."

"But I…I can't repay the money."

"What money?"

She glanced away and moved to the window that looked

out over the street. "They paid me a portion of the fee up front. And it's already been spent. I can't repay them."

That wasn't his problem. But his conscience niggled at him. All in all, Lizzie wasn't bad. In fact, she was smokin' hot. And when she smiled it was as though a thousand-watt lightbulb had been switched on. But when she opened her mouth—well, that was a different story. She knew instinctively which buttons of his to push.

He wanted to think that she was lying to him just to gain his sympathy, but his gut was telling him that she was being truthful. Those unshed tears in her eyes—those were genuine. There had to be a compromise but he didn't know what that would be at this point.

Until he figured out what that was, he had to say something to ease her worry. "I can't promise you this will work out for you. But if you quit worrying while we're away, I give you my word that I'll share what my solicitor uncovers before I make any moves."

She hitched a slender hip and tilted her head to the side. He couldn't help but smile at the way she was eyeing him, trying to decide if she should trust him. He supposed he deserved it. He had just done the same thing to her.

The strained silence stretched on, making him uncomfortable. "Okay, you've made your point. I'll trust you not to pull the *poor pitiful me* card around my grandfather, if you'll trust me not to take any action without consulting you."

Why did he feel as if he'd just struck up a losing deal? For a man used to getting his way, this was a very unsettling feeling.

CHAPTER SIX

THIS WOULD IMPRESS HER.

Dante maneuvered his low-slung, freshly waxed, candy-apple-red sports car around the street corner and slowed to a crawl as he approached the front of the *ristorante*. Lizzie stood on the sidewalk with an overnight bag slung over her shoulder and her face lifted toward the sun. She didn't appear to notice him. The sun's rays gave her golden mane a shimmery glow. He wondered if she had any clue how her beauty commanded attention. Something told him she didn't. There was an unassuming air about her.

Without taking time to consider his actions, he tramped the brakes and reached for his smartphone to snap her picture. It wasn't until he returned it to the dash that he realized how foolish he was acting. Like some schoolkid with a crush on the most popular girl in school.

Back then he'd been so unsure of himself—not knowing how to act smooth around the girls. That all changed after he moved to Rome. Away from his father and brother, he'd grown more confident—more at ease with the ladies.

His older brother, though, always had a way with the women…but Stefano had eyes for only one girl, even back in school. They'd been childhood sweethearts until it came to a devastating end. The jarring memory brought Dante up short.

He eased the car forward and parked next to Lizzie.

He jumped out and offered to take her bag, but she didn't release her hold. In fact, her grip tightened on the straps. What in the world?

"I just want to put it in the boot. There's no room inside the car. As you can see, it's rather compact."

She cast him a hesitant look before handing over the bag. He opened the door for her. Once she was seated, he stowed her bag with his. He was surprised how light she packed. He'd never met a woman who didn't need everything including the kitchen sink just to go away for the night. Lizzie was different in so many ways.

And now it was his chance to impress her with his pride and joy. Anytime he wanted to make a surefire impression on a woman, he pulled out Red. He'd bestowed the name upon the luxury sports car, not just because of its color but because the name implied an attitude, a fieriness, and that was how he felt when he was in the driver's seat.

"Ready?" He glanced at her as she perched a pair of dark sunglasses on her face, hiding her expressive eyes.

"Yes. I'm surprised you'd choose to drive."

"Why wouldn't I drive?" He revved the engine just because he could, and he loved how the motor roared with power.

Who complained about riding in a fine machine like this one? He'd dreamed about a powerful car like this all of his life, but his father made him wait—made him earn it on his own without dipping into his trust fund. At the time Dante had resented his father for standing in his way. Now Dante found himself grateful for the challenge. He'd learned an important lesson—he could accomplish whatever he set his mind to. Even his father had been impressed with the car, not that he'd said much, but Dante had seen it in his eyes the first time he'd driven up to the villa.

Lizzie adjusted her seat belt. "I thought I read somewhere that people utilize public transportation here."

He glanced at her as he slowed for a stop sign. Was she

serious? She'd prefer the train to his car? Impossible. "I thought the car would be more convenient. We can come and go as we need."

"Oh. Right. And do you always run stop signs?"

"What?"

"There was a stop sign back there. Didn't you see it?"

"Of course I did. Didn't you notice how I slowed down and checked that there was no cross traffic?"

"But you didn't stop."

His jaw tightened as he adjusted his grip on the steering wheel. "Are you always such a stickler for rules?"

"Yes. Is that a problem?"

"It depends."

Silence settled over them as Dante navigated them out of the city. Every now and then he sneaked a glance at Lizzie. She kept her face turned to the side. The tires clicked over the brick roadway as Rome passed by the window. The cars, the buildings and the people. He'd never been to New York City and he couldn't help but wonder if it was as beautiful as Rome. The lush green trees planted along stretches of roadway softened the view of block-and-mortar buildings. Thankfully it was Sunday, so the roadway wasn't congested with standstill traffic.

They quickly exited the city. Now was his chance to find out a little bit more about her before she met his grandfather. His gut told him there was a lot she was holding back. It was his duty to make sure there weren't any unpleasant surprises that might upset his grandfather. Dante assured himself that his interest was legitimate. It had absolutely nothing to do with unraveling the story behind the sad look in her eyes when she thought no one was watching her.

"Where in New York do you come from?"

Out of the corner of his eye he noticed how her head swung around quickly. "The Bronx. Why?"

"Just curious. I figured if we're going to be spending

some time together, we might as well get to know a little about each other."

There was a poignant moment of silence as though she were deciding if this was a good idea or not. "And were you raised at this vineyard we're going to visit?"

Fair was fair. "Yes, I was. It's been in my family for generations. But it has grown over the years. And now our vino is a household name."

"That's an impressive legacy. So how did you end up in Rome helping your grandfather run a restaurant?"

How in the world did this conversation get totally turned around? They were supposed to be talking about her—not him. "It's a long story. But I really enjoyed the time I spent working with my grandfather. I'll never forget my time at Ristorante Massimo."

"You make it sound like you're leaving."

Dante's fingers tightened on the steering wheel. He had to be more careful with what he said. He could feel her puzzled gaze as she waited for him to affirm or deny her suspicions. That he couldn't do. He hadn't even told his family yet that he was planning to sell the place. There was always one excuse or another to put off the announcement.

But now that the negotiations were winding down, he was out of time. He needed to get his grandfather's blessing to include the family's recipes as part of the sale. Dante's gut tightened.

And the other reason he hesitated to bring it up was that he knew his father would use it as one more thing against him. His father always blamed him for Dante's mother's death during childbirth. Though logically Dante knew he wasn't responsible, he still felt the guilt of playing a part in his father's unhappiness. The man he'd known as a child wore a permanent scowl and he couldn't recall ever seeing his father smile. Not once.

When they communicated it was only because Dante

hadn't done a chore or hadn't done it "correctly." Who could blame him for moving away to the city?

But over the years, his father seemed to have changed—mellowed. He wasn't so critical of Dante. But was it enough to rebuild their relationship?

"Dante, are you planning to leave the restaurant? Is that why you're hesitant to help me?"

What was it about this woman that she could read him so well? Too well. "Why would you say that?"

Before she could respond, the strums of music filled the car. He hadn't turned on the stereo and that certainly wasn't his phone's ringtone.

"Oh, no!" Lizzie went diving for her oversize black purse that was on the floor beneath the dash.

"Something wrong?"

"I told my sister to only call me if there was an emergency." She scrambled through her purse. With the phone pressed to her ear, she sounded breathless when she spoke. "Jules, what's the matter?"

Dante glanced at Lizzie, noticing how the color had drained from her face. He wasn't the sort to eavesdrop, but it wasn't as if he could go anywhere. Besides, if she was anything like his younger cousins, it was most likely nothing more than a romantic crisis or a hair emergency—at least he hoped so for Lizzie's sake.

Most of the time when he was out in public, he grew frustrated with people who had their phones turned up so loud that you could hear both sides of the conversation. Lizzie obviously felt the same way as him, as hers was turned down so low that he couldn't hear the caller's voice. Lizzie wasn't much help as she only uttered things like: "Okay."

"Yes."

"Mmm…hmm…"

When her hand started waving around as she talked, Dante didn't know if he should pull over or keep driving.

"He can't do that!"

Who couldn't do what? Was it a boyfriend? Had he done something to her sister? The fact that Lizzie might have a man waiting for her in New York gave him an uneasy sensation.

At last, Lizzie disconnected the call and sank back against the leather upholstery. He wasn't sure what to say because he didn't have a clue what the problem might be. That, and he wasn't very good with upset women. He didn't have much experience in that department as he preferred to keep things light and casual.

Unable to stand the suspense, he asked, "Problems with your boyfriend?"

"Not a chance. I don't have one."

He breathed a little easier. "But I take it there's an emergency?"

"That depends on if you call getting tossed out of your apartment a problem."

"That serious, huh?"

"That man is so greedy, he'd sell his own mother if it'd make him an easy dollar."

"Who's greedy?"

"The landlord. He says he's converting the building into condos."

Dante was truly sorry for Lizzie's plight. He couldn't imagine what it'd be like to get kicked out of your home. Even though he and his father had a tenuous relationship, leaving the vineyard had been completely Dante's idea.

He pulled the car off the road. "Do I need to turn the car around?"

She glanced at him, her brows scrunched up in puzzlement. "Why would you do that?"

"So that you can catch a flight back to New York."

"That's not necessary."

Not necessary. If he was getting evicted, he'd be hightailing it home to find a new place to live. He must be missing something. But what?

"Don't you want to go back and figure out where you're going to live? I can't imagine in such a populated city that it'll be easy to find another place to your liking."

She clucked her tongue. "Are you trying to get rid of me?"

"What?" His tone filled with indignation, but a sliver of guilt sliced through him. "I'm just concerned."

"Well, you don't have to be concerned because the landlord gave us plenty of notice."

"He did?" Lizzie's gaze narrowed on him as he stammered to correct himself. "I…I mean, that's great. Are you sure you'll have time to find another place?"

"My, aren't you worried about my welfare. What could have brought on this bit of concern? Wait, could it be that you thought this might be your out with the contract?"

"No." The word came out far too fast. He wished he were anywhere but in this much-too-small car. There was nowhere to go. No way to avoid her expectant look. "Okay, it might have crossed my mind. But I still wouldn't wish someone to get kicked out of their home just to save me grief."

She laughed.

The sound grated on his nerves. "What's so funny?"

"The guilty look on your face. You're cute. Like a little boy caught with his hand in the proverbial cookie jar."

Great. Now he'd just been reduced to the level of a cute little kid. Talk about taking direct aim at a guy's ego. He eased the car back onto the road. If he'd ever entertained striking up a more personal relationship with Lizzie, it just came to a screeching halt right there. How did one make a comeback from being "cute"?

"So you aren't mad at me now?" He chanced a quick glance her way as she shook her head.

"I can't blame you for wanting an easy solution to our

problem. And after watching how much you worry about your grandfather, I realized that you aren't the sort to revel in others' misfortune."

Wow, she'd read all of that into him not wanting her to drag his grandfather into the middle of their situation? He was truly impressed. But that still didn't erase the *cute little boy* comment. His pride still stung.

After a few moments of silence passed, he turned to the right onto a private lane. "We're here. Are you up for this?"

CHAPTER SEVEN

SHE WAS MOST definitely ready for this adventure.

Lizzie gazed out the car window at the rolling green hills and lines of grapevines. This place was a beauty to behold. Did a more picturesque place exist? She didn't think so.

Of course, it didn't hurt that she was in the most amazing sports car, being escorted by the sexiest man on the planet. But she refused to let Dante know how truly captivated she was by him. She couldn't let him have any more leverage. They still had a contract to iron out.

And whereas he appeared to have plenty of money to hire his own legal dream team, she didn't have two pennies to rub together. She had to play her cards carefully, and by letting him know that she was vulnerable to his gorgeous smile and drawn in by his mesmerizing gaze, she would have lost before she even started.

They pulled to a stop in front of a spacious villa situated atop a hill overlooking the sprawling vineyard and olive grove. The home's lemon-yellow exterior was offset by a red tile roof and pale blue shutters lining the windows and doors. The three-story structure gave off a cheerful appeal that called to Lizzie.

Her gaze came to rest on a sweeping veranda with blue-and-white lawn furniture, which added an inviting quality. What a perfect place to kick back while enjoying a gentle breeze over her sun-warmed skin and sipping an icy lemonade.

"This is where you live?"

Dante cut the engine. "This is where my family lives."

"It's so big."

"It has to be to accommodate so many generations. It seems like every generation expands or adds something."

She especially liked the private balconies. She could easily imagine having her morning coffee there while Dante read the newspaper. "I couldn't even imagine what it would be like to call this my home."

"A little smothering."

"Smothering? You can't be serious." She turned, taking in the endless fields.

He shrugged. "When you have so many people keeping an eye on you constantly, it can be."

"But there's just your grandfather, father and brother, isn't it?"

"You're forgetting about all of my aunts, uncles and cousins. They stop over daily. There's never a lack of relatives. In fact, the dinner table seats twelve and never has an empty chair. They disapproved of my father not remarrying. So they made a point of ensuring my brother and I had a woman's influence."

"And did it work?"

"What? Oh, you mean the woman's-influence thing. I guess it helped. I just know that it was annoying always tripping over family members."

She frowned at him. "You should be grateful that they cared enough!"

His eyes grew round at her agitated tone. "I…I am."

She didn't believe him.

She couldn't even imagine how wonderful it would be to have so much family. He took it all for granted, not having sense enough to count his blessings. She'd have done anything to have a big, loving family.

"Not everyone is as lucky as you." With that, she got

out of the car, no longer wanting to hear how hard Dante had it putting up with his relatives.

He was the luckiest person she knew. He wasn't much older than herself and he already owned his very own restaurant—a successful one at that. Not to mention his jaw-dropping apartment. And she couldn't forget his flashy sports car. And on top of all that, he had a family that cared about him. Stacked up against her life, she was left lacking. She was up to her eyeballs in debt. And without the money from this television spot, she didn't know how she'd survive.

But how did she explain any of that to him? How would he ever understand when he couldn't even appreciate what he had? She'd met people like him before—specifically a guy in college. He was an only child—and spoiled. He thought he understood what hardship was when he had to buy a used car to replace the brand-new one his parents had bought him—a car he'd wrecked while out partying with the guys. She stifled the groan of frustration that rose in her throat. Hardship was choosing between paying the rent or buying groceries.

A gentle breeze brushed over her cheeks and whipped her hair into her face. She tucked the loose strands behind her ear. The air felt good. It eased her tense muscles, sweeping up her frustration and carrying it away.

In this particular case, she'd overreacted. Big-time. She had better keep a firmer grip on her emotions or soon Dante would learn about her past. She didn't want him to look down on her like she was less than everyone else since her mother hadn't loved her enough to straighten out her life and her father was someone without a name—a face. The breath caught in her throat.

She hated that being around Dante was bringing all of these old feelings of inadequacy to the surface. She'd buried them long ago. Coming here was a mistake. Nursing her dream of finding out what it would be like to have a grandfather—a family—was opening Pandora's box and her past was spilling out.

What had set her off?

Dante darted out of the car, but then froze. Lizzie's back was to him. Her shoulders were rigid. Her head was held high. He didn't want to do battle with her. Especially not here, where his family could happen upon them at any moment.

But more than that, he didn't have a clue what he'd done wrong. Did she have that strong an opinion about families? And if so, why?

His questions about her only multiplied. And as much as he'd set out to learn more about his flatmate on the ride here, he truly believed he had gained more questions than answers. Sure, he'd learned that she appeared to be very close with her sister and that she was about to get evicted. Oh, and she was a stickler for following the rules—especially the rules of the road. But there was so much more she was holding back. Things he wanted to know. But that would have to wait.

He could only hope that he could smooth things over with her before his father descended upon them. He didn't need her giving his family the impression that he didn't know how to treat a lady. His father already held enough things against him without adding to the list.

He rounded the car and stopped in front of her. "Hey, I don't know what I said back there, but I'm sorry. You must miss your family."

Her head lowered and her shoulders drooped. "It's me that should apologize. I guess it was just hearing Jules's voice made me realize it's going to be a long time before I will see her again. We've never been apart for an extended period like this."

So that was it. She was homesick. That was totally understandable. Maybe his family could help fill that gap. They certainly were a chatty, friendly bunch—even if they could be a bit overbearing at times.

"Why don't we go inside? I'm sure my father and brother are out in the fields. They keep a close eye on the vines and soil. But my grandfather will be around. Not to mention an aunt or two."

She smiled. "Thanks for including me. I'm really excited to meet your family."

"They're looking forward to meeting you, too."

"They know I'm coming?" When he nodded, she said, "But you made it sound like you'd planned to come without me."

"I had, but my grandfather had other ideas. He insisted I bring you to meet him. He told the family while I was on the phone."

"Would you have really left me behind if I hadn't promised to keep quiet about the contract?"

Dante shrugged. "I guess we'll never know. Just remember our agreement. Don't say or do anything to upset my grandfather."

Her eyes flared with indignation. But before she could say a word, there were footsteps on the gravel.

"Dante, who's your guest?"

He didn't even have to turn around to recognize his older brother's voice. Stefano was the eldest. The son who did no wrong. He'd stayed on at the villa and helped their father run the vineyard as was expected of the DeFiore men. But what no one took into consideration was that Stefano always got along with their father. He wasn't the one their father held responsible for their mother's death.

Dante turned on his heels. "Stefano, this is Lizzie."

Stefano stepped up, and when she extended her hand, he accepted it and kissed the back of it. Dante's blood pressure spiked. What was his brother doing? Wasn't he the forlorn widower?

Not that Dante wished for his brother to be miserable the rest of his life. In fact, he wished that Stefano would be able to move past the nightmare and get on with his life, but Stefano seemed certain that he would remain a bachelor…which seemed to be the destiny of the DeFiore men.

Dante had learned much from his family, especially to keep his guard up around women. He had zero intention of getting caught up in the tangled web of love. It only led to pain. Something he could live without.

While Stefano made idle chitchat with Lizzie, Dante noticed how her face lit up. He swallowed down his agitation. "Is Nonno in the house?"

Stefano turned to him. His whole demeanor changed into something more stoic—more like the brother he knew. "Of course. Where else would you expect him to be?"

Dante rolled his eyes and started for the house. When he realized that Lizzie had remained behind with his brother, he turned and signaled for her to follow him. She smiled at Stefano—a great big, ear-to-ear, genuine smile that lit up the world like a starburst. Dante's jaw tightened.

Why couldn't she be that happy around him? Why did she have to act so reserved—so on guard? After all, he was a nice guy, too. Or so he'd been told by some lady friends. Surely he hadn't lost his touch with the women. Maybe he'd have to try a little harder.

When Lizzie joined him, he said, "My grandfather is probably getting impatient. We should go see him."

Lizzie kept her smile in place and he couldn't help but wonder if it was part of their agreement to keep the mood light and happy. Or perhaps it was lingering happiness from meeting his older brother—Mr. Tall, Dark and Persuasive.

Not that it mattered if Lizzie had a thing for Stefano. It wasn't as if Dante was interested in the woman who was threatening the deal he'd been working for weeks to finalize. And it rankled him that he now felt some sort of responsibility toward Lizzie. Not only did he have to take into consideration what was best for the business, but also he felt compelled to take into account how it impacted her.

Dante stepped into the sunroom. "Nonno."

His grandfather's silver head lifted from reading a newspaper. He removed his reading glasses, focused on Dante and then his gaze moved to Lizzie. A lopsided smile pulled at his lips. Dante inwardly sighed at the effect Lizzie had over the men in his family. They stared at her as if she were a movie star. Well…she was pretty enough. Still, they didn't have to act as though they'd never seen a beautiful female before. Then again, it had been a very long time since a woman that wasn't a relative had visited the DeFiore villa. Okay, so maybe they had a reason to sit up and take notice. He just wished they didn't make it so noticeable.

"Come here." Nonno's deep voice was a bit slurred from the stroke.

His grandfather's gaze clung to Lizzie. She moved forward without hesitation and came to a stop in front of his chair. Then something happened that totally surprised Dante. She bent over and hugged his grandfather. It was as though they'd known each other forever. How did that happen?

The two of them chatted while Dante sat on the couch. He really wasn't needed as neither of them even noticed that he was in the room. And he could plainly see that Lizzie's presence had an uplifting effect on his grandfather. In fact, this was the happiest he'd seen his grandfather since he'd been forced into retirement.

"So that's why you changed your mind about visiting this weekend?" Dante's father entered the room and came to a stop by the couch before nodding in Lizzie's direction.

Dante instinctively followed his father's gaze back to the woman who'd thrown his life into turmoil. "She knows Nonno. He asked me to bring her here."

His father nodded. "If I had that sort of distraction, I might stay in the city, too. After all, it's a lot easier to have a good time with a beautiful woman than it is to do the hard work needed to keep the family vineyard running."

Dante's jaw ratcheted tight. It didn't matter what he said; it never seemed to be the right thing where his father was concerned. Some things never changed.

"At least you have good taste." That was the closest his father had ever come to giving him a compliment.

"Lizzie and I are working together, nothing more."

His father sent him a *you are crazy* look. Dante wasn't going to argue with the man—it wouldn't change things. He never lived up to his father's expectations—not like his brother, Stefano, always did. Just once, he'd like his father to clap him on the back and tell him he'd done something right—something good.

Dante sat rigidly on the couch. Not even his father's jabs were enough to make him leave the room. He assured himself that it was just to keep an eye on what Lizzie said to his grandfather. Because there couldn't be any other reason. Unlike the rest of his family, he was immune to her charms.

Sure, he knew how to enjoy a woman's company. Her smiles. Her laugh. Her touch. But that was as far as it went. He refused to let himself become vulnerable. He'd seen too much pain in his life. It wouldn't happen to him. The *L* word wasn't worth the staggering risks.

CHAPTER EIGHT

"THIS PLACE IS AMAZING."

Lizzie didn't bother to hide her enthusiasm as she glanced around the spacious living room with a high ceiling and two sets of double doors that let the afternoon sun stream in. She'd trade her Bronx apartment in a heartbeat for this peaceful retreat.

"I love it here." She spoke the words to no one in particular. "Very different from city life."

"It is different." Massimo's words took her full attention between the accent and the slight slur from his stroke. "I'm glad you're here. Is my grandson treating you well?"

Her thoughts flashed back to their first meeting. But she wasn't so sure that Massimo would find it amusing that Dante mistook her presence at the restaurant and put her to work as a hostess. She opted to save that story for a later date.

She glanced across to where Dante was pretending to read a cooking magazine. "Yes. He…he's been a gentleman."

Massimo gave her a quizzical look. "My grandson is a good man. He knows a lot. Make him teach you."

His choice of words struck her as a bit odd. Either the man was eager to shorten his sentences or he sensed that things between her and Dante weren't going smoothly.

"I will. I just wish you could be there. I was really looking forward to working next to such a legend."

Massimo attempted to smile but the one side of his

mouth would not cooperate. Her heart pinched. She had no idea how frustrating it must be for your body not to cooperate. But beyond that, the man's face spoke of exhaustion. Dante had warned her not to overtax him. And she wouldn't do anything to harm Massimo. The place in her heart for him had only grown exponentially since meeting him in person.

"I'll let you get some rest." Lizzie went to stand when Massimo reached for her hand.

His grip was strong but not painful. But it was the look in his eyes that dug at her heart. "Promise me you won't give up. Promise me you'll see through our deal."

"But—" She'd almost uttered the fact that Dante was opposed to the whole idea. "I'll do my best." It was all she could offer the man.

"My grandson needs someone like you."

The following morning Lizzie hit the ground running.

She wasn't about to waste a minute of her time at the villa. The big, brilliant ball of orange was still low in the distant horizon. She stood just outside the kitchen door with a cup of steamy black coffee in hand.

She wandered across to an old wooden fence and gazed out at the endless acres of grapes. The golden rays gave the rows and rows of vines a beauty all of their own. She'd never been someplace so wide open. She reveled in the peacefulness that surrounded her. And that was something she truly found amazing. Normally her nights were full of restless dreams and her days full of running here and there, doing this and that. But here she could take a moment to breathe—just to be.

Her thoughts trailed back to her unusual conversation with Massimo. Was the man some sort of matchmaker? But why? He hardly knew her. How would he know if she would be good for Dante? And why would Dante need her?

The questions followed one after the other. The most

frustrating part was that she didn't have an answer for any of them. Dante was even more of a mystery to her now than he was before.

She'd noticed from the moment they'd arrived here that everything wasn't so perfect in Dante's life. Though she hadn't been able to hear the conversation between father and son, she'd clearly seen the dark look that had come over Dante's handsome face while talking with his father. There was a definite distance between him and his family. Was that what Massimo thought she could help Dante with? But how? She was here for only a matter of weeks, certainly not long enough to change someone's life. And what did she know about the inner workings of families?

Still, she couldn't get her mind to stop replaying the events from the prior evening. When his family grew boisterous talking of the vineyard, she noticed how Dante had become withdrawn as if he didn't feel as though he fit in—or was it that he didn't want to fit in? Either way, she couldn't imagine Dante willingly walking away from such an amazing place.

There had to be something more to his story—something he wasn't willing to share. But what could drive him from the peacefulness of the countryside and the bosom of his family to the city? Unless… Was it possible? Her mind raced. Could he have a passion for cooking that rivaled hers? Was it possible that they at last had something in common?

The thunk of the kitchen door swinging shut startled her. She spun around and there stood the man who'd filled her every thought since arriving here. The heat crept up her neck and settled in her cheeks. She realized that she was being silly. It wasn't as if he could read her mind.

Their gazes met and held. His stare was deep and probing. Unease inched up her spine. There was no way that he could know that just moments ago, she'd been daydreaming about his grandfather's suggestion that she and Dante might be a perfect fit.

"I didn't know if you'd be up yet." His voice was deep and gravelly.

"I set my phone alarm. I didn't want to miss the sunrise."

"And was it worth the effort?"

She nodded vigorously. "Definitely. I'm in love." When his eyes widened in surprise, she added, "With the villa and the vineyard. With all of it."

"I'm glad you like it here."

"I was considering going for a walk."

"Would you care for some company?"

Her gaze jerked back around to his to see if he was serious. "You really want to escort me around? I mean, it isn't like I'll be running into any of your family. You don't have to babysit me."

"I didn't offer so I could play babysitter. I thought maybe you'd want some company, but obviously I was wrong." He turned back to the house.

"Wait." He paused, but he didn't turn around. She swallowed down a chunk of pride. "I would like your company."

He turned to her but his lips were pressed together in a firm line. He crossed his arms and looked at her expectantly. He had a right to expect more. She'd been snippy and he hadn't deserved it. But it wasn't easy for her. For some reason, she had the hardest time dealing with him. His mere presence put her on edge. And he always scattered her thoughts with his good looks and charming smile.

"Okay, I'm sorry. Is that what you want to hear?"

"Yes, it is." He stepped up to her. "Shall we go?"

She glanced down at the almost empty cup. "I need to put this in the house."

He took it from her, jogged back to the kitchen and returned in no time. He extended his arm like a total gentleman, which sent her heart tumbling in her chest. Without hesitation, she slipped her hand into the crook of his arm.

When her fingers tightened around his biceps, she noticed his rock-hard strength.

This wasn't right. She had no business letting her guard down around him. Nothing good would come of it. She considered pulling away, but part of her refused to let go. With a quick glance at his relaxed features, she realized she was making too much of the situation.

He led her away from the house and down a dirt path. "You made quite an impression on my family."

"Is that a good thing?"

"Most definitely. They're all quite taken with you. It was the most excitement they've had around here in quite a while."

Normally she kept up her walls and held everyone at bay, but being here, being around Massimo, she'd let down her defenses a bit. "I noticed you were quiet last night. Was there something wrong?"

"No, not at all. And you were amazing, especially with Nonno. He's been really down in the dumps, but you cheered him up. So I owe you a big thank-you."

She noticed how he didn't explain his quietness. She wondered if he was always so reserved around his family. Granted, she didn't understand how traditional families worked as her life had consisted of foster homes where kids came and went and there wasn't that deep, abiding love that came naturally. But she had Jules and they were as close as any blood relatives.

"Your brother, he's older than you, isn't he?" She wanted to get Dante to open up about his family. She couldn't help it. She was curious.

"Yes. He's a couple of years older."

Well, that certainly didn't strike up the hoped-for conversation. "Are you two very close?"

Dante slanted a gaze her way but she pretended not to notice. "I don't know. We're brothers."

She knew none of this was any of her business but everything about Dante intrigued her. He was like an artichoke and she'd barely begun to pull at the tough outer layer. There was so much to learn before she got to the tender center that he protected from everyone.

"They care a lot about you."

He stopped and pulled her around to look at him. "Why all of this curiosity about my family? What's going on in that beautiful mind of yours?"

Did he just say she was beautiful? Her gaze met his and her breath became shallow. No, he'd said her mind was beautiful. But was that the same thing as saying she was beautiful?

"I was just making small talk." She tried to act innocent. "Why do I have to have ulterior motives?"

"I didn't say you did. But sometimes you make me wonder." He peered into her eyes and for a moment she wondered if he could read her thoughts.

Heat filled her cheeks and she glanced away. "Wonder about what?"

"You. There's more to you than meets the eye. Something tells me that you have an interesting past."

She couldn't hold back a laugh. "You make me sound very mysterious. Like Mata Hari or something." She leaned closer to him and whispered in his ear. "I'm here to find out your secrets."

He grabbed her upper arms and moved her back, allowing her the opportunity to see the worry lines ingrained on his face. "What secrets?"

His hard, sharp tone startled her. "Your secrets in the kitchen, of course. What else did you think I meant?"

His frown eased. "You're having far too much fun at my expense."

So the man was keeping secrets. From her? Or from the whole world? She didn't think it was possible but she was even more intrigued by him.

She gazed into his bottomless brown eyes. "You need

to let your hair down and have some fun. It won't hurt. I promise."

"Is that what all of the smiling and laughing was about last night? Or are you trying to sway my family over to your side so they'll pressure me into agreeing to follow through with the contract?"

She pulled back her shoulders. She knew she shouldn't but she just couldn't help herself. His gaze dipped as her fingers once again made an X over her chest. "I promised not to do that."

The vein in his neck pulsated and when his eyes met hers again, there was a need, a passion in his gaze. Her line of vision dipped to his lips.

"You do know that you're driving me crazy, don't you?"

"Who, me?" This was the most fun she'd ever had. She'd never flirted with a guy before. Sure, they'd flirted with her but she never felt the desire to return the flirtations.

Until now.

His hands encircled her waist. "Yes, you. Do you have any idea what I'd like to do to you right now?"

A few scintillating thoughts danced and teased her mind. She placed her hands on his chest and felt the pounding of his heart. She was certain that hers could easily keep time with his. It was pumping so fast that it felt as if she'd just finished a long run on a hot, muggy day. In that moment she was overcome by the urge to find out if his kiss was as moving in real life as it had been in her dreams last night.

"You know, we really shouldn't do this." His voice was carried like a whisper in the breeze.

"When have you ever done what was expected of you?"

"Not very often." His gaze bored deep into her, making her stomach quiver with need.

"Then why start now? I won't tell, if you won't."

That was all it took. His head dipped and then his lips were there. He stopped just a breath away from hers. She could practically feel the turbulent vibes coming off him.

It was as though he was fighting an inner battle between what was right and what he wanted. She needed to put him out of his misery—out of her misery.

Acting on total instinct and desire, she leaned up on her tiptoes and pressed her mouth to his. His lips were smooth and warm. He didn't move. He wanted it. She knew that as well as she knew that the sun would set that evening. Perhaps he needed just a touch more enticement.

She let her body lean into his as her hands slipped up over his broad shoulders. Her fingertips raked through his dark hair as her lips gently moved over his. And then she heard a hungry moan swell in his throat as he pulled her snug against him.

Perhaps it was the knowledge that this kiss should be forbidden that made it the most enticing kiss she'd ever experienced. Then again, it could be that she was lonely and missing her sister, and being in Dante's arms made her feel connected to someone. Or maybe it was simply the fact that he was the dreamiest hunk she'd ever laid her eyes on, and she just wanted to see what she'd be missing by holding herself back.

He stroked and prodded, sending her heart pounding against her ribs with pure desire. His hard planes fit perfectly against her soft curves. And for the moment, she felt like the most beautiful—most desired—woman in the world.

Dante moved, placing his hands on each side of her face. When he pulled his lips from hers, she felt bereft. She wanted more. Needed more.

He rested his forehead against hers. His breathing was deep and uneven. He'd been just as caught up in the moment as she'd been, so why had he stopped? What had happened?

His thumb gently stroked her cheek. "Lizzie, we can't do this. You know that it's wrong."

"But it felt so right."

She couldn't help it. She wasn't ready for the harsh light of reality. She lived every single day with the sharp edges of reality slicing into her dreams. Just once, she wanted to know what it was like not to have to worry about meeting the monthly bills. She just wanted this one blissful memory.

"Lizzie, this can't happen. You and I…it's impossible."

His words pricked her bubble of happiness. Once again she was being rejected. And the worst part was he was right. And that thought made the backs of her eyes sting.

When was it going to be her turn for just a little bit of happiness without the rug being pulled out from under her? This trip to Rome should be the trip of a lifetime, but now the entire arrangement was in jeopardy and she had no job to return to.

She blinked repeatedly, keeping the moisture in her eyes in check. If she was good at one thing in life, it was being a trooper. When life dropped lemons on her, she whipped up a lemon meringue pie with the fluffiest, tallest peaks. She could do it again.

She pulled back until her spine was straight and his hands fell away. "You're right. I don't know what I was thinking." Her voice wobbled. She swallowed down the lump of emotion. "It won't happen again."

Without meeting his gaze, she moved past him and started for the villa. The tip of her tongue ran over her lower lip, where she found the slightest minty taste of toothpaste he'd left behind. She stifled a frustrated moan, knowing that he was only a few steps behind her.

CHAPTER NINE

HE'D TOTALLY BLOWN IT.

Dante stowed their bags in the car's boot and then glanced back at the villa. Lizzie smiled at his grandfather before hugging him goodbye. A stab of jealousy tore into Dante. She'd barely spoken to him after they'd kissed, and even then, it'd only been one-word answers. Why in the world had he let his hormones do the thinking for him?

He had absolutely no desire to toy with her feelings. Hurting Lizzie was the last thing in the world he wanted to do. And though she appeared to have it all together, he knew that she had a vulnerable side, too. He'd witnessed the hurt that had flashed in her eyes when she realized that he didn't trust her with his grandfather. She wanted him to think she was tough, but he knew lurking beneath the beautiful surface lay a vulnerable woman—a woman that he was coming to like a bit more than he should.

When she at last joined him in the car, she stared straight ahead. The unease between them was palpable. Dante didn't like it one bit, but he had no one to blame but himself. There was no way he could go back in time and undo the kiss. And if he could, he wasn't so sure he would. Their kiss had been something special—something he'd never experienced before.

He cut his thoughts off short. He realized that it was thoughts like this that had gotten him into trouble in the first place. But he couldn't ignore the fact that this silent treatment was doing him in.

"Are you ever going to speak to me again?" He struggled to keep the frustration out of his voice.

"Yes."

More of the one-syllable answers. "Did you enjoy your visit to the vineyard?"

"Yes."

"Enough with the yeses and nos." His hands tightened on the steering wheel, trying to get a grip on his rising frustration. Worst of all was the fact he had no clue how to fix things between them. And whether it was wise or not, he wanted Lizzie to like him. "My grandfather seemed quite taken with you. In fact, the whole family did."

Nothing.

She crossed her arms and huffed. What did that mean? Was she about to let him have it? His muscles tensed as he waited for a tongue-lashing. Not that he could blame her. He deserved it, but it wouldn't make it any less uncomfortable.

Her voice was soft and he strained to hear her. "How do you do it?"

Well, it was more than one syllable, but he didn't have a clue what she meant. And he was hesitant to ask, but what choice did he have?

"How do I do what?" The breath caught in his throat as he waited for what came next.

"How do you drive away from that little piece of heaven at the end of each weekend and return to the city?"

This wasn't the direction he'd expected the conversation to take. His family wasn't a subject he talked about beyond the generalities. *How's your father? Is your brother still working at the vineyard? Did they have a good harvest?* But no one ever probed into his choice to move away—to distance himself from his family.

"I prefer Rome." It wasn't necessarily a lie.

"Don't get me wrong. I love the city life. But I was born and bred in a city that never sleeps. I think it's in my bones to appreciate the chatter of voices and the hum of vehicles. But you, you were raised in the peace and tranquillity."

"It isn't the perfect slice of heaven like you're thinking." He tried not to think about his childhood. He didn't want to remember.

"What wasn't perfect about it?"

He glanced her way, giving her a warning stare to leave the subject alone.

"Hey, you're the one who wanted me to talk. I'm talking. Now it's your turn."

He could see that she wasn't going to leave this subject alone. Not unless he let her know that she was stepping on a very tender subject.

"Life at the DeFiore Vineyard wasn't idyllic when I was a kid. Far from it."

"Why?"

She really was going to push this. And for some unknown reason, he wanted to make her understand his side. "I'm the reason my mother died."

"What?" She swung around in her seat, fighting with the seat belt so that she was able to look directly at him. "But I don't understand. How?"

"She died after she gave birth to me."

"Oh. How horrible." There was an awkward pause. "But it wasn't your fault."

"No, not directly. But my father blamed me. He told me that I took away the best part of his life."

"He didn't mean it. That…those words, they were part of his grief."

Dante shoved his fingers through his hair. "He meant it. I can't help but feel that I bring sadness and misery to those closest to me—"

"Nonsense. Listen, I'm so sorry for your loss. I know

how tough that can be, but you're not to blame for her death or how your father handled his grief. We all handle the death of family members differently."

That caught his attention. A chance to turn the tables away from himself and back to her. "Have you lost a parent?"

Silence enveloped the car. Only the hum of the engine and the tires rolling over the blacktop could be heard. Lizzie turned away to stare out the side window as Dante drove on, waiting and wondering.

"Lizzie, you can talk to me. Whatever you say won't go any further."

He took his focus off the road for just a moment to glance her way. She cast him a hesitant look. He had a feeling she had something important to say—something she didn't normally share. He really hoped she'd let down her guard and let him in. He wanted so badly to understand more about her.

"My mother died." Her voice was so soft.

"I'm sorry. I guess we've both had some hard knocks in life."

"Yes, but at least you have a loving family. And you can always go home when you want to..." It seemed as though she wanted to say more but stopped.

This conversation was much deeper—much more serious than he'd ever expected. He wanted to press for more information, but he sensed now wasn't the time. Spotting a small village up ahead with a trattoria, he slowed down.

"You know, we left without eating. Would you care for a bite of food? And they have the best *caffé* around. I noticed that you have quite a fondness for cappuccino."

"I do. And I'd love to get some."

He eased off the road and maneuvered the car into the lot. Before he got out, he knew there was something more he had to say. "I'm sorry about what happened back at the vineyard. The kiss was a mistake. I didn't mean to cross the line. The last thing I want to do is hurt you."

She turned to him and smiled, but the gesture never quite reached her eyes. "Don't worry. You'd have to do a lot more than that kiss to hurt me. Now let's get that coffee."

Without giving him a chance to say anything else, she alighted from the car. Her words might have been what he wanted to hear, but he didn't believe her. His gut told him that he'd hurt her more deeply than her stubborn pride would let on.

He didn't know what it was about Ms. Lizzie Addler from New York, but she was getting to him. He longed to be a good guy in her eyes, but he was torn between his desire to help her and his need to sell the *ristorante* in order to return to the vineyard and help his family. How was he supposed to make everyone happy? Was it even possible?

How had that happened?

Lizzie had entered the quaint restaurant with no appetite at all. And now as they exited the small family establishment, her stomach was full up with the most delicious sampling of pastas, meats and cheeses.

It had all started when they'd been greeted by the sweetest older woman. She'd insisted that they have a seat while she called to her husband, who was in the kitchen. Apparently they'd known Dante all of his life and were thrilled to see that he'd brought his lady friend to meet them. When Lizzie tried to correct the very chatty woman, her words got lost in the conversation.

"Are they always so outgoing?" Lizzie asked Dante as they approached the car.

"Guido and Luiso Caruso have known my family for years, and yes, they are always that friendly. Did you get enough to eat?"

Lizzie gently patted her rounded stomach. "I'm stuffed."

Dante snapped his fingers. "I forgot to give them a message from my grandfather. I'll be right back."

While Dante rushed back inside, Lizzie leaned against the car's fender and lifted her face to the sun. Perhaps she was hungrier than she thought because now that she'd eaten, her mood was much lighter. And it'd helped that Dante had opened up to her about his family. No matter how little he cracked open the door to his past, every bit he shared meant a lot to her.

But nothing could dislodge the memory of that earth-shattering kiss. It was always there, lurking around the edges of her mind. But the part that stung was how Dante had rejected her. And his reasoning did nothing to soothe her.

Somehow she'd get past this crazy infatuation. Because in the end, he was right. They did have to work together over the next eight weeks. Not to mention that they shared an apartment—anything else, no matter how casual, would just complicate matters.

"Ready to go?" Dante frowned as he noticed her leaning against the flawless paint job.

"Yes, I am."

As he got closer, she noticed how he inspected where she'd been leaning, as if she'd dented the car or something. His hand smoothed across the paint.

"Are you serious?" she asked incredulously.

He turned to her, his face perfectly serious. "What?"

He really didn't get it. She smiled and shook her head. Men and their cars. "Nothing."

"If we get going we should be home in no time. There's not much traffic. And the weather is perfect." He repeatedly tossed the keys in the air.

Lizzie moved in to catch them. "Let me drive."

"What? You're joking, right?" He reached out to take the keys from her.

She pulled her hand behind her back, which drew her

blouse tight across her chest. His gaze dipped and lingered just a moment. When his gaze met hers again, she smiled.

"Come on. You said yourself there is hardly any traffic."

And she'd love to drive an honest-to-goodness exclusive sports car, the kind that turned heads—both men and women, young and old. She may not be a car junkie, but that didn't mean she couldn't appreciate a fine vehicle. And this car was quite fine. Jules would never believe she'd gotten to drive such an amazing sports car.

"I don't think so." The smile slipped from his face. "Can I have the keys so we can get going?"

Enjoying having him at a disadvantage, she felt her smile broaden. She backed up a few steps. She was in the mood to have a little fun, hoping it'd get them back on track. "If you want them, you'll have to come and get them."

He didn't move. "This isn't funny." His tone grew quite insistent. "Hand over the keys."

Her good mood screeched to a halt. He wouldn't even consider letting her behind the steering wheel. Did he really think so little of her that she couldn't drive a car in a straight line?

Hurt balled up in her gut. She dropped the keys in his outstretched hand and strode around the car. "I assume I'm still allowed to sit in the passenger seat."

"Hey, you don't have to be like that. After all, I don't let anyone drive Red."

Her head snapped around to face him. "You named your car?"

"Of course. Why wouldn't I?"

She shook her head, having no words to describe her amazement.

"Besides, I'm sure that you'll enjoy riding in the passenger seat more. You can take a nap or check out the passing scenery."

It hurt her how easily he brushed off her request as though she couldn't possibly be serious about wanting to drive such a fine machine. All of her life people had never seen past her foster-kid status and used clothes. Even now as she sat on the butter-soft upholstery of a car that she would never be able to afford in her entire life, she was wearing hand-me-downs. But at least these clothes fit her and they didn't look as though they'd seen a better day.

She was tired of people underestimating her. She refused to sit by and take it. She would show Dante that she was just as capable as him.

CHAPTER TEN

"I KEPT MY WORD."

The sound of Lizzie's voice startled Dante.

She'd resumed her quiet mode after he'd asked for the keys. He had no idea she was so intent on driving his car—his gem. She obviously didn't know how precious it was to him and he didn't know how to describe it to her. The fact that his father liked this car almost as much as Dante did meant the world to him. And the fact that he'd bought it all on his own had earned him some of his father's respect. He couldn't afford to lose that one small step.

Dante unlocked the penthouse door. "You kept your word about what?"

"The contract. I didn't say a word while we were at the villa. But now that we're back and the film crew will be here tomorrow at 6:00 a.m., I need to know if you're on board with the whole thing." Lizzie strode into the living room. She fished around in her purse, eventually producing her cell phone. Her gaze met his as her finger hovered over the touch screen.

His curiosity was piqued. "Who are you planning to call?"

"My contact at the studio."

"Did you already tell them about my grandfather not being able to fulfill his obligation?"

She nodded. "I told them right away."

He kind of figured she would. "And what did they say?"

He wasn't so sure he wanted to hear the answer because Lizzie looked far too confident. What did she know that he didn't?

Lizzie perched on the arm of the couch. "They were sorry to hear about your grandfather."

"And?"

"And when I mentioned that you'd taken over the restaurant, they were intrigued. They pulled up some old footage of you with your grandfather and they're convinced transitioning the spotlight from your grandfather to you will work."

He should have known that eventually being on television even for a few seconds would come back to bite him. He just never expected this. Who would want him on television? He knew nothing of acting. And he wasn't inclined to learn.

"Lizzie, I haven't agreed to this. Any of it." And he didn't want to either.

"But what choice do you have at this point? If your attorney was going to uncover an easy out, he'd have told you by now."

Dante's hands pressed down on the granite countertop. He wanted to argue with her. He wanted to point out that this idea didn't have a chance to be a success. But even his solicitor wasn't rushing in, promising that all would be fine. In fact, his solicitor had said quite the opposite. That trying to break the contract would cost him money and time.

The television exposure would definitely give the *ristorante* added publicity and the asking price could easily be inflated. As it was, he'd been forced to lower the price to unload it quickly, but now there wouldn't be a rush. He could ask for a more realistic price and perhaps someone else would step forward that would want the *ristorante* without buying the family recipes.

Lizzie tossed her oversize purse on the couch. "Besides, if you help me out, I'll help you out."

"What do you have in mind?"

"If you agree to do the filming each morning before the restaurant opens, I can help you around Ristorante Massimo."

His brows rose. "You're offering to work for me?"

"Sure. What else do I have to do with my time?"

There had to be a catch. There always was. Everybody wanted something. "And what are you expecting me to pay you?"

She shrugged. "Nothing."

"Nothing?"

"I'd just like a chance to do what I would have done with your grandfather."

"And that was?"

"To learn from him. He was planning to teach me as much as he could while I was in town. I came to Italy with the sole intent to work my butt off."

Dante eyed her up. "You really don't want anything else but to learn?"

"Why do you sound so skeptical?"

He shrugged. "I'm not used to people offering me free help."

"I wouldn't get used to it. Not everyone can afford to do it. But the studio is paying me to be here, and with you providing free room and board, it should all work out."

At last he found the rub. "You intend to continue to live here? With me?"

"Is this your way of saying that you plan to kick me out?"

"You have to admit that after what happened in the vineyard the idea of us living and working together isn't a good one."

"Why? Are you saying that you want to repeat that kiss?" She moved forward, only stopping when she stood on the other side of the counter. "Are you wishing that you hadn't stopped it?"

His gaze dipped to her pink frosted lips. Oh, yes, he

definitely wanted to continue that kiss. He wanted it to go on and on. "No. That's not what I'm saying. Quit putting words in my mouth."

Her eyes flashed her disbelief. "I only call 'em like I see 'em."

"It has nothing to do with the kiss. I'd already forgotten about it." No, he hadn't. Not in the least. "It's just…"

"Just what?" Lines bracketed her icy blue eyes as she waited for his answer.

"I just don't know if you understand what will be expected from you."

"You mean you think I'm just another pretty face without anything between my ears."

"Hey, I didn't say that. There you go again, making assumptions."

"Then what did you mean?"

"I have my way of doing things. And I expect you to pay attention to the details—no matter how small or meaningless you might find them." He needed time alone to get his head on straight. There was a lot here to consider. "I'm going to my office. We'll talk more later."

"Do you mind if I go downstairs and have a look around. I want to know what I'm getting myself into."

"Be my guest. Here's the key." He tossed her a key card and rattled off the security pass code.

Her lips pressed into a firm line as she clutched the key card and turned for the door. He stood there in the kitchenette. He couldn't turn away as his gaze was latched on the gentle sway of her hips as she strode away. His pulse raced and memories of holding her and tasting her sweet kisses clouded his mind. How had he ever found the willpower to let her go?

The snick of the door closing snapped Dante back to the here and now. What was so different about her? He'd dated his share of women and none of them had gotten to him like her. But if there was any possibility of them working together and sharing this apartment, he needed to see her as just another coworker. Someone who couldn't get under his skin and give him that overwhelming urge to scratch his itch. Because that would only lead them both into trouble as had already happened back at the vineyard.

He should just show Lizzie the door and forget trying to fulfill his grandfather's wishes. If he was logical, that was what he'd do. But when it came to family, nothing was logical.

Combine that with the desperation he'd witnessed in Lizzie's gaze, and he felt an overwhelming urge to find a way to make this work for both of them. But could he keep his hormones in check around her? Suddenly his apartment wasn't looking so big after all.

She'd prove him wrong.

Lizzie strode into the impressive kitchen of Ristorante Massimo. It was more spacious than it had appeared on television. And she immediately felt at home surrounded by the stainless-steel appliances. She just wished that Massimo would be there instead of his stubborn grandson.

But she had a plan. She was going to prove to Dante that she was talented—that she could hold up her end of the agreement. She looked over the ingredients in the fridge and the freezer. Slowly a dinner menu took shape in her mind. She didn't want it to be pasta as she didn't want to compete in his arena. No, she would whip up something else.

She set to work, anxious to prove to Dante that she belonged here in Massimo's kitchen. She had the ability; she just needed to broaden her horizons with new culinary skills.

She didn't know how much time had passed when she heard a sound behind her. She turned and jumped when she saw Dante propping himself up in the doorway.

"What are you doing there?" She set aside the masher she'd used to whip up the cauliflower.

"I think I'm the one who should be asking you that question."

She glanced around at the mess she'd created. Okay, so she wasn't the neatest person in the kitchen. But to be honest, she had seen worse. And she was in a hurry. She'd wanted it all to be completed before he arrived. So much for her plan.

"I thought I'd put together dinner."

He walked closer. "And what's on the menu?"

She ran over and pressed a hand to his chest to stop him. The warmth from his body and the rhythm of his heart sent tingles shooting up her arm. Big mistake. But her heart wasn't listening to her head. A bolt of awareness struck her and all she could think about was stepping a little closer. The breath caught in her throat as she looked up at his tempting lips.

Memories of his caresses dominated her thoughts. She'd never been kissed like that before. It had meaning. It had depth. And it had left her longing for more. But this wasn't the time or the place. She had to make a point with him. And caving in to her desires would not help her cause.

She pulled her hand back. "I have a table all set in the dining room. Why don't you go make yourself comfortable? The food will be in shortly."

He strained his neck, looking around. "Are you sure I shouldn't stay and help?"

She pressed her hands to her hips. "I'm positive. Go."

He hesitated and she started to wonder if he was going to trust her. But then he relented. And turned. When he exited the kitchen, she rushed to finish up with the things on the stove. She placed them in the oven to keep them warm.

At last, it was time to start serving up the most important meal of her life. Since when had impressing Dante become more about what he thought of her and less about gaining the job? She consoled herself with the thought that it was just nerves. It wasn't as if he was the first man to kiss her. Nor would he be the last.

She pushed aside the jumbled thoughts as she moved to the refrigerator and removed the crab-and-avocado salad. She placed the dish on the tray, took off her apron and smoothed a hand over her hair, worrying that she must look a mess. Oh, well, it was too late to worry about it now.

Then, realizing that she'd forgotten something for him to drink, she grabbed both a glass of chilled water and a bottle of DeFiore white wine she'd picked out to complement the meal.

She carried the tray into the dining room and came to a stop when she noticed the lights had been dimmed and candles had been added to the table as well as some fresh greens and dahlias with hearty yellow centers and deep pink tips. The breath caught in her throat.

The table was perfect. It looked as though it was ready for a romantic interlude. And then her gaze came to rest on Dante. He'd changed clothes. What? But why?

She glanced down at the same clothes she'd worn all day that were now smudged with flour and sauce. She resisted the urge to race out of the room to grab a shower and to change into something that would make her feel sexy and alluring.

She turned her attention to Dante, taking in his creased black slacks, a matching jacket and a gray button-up shirt. Wow. With his tanned features and his dark hair, he looked like a Hollywood star. She swallowed hard. She wondered if he'd remembered to put on a touch of cologne, too. The thought of moving close enough to check was oh, so tempting.

She gave herself a mental jerk. She wasn't here for a date. This was business. She couldn't blow her chance to show him that she was quite competent in the kitchen. She would impress him this evening, but it would be through her culinary prowess and not through flirting or any of the other tempting thoughts that came readily to mind.

"If you'll have a seat, I'll serve you." She tried to act as though her heart wasn't thumping against her ribs.

He frowned. "But I want to get your chair for you."

"You don't need to do that."

"Aren't you joining me?"

She shook her head.

"But you've got to be hungry, too."

She was but it wasn't the food she'd slaved over for the past couple of hours that had her salivating. "I'm fine."

"Oh, come on. You surely don't think that I'll enjoy this meal with you rushing around waiting on me. Now sit."

What was up with him? She eyed him up as she sat in the chair he'd pulled out for her. Was he having a change of heart about teaching her what he knew—in the kitchen, that was?

"I only brought out enough food for one."

"Not a problem." Before she could utter a word, he moved to the kitchen.

This wasn't right. This was not how she'd planned to prove to Dante that she was up to the task of working in Ristorante Massimo. Frustration collided with the girlie part of her that was thrilled to be pampered. It was a totally new experience for her. But it also left her feeling off-kilter. Was she supposed to read something into his actions? The clothes? The flowers and candles? Did any of it have anything to do with their kiss?

When he returned, she gazed at him in the glow of the candle. The words caught in her throat as she realized this was her first candlelit dinner. Romance had never been part of her other relationships. She could definitely get used to this and to Dante—

No. No. She couldn't get distracted again. This was not a date. It was business. So why was Dante acting so strange? So kind and thoughtful?

"Is there something I should know?" she asked, bracing herself for bad news.

A dark brow arched. "Know about what?"

She didn't want to put words in his mouth, especially if they were not what she wanted to hear. "I don't know. I just wondered about your effort to be so nice."

He frowned. "So now you think that I'm not nice."

She groaned. "That isn't what I meant. You're taking my words out of context."

"I am?" He placed a plate and glass in front of her. "Perhaps we should talk about something else, then."

"No. I want to know why you're in such a good mood. Have you made up your mind about the television show?"

Please let him say that he had a change of heart.

His gaze lowered to the table as he took his seat. "Are you sure you know what you're asking?"

"Of course I do. All you have to do is fill in for your grandfather. And teach me everything you know." Did this mean he was truly considering the idea? Were her dreams about to come true?

"You really want to learn from me?"

She nodded.

The silence dragged on. Her stomach knotted and her palms grew damp. Why wasn't he saying anything?

"Well?" She couldn't bear the unknown any longer. "Where does that leave us?"

"It leaves us with a meal that's going to get cold if we don't get through this first course soon."

"But I need to know."

"And you will. Soon."

Was that a promise? It sounded like one. But what was soon in his book? She glanced down at her salad. How in the world was she supposed to eat now?

CHAPTER ELEVEN

HE MUST HAVE lost his mind.

That had to be it. Otherwise why would he even consider going along with this arrangement?

Dante stared across the candlelit table at Lizzie. He noticed how she'd moved the food around on her plate, but she'd barely eaten a bite. She had to be hungry because it'd been hours since they'd stopped at the trattoria on their way back to Rome.

And this food was really good. In fact, he had to admit that he was impressed. Maybe taking her under his wing wouldn't be such a hardship after all. His solicitor definitely thought it was the least painless course of action. Easy for him to say.

But the deciding factor was when the potential buyer of the *ristorante* had been willing to wait the two months. His solicitor said that they'd actually been quite enthusiastic about the *ristorante* getting international coverage.

But what no one took into consideration was the fact that Dante was totally drawn to Lizzie. And that was a serious complication. How in the world were they to work together when all he could think about was kissing her again? He longed to wrap his arms around her and pull her close. He remembered vividly how the morning sun had glowed behind her, giving her whole appearance a golden glow. It had been an experience unlike any other. And when their lips had met—

"Is something wrong with the food?"

Dante blinked before meeting Lizzie's worried gaze. He had to start thinking of her in professional terms. He supposed that if he were going to take her on as his protégée, he might as well get started. He'd teach her as much as possible within their time limit.

"Now that you'll be working here, there'll be no special treatment. You'll be expected to work just like everyone else."

"Understood."

"As for the food, the chicken is a little overcooked. You'll need to be careful of that going forward."

A whole host of expressions flitted across her face. "Is there anything else?"

It wasn't the reaction he'd been expecting. He thought she'd be ecstatic to learn that she'd be working there. And that she'd get her television spot. Women. He'd never figure them out. In his experience, they never reacted predictably.

"And use less salt. The guest can always add more according to their taste and diet."

Her face filled with color. Without a word, she threw her linen napkin on the table and rushed to the kitchen.

He groaned. He hadn't meant to upset her. Still, how was he supposed to teach her anything if he couldn't provide constructive criticism? His grandfather should be here. He would know what to say and how to say it.

Dante raked his fingers through his hair. He'd agreed to this arrangement far too quickly. He should have gone with his gut that said this was going to be a monumental mistake. Now he had to fix things before the camera crew showed up. The last thing either of them needed was to start their television appearances on a bad note—with all of the world watching.

He strode toward the kitchen and paused by the door. What did he say to her? Did he apologize even though he hadn't said anything derogatory? Did he set a precedent that she would expect him to apologize every time she got upset when he pointed out something that she could improve on? An exasperated sigh passed his lips. He obviously wasn't meant to be a teacher.

He pushed the door open, prepared to find Lizzie in tears. Instead he found her scraping leftovers into the garbage and piling the dishes in the sink.

"What are you doing?"

She didn't face him. "I'm cleaning up. What does it look like?"

"But we weren't done eating. Why don't you come back to the table?"

She grabbed the main dish and dumped it in the garbage. "I don't want anything else."

"Would you stop?"

"There's no point in keeping leftovers." With that, she grabbed the dessert.

He knew where she was headed and stepped in her way. What in the world had gotten into her? Why was she acting this way?

"Lizzie, put down the dessert and tell me what's bothering you."

She tilted her chin to gaze up at him. "Why should something be bothering me? You tore to shreds the dinner I painstakingly prepared for you."

"But isn't that what you want me to do? Teach you?"

Her icy gaze bored into him. The temperature took an immediate dive. "Move."

"No. We need to finish talking."

"So you can continue to insult me. No, thank you." She moved to go around him but he moved to block her.

"Lizzie, I don't know what it is you want from me. I thought you wanted me to teach you, but obviously that isn't the case. So what is it you want? Or do you just want to call this whole thing off?"

"I didn't know we were starting the lessons right away.

Or did you just say those things in hopes of me calling off the arrangement?"

"No, that isn't what I had in mind." How the heck had he ended up on the defensive? He'd only meant to be helpful.

"So you truly think I'm terrible in the kitchen?"

He took the tray from her and set it on the counter. Then he stepped up to her, hating the emotional turmoil he saw in her eyes. He found himself longing to soothe her. But he didn't have a clue how to accomplish such a thing. He seemed to keep making one mistake after the other where she was concerned.

"I think that you're very talented." It was the truth. And he'd have said it even if he didn't find her amazingly attractive.

Her bewildered gaze met his. "But you said—"

"That there were things for you to take into consideration while working here. I didn't mean to hurt your feelings."

Disbelief shimmered in her eyes.

He didn't think. He just acted, reaching out to her. His thumb stroked her cheek, enjoying its velvety softness. She stepped away from his touch and his hand lowered to his side.

"Lizzie, you have to believe me. If you're going to be this sensitive, how do you think we'll be able to work together?"

This was all wrong.

Lizzie crossed her arms to keep from reaching out to him. The whole evening had gone off the rails and she had no idea how to fix things. And the worst part was that she'd overreacted. Big-time.

She'd always prided herself on being able to contain her feelings behind a wall of indifference. And Dante wasn't the first to criticize her skills. But he was the first whose opinion truly mattered to her on a deeply personal level. He was the first person she wanted to thoroughly impress.

The thought brought her up short. Since when had his thoughts and feelings come to mean so much to her? Was it the kiss? Had it changed everything? Or was it opening up to him in the car? Had their heart-to-heart made her vulnerable to him?

Panic clawed at her. She knew what happened when she let people too close and she opened up about her background. She'd been shunned most of her life. She couldn't let Dante do that to her. She couldn't stand the thought of him looking at her with pity while thinking that she was less than everyone else—after all, if her own parents couldn't love her, how was anyone else supposed to?

Not that she wanted Dante to fall in love with her. Did she? No. That was the craziest idea to cross her mind in a long time—probably her craziest idea ever.

The walls started to close in on her. She needed space. Away from Dante. Away from his curious stare. "I need... need to make a phone call. I...I'll clean this all up later."

And with that, she raced for the door. She didn't have to call Jules, but she did need the excuse to get away from him. It was as if he had some sort of magnetic field around him and it drew out her deepest feelings. She needed to stuff them back in the little box in her heart.

Being alone in a strange city in a country practically halfway around the world from her home made her choices quite limited. She thought of escaping back to the vineyard and visiting some more with Massimo. He was so easy to talk to. He was her friend. But he was also Dante's grandfather. And the vineyard was Dante's home.

Her shoulders slumped as she headed for the apartment. What she needed now was to talk to Jules. It would be good to hear a familiar voice. She made a beeline for her room and pulled out her phone. She knew the call would cost her a small fortune but this was an emergency.

She dialed the familiar number. The phone rang and

rang. Just when she thought that it was going to switch to voice mail, she heard a familiar voice.

"Lizzie, is that you? What's wrong?"

The concern in Jules's voice had her rushing to reassure her. "I just wanted to check in."

"But you said that we needed to watch how much we spend on the phone. You said we should only call when something was wrong. So what happened?"

"Nothing. I just wanted to hear your voice and make sure you are doing okay."

There was a slight pause. "Lizzie, this is me. You can't lie to me. Something is bothering you. So spill it."

Calling Jules had been a mistake. She knew her far too well. And now Jules wasn't going to let her off the hook. "It's Dante. I think I just blew my chance to work with him."

"Why? What did you do?"

"I…I overreacted. Instead of taking his feedback on my cooking like a professional, I acted like an oversensitive female." Her thoughts drifted over the evening. "All I wanted to do was impress him and…and I failed."

"Don't worry about him. Just come home."

"I can't do that. Remember, I quit my job. And your tuition is due soon."

"You don't have to worry about that. I don't have to go to grad school."

"You do if you want to be a social worker and help other kids like us." The remembrance of her promise to her foster sister put things in perspective. She couldn't let her bruised ego get the best of her. She couldn't walk away. "Just ignore what I said. I'm tired. Everything will work out."

"But, Lizzie, if he's making things impossible for you, what are you going to do?"

There was a knock at her bedroom door.

"Jules, I have to go. I'll call you later."

With a quick goodbye, she disconnected the call. She

worried her bottom lip and waited. Maybe Dante would go away. She wasn't ready to talk to him. Not yet.

Again the tap at the door. "I'm not going away until we talk."

"I don't have anything to say to you."

"But I have plenty to say to you."

That sparked her curiosity, but her bruised ego wasn't ready to give in. She wanted to tell herself that his words and his opinions meant nothing. But that trip to the vineyard and that kiss in the morning sunshine had cast some sort of spell over her—over her heart.

"Lizzie, open the door."

She ran a hand over her hair, finding it to be a flyaway mess. What was she doing hiding away? She was a foster kid. She knew how to take care of herself. Running and hiding wasn't her style. She straightened her shoulders. And with a resigned sigh, she moved to the door and opened it.

Dante stood there, slouched against the doorjamb. Much too close. Her heart thumped. Her gaze dipped to his lips. She recalled how his mouth did the most exquisite things to her and made her insides melt into a puddle. If she were to lean a little forward, they'd be nose to nose, lip to lip, breath to breath. But that couldn't happen again. It played with her mind and her heart too much.

With effort she drew her gaze to his eyes, which seemed to be filled with amusement.

"See something you like?" A smile pulled at his lips and made him even sexier than the serious expression he normally wore like armor.

"I see a man who insists he has to talk to me. What do you want?"

He shook his head. "Not like this. Join me in the living room."

"I have things to do."

"I think this is more important. Trust me." With that, he walked away.

She stood there fighting off the urge to rush to catch up with him. After all, he was the one who'd ruined a perfectly amazing dinner, nitpicking over her cooking. The reminder had her straightening her spine.

Refusing to continue to let him have the upper hand, she closed the door and rushed over to the walk-in closet to retrieve some fresh clothes that didn't smell as if she'd been working in the kitchen for hours. She wished she had time for a shower, but she didn't want to press her luck.

With a fresh pair of snug black jean capris and a black sheer blouse that she knotted at her belly button, she entered the en suite bathroom that was almost as big as her bedroom. She splashed some water on her heated face. Then she took a moment to run a brush through her hair. Not satisfied with it, she grabbed a ponytail holder and pulled her hair back out of her face. With a touch of powder and a little lip gloss to add a touch of color to her face, she decided that she wasn't going to go out of her way for him.

Satisfied that she'd taken enough time that it didn't seem as though she was rushing after him, she exited her room. She didn't hear anything. Had he given up and disappeared to his office?

Disappointment coursed through her. The fact that she was so eager to hear what he had to say should have been warning enough, but curiosity kept her moving forward. When she entered the wide open living area, she was surprised to find Dante kicked back on the couch with his smartphone in his hand. He glanced up at her with an unidentifiable expression.

"What?" she asked, feeling self-conscious about her appearance.

He shook his head, dismissing her worry. "Nothing. It's just that when I think I've figured you out, you go and surprise me."

"And how did I do that?"

He shook his head. “It doesn’t matter.”

“Yes, it does. Otherwise you wouldn’t have mentioned it.”

“It’s just that as tough as you act, on the inside you’re such a girl.” His gaze drifted over her change of clothes down to her strappy black sandals. “And a beautiful one at that.”

She crossed her arms and shrugged. “I…I’m sorry for being sensitive. I’m not normally like that. I swear. It won’t happen again.”

But the one subject she didn’t dare delve into was that her appearance was an illusion. Unlike his other women friends, her clothes didn’t come from some Rome boutique. Her clothes were hand-me-downs. For a moment, she wondered what he’d say if he knew she was a fraud. Her insides tightened as she thought of him rejecting her.

“Apology accepted.” He patted a spot on the black leather couch next to him. “Now come sit down.”

It was then that she noticed the candles on the glass coffee table. And there were the dishes of berries and fresh whipped cream and a sprig of mint. Why in the world had he brought it up here?

When she sat down, it was in the overstuffed chair. “I don’t understand.”

He leaned forward. His elbows rested on his knees. Her instinct was to sit back out of his reach, but steely resistance kept her from moving. She wasn’t going to let him think that he had any power over her.

“Dante, what’s this all about? Are you trying to soften the blow? Are you calling off the television spot?”

CHAPTER TWELVE

LIZZIE'S HARD GAZE challenged him.

Dante wondered if she truly wanted him to step away from this project. Had she gotten a taste of his mentoring skills and changed her mind? Not that it mattered. It was too late for either of them to back out.

Somehow he had to smooth things out with her. And he wasn't well versed with apologies. This was going to be harder than he'd imagined.

"It's my turn to apologize." There. He'd said it. Now he just hoped that she'd believe him.

"For what?"

This was where things got sticky. He didn't want to talk about feelings and emotions. He swallowed hard as he sorted his thoughts.

"I didn't mean to make you feel bad about dinner." Her gaze narrowed in on him, letting him know that he now had her full attention. "See, that's the thing. I'm not a teacher. I have no experience. My grandfather always prided himself on being the one to show people how to do things. He has a way about him that makes people want to learn. If he hadn't been a chef, he should have been a teacher."

The stiffness in her shoulders eased. "But I didn't make you dinner so that you could teach me. I…I wanted… Oh, never mind."

She clammed up quickly. What had she been about to say? He really wanted to know. Was she going to say that she'd made him dinner because she liked him? Did she want to continue what they'd started earlier that day?

No. She wouldn't want that...would she? He had to resolve the uncertainty. The not knowing would taunt him to utter distraction. And if they were going to work together, he had to know where they stood.

He cleared his throat. "What is it you wanted?"

"I just wanted to prepare you a nice dinner as a thank-you for what you did by introducing me to your family. And...and I wanted to show you that you wouldn't be making a mistake by taking me on to work here. But obviously I was wrong."

"No, you weren't."

"Yes, I was. You made it clear you don't care for my cooking."

He shook his head. "That's not it. I think you're a good cook."

"So then why did you say those things?"

"Because good is fine for most people, but you aren't most people."

Her fine brows drew together. "What does that mean? Do you know about my past? Did your grandfather tell you?"

Whoa! That had him sitting up straight. "Nonno didn't tell me anything." But Dante couldn't let it end there. He wanted to believe that he was being cautious because of the business but it was more than that. He wanted to know everything there was about her. "I'm willing to listen, if you're willing to tell me."

Her blue eyes were a turbulent sea of emotions. "You don't want to hear about me."

"Yes, I do." The conviction in his voice took him by surprise.

She worried her lip as though considering what to tell him. "I don't know. I've already told you enough. I don't need to give you more reason to look at me differently."

Now he had to know. "I promise I won't do that."

"You might try, but it'll definitely color the way you see me." She leaned back in the chair and crossed her arms.

He wanted her to trust him although he knew that he hadn't given her any reason to do so. But this was important. On top of it all, if he understood her better, maybe he'd have an easier time communicating with her when they were working together. He knew he was kidding himself. His interest in her went much deeper than employer and employee.

"Trust me, Lizzie."

He could see the conflicted look in her eyes. She obviously wasn't used to opening up to people—except his grandfather. Nonno had a way with people that put them at ease. Dante was more like his father when it came to personal relationships—he had to work to find the right words. Sure, he could flirt with the women, but when it came down to meaningful talks, the DeFiore men failed.

But this was about Lizzie, not himself. And he didn't want to fail her. More than anything, he wanted her to let him in.

Should she trust him?

Lizzie studied Dante's handsome face. Her brain said that she'd already told him more than enough, but her heart pleaded with her to trust him. But to what end? It wasn't as if she was going to build a life here in Rome. Her life—her home—was thousands of miles away in New York.

But maybe she'd stumbled across something.

Whatever she told him would stay here in Rome. So what did it matter if she told him more about her past? It wasn't as if it was a secret anyway. Plenty of people knew her story—and plenty of those people had used it as a yardstick to judge her. Would Dante be different?

With every fiber of her being she wanted to believe that he would be. But she'd never know unless she said the words—words that made her feel as though she was less than everyone else. Admitting to her past made her feel as though she wasn't worthy of love.

She took a deep breath. "Before my mother died, I was placed in foster care."

Dante sat there looking at her as though he were still waiting for her big revelation.

"Did you hear me?"

"I heard that you grew up in a foster home, but I don't know why you would think that would make me look at you differently."

Seriously? This was so not the reaction she was expecting. Growing up, she'd learned to keep this information to herself. When the parents of her school friends had learned that she came from a foster home, they'd clucked their tongues and shaken their heads. Then suddenly her friends had no time for her. And once she'd overheard a parent say to another, *"You can never be too careful. Who knows about those foster kids. I don't want her having a bad influence on my kid."*

The memory made the backs of Lizzie's eyes sting. She'd already felt unwanted by her mother, who'd tossed her away as though she hadn't mattered. And then to know that people looked down on her, it hurt—a lot. But Lizzie refused to let it destroy her. Instead, she insisted on showing them that they were wrong—that she would make something of herself.

"You don't understand what it's like to grow up as a foster kid. Trust me. You had it so good."

Dante glanced away. "You don't know that."

"Are you serious? You have an amazing family. You know where you come from and who your parents are."

"It may look good from the outside, but you have no idea what it's like to live in that house and never be able to measure up." He got to his feet and strode over to the window.

"Maybe your family expected things from you because

they knew you were capable of great things. In my case, no one expected anything from me but trouble."

"Why would they think that?"

"Don't you get it? My parents tossed me away like yesterday's news. If the two people in the world who were supposed to love me the most didn't want me, it could only mean there's something wrong with me—something unworthy." Her voice cracked with emotion. "You don't know what it was like to be looked at like you are less than a person."

In three long, quick strides Dante was beside her. He sat down next to her and draped his arm around her. Needing to feel his strength and comfort, she lowered her head to his broad shoulder. The lid creaked open on the box of memories that she'd kept locked away for so many years.

Once again she was that little girl with the hand-me-down jeans with patches on the knees and the pant legs that were two inches too short. And the socks that rarely matched—she'd never forget those. She'd been incessantly taunted and teased about them.

But no longer.

Her clothes may not come from high-class shops, but they were of designer quality and gently worn so that no one knew that they were used—no one but Jules. But her foster sister was never one to judge. Probably because Jules never went for the sophisticated styles—Jules marched to a different drummer in fashion and makeup.

"I…I never had any friendships that lasted, except Jules. We had similar backgrounds and we leaned on each other through thick and thin."

"I'm so glad she was there for you. If I had been there I'd have told those people what was up."

Lizzie gave a little smile. "I can imagine you doing that, too."

"I don't understand why people have to be so mean."

She swallowed down the lump in her throat. "You can't

imagine how awful it was. At least when I was little, I didn't know what the looks and snide little comments by the mothers were about, but as I got older, I learned."

Dante's jaw tightened and a muscle in his cheek twitched. "Unbelievable."

"The kids were even meaner. If you didn't have the right clothes, and I never did, you'd be picked on and called names. And the right hairstyle, you had to have the latest trend. And my poker-straight hair would never cooperate. It seemed one way or another I constantly failed to fit in."

"I think they were all just jealous. How could they not be? You're gorgeous."

His compliment was like a balm on her old wounds. Did he really mean it? She gazed deep into his eyes and saw sincerity, which stole her breath away. Dante thought she was gorgeous. A warmth started in her chest and worked its way up her neck and settled in her cheeks.

"It's a shame they missed getting to know what a great person you are. And how caring you are."

She lifted her head and looked at him squarely in the eyes. "You're just saying that to make me feel better."

"No, I'm not." His breath brushed against her cheek, tickling it. "You're special."

She moved just a little so that she was face-to-face with him. She wanted to look into his eyes once more. She wanted to know without a doubt that he believed what he was saying. But what she found in his dark gaze sent her heart racing. Sincerity and desire reflected in his eyes.

He pulled her closer until her curves were pressed up against his hard planes. She knew this place. Logic said she should pull away. But the pounding of her heart drowned out any common sense. The only recognizable thought in her head was that she wanted him—all of him, and it didn't matter at that moment what happened tomorrow.

His gaze dipped to her lips. The breath caught in his throat. Her eyelids fluttered closed and then he was there pressing his mouth to hers. Her hands crept over his sturdy shoulders. Her fingertips raked through his short strands.

She followed his gently probing kisses until her mounting desire drove her to become more assertive. As she deepened their kiss, a moan sounded from him. She reveled in the ability to rouse his interest. Sure, she'd attracted a few men in the past, but none had gotten her heart to pound like it was doing now. She wondered if Dante could hear it. Did he know what amazing things he was doing to her body?

Did he know how much she wanted him?

The knowledge that she was willing to give herself to him just for the asking startled her back to reality. She pulled back. She wanted Dante too much. It was too dangerous. And after being a foster kid, she liked to play things safe—at least where her heart was concerned. She'd been burned far too many times.

"What's wrong?" Dante tried to pull her back to him.

She'd been here before, putting her heart on the line. Only then, she'd been a kid wanting to have a best friend and thinking that all would be fine. Then the parents had stepped in and she was rejected.

She remembered the agonizing pain of losing friend after friend. She'd promised herself that she'd never let herself be that vulnerable again. Not for anyone. Not even for this most remarkable man.

She struggled to slow her breathing and then uttered, "We can't do this. It isn't right."

"It sure felt right to me." He sent her a dreamy smile that made her heart flip-flop.

"Dante, don't. I'm being serious."

"And so am I. What's wrong with having a little fun?"

"It's more than that. It's… Oh, I don't know." Her insides were a ball of conflicting emotions.

"Relax. I won't push you for something you don't want to do."

The problem was that she did want him. She wanted him

more than she'd wanted anyone in her life. But it couldn't happen. She wouldn't let it. It would end in heartbreak—her heartbreak.

Dante placed a thumb beneath her chin and tilted it up until their gazes met. "Don't look so sad."

"I'm not." Then feeling a moment of panic over how easy it'd be to give in to these new feelings, she backed away from him. "You don't even know me. Why are you being so nice?"

"Seriously. Are you really going to play that card?" He smiled and shook his head in disbelief. "You aren't that much of a mystery."

She crossed her arms, not sure how comfortable she was with him thinking that he knew so much about her. "And what do you think you know about me?"

"I know that you like to put on a tough exterior to keep people at arm's length, but deep down you are sweet and thoughtful. I saw you with my family and especially Massimo. You listened to him and you didn't rush him when he had problems pronouncing some words. You made him feel like he had something important to say—like he was still a contributing member of the family."

"I'm glad to hear that my visit helped. I wish I could go back."

"You can…if you stay here."

What? Had she heard him correctly? He wanted her to stay? She didn't understand what was happening here. Not too long ago she'd been the one pushing for this arrangement to work and he was the one resisting the arrangement. Now suddenly he wanted her to stay. What was she missing?

"Why?" She searched his face, trying to gain a glimmer of insight.

"Why not?"

"That's not an answer. Why did you suddenly have this change of heart?"

He shifted his weight from one foot to the other. "I've had a chance to think it over. And I think that we can help each other."

"Are you saying this because I told you about my background? Is this some sort of sympathy?"

"No." The response came quickly—too quickly. "Why would you say that?"

She shrugged. "Why not? It's the only reason I can see for you to want this arrangement to work. Or is there something I don't know?"

There was a look in his eyes. Was it surprise? Had she stumbled across something?

"Tell me, Dante. Otherwise, I'm outta here. If you can't be honest with me, we can't work together." And she meant it. Somehow, someway she'd scrape together the money for Jules to go to grad school, to reach her dreams and to be able to help other unfortunate children.

He exhaled a frustrated sigh. "I talked with my solicitor before dinner."

When he paused, she prompted him. "And."

"He said that we could break the contract but it wouldn't be quick or cheap."

Her gut was telling her that there was more to this than he was telling her. "What else?"

Dante rubbed the back of his neck. "Did anyone ever tell you that you're pushy?"

"I am when I have to be—when I can tell that I'm not being given the whole truth."

"Well, that's it. My solicitor advised me that it would be easier to go through with your project. And he mentioned that in the end it would benefit the *ristorante* and bring in more tourist traffic."

So that was it. He was looking at his bottom line. She couldn't fault him for that because technically she was doing the same thing. She was looking forward to the money she earned to help her foster sister. But she just couldn't shake the memories of the past.

"And you're sure this has nothing to do with what I told you about my past."

"I swear. Now will you stay?"

She didn't know what to say. She wasn't sure how this would work now that they'd kissed twice and were sharing an apartment, regardless of its spaciousness. When she glanced into Dante's eyes, the fluttering feeling churned in her stomach. And when her gaze slipped down to his lips, she was tempted to steal another kiss.

"What's the matter?" Dante asked, arching his brow. "Are you worried about us being roommates?"

"How did you know?"

The corner of his tempting mouth lifted in a knowing smile. "Because you aren't the only one wondering about that question. But before you let that chase you off, remember the reason you came here—to learn. To hone your cooking skills."

"But I can't do that if you and I are…you know…"

"How about I make you a promise that I won't kiss you again…until you ask me. I will be the perfect host and teacher— Well, okay, the teaching might be a bit rough at first but I will try my best."

She looked deep into his eyes, finding sincerity. Her gut said to trust him. But it was these new feelings that she didn't trust. Still, this was her only viable option to hold up her promise to Jules, who'd helped her through school and pushed her to reach for her dreams. How could she do any less in return?

With a bit of hesitancy, she stuck out her hand. "You have a deal."

CHAPTER THIRTEEN

WHAT EXACTLY HAD he gotten himself into?

The sun was flirting with the horizon as Dante yawned and entered the kitchen of Ristorante Massimo. The film crew was quite timely. Dante stood off to the side, watching the bustle of activity as a large pot of *caffé* brewed. The large kitchen instantly shrank as the camera crew, makeup artist and director took over the area. In no time, spotless countertops were covered with equipment, cases and papers. The place no longer looked like the kitchen his grandfather had taught him to cook in—the large room that held some of his happiest memories.

Dante inwardly groaned and stepped out of the way of a young assistant wheeling in another camera. So much for the peace and tranquillity that he always enjoyed at this time of the day. He slipped into the office to enjoy his coffee.

"Hey, what are you doing in here?" Lizzie's voice called out from behind him.

He turned to find her lingering in the doorway. The smile on her face lit up her eyes. She practically glowed. Was it the television cameras that brought out this side of her? The thought saddened him. He wished that he could evoke such happiness in her. But it was best that they'd settled things and agreed that from now on she was hands off for him.

"I'm just staying out of the way. Is all of that stuff necessary?"

"There's not much. You should see what they have in the studio."

"I don't remember all of those things when they filmed here before."

She shrugged. "Are you ready for this?"

He wasn't. He really didn't want to be a television star, but he'd given his word and he wouldn't go back on that—he wouldn't disappoint Lizzie. She'd been disappointed too many times in her life.

"Yes, I am. We need to get this done before the employees show up to get everything started for the lunch crowd. What do we need to do first?"

"You need makeup."

"What?" He shook his head and waved off the idea. "I don't think so."

His thoughts filled with images of some lady applying black eyeliner and lipstick to him. His nose turned up at the idea. No way. Wasn't happening. Not in his lifetime.

"Is it really that bad?" Lizzie's sweet laugh grated on his taut nerves.

"I agreed to teach you to cook in front of the cameras, but I never agreed to eyeliner."

Lizzie stepped closer. "What? You don't think you need a little cover stick and maybe a little blush."

His gaze narrowed on her as she stopped right in front of him. The amusement danced in her eyes. He truly believed, next to her visit with his grandfather, this was the happiest he'd seen her. He didn't want it to end, but he had to draw a line when it came to makeup.

"I'm not doing it. And you can keep smiling at me, but it isn't going to change my mind."

Her fingertip stroked along his jaw. "Mmm, nice. Someone just shaved."

Yes, he had. Twice. "That doesn't have anything to do with makeup."

Her light touch did the craziest things to his pulse. And was that the sweet scent of her perfume? Or was it the lingering trace of her shampoo? He inhaled deeper. Whatever it was, he could definitely get used to it.

Her fingertip moved to his bottom lip, which triggered nerve endings that shot straight through to his core. Her every touch was agonizing as he struggled not to pull her close and replace her finger with her lips. But he'd once again given his word to be on his best behavior.

He caught her arm and pulled it away from his mouth. "You might want to stop doing that or I won't be responsible for what happens next."

Her baby blues opened wide and her pink frosty lips formed an O.

She withdrew her arm and stepped back. He regretted putting an end to her fun as she seemed to regress back into her shell. He wished she'd let that side of her personality out more often. But obviously he'd have to get a better grip on himself so that next time he didn't chase her away.

She was so beautiful. So amazing. So very tempting. And he'd been the biggest fool in the world to promise to be a gentleman. But he had no one to blame for this agonizing torture except himself.

"You need to loosen up. Act natural."

Lizzie glanced up at the director, thinking he was talking to Dante. After all, she'd done this sort of thing before—acting in front of the cameras. But instead of the young guy giving Dante a pointed look, the man was staring directly at her. Her chest tightened.

"I…I am."

The man shook his head and turned to his cameraman to say something.

Dante moved to her side. “What’s the matter, Lizzie? Where’s the woman who just a little bit ago was teasing me about makeup?”

She refused to let him get the best of her. “Speaking of which, I see that you’re wearing some. Looks good. Except you might want a little more eyeliner.”

“What?” He grabbed a stainless-steel pot and held it up so he could see his reflection. His dark brows drew together. “I’m not wearing eyeliner.”

She smiled.

“That’s what I want.” The director’s voice drew her attention. “I want that spark and easy interaction on the camera.”

Lizzie inwardly groaned. The man didn’t know what he was asking of her. She chanced a glance at Dante as he returned the pot to a shelf. She wasn’t the only one who’d reverted back behind a wall. He had been keeping his distance around her, too. She wondered if he regretted their kissing? Or was it something deeper? Did it have something to do with the reason Dante lived all alone in that spacious apartment that was far too big for just one person?

“Okay, let’s try this shot again.”

Lizzie took her position at the counter, trying her best to act relaxed and forget about the camera facing her. But as Dante began his lines and moved around her, showing her how to prepare the *pasta alla gricia*, she could smell his spicy aftershave. It’d be so easy to give in to her desires. But where would that leave her? Brokenhearted and alone. Her muscles stiffened.

“Cut.” The director walked up to her. “I don’t understand. We’ve worked together before and you did wonderfully. What’s the problem now?”

The problem was Dante looked irresistibly sexy in his pressed white jacket. She swallowed hard. As she took a deep calming breath, she recalled his fresh, soapy scent.

Mmm…he smelled divine. What was she supposed to do? When he got close enough to assist her with the food prep, she panicked—worried she'd end up caring about him. That she'd end up falling for him. And that just couldn't happen. She wouldn't let it.

"Nothing is wrong." She hoped her voice sounded more assured than she felt at the moment. "I'll do better."

The director frowned at her. "Maybe you should take a break. We'll shoot the next segment with just Dante."

Lizzie felt like a kid in school that had just gotten a stern warning from the principal before being dismissed to go contemplate her actions. Keeping her gaze straight ahead and well away from Dante, she headed for the coffeepot, where she filled up a cup. After a couple of dashes of sugar and topping it off with cream, she headed for the office. It was her only refuge from prying eyes.

She resisted the urge to close the door. She didn't need them speculating that she'd dissolved into a puddle of tears. It would take a lot more than messing up a shot to start the waterworks.

More than anything, she was frustrated. She grabbed for her cell phone, wanting to hear Jules's voice. Her foster sister always had a way of talking her off ledges. But just as she was about to press the last digit, she realized that with the time difference, Jules would still be sound asleep.

Lizzie slid the phone back in her pocket. What was she going to do now? Dante was totally showing her up in there. The thought did not sit well with her at all.

Since when did she let a man get to her? She could be a professional. She wasn't some teenager with a crush. She was a grown woman with responsibilities. It was time she started acting that way before this whole spotlight series went up in flames.

"Are you all right?" Dante's voice came from behind her.

"I'm fine. Why does everyone keep asking me that?"

"Because you haven't been acting like yourself." Concern reflected in his eyes. "Tell me what's bothering you. I'll help if I can."

"Don't do that."

His forehead wrinkled. "What?"

"Act like we're something we're not." If he continued to treat her this way, her resolve would crack. And she didn't want to rely on him. She knew what would happen then. He'd pull back just like her ex had done. Men were only into women for an uncomplicated good time.

And she was anything but uncomplicated.

"I don't know what you're talking about." Dante's voice took on a deeper tone. "All I wanted to do was help." He held up his hands innocently. "But I can tell when I'm not wanted."

He stormed back out the door.

Good. Not that she was happy that he was upset. But she could deal with his agitation much easier than she could his niceness. Each kind word he spoke to her was one more chip at the wall she'd carefully built over the years to protect herself. And she wasn't ready to take it down for him or anyone.

At last, feeling as though she had her head screwed on straight, she returned to the kitchen. The director looked at her as though studying her. "You ready?"

She nodded. "Yes, I am."

The director had them take their places as Lizzie sensed Dante's agitation and distance. She was sorry that it had to be this way, but she could at last think straight. And when the director called a halt to the filming, it was Dante who fouled up the shot. They redid it a few times until the director was satisfied.

This arrangement may have been her idea, but at the time she hadn't a clue how hard it was going to be to work so closely with Dante. Still, she had to do this. She didn't have a choice. There were bills to meet and grad school to pay.

She just had to pretend that Dante was no one special. But was that possible in the long run? How was she supposed to ignore these growing feelings when she found Dante fascinating in every way?

She was in trouble. Deep trouble.

CHAPTER FOURTEEN

NOT TOO BAD.

Lizzie stifled a yawn as she poured herself a cup of coffee. Thankfully it was late Friday night and the restaurant was at last closed. She was relieved that there was no filming in the morning. Those early wake-up calls were wearing her down. The next morning the crew was off to shoot some footage of Rome to pad their spotlights. And she couldn't be happier.

Lizzie pressed a cup of stale coffee to her lips.

"You might not want to drink that."

She turned at the sound of Dante's voice. "Why not?"

"That stuff is strong enough to strip paint off Red. You'll never get to sleep if you drink it."

She held back a laugh. "Don't worry. I'll be fine."

Dante raised a questioning brow before he turned back to finish cleaning the grill. He really was a hands-on kinda guy. She didn't know why that should surprise her. He'd never once sloughed off his work onto his staff. Everyone had their assigned duties and they all seemed to work in harmony.

Dante had been remarkable when it came to the filming, too. He may grump and growl like an old bear about things like makeup, but when the cameras started to roll, he really came through for her—for them. Maybe he hadn't nailed every scene but he'd been trying and that was what counted. And if she didn't know better, she'd swear he'd been enjoying himself in front of the cameras.

It was amazing how long it took to shoot a short segment to splice into the station's number-one-rated cooking show. But it was so worth it. What a plum spot they'd been given. It'd definitely make her credentials stand out from the competition when she returned to New York and searched for a chef position at one of the upscale restaurants in Manhattan.

She took the cup of coffee to the office and cleared off a spot at the end of the couch. No sooner had she gotten comfortable than Dante sauntered into the room.

"See, you should have taken me up on my offer to take the afternoon off." He sent her an *I told you so* look.

She shrugged. "I wanted to get a feel for how everything works around here."

"And now you're exhausted."

"Listen to who's talking. You worked just as many hours as I did."

"But I'm used to it."

Now, that did surprise her. What was a young, incredibly sexy man doing spending all of his time at the restaurant? Surely he must have an active social life away from this place. The image of him dressed in a sharp suit filled her mind. And then a beautiful slip of a woman infiltrated her thoughts. The mystery woman sauntered over and draped herself on his arm. Lizzie's body tensed.

"Is something the matter?"

She glanced up at Dante. "What?"

"You were frowning. Is it the *caffé*? I told you not to drink it."

Not about to tell him her true thoughts, she said, "Yes, it's cold. I'll just dump it out and head upstairs. Are you coming?"

He glanced around at the messy office. "I should probably do a little work in here."

She stifled a laugh. This place needed a lot more than a "little" help. "Have you ever thought of hiring someone to sort through all of these old papers?"

"I don't think there's a person alive that would willingly take on this challenge. My grandfather was not much of a businessman. He did the bare minimum. And I'm afraid that I'm not much better. I'd rather be in the kitchen or talking with the patrons."

She could easily believe that of him and his grandfather. They were both very social people, unlike her. She could hold her own in social scenes but her preference was the anonymity of a kitchen or office.

"Well, don't stay up too late." She headed for the door. "We wouldn't want you having bags under your eyes for the camera."

"Is there an in-between with you?"

She turned. "What do you mean?"

"You are either very serious or joking around. Is there ever a middle ground?"

She'd never really thought that much about it. "Of course. See, I'm not making any jokes now."

"And you're also being serious. You're wondering if I'm right."

Her lips pursed together. Did Dante see something that she'd been missing all along? And was he right?

He stepped closer. "If you control the conversation then nothing slips out—those little pieces of your life that let a person really know you. You can then keep everyone at a safe distance."

Her gaze narrowed in on him. "Since when have you become such an expert on me?"

"I'm good at reading people. And you intrigue me."

Any other time she might have enjoyed the fact that she intrigued a man but not now. Not when he could see aspects of her that made her uncomfortable.

"Are you trying to tell me that you're a mind reader—

no, wait, maybe a fortune-teller? I can see you now with a colorful turban, staring into a glass ball." She forced a smile, hoping to lighten the conversation.

"And there you go with the jokes. My point is proven."

He was right. Drat. She'd never thought about how she'd learned to shield herself from other people. When conversations got too close, too personal, she turned them around with a joke. Anything to get the spotlight off herself.

After all this time of putting up defensive postures, she didn't know if she could let down those protective walls and just be—especially around a man who could make her heart race with just a look. But something within her wanted things to be different with Dante. It was lonely always pushing people away.

"I'm just me." She didn't know how to be anyone else. "I'm sorry if that doesn't live up to your idea of the perfect woman."

He stepped closer to her. It'd be so easy to reach out to him—to lean into his arms and forget about the world for just a moment. Every fiber of her body wanted to throw herself into his arms and feel his lips against hers.

"Lizzie, you don't have to be perfect." His voice was soft and comforting. "You just have to be honest with yourself and realize that not everyone is out to hurt you. I won't hurt you."

Hearing those last four words was like having a bucket of ice water dumped over her head. Her ex had said the same thing to her to get her into bed. But when opportunity came knocking on his door, she was relegated to nothing more than an afterthought. He couldn't wait to leave New York—to leave her. The realization of how little he'd cared for her cut deep.

She wasn't going to fall for those words again.

She stepped back out of Dante's reach.

His dark gaze stared straight at her as though searching for answers to his unspoken questions.

When his gaze dipped to her lips, the breath hitched in her throat. What was he going to do? He'd promised not to kiss her until she asked him to. Would he keep that promise?

Factions warred within her. One wanted to remain safe. The other part wanted to sweep caution aside and lean into his arms. Was it possible that being safe wasn't always the best choice? Was a chance at happiness worth the inherent risks?

Dante cleared his throat. "You better go upstairs now." His voice was deeper than normal and rumbled with emotion. "If you don't, I might end up breaking my word. And a DeFiore never goes back on his word."

She turned on legs that felt like rubber and headed for the door. The warm night air did nothing to soothe her heated emotions. She needed a shower to relax her or she'd never get any sleep tonight. And Dante was worried the coffee would be stimulating. It was nothing compared to his presence.

It was on the elevator ride upstairs that she realized if he had reached out to her, she wouldn't have resisted. She wanted him as much as he wanted her. He didn't have to say the words. It was all there in his eyes. The need. The want. The desire.

Sleep was not something that was going to come easily that night.

What was wrong with him?

Dante got up from the desk in his study and strode to the window. The lights from the city obscured the stars, but he knew they were there, just like he knew there was something growing between him and Lizzie. He couldn't touch it. He couldn't see it. But there was definitely something real growing between them.

She'd appeared in his life out of nowhere. At every turn, she challenged everything he believed he wanted in life.

But above and beyond all of that, she brought the "fun factor" back to his life. He enjoyed sharing the kitchen with her. He even went to bed each night anticipating the next morning. What was it about Lizzie that had him feeling things that he'd never experienced before?

Images of her curled up in bed just down the hall from him had him prowling around his study instead of sleeping. The only good news was that there was no filming tomorrow. But it wasn't as if they had the next day off. It was Saturday, the busiest day of the week for the *ristorante*. The responsible side of him told him to go to bed this second or he'd pay for it in the morning. But he didn't relish the idea of lying there in the dark while images of the alluring woman who now shared his apartment teased and danced through his mind.

He clenched his hands as a groan rose in his throat. Pacing around his study was not doing him a bit of good. At least if he went and lay down, his body would get some much-needed rest. If he was lucky, maybe sleep would finally claim him. But first he needed a drink.

In nothing but his boxers, he quietly padded to the darkened kitchen. When he rounded the corner, the door of the fridge swung open and he stopped in his tracks, thoroughly captivated with the sight before him.

Lizzie bent over to rummage through the contents of the fridge. A pair of peach lacy shorts rode up over her shapely thighs and backside. He swallowed hard, unable to pry his eyes away from her.

Then, realizing he was spying on her, he cleared his throat. His mouth suddenly went dry. He hoped when he spoke that his voice would come out clearly. "Something you need?"

Lizzie jumped and turned around. "I didn't mean to wake you."

"You didn't."

She closed the fridge, shrouding them in darkness.

Dante moved to switch on the light over the stove. He couldn't get enough of her beauty.

She turned, casting him a questioning stare. "You couldn't sleep either?"

"Too much on my mind." He wasn't about to admit that she was on his mind. Her image had been taunting him. But those images had been nothing compared to the real thing that was standing in front of him.

The spaghetti straps of her top rested on her ivory shoulders as her straight flaxen hair flowed down her back. He didn't know that she could look even more beautiful, but he'd never be able to erase this enchanting image from his mind. He stifled a frustrated sigh and turned to the fridge. He pulled it open but nothing appealed to him. When he turned back around, her intent gaze met his.

Her fingers toyed with the lace edging of her top. "What are you worried about?"

"Nothing in particular." He really didn't want to discuss what was on his mind. "I just came out to get a snack."

He was hungry but it wasn't food he craved. When his gaze returned to her face, he noticed how she crossed her arms over her breasts. It was far too late for modesty.

"You know, you don't have to be so uncomfortable around me." He stepped forward. "I promise I just want to be your friend."

"I think it's more than that." She arched a brow. "More like friends with benefits?"

"Hey, now, that's not fair. I've kept my word. I haven't touched you." His voice grew deep as his imagination kicked into high gear. "I haven't wrapped my arms around you and pulled you close." He took another step toward her. "I haven't run my fingers up your neck and over your cheeks or trailed my thumb over your pouty lips."

Her gaze bored deep into his. The desire flared in her baby blues. He knew she wanted this moment as much as he did. He also knew that opening this door in their relationship would change things between them dramatically. But that didn't stop him. He'd gotten a glimpse of life with Lizzie in it and he wanted more of her—no matter the cost.

Damn. Why had he given his word to keep his hands to himself? Now all he had to work with were his words. He wasn't a poet, but suddenly he felt inspired.

"I…I thought you said you were going to be a gentleman?" Her gaze never left his.

"I said that I wouldn't touch you—wouldn't kiss you—not until you asked me to. But I never said anything about telling you how I feel."

She took a step toward him until their bodies were almost touching. "And how do you feel?"

His heart slammed into his ribs. He swallowed hard. "I want you so much that it's all I can think about. I can't eat. I can't sleep. All I can think about is you. Do you have any idea how much I want to wrap my arms around you and pull you close? Then I'd press my mouth to yours. I'd leave no doubt in your mind about how good we can be. Together."

She looked deep into his eyes as though she could see clear through to his soul. No one had ever looked at him that way before. The breath caught in his throat as he waited, hoping she'd cave. He wasn't so sure how long his willpower would hold out.

Her head tilted to the left and her hair swished around her shoulder. "Do you really mean it?"

"Yes, I mean it." Second by second he was losing his steadfast control. "You are driving me to distraction. It's a miracle I haven't accidentally burned the *ristorante* down."

Her lips lifted. "You're too much of a professional to do something like that."

"We'll have to wait and see. After tonight, I don't know if I'll ever get the image of you in that barely-there outfit out of my mind." He groaned in frustration. "Talk about a major distraction."

A sexy smile tugged at her lips as desire sparkled in her

eyes. Her hands reached out to him, pressing against his bare chest. He sucked in an even breath as her touch sent tremors of excitement throughout his body. Did she have any idea what she was doing to him?

This was the sweetest torture he'd ever endured. It'd take every bit of willpower to walk away from her. But he had to keep his promise to her—he couldn't be like those other people in her life who'd let her down. But he didn't want it to end—not yet.

She tilted her chin and their gazes locked. All he could think about was pressing his mouth to hers. He desperately wanted to show her exactly how she made him feel.

He was in trouble—up to his neck in it. And as much as he savored having Lizzie this close and looking at him as if he was the only man in the world for her, his resolve was rapidly deteriorating. Was this what it was like to fall in love?

Not that he was going there. Was he?

He gazed deep into her eyes, and in that moment, he saw a flash of his future—a future with Lizzie. He wanted her to look at him with that heated desire for the rest of their lives. The revelation shook him, rattling his very foundation and jarring him back to reality.

He shackled his fingers around her wrists and pushed her away from him, hoping he'd be able to think more clearly.

"You're really as good as your word, aren't you?" There was a note of marvel in her voice.

"I'm trying. But if you keep this up, I'm going to lose the battle."

"Maybe I want you to lose."

What? His gaze studied her face. A smile tugged at her lips and delight danced in her eyes. He honestly didn't know if this was another of her tests. Or was it an invitation. With a frustrated groan, he let go of her wrists and backed up until the stove pressed into his backside. He slouched against it. Defeat and frustration weighed heavy on his shoulders.

"Don't look so miserable." She stepped toward him.

When she went to touch him again, he said, "Don't, Lizzie. You've had your fun but now let me be… Please go."

"I don't want to leave you alone. Maybe I want you to pull me into your arms and do those things you mentioned."

His back straightened. "Is that an invitation?"

She nodded. "Dante, I want you just as much—"

That was all he needed to hear. In a heartbeat, he had her in his arms and his mouth claimed hers. She tasted of mint and chocolate like the after-dinner treats they handed out with the checks. He'd never taste another of those little chocolates without thinking of her.

And though the thought of letting her slip through his fingers was agonizing, he had to be absolutely sure that she wanted this, too. With every last bit of willpower, he moved his mouth from hers. "Are you sure about this? About us?"

Her big round eyes shimmered with desire. "Yes, I'm positive."

In the next instant, he swung her up into his arms and carried her back down the hallway to his master bedroom—a room he'd never shared with another woman.

But Lizzie was different. Everything about her felt so right. It was as though he'd been waiting for her to step into his life. Things would never be the same.

But exactly where they went from here, he wasn't quite certain.

He'd think about it later.

Much later.

CHAPTER FIFTEEN

DROP BY DROP...

The icy walls around her heart had melted.

Lizzie felt exposed. Vulnerable. A position she'd promised herself she'd never put herself in again. She rushed downstairs to the restaurant. When she got there she couldn't fathom how she'd found the willpower to leave Dante's side—where she longed to be right now. But she couldn't stay there. She couldn't afford to get in even deeper.

Her time in Italy was limited. In just a few weeks, she'd be preparing to return to the States—back where her responsibilities were awaiting her. And then what? She'd leave her heart in Italy. No, thank you. She had no intention of being some kind of martyr to love.

What she and Dante had was...was a one-night stand. This acknowledgment startled her. She'd never thought of herself as the type to have a fling. And now that the scratch had been itched, they'd be fine. They could go back to being coworkers.

With a fresh pot of coffee, she filled a mug and headed to the office. She had no idea how Dante could stand such a mess. It was the exact opposite of the immaculate study in his apartment, which probably explained why almost everything in here dated back years. And she couldn't find any current invoices or orders. He probably did his work upstairs and left this place as a reminder of his grandfather. Dante must miss him terribly. Her heart went out to both of them.

She knew what it was like to miss someone terribly. Her thoughts strayed to Jules. She wondered if she was still awake. She glanced at the big clock on the wall. It should be close to midnight now. Jules wasn't a partyer, but she was a night owl who had a thing for watching old movies until she fell asleep.

Needing to hear her foster sister's voice to remind her of why she should be down here instead of snug in bed with Dante, she reached for her phone. It rang once, twice, three times—

"Hey, Lizzie, what's going on?" Jules's voice was a bit groggy. "Is what's-his-face still giving you a hard time?"

"I…I just wanted to touch base and make sure things are okay with you." Her voice wobbled. Usually she told Jules everything, but suddenly she felt herself clamming up.

A groan came through the phone, the sound Jules made when she was stretching after waking up. Lizzie smiled. She could just imagine Jules stretched out on the couch. She really did miss her. They were like two peas in a pod. She couldn't imagine they'd ever move far from each other—no matter what happened in life.

"Lizzie, I can hear it in your voice. Talk to me." Her concern rang through the phone, crystal clear and totally undeniable.

This call had been a mistake. How could she tell Jules—that she'd slept with the dreamiest man on earth? She didn't want Jules adding one plus one and ending up with five.

Because there was no way she was in love with Dante. He liked fast cars and beautiful women draped on his arm. She recalled the photos of him with various stunning women hanging in the dining room. The strange thing was she hadn't found any evidence that he was anything more than a caring, compassionate man who appeared to be as commitment-phobic as herself.

"Stop worrying. I'm fine. Dante and I worked things out." Lizzie ran her thumb over the edge of a tall stack of papers. "What's new with you?"

There was a moment of strained silence.

"I had an interview for grad school. Actually, it was an all-day event. They even took the candidates out for a fancy dinner."

"I hope you didn't scare them off with all of your makeup and your black-and-white ensemble," she said in a teasing tone.

Jules sighed. "You ought to give me more credit. Actually, I borrowed some of your clothes. I even received a couple of compliments."

Excitement swirled in Lizzie's chest and had her smiling. "Does that mean you're ready for a wardrobe makeover?"

"Not a chance. I'm good the way I am."

"Yes, you are."

Jules used the makeup and clothes as camouflage—so people couldn't see the real her. But someday she hoped Jules would feel secure enough to move beyond the walls she hid behind. Whereas Lizzie's scars were all on the inside, Jules wasn't so lucky—she had them both inside and out, and she took great care to hide them.

"Anyway, it went really well and I was told unofficially that I got in. But it'll take a bit of paperwork before I get my official notification." There was a distinct lack of excitement in Jules's voice. "Lizzie? Are you still there?"

"Uh, yes. That's great! I knew you could do it. And don't worry about anything but getting through your final exams. I've got everything else under control."

"I can tell you have something on your mind. If you aren't happy there, come home."

"It's not that." And it wasn't even a lie. "I'm just tired. I didn't sleep much. That's all it is."

"Are you sure that Dante guy doesn't have anything to do with it?"

"I promise he's been great." Lizzie blinked repeatedly, keeping her emotions at bay. "If you must know, I'm a bit homesick. I miss my sidekick."

"I miss you, too. But you'll be home soon."

"I know. I'm looking forward to it."

"And here I thought Rome would be your trip of a lifetime. I was worried that you'd fall in love and I'd never see you again."

Jules was so close to the truth. Perhaps she really could use someone else's thoughts. "The truth is, Dante and I… we…umm…"

"You slept together?" The awe in Jules's voice echoed through the phone.

"Yes. But it was a one-time thing. It didn't mean anything." In her heart she knew it was a lie, but it was the reassurance Jules needed to hear to keep her calm before her finals. "Don't worry. I'll be home soon."

And the truth was it wouldn't happen again. They'd gotten away with making love once, but to have a full-blown affair with him would run the real risk of breaking her heart. Already she felt closer to him than any other man she'd ever known.

It didn't mean anything.

Those words smacked Dante across the face.

When he'd woken up, he'd reached out and found a cold, empty spot next to him. He'd begun to wonder if he'd just dreamed the incredible night. If it hadn't been for the impression of Lizzie's head in the pillow next to his and the lingering floral scent, he might have written it off as a very vivid dream. Maybe that would have been best for both of them.

By the time he'd searched the whole apartment, he'd started to panic. Where could she have gone? Why had she left? Did she regret their moment of lovemaking?

And now as he stood in the doorway with the doorjamb

propping him up, his worst fears were confirmed. Lizzie regretted last night. While he was thinking that this could possibly be the start of something, she was thinking that it would never happen again. His gut twisted into a painful knot.

Gone were the illusions that last night meant something special—for both of them. He'd been so wrong about so many things. He knew that Lizzie wouldn't intentionally hurt him. She had a good heart even though she kept it guarded.

Hearing those painful words was his own fault. He shouldn't be eavesdropping. Still, not even Red could drag him away from the spot on the white tiled floor. It was better to hear the truth than to misread things and get lost in some fantasy that wasn't real.

How could he have been such a fool? He couldn't believe he'd given in to his desires. He never lost control like that. But when he'd thought she'd finally let down her guard and let him in, he'd gotten carried away. In the end, it had all been in his imagination.

She had only one goal. To finish her job here and return to New York. Well, that was fine with him. She didn't have to worry about him clinging to her. That wasn't about to happen. No way.

Finding this out now was for the best. In the end, committed relationships didn't work out for DeFiore men. One way or another, when one of them got too close, they ended up getting burned. Luckily he'd only gotten singed, unlike his father and brother, who'd had their hearts and lives utterly decimated.

Dante stepped into the office. "So this is where you're hiding."

Lizzie jumped and pressed a hand to her chest. "I'm not hiding. And how long have you been standing there?"

"Long enough. A more important question is why did

you disappear without a word?" He should leave the subject alone but he couldn't.

His pride had been pricked and it demanded to be soothed. Because his bruised ego had to be what was causing him such discomfort. It couldn't be anything else. He refused to accept that he'd fallen for a woman who had used him for a one-night stand.

Lizzie's gaze moved to the papers on the desk. "I couldn't sleep."

Because she was horrified by what she'd let happen between them. He stifled a groan of frustration. "Something on your mind?"

Her gaze avoided his. "Uhh…no. I…ah, you must have been right. I had too much caffeine last night."

He cleared his throat, refusing to let his voice carry tones of agitation. "And you thought you'd come down here and what? Clean up the office?"

Her slender shoulders, the ones he'd rained kisses down on just hours ago, rose and fell. "I thought maybe I could organize it for you."

"And you were so excited to sort papers that it had you jumping out of bed before sunrise?"

Her gaze didn't meet his. "I like office work."

"You must."

She nodded. "I have a business degree."

He struggled to keep the surprise from showing on his face. Just one more thing to prove how little he knew about her…and yet he couldn't ignore the nagging thought that he still wanted to learn more about the beautiful blonde with the blue eyes that he could lose himself in.

He crossed his arms as his gaze followed her around the office as she moved stacks of papers to the desk. "You know, office work isn't part of the contract."

"I didn't know that we were being formal about things."

"I think it would be for the best. We don't want to forget the reason you're here."

Her forehead crinkled. "If it's about last night—"

"It's not. That was a fun night, but I'm sure neither of us plans to repeat it." *Liar. Liar.*

"So we're okay?" Hope reflected in her eyes.

"Sure." He was as far from "sure" about this as he could get, but he'd tough it out. After all, he'd given his word. A DeFiore wasn't a quitter. "You still want to complete the filming, don't you?"

There was a determined set of her jaw as she nodded. He didn't want to admit it, but he admired the way she stuck by her commitments, even if she didn't want to be around him. But there was something more. He peered closer at her, noticing the shadows beneath her eyes.

"You don't need to waste your time in here." He didn't want her wearing herself out on his behalf. "You should get some sleep since you…you were up most of the night. I don't need you walking around here in a sleep-filled haze."

"I'll be fine. I…I don't sleep much."

He wasn't going to argue with her. If she found some sort of comfort in sorting through this mound of paperwork that stretched back more years than he wanted to know, why should he stop her?

"Fine. Sort through as many papers as you like."

Her brows lifted as her eyes widened. "You mean it?"

"Sure. But I do have one question. How do you plan to sort everything when it's in Italian?"

She shrugged. "I'll muddle through. I took Italian in school."

And yet another surprise. They just kept coming, and without the aid of caffeine, he had problems keeping the surprise from filtering onto his face. He scrubbed his hand over his head, not caring that he was making a mess of his hair.

He noticed the eager look on her face. "Whatever. It has to be done soon anyway if I plan to…"

"Plan to what?"

He couldn't believe that he'd almost blurted out his plans to sell the *ristorante*. He hadn't even discussed it with Nonno. There was just something about Lizzie that put him at ease and had him feeling as though he could discuss anything. But obviously the feeling didn't go both ways.

"Once there's room, I was planning to move the business files I have upstairs in my study down here."

"Understood." She gave him a pointed look. "Before you go, we really should talk about last night—"

"It was late. Neither of us were thinking clearly. It's best if we forget about it. We still have to work together."

Her mouth gaped but no words came out. The look in her eyes said there were plenty of thoughts racing round in her mind, but that wasn't his problem. By admitting it'd been a mistake, he'd beaten her to the punch. That was fine with him.

He refused to think about how she'd discarded him and his lovemaking so readily. Soon she'd be gone. He'd just have to figure out how they could avoid each other as much as possible between now and then.

CHAPTER SIXTEEN

PRETEND IT HADN'T HAPPENED?

Was he kidding? The thought ricocheted through Lizzie's mind for about the thousandth time since Dante had spoken the words. His solution was paramount to pretending there wasn't a thousand-pound pink polka-dot elephant in the room. Impossible.

How could he just forget their lovemaking?

As the days rolled into weeks, he acted as though that earth-moving night had never happened. And he didn't leave her any room to explain or make amends. He only interacted with her on a minimal basis. The easy friendship they'd developed had crashed upon rocky shores. She missed her newfound friend more than she thought possible.

And worse yet, their chilly rapport was now apparent on the filmed segments. The director appeared to be at a loss as to how to regain their easy camaraderie. Their television segment was in jeopardy. And Lizzie couldn't let things end like this—too much was riding on their success.

While spending yet another sleepless night staring into the darkness, she'd stumbled across an idea. A chance to smooth things out with Dante.

Instead of spending another lonely weekend sightseeing while Dante visited the vineyard, she'd invited herself to accompany him to the country. Armed with an old family recipe she'd found while straightening the office and with

Massimo by her side, she'd commandeered the kitchen. She would cook the family a feast and in the process hopefully she'd mend a fence with Dante.

"Do you really think they'll like it?" She glanced at Massimo as he sat at the large kitchen table near the picture window.

"Don't you mean will Dante like it?"

The more time she spent with Massimo, the less she noticed his slurred speech and the more he could read her mind. "Yes, I want Dante to like it, too."

A knowing gleam glinted in the older man's eyes. "Something is wrong between you two."

It wasn't a question. It was a statement of fact. She glanced away and gave the sauce a stir. She didn't want Massimo to read too much in her eyes. Some things were meant to stay between her and Dante.

"We'll be fine."

Massimo got to his feet and, with the aid of his walker, moved next to her. "Look at me."

She hesitated before doing as he'd asked. She didn't know what he was going to say, but her gut told her that it would be important.

"My grandson has witnessed a lot of loss in his life. He's also been at the wrong end of his father's grief over losing my daughter. I know all about grief. When I lost my dear, sweet Isabelle, it nearly killed me. It can make a good man say things he shouldn't. It can cause a person to grow a tough skin to keep from getting hurt again."

The impact of his words answered so many questions and affirmed her suspicions. "But why are you telling me all of this? It's none of my business."

"I see how my grandson looks at you. It's the same way I looked at his grandmother. But he's afraid—afraid of being hurt like his father and brother. If you care about my grandson like I think you do, you'll fight for him."

"But I can't. Even if there was something between Dante and me, my life—it's in New York."

"Love will always find a way—"

"Mmm… What smells so good?"

Stefano strode into the kitchen, followed closely by Dante and his father. Their hungry gazes roamed over the counter and stove. She shooed them all away to get washed up while she set the dining room table.

Soon all four men were cleaned up in dress shirts and slacks. Thankfully, she'd had a couple of minutes to run to her room and put on a dress. Still, next to these smartly dressed men, she felt underdressed.

"I hope you all like tonight's dinner. Thanks to Massimo, I was able to cook some old family recipes."

"I'm sure it will be fantastic," Dante's father said as he took a seat at the head of the table.

She wished she was as confident as he sounded. It felt like a swarm of butterflies had now inhabited her stomach as she removed the ceramic lids from the serving dishes. This just had to work. She had to impress them—impress Dante.

She sat back, eagerly watching as the men filled their plates. It seemed to take forever. She didn't bother filling hers yet. She already knew what everything tasted like as she'd sampled everything numerous times in the kitchen. In fact, she wasn't even hungry at this point.

But as they started to eat, a silence came over the table. The men started exchanging puzzled looks among themselves. Lizzie's stomach tightened. What was wrong?

She glanced Dante's way but his attention was on the food. She turned to Massimo for some sort of sign that all would be well, but before he could say a word, Dante's father's chair scraped across the tiles. In the silent room, the sound was like a crescendo.

The man threw down his linen napkin and strode out

of the room. Lizzie watched in horror. She pressed a hand to her mouth, holding back a horrified gasp.

Dante called out, "Papa."

The man didn't turn back or even acknowledge him.

"Let him go." Stefano sent Dante a pointed look.

As more forks clattered to their plates, the weight of disappointment weighed heavy on Lizzie. Her chest tightened, holding back a sob. This was absolutely horrific. Instead of the dinner bringing everyone together and mending fences, it'd only upset them.

Unable to sit there and keep her emotions under wraps, Lizzie pushed back her chair. She jumped to her feet, and as fast as her feet would carry her, she headed for the kitchen.

Her eyes stung and she blinked repeatedly. She'd done something wrong. How could she have messed up the recipe? She'd double-checked everything. But her Italian was a bit rusty. Was that it? Had she misread something?

Not finding any solace in the room where she'd created the dinner—the disaster—she kept going out the back door. She had no destination in mind. Her feet just kept moving.

The what-ifs and maybes clanged about in her head. But the one thought that rose above the others was how this dinner was supposed to be her peace offering to Dante. This was what she'd hoped would be a chance for them to smooth over their differences. But that obviously wasn't going to happen when no one even wanted to eat her food.

She kept walking. She didn't even know how much time had passed when she stopped and looked around. The setting sun's rays gave the grape leaves a magical glow. Any other time she'd have been caught up in the romantic setting, but right now romance was the last thing on her mind.

She should turn back, but she wasn't ready to face anyone. Oh, who was she kidding—she wasn't willing to look into Dante's eyes and to find that once again in her life, she didn't quite measure up.

When others looked at her as though she were less than

everyone else, she could choke it down and keep going. After all, those people hadn't meant anything to her. It'd hurt—it'd hurt deeply, but it hadn't destroyed her. And she'd clung to the belief that whatever didn't destroy you made you stronger.

But Dante was a different story. A sob caught in her throat. She couldn't stand the thought of him thinking that she was inept at cooking—the one ability that she'd always excelled in—her one hope to gain his respect.

And now she'd failed. Miserably.

"Are you serious?"

Dante sent Stefano a hard stare. The main dish Lizzie had prepared was his mother's trademark dish. She only prepared it on the most special occasions.

"Of course I'm serious. Did you see how all of the color drained from Papa's face? It was like he'd seen a ghost or something."

Dante raked his fingers through his hair. "I guess I was too busy watching the horrified look on Lizzie's face. She worked all day on that meal. She wouldn't say it but I know that she was so anxious to please everyone—"

"You mean anxious to please you, little brother."

"Me? Why would she do that?" He wasn't about to let on to his older brother that anything had gone on between him and Lizzie. No way! He'd never hear the end of it. "We're working together. That's all."

Stefano elbowed him. "Whatever you say."

Dante leaned forward on the porch rail and stared off into the distance, but there was no sign of Lizzie.

"I just have one question."

Dante stifled a groan. "You always have a question and most of the time it's none of your business."

"Ah, but see, this does have to do with me. Because while you're standing there insisting that you don't care about Lizzie, she's gotten who knows how far away. So is it going to be me or you that goes after her?"

Dante hated when his brother was right. She had been gone a long time. Soon it'd be dark out. He'd attempted to follow her right after the incident, but Massimo had insisted she needed some time alone. But the thing was she didn't understand what had happened to her special dinner and he needed to explain that it had nothing to do with her. Still, he figured that after her walk she'd be more apt to listen to him.

"Dante, did you hear me?"

He turned and glared at Stefano. "How could I help but hear you when you're talking in my ear?"

"You're ignoring the question. Are you going? Or should I?"

"I'm going."

"You might want to take your car. Hard to tell how far she's gotten by now."

"Thanks so much for your expert advice."

Stefano sent him a knowing smile. "You always did need a little guidance."

They'd probably have ended up in a sparring match like they used to do as kids, but Dante had more important matters than showing his big brother that he was all grown up now. Dante jumped in Red and fired up the engine. He headed down the lane to the main road, not sure he was even headed in the right direction. No one had watched Lizzie leave, but he couldn't imagine that she'd go hiking through the fields in a dress and sandals.

He slowly eased the car along the lane, doing his best to search the fields while trying to keep the car from drifting off the road. Thankfully it was a private lane as he was doing a good deal of weaving back and forth.

Where was she?

As he reached the main road, his worries multiplied. Had he missed her? Had she wandered into the fields and somehow gotten lost? He pulled to a stop at the intersection and pounded his palm against the steering wheel. Why had he listened to his grandfather? He should have gone after her immediately.

A car passed by and his gut churned. Was it possible she was so upset that she hitched a ride from a passing motorist? A stranger?

His whole body stiffened. This was his fault. He'd been so upset by her rejection that he'd built up an impenetrable wall between them. Maybe if he hadn't been so worried about letting her hurt him again, she wouldn't have been trying so hard to impress him and his family—his dysfunctional family. If he couldn't please his father—his own flesh and blood—how was she supposed to succeed?

Dante's gaze took in the right side of the main road, but there was no sign of Lizzie. And then he proceeded to the left, the direction they'd come from the city. That had to be the way she'd gone. He could only hope that she was wise enough to keep to herself and not trust any strangers. If anything happened to her—

He cut off the thought. Nothing would happen to her. She would be fine. She had to be.

And then he spotted the back of her red dress. He let out a breath that had been pent up in his chest. He sent up a silent thank-you to the big man upstairs.

He pulled up next to her and put down the window. "Lizzie, get in the car."

She didn't stop walking. She didn't even look at him. He was in a big mess here. He picked up speed and pulled off the road. He cut the engine and jumped out of the car.

By this point, Lizzie was just passing the car. She was still walking and he had no choice but to fall in step next to her. It was either that or toss her over his shoulder. He didn't think she'd appreciate the latter option. And he didn't need any passing motorists calling the *polizia*.

"Lizzie, would you stop so we can talk?"

Still nothing. Her strides were long and quick. His car was fading into the background. He should have locked it up, but he never imagined she'd keep walking.

"What are you going to do? Walk the whole way back to Rome?"

She came to an abrupt halt and turned to him with a pained look. "It's better than going back and facing your family."

"Lizzie, they didn't mean to hurt you. It's just…just that your food surprised them."

"I know. I saw the looks on their faces. Your father couldn't get away from the table fast enough. It was as if he was going to be sick." A pained look swept over her face. "Oh, no. He didn't get sick, did he?"

"Not like you're thinking." Dante really didn't want to discuss his family's problems here on the side of the road. "Come back to the car with me. We can talk there."

She crossed her arms. "We can talk here."

"Fine. The truth is your cooking was fantastic."

She rolled her eyes. "Like I'm going to fall for that line."

She turned to start walking again when he reached out, grabbing her arm. "Wait. The least you can do is hear me out."

Her gaze moved to his hand. He released his hold, hoping she wouldn't walk away.

"I'm listening. But don't feed me a bunch of lies."

"It wasn't a lie," he ground out. "The honest-to-goodness truth is your dinner tasted exactly like my mother's cooking. At least that's what I'm told since I never had the opportunity to taste anything she prepared."

Lizzie pressed a hand to her mouth.

"It seems that particular dish was her favorite. She made it for special occasions—most notably my father's birthday. He hasn't had it since she was alive. So you can see how it would unearth a lot of unexpected memories."

She blinked repeatedly. "I'm so sorry. I never thought—"

"And you shouldn't have to know these things. It's just that my family doesn't move on with life very well. They have a tendency to stick with old stories and relish memories. If you hadn't noticed, my mother's memory is quite alive. And Massimo had no clue that the dish was special to my mother and father."

"I feel so awful for upsetting everyone."

"You have nothing to worry about. In fact, you might be the best thing that has happened to my family in a very long time."

Her beautiful blue eyes widened. "How do you get that?"

"My family has been in a rut for many years. And you're like a breath of fresh air. Instead of them going through the same routine day in and day out, now they have something to look forward to."

"Look forward to what?"

"To you."

"Really?" When he nodded, she added, "But the dinner was supposed to be special—for you."

"For me?" He pressed a hand to his chest. "But why?"

"Because ever since that night when we…uhh…you know…"

"Made love." It had been very special for him—for both of them. There was no way he could cheapen it by calling it sex. No matter what happened afterward.

"Uh, yes…well, after that you grew cold and distant. I was hoping that this dinner would change that."

"But isn't that what you wanted? Distance?"

Her fine brows rose. "Why would you think that?"

Now he had to admit what he'd done and he wasn't any too proud of it. "I heard you."

"Heard me say what?"

He kicked at a stone on the side of the desolate road. It skidded into the field. "When I found you gone that morning, I went searching for you. I knew that the night wasn't anything either one of us planned and I was worried that maybe you'd regretted it."

"But I didn't…not like you're thinking."

He pressed a finger to her lips. "Let me finish before I lose my nerve." He took a deep breath. "I'm not proud of what I have to say."

Her eyes implored him to get to the point.

"After I'd searched the whole apartment including your bedroom and found it empty, I panicked. I'd thought you'd left for good. But then I saw your suitcase. So I went down to the *ristorante* and that's when I heard your voice. When I moved toward the office, I heard you on the phone. And when you said that what we had was a one-time thing—that it didn't mean anything—I knew you regretted our lovemaking."

"Oh, Dante. I'm so sorry you overheard that."

Hope swelled in his chest. "Are you saying that all of this time I misunderstood?"

Her gaze dipped. "I wish I could tell you that, but I can't."

Piercing pain arrowed into his chest. His jaw tightened as he took a step back. He was standing here making a fool of himself for a lady who wanted nothing but to put thousands of miles between them.

"We should get back to the house and get your things." He turned for the car feeling lower than he'd ever felt in his life.

"Wait! Please." The pleading tone in her voice caused him to pause. She rushed to his side. "When I said those words, I was in the midst of a panic attack. That night had been so special. It had me reconsidering my future. I didn't know what I was feeling for you. I just knew that I didn't want to get hurt."

"And then I turned around and hurt you by putting so much distance between us."

She bit down on her lower lip and nodded.

Damn. What he knew about dealing with women and relationships couldn't even fill up the thimble his father kept on his dresser as a reminder of his mother. "I'm sorry. I didn't mean to hurt you. That's the last thing in the world I wanted to do."

"I never wanted to hurt you either. Is there any way we can go back to being friends?"

"I think we can do better than that." His head dipped and caught her lips.

Not sure that he'd made the right move and not wanting to scare her off, he restrained himself, making the kiss brief. It was with great regret that he pulled away. But when she looked up at him and smiled, he knew that he'd made the right move. There was still something there. Something very special.

"See. Your dinner was very successful. It brought us back together. Thank you for not giving up on me and for going to all of the trouble to get through my thick skull."

She lifted up on her tiptoes and pressed her lips to his. No way was he letting her get away twice. His arms quickly wrapped around her waist and pulled her close. It seemed like forever since he'd tasted her and held her. He didn't ever want this moment to end. When she was in his arms, the world felt as if it had righted itself.

The blare of a horn from a passing motorist had Lizzie jumping out of his arms. Color filled her face. "I don't think we should put on a show for everyone."

"Why not?" He didn't feel like being proper at the moment. He had more important things on his mind, like getting her back in his arms. "Who doesn't enjoy a couple—" he'd almost said "in love" but he'd caught himself in time "—a couple enjoying themselves on a summer evening."

"Is that what we were doing?"

Not comfortable exploring the eruption of emotions that plagued him when they'd kissed, he didn't answer her question. Instead he slipped his arm over her shoulders and pulled her close. "How about you and I head back to the villa?"

"I don't know. Couldn't we just go back to the city?"

"But your things are still there."

She didn't move. Then he noticed her gaze searching out his car that was a ways back the road. In that moment he knew how to get her back to the vineyard.

He jangled the car keys in front of her. "I'll let you drive Red."

Her surprised gaze searched his face. "Are you serious?"

"I'd never joke about driving Red."

She snatched the keys from his hand and started for the car.

"That's it?" He started after her. "You just take the keys and don't say a word. You know I never let anyone drive Red, right?"

"I know. But you owe me."

"And how do you get that?"

"I put up with your moodiness lately." She smiled up at him, letting him know that her sense of humor had returned. "And I didn't complain."

He stopped in his tracks and planted his hands on his sides. "I wasn't moody!"

"Oh, yes, you were," she called over her shoulder. "Worse than an old bear awakened during a snowstorm. You better hurry or you'll miss your ride."

"You wouldn't..."

Then again, she just might, depending on her mood. He smiled and shook his head. Then, realizing that she hadn't slowed down for him, he took long, quick strides to catch up with her.

CHAPTER SEVENTEEN

LIZZIE CHECKED HER tattered pride at the door. With her shoulders pulled back, she entered the DeFiore home once again. She didn't know what she expected but it certainly wasn't everyone relaxing. Massimo was reading the newspaper. Stefano was in another room watching a soccer game on a large-screen television. She'd been corrected numerous times that on this side of the pond, it was referred to as football. Not that it mattered one way or the other to her. She'd never been a sports fan.

"See. Nothing to worry about." The whisper of Dante's voice in her ear sent a wave of goose bumps down her arms.

She moved to the kitchen. Everything had been cleaned and put away. "I still haven't seen your father anywhere."

Dante shrugged. "He isn't one for sitting around. He's always complaining that there aren't enough hours in the day."

"I'd really like a chance to talk to him—to apologize."

Dante moved in front of her. "You have nothing to apologize about."

"Yes, I do. I made him unhappy and that's the last thing I meant to do."

"He should be the one apologizing to you. That man always has to have things his way—even if it makes the rest of us miserable."

She studied Dante's furrowed brow and darkened eyes. He wasn't talking about her or the disastrous dinner. There was something else eating at the relationship he had with his father.

Maybe she could do something to help. “Have you tried talking to him? Telling him how you feel?”

“Don’t go there.” Dante’s brusque tone caught her off guard.

She took a second to suck down her emotional response. “Listen, I know there’s something wrong between you and your father. When he enters the room, you leave. Your contact is bare minimum.”

Dante shrugged. “It’s nothing.”

“No. It’s definitely something. And take it from someone who never knew their father and would have moved heaven and earth to get to know him—you need to fix this thing before it’s too late.”

“But it’s not me. It’s him. There’s nothing about me that he approves of.”

“Aren’t you exaggerating just a bit?”

“Not really.” Dante raked his fingers through his hair. “But you don’t want to hear any of this. Compared to you, I have nothing to complain about.”

She worried her bottom lip. In her effort to make him realize how lucky he was to have a family, she’d made him feel worse. “My background has nothing to do with yours. But I would like to hear more about you and your father, if you’ll tell me.”

Dante stared at her as though trying to decide if she was being on the level or not. The silence grew oppressive. And just when she thought he was going to brush her off, he started to talk.

“We didn’t exactly get off to a good start as he got stuck with a newborn baby in exchange for losing his wife. Not exactly a fair trade.”

“Still, it’s nothing that you can be held responsible for.”

“I resemble my mother in more than just my looks. Instead of being drawn into the vineyard like my brother, I got restless. My father didn't understand why I wasn't interested in the family business. We fought about it continually until I moved to Rome."

"And that's where you found your passion for cooking."

He nodded. "I thought I had found my calling until Massimo left. It hasn't been the same since." Dante turned to her and looked her straight in the eyes. "If I tell you something, will you promise it'll go no further?"

She crossed her heart just like she used to do as a kid with Jules. "I promise."

"I'm in negotiations to sell the *ristorante*—"

"What? But why?"

"I figured that it's time I moved home. Make amends. And do my part."

"And you think that'll make you happy?"

He shrugged and looked away from her. "I think it's the best thing I can do for my family. Maybe at last it'll make my father happy."

Lizzie bit back her opinion. She'd have to think long and hard about what to say to him because she didn't have much experience when it came to families. With it just being her and Jules, they'd been able to work things out pretty easily. But this bigger family dynamic had her feeling like a fish out of water.

"Why don't you talk to your father? Tell him your plan."

He shrugged. "Every time I try, we end up arguing. Usually over the choices I've made in my life."

She heard the defeated tone in his voice and it dug at the old scars on her heart. "Don't give up. Promise me. It's too important."

Dante's eyes widened at her plea. "I'll do my best."

That was all she could ask of him. And she believed him. Though she didn't think that selling the restaurant and moving back here was the answer to his problems. But that was for Dante to figure out on his own.

"Now, where did you say I could find your father?"

* * *

Was she right?

Dante rolled around everything they'd talked about in his mind as he led Lizzie to the barrel cellar. When his father wasn't out in the fields checking the grapes or the soil, he was in the cellar—avoiding his family. As a young child, Dante resented anything and everything that had to do with the vineyard. He blamed the grapes for his father's notable absence.

But as Dante grew up, he realized it wasn't the vineyard he should blame—it was his father. It was his choice to avoid his children. And though his father wasn't as remote as he used to be, some habits were hard to change.

Dante glanced over at Lizzie. "Are you sure you want to do this?"

She threaded her fingers with his. With a squeeze, she smiled up at him. "I'm positive. Lead the way."

He wanted to lean over and press his mouth to hers—to feel the rightness of holding her in his arms. But with his father close by, Dante would settle for the comfort of her touch. He tightened his grip on her much smaller hand and led her down the steps.

As they walked, Lizzie asked about the wooden barrels containing the vineyard's bounty. The fact that she was truly interested in his family's heritage impressed him. He and his father may not hit it off, but he still had pride in his family's hard work. It was why he showcased DeFiore vino exclusively at the *ristorante*.

"This is so impressive." Lizzie looked all around at the walls of barrels. "And they're all full of wine?"

He nodded. "This place has grown a lot since I was a kid."

"Dante, is that you?"

They both turned to find his father holding a sample of vino. "Hey, Papa. I thought we'd find you down here."

"I was doing some testing." His father glanced at Lizzie.

"We do a periodic analysis of the contents and top off the barrels to keep down the exposure to oxygen due to evaporation."

"With all of these barrels, I'd say you have a lot of work to stay on top of things."

"It keeps me busy." His father smiled, something he didn't do often. "Is there something you needed?"

Lizzie glanced at Dante, but if she thought he was going anywhere, she was mistaken. He wasn't budging. He crossed his arms and leaned against a post. His father could be gruff and tactless at times. Dante wasn't about to let him hurt Lizzie's feelings any more than had already been done.

Lizzie turned to his father. "Mr. DeFiore, I owe you an apology for tonight. I'm so sorry I ruined your dinner and…and brought up painful memories. I had absolutely no idea that the recipe held such special meaning for you. If I had, I never would have cooked that meal."

There was an awkward pause. Dante's body tensed. Please don't let his father brush her off as though her apology meant nothing. Lizzie didn't say it, but she wanted his father's approval. And Dante wanted it for her. He didn't want her to feel the pain of once again being rejected.

Dante turned his gaze on his father, planning to send him a warning look, but his father was staring down at the vino in his hand.

The breath caught in Dante's chest as tension filled the room. When his father spoke, his voice was softer than normal and Dante strained to hear every word.

"I am the one who owes you an apology. I reacted badly. And I'm sorry. The meal, it…it caught me off guard. It tasted exactly like my wife's."

The pent-up breath released from Dante's lungs like a punctured balloon. He didn't know what was up with his father, but Dante was thankful he'd paid Lizzie such a high compliment. As far as Dante knew, there was no higher compliment than for his father to compare Lizzie's cooking to that of his mother. Was it possible his father truly was changing for the better?

"I'll try not to cook any of your wife's favorites in the future—"

"No. I mean I'd like you to. I know this meal caught me off guard, but it brought back some of the best memories." His father set aside the vino and reached for Lizzie's hand. "I hope I haven't scared you off. I'd really like you to come back and cook for us. That is, if you'd still like to."

"I would…like to cook for you, that is."

"Maybe next weekend?"

Dante at last found his voice. "Papa, we can't be here next weekend. There's been a change in the filming schedule and they're pushing to wrap up the series, so we'll be working all next weekend."

"Oh, I see." His father turned to Lizzie. "So what do you think of my son? Is he good in the kitchen?"

Lizzie's eyes opened wide. "You don't know?"

His father shook his head. "He never cooks for us. Always says it's too much like work."

Lizzie turned an astonished look to Dante. Guilt consumed him. He shrugged his shoulders innocently.

The truth was that cooking was an area where he'd excelled and he didn't want his father's ill-timed, stinging comments to rob him of that special feeling. But witnessing this different side of his father had him rethinking his stance.

"We'll have to change that." Lizzie turned back to his father. "Your son is an excellent cook and he's turning out to be an excellent teacher."

"I have an idea." There was a gleam in his father's eyes. "I'm sure Dante has told you that Massimo hasn't had an easy time moving away from the city and leaving the *ristorante* behind."

Lizzie nodded. “He mentioned it. What can I do to help?”

“That’s the spirit.” Papa smiled. “I was thinking that we should celebrate his birthday.”

“You mean like a party.”

He nodded. “Something special to show him that…well, you know.”

“To let him know that everybody loves him.”

Papa nodded. “I’ll hire the musicians.”

Lizzie’s face lit up and she turned to Dante. “What do you think? Would you be willing to bring me back here?”

He couldn’t think of anything he’d like more. “I think it can be arranged.”

She smiled at him and a spot in his chest warmed. The warmth spread throughout his body. And he realized that for the first time he was at total ease around his father. Lizzie was a miracle worker.

“Don’t worry about a thing.” She patted his father’s arm. “Dante and I will take care of all the food. Although your son might have to get a bigger vehicle to haul everything.”

That was not a problem. Her wish was his command. He had a feeling that this party was going to be a huge deal and not just for his grandfather. He had a feeling his own life would never be the same again.

CHAPTER EIGHTEEN

AND THAT WAS a wrap!

Two weeks ahead of schedule, the filming was over. Lizzie was exhausted. They'd worked every available minute to get enough footage for the studio to splice together for the upcoming season.

And so far Dante hadn't said a word about everything they'd shared at the vineyard. Every time she'd worked up the courage to ask him about it, there was no opportunity for them to talk privately. And it was driving her crazy wondering where they went from here. Technically, she still had another two weeks in Rome to learn as much as she could from him. But her biggest lessons hadn't been taught in the kitchen.

Somewhere along the way, she'd fallen in love with Dante. Oh, she'd been in love with him for longer than she'd been willing to admit. And she accepted that was the reason she'd been so freaked out after they'd made love. She just couldn't bear to have him reject her, so she did the rejecting first. Not her best move.

"Something on your mind?" Dante asked as he strolled into the living room Saturday morning.

"I was thinking about you." She watched as surprise filtered across his handsome features.

"You were?" In a navy suit, white dress shirt and maroon tie, he looked quite dashing. "Only good thoughts, I hope."

"Definitely." Her gaze skimmed down over him again, enjoying the view. "You look a bit overdressed to be heading downstairs to help with the lunch crowd."

"That's because I'm not. I made arrangements so the kitchen is covered today. You, my pretty lady, have the day off." His smile sent her heart tumbling.

To spend with him! She grinned back at him.

She shouldn't have worried. It'd been the rush of the filming and keeping up with the increasing crush of patrons that had kept him from following up on those kisses at the vineyard. She was certain of it now.

"I like the sounds of that. What shall we do with the day?"

"I don't know about you, but I have a meeting."

"A meeting?" The words slipped past her lips.

A questioning brow lifted. "Is that a problem?"

"Umm…no. I just thought we could do something, you know, together." Did she really have to spell it out for him?

The intercom buzzed. Who in the world could that be? From what she'd gathered living here for the past several weeks, Dante didn't entertain much, and when he did, it was down in the restaurant.

"That'll be for me. They sent a car."

"Who did?"

His face creased with stress lines. "The people interested in buying the *ristorante*."

His words knocked her off-kilter. She sat down on the arm of the couch. And here she'd been daydreaming about them one day running the restaurant together. She didn't have a clue how she'd work things out with Jules being so far away, but Massimo's words came back to her: *Love will always find a way.* Now all of her daydreams were about to be dashed.

"You're really going through with it?" Her voice was barely more than a whisper.

"Why do you seem so surprised? I told you I was considering it. And thanks to you, things between me and my father are looking up. It's time I do what's expected of me."

He was trying to be noble and earn his father's respect and love. That she could admire. But at what cost?

"Dante, do you really think that you'll be happy working at the vineyard? After all, you couldn't wait to leave when you were younger. Do you really think it'll have changed?"

His gaze darkened. "Maybe I've changed."

"And you aren't going to miss the restaurant—your grandfather's legacy? Have you even told Massimo?"

Dante's brows gathered. "When I took over the *ristorante*, he gave me his blessing to do what I thought was appropriate with it. And that's what I'm doing."

She knew the decision was ultimately up to him, but if she didn't say something now, she'd regret it—they both might regret it. "Don't do it. Don't sell the restaurant."

Dante grabbed his briefcase and headed for the door. "I've got to go."

"Wait." She rushed over to him. "I'm sorry. I'm butting in where I don't belong, but I don't want you to have any regrets."

"I won't. I know what I want."

And it wasn't working here side by side with her. Her heart sank.

"We'll do something when I get back." The buzzer sounded again. "I really do have to go."

He rushed out the door. She willed him to come back, but he didn't. Deep down she had a bad feeling that Dante was about to make a decision that he would come to regret. But there was nothing else she could do to stop him.

Not quite an hour later, as Lizzie was trying to find a television show to distract her from thinking of Dante, the phone rang. Maybe it was him. Maybe he had come to his senses and couldn't wait to tell her.

"Hello."

"Lizzie, is that you?" Definitely not Dante's voice, but still it was familiar.

"Yes."

"This is Dante's father."

"Oh, hi. Dante isn't here. But I can give him a message."

"Actually, you're the one I wanted to speak to. I wanted to know if you needed any help with the food for the party tomorrow. My sisters have been pestering me to know how they can help."

How in the world had she let Massimo's party slip her mind? Of course, with the crazy filming schedule and the vibes of attraction zinging back and forth between her and Dante, it culminated into a surge, short-circuiting her mind.

"Don't worry about a thing. I have everything under control." No way was she telling him the truth. Not after that disastrous dinner.

"I knew I could count on you." His confidence in her only compounded her guilt. "This party is going to be just what Massimo needs. A houseful of family and friends with great food, music and the best vino."

They talked for a few more minutes before she gave in and said that his sisters could do the appetizers, but the entrées were her and Dante's responsibility.

As she hung up the phone, her mind was racing. That was when she realized they hadn't picked up the collage of photos of the restaurant through the years to hang in Massimo's room at the vineyard. A quick call assured her that the order was complete, but she'd have to get there right away. In twenty minutes, they closed for the weekend. She tried calling Dante's cell phone but it went straight to voice mail.

A glance at the clock told her that she didn't have time to wait. She needed to go right now. She wouldn't let Dante down in front of his family. Not when he was so anxious to fix things with his father. This gift was from the both of them, but it was more Dante's idea than hers.

Spotting the keys to Red on the counter, she wondered

if Dante would mind if she borrowed the car. After all, this was an emergency and he had let her drive it when they were in the country. What could it hurt? The shop wasn't too far away.

Before she could change her mind, she grabbed the keys and headed out the door. Her stomach quivered with nerves as she fired up the engine. As she maneuvered Red down the street, heads turned. She could only ever dream of having a luxury sports car for herself. Without even checking, she knew that the price tag on this gem was not even in her realm of possibilities…ever.

In no time, she placed the large framed collage in the passenger seat. Being cautious, she used the seat belt to hold it in place. She didn't want anything to happen to the gift. It was perfect. And she was certain that Massimo would treasure it.

Mentally she was listing everything she needed to start preparing as soon as she got home. The fact that there would be a hundred-plus people at this "small" gathering totally boggled her mind. When she and Jules had a birthday party, it usually ended up being them and a handful of friends—less than ten people total. The DeFiore clan was more like a small village.

She would need at least four trays of lasagna alone. Thankfully the restaurant was kept well stocked. When they'd talked about the party previously, Dante had told her to take whatever she needed and just to leave him a list of what she used. That was a big relief—

The blur of a speeding car caught her attention. Lizzie slammed on the brakes. Red immediately responded. Her body tensed. The air became trapped in her lungs.

The blue compact car cut in front of her, narrowly missing her.

Lizzie slowed to a stop. She blew out the pent-up breath.

Thank goodness nothing had happened to Red. Dante

would have freaked out if she'd damaged his precious car. The man truly loved this fine vehicle—

Squeal!

Thunk!

Lizzie's body lurched forward. Her body jerked hard against the seat belt. The air was knocked out of her lungs.

CHAPTER NINETEEN

"THAT'S NOT POSSIBLE. Lizzie wouldn't be out in Red." Dante gripped the phone tighter. "You're sure it was her?" He listened intently as though his very life depended on it. "What do you mean you don't know if she's okay?" His gut twisted into a painful knot. "I'm on my way."

Was it possible his newly hired busboy was mistaken? Lizzie had been in a car accident with Red? The kid didn't know Lizzie very well. He had to have her mixed up with someone else.

Dante strode toward the elevator of the corporate offices after his meeting. He could only hope the hired car would be waiting for him. When the elevator didn't come fast enough, he headed for the stairwell. Lizzie just had to be okay. His feet barely touched the steps as he flew down the two flights of stairs.

After nearly running into a half-dozen people, he made it to the street. The black car was waiting for him. When the driver went to get out to open his door for him, Dante waved him off. There wasn't time for niceties. He had to know if Lizzie was okay.

It seemed to take forever for the car to get across the city. He tried calling her. She didn't answer at the apartment and she didn't pick up her cell phone. Dante's body tensed. Was the kid right? Had she been in an accident? Was she hurt?

Then feeling utterly helpless, Dante did something he

hadn't done since he was a kid. He sent a prayer to the big guy upstairs, pleading for Lizzie's safety.

What had she been doing? Where had she gone? And what was she doing with Red? He couldn't come up with any plausible answers. All he could do was stare helplessly out the window as they slowly inched closer to the accident site.

"This is as close as I can get, sir. Looks like they have the road shut down up ahead." The driver sent him an apologetic look in the rearview mirror.

"Thank you."

Dante sprang out of the car and weaved his way through the throng of people on the sidewalk, sidestepping a cyclist and a few strollers. He inwardly groaned. Just his luck. Everyone seemed to be out and about on such a sunny day.

And then he saw the familiar candy-apple-red paint, but his gaze kept moving, searching for Lizzie's blond hair. She wasn't by the car. And she wasn't standing on the sidewalk.

And then he spotted the ambulance. His heart tightened. *Please. Please. Don't let her be hurt.*

He ran to the ambulance and moved to the back. Lizzie was sitting there with a stunned look on her face. His gaze scanned her from head to foot. No blood. No bandages.

Thank goodness.

"Lizzie."

It was all he got out before she was rushing into his arms and he nearly dropped to the roadway with relief. As his arms wrapped around her, he realized that he'd never been so scared in his entire life. If he had lost her— No, he couldn't go there. Losing her was unimaginable.

As he held her close and felt her shake, he realized that he loved her. Not just a little. But a whole lot. In that moment, he understood the depth of love his father had felt for his mother. He'd never before been able to comprehend why his father never remarried—why his father kept all of the memories of his mother around the house. Now he understood.

Lizzie pulled back. "Dante, I'm so sorry. I…I—"

"Are you okay?" When she didn't answer right away, his gaze moved to the paramedic. "Is she okay? Does she need to go to the hospital?"

"She refused to go to the hospital."

Dante turned to her. "You've got to go. What if something is wrong?"

"It looks like she's going to be bruised from the seat belt and a bit sore in the morning, but she should be okay."

Lizzie patted Dante's arm to get his attention. "He's right. I'm fine. But…"

"But what?" If she so much as had a pain in her little finger, he was going to carry her into that ambulance himself.

"But Red isn't in such good condition. Oh, Dante, I'm sorry…" She burst out in tears.

What did he do now? He didn't know a thing about women and tears. He let his instincts take over as he pulled her against his chest and gently rubbed her back. "It's okay. I'm just glad you're okay."

He truly meant it.

While she let her emotions flow, he realized how close he'd come to losing her in a car accident. He knew this scene. He'd lived through it with his brother. Stefano's wife had died so tragically—so unexpectedly.

The memory sent a new cold knife of fear into Dante's heart. He'd watched the agony his brother had endured when he'd joined the ranks of the DeFiore widowers' club. Dante had sworn then and there that wouldn't be him. He'd never let someone close enough to make him vulnerable. And that was exactly what was happening with Lizzie. Every moment he was with her. Every time he touched her, she got further under his skin and deeper in his heart.

He had to stop it.

He couldn't go through this again. Because next time they both might not be so lucky.

As though sensing the change in him, Lizzie pulled back and swiped quickly at her cheeks. "Dante, I'm so sorry."

"It's not your fault."

"Of course it is. I didn't ask you…I tried. But your phone was off. And I had to hurry."

"I had my phone switched off for the meeting."

"I'd forgotten. Then your dad called. And there wasn't time to wait. Then this car cut me off—"

"Slow down. Take a breath." In her excitement she wasn't making much sense and he was worried she might hyperventilate.

"The car—Red—it's not drivable. They called for a flat-bed."

This was the first time he truly looked at Red. Any other time that would have been his priority. Warning bells went off in his head. He loved Lizzie more than anything in the world. When his gaze landed on the crumpled rear corner panel, he didn't feel anything. Maybe he was numb with shock and worry after seeing Lizzie in the back of the ambulance.

She sniffled. "I can't believe it happened. I was on my way home when this little car cut me off. I braked just in time. Before I could get moving again, I was hit from behind by that delivery truck."

Dante's gaze moved to the nearby white truck. The size of it was much, much larger than he'd been anticipating. The damage could have been so much worse. The thought that Lizzie could have been seriously injured…or worse hit him in the gut with a sharp jab.

"I don't know if they can repair the car but…but I'll pay the bill or replace it. Whatever it takes."

She didn't have that kind of money. Not that he'd accept it even if she did. The only important part was that she was safe. He'd be lost without her. The words teetered on his tongue, but he couldn't vocalize them. Telling her that would just be cruel. He refused to get her hopes up and have her think they were going to have a happily-ever-after ending. That simply couldn't happen.

Stifling his emotions, he said, "I still don't understand why you took the car without asking."

She turned and stared directly at him. "I told you. I tried to call you but it went straight to voice mail. And I couldn't be late. Otherwise they would have closed."

"Who would have closed? What was so damn important that you almost got yourself killed?"

Pain flashed in her eyes. "Listen, I know you're worked up about your car, but I was trying to do you a favor."

"A favor? You call totaling my car and scaring me *doing me a favor*?" He rubbed the back of his neck. His words were coming out all wrong. His gut continued to churn with a ball of conflicting emotions.

Lizzie glared at him. "I told you I'm sorry."

"But that won't fix anything." And it wouldn't ease the scare she'd given him.

The groan of the motor hauling his car up onto the back of the tow drew his attention. The bent, broken and cracked car was slowly rolled onto a flatbed. It was a miracle Lizzie had escaped serious injury.

If this worry and agony was what loving someone was about, he didn't want it. He didn't want to have to care so deeply—to depend on someone. The price of loving and losing was too steep. He didn't care if that made him a wimp or worse. He wasn't going to end up a miserable old man like the rest of his family—with only memories to keep him company on those long lonely nights. No way.

"Stay here." He wanted to keep her in sight just in case she started to feel ill. "I need to speak to the *polizia* and the tow driver."

In truth, he needed some distance. A chance to think

clearly. He had to break things off with Lizzie. It was the only logical thing to do. But why did it feel so wrong?

What was his problem?

Lizzie had never seen Dante in such a black mood. Did he really care about his car that much? She glanced over to see broken bits of the car being cleaned up. Okay. So she had totally messed up today. She knew it was her fault, but did he have to be so gruff? This wasn't the man—dare she say it—the man she loved.

After he spoke with the tow driver and the *polizia*, he returned to Lizzie. His face creased into a frown. "I'll call us a taxi."

There was no way she wanted to spend any more time around him. She already felt bad enough and had offered to pay for the damages. There was nothing else she could do to make things better. "I'd rather walk."

"You aren't up for walking." His gaze wouldn't even meet hers. "You were just in an accident."

His body was rigid. A vein pulsated in his neck. He was doing his best to bottle up his anger but she could feel it. And she couldn't stand it. He hated her for wrecking his car. "Just say it."

"I don't know what you're talking about, but I'm calling a taxi." He placed the call, ignoring her protests. "The taxi will be here shortly."

She wished he'd get it off his chest. If they couldn't even talk to each other, how in the world did she think they were going to have an ongoing relationship? Her mind was racing. She had to calm down. Everything was under control… except Massimo's birthday party.

And that was when she realized that the gift—the whole reason for this illuminating calamity—was about to be hauled away inside Red. Her gaze swung around to the damaged car atop the tow. Anxious to get to the truck before it pulled out, she took off at a brisk pace. Her heeled black boots kept her from moving quicker.

"Lizzie!" Dante called out behind her. "What's wrong? Would you talk to me?"

She kept moving until she was next to the truck. She reached up and knocked on the window. When the driver rolled down his window, she explained that she needed a package out of the vehicle.

"Couldn't this have waited?" Dante sighed.

"No. It couldn't." Lizzie stood there ramrod-straight, staring straight ahead. She refused to let Dante get to her. Instead she watched as the driver climbed up to the car and retrieved the large package.

When the man went to hand it down, Dante intercepted it. "Let me guess. This is the reason you couldn't wait for me."

She nodded. "It's the gift for your grandfather."

The tension on his face eased. It was though at last he realized she'd been trying to do something for him and she hadn't taken his car for a joyride.

When the taxi pulled up and they climbed inside, exhaustion coursed through Lizzie's veins. It was so tempting to lean her head against Dante's shoulder. They'd both been worked up. They'd both said things that they regretted. Everything would be all right when they got back to the apartment.

Satisfied that everything would work itself out, she leaned her head against him. She enjoyed the firmness of his muscles against her cheek and the gentle scent of his fresh cologne. She closed her eyes, noticing the beginning of the predicted aches setting in. But if that was all she ended up with, she'd be grateful. It could have been so much worse.

But she noticed how Dante didn't move. He didn't attempt to put his arm around her and draw her closer. He sat there stiffly and stared out the window. Maybe he was embarrassed about his heated reaction. That was understandable. She was horrified that she'd wrecked his car. Once they were home and alone, they could sort this all out.

CHAPTER TWENTY

IF THERE WAS another way to do this, he didn't know what it was.

Guilt ate at Dante. Though the ride back to the apartment was only a few minutes, it felt more like an eternity. And having Lizzie nestled against him only made him feel worse about his decision to end things. But he just couldn't live like this—always wondering when the good times would come to a crashing halt. And now that he'd had a small sample of what the pain and agony would be like—he just couldn't commit himself to a relationship.

The sooner he did this—laid everything on the table with Lizzie—the less pain they'd both experience. It was what he kept telling himself on the elevator ride to the penthouse. But somehow he was having trouble believing his own words.

It was nerves. That was it. He didn't want to hurt Lizzie any more than he had to. But in the end, this was what was best for both of them. After all, her life was in New York.

Once they stepped inside the apartment, Lizzie moved to the kitchen area. "I'll need to make a list of what we need from downstairs."

"For what?"

"The party. Remember, we're in charge of the food. Your father wants to taste your cooking."

The party where she would be introduced to his extended family—the party where people would start hint-ing about a wedding. His aunts were notorious for playing the part of matchmakers. That was why he ducked them as much as possible.

Dante sighed. This was all getting so complicated now. “Lizzie, can you come in here so we can talk?”

She rummaged through a drawer, pulling out a pen and paper. “It’s already getting late. We really need to get to work on the food prep. You never did say how we’re going to get all of this to the vineyard. You know, it might be easier if we’d take the supplies there and prepare it—”

He’d heard her ramble on a few occasions and each time she’d been nervous. “Lizzie, stop!”

She jumped and turned wide eyes in his direction. He felt even worse now that he’d scared her than he did before. He was making a mess of this.

“I’m sorry. I didn’t mean to startle you. I just wanted your attention.” He walked toward the black leather couch. “Come here. There’s something I need to say.”

Lizzie placed the pen and paper on the kitchen counter and hesitantly walked toward him. She knew what was coming, didn’t she? It was obvious this wasn’t going to work. He just wasn’t cut out to be anyone’s better half. He’d laugh at the thought if he wasn’t so miserable.

She perched on the edge of the couch with her spine straight. “Is this about the restaurant? About your meeting today. Did you go through with the sale?”

That was what she thought he wanted to talk about? He scrubbed his hand over his face. “No, this isn’t about that.”

“Oh. But did you sell it? Not that it’s any of my business. But I was just curious because of Massimo—”

“You don’t have to remind me. I know that my grandfather put his whole life into that business.” And this was just one more reason why he needed to end this relationship. She was already influencing his decisions—decisions that only a couple of months ago he hadn’t needed or wanted anyone’s input. “No, I didn’t sell the place.”

"I didn't think you could part with it. It's in your blood. You'd be lost without the restaurant." A hesitant smile pulled at the edges of her lips. "Massimo will be so pleased to know the restaurant is in safe hands. It will make his birthday gift even more special."

The collage. She'd been hurt because of him—because he'd forgotten to pick up the present. Guilt ate at him. An apology teetered on the tip of his tongue, but at the last second he bit it back. Comforting her would only muddy things. He had to end things as cleanly as possible—it would hurt her less that way.

"There's something else we need to talk about." There, he'd gotten the conversation started.

Lizzie sent him a puzzled look. "But we have so much to do for the party—"

"Don't you see, we can't do this? I can't do this." He turned his back to her, unable to bear the weight of seeing the inevitable disillusionment on her face. "We were kidding ourselves to think that we could ever have something real."

"What's going on, Dante? I thought that we were getting closer. I thought—"

"You thought wrong," he ground out. He hated himself for the pain and confusion he was causing her.

"You…you're ending things because I screwed up and wrecked your car?" The horror came across in the rising tones of her voice.

"It's not that."

He turned around then and saw the shimmer of unshed tears in her eyes. It was almost his undoing. But then he recalled the paralyzing fear of thinking that something serious had happened to her. He just couldn't cave in. It would mean risking his heart and waiting for the day that his whole world would come crashing down around him.

"Then it's my past." She looked at him with disbelief

reflected in her eyes. "I should have never told you. Now you think that I'm damaged goods."

"I never thought that. Ever." He stepped closer to her. No matter what it cost him, he was unwilling to let her think such a horrible thing. "You're amazing." His fingers caressed her cheek. "Any man who is fortunate to have you in his life will be the luckiest man in the world."

She stepped back out of his reach. "You expect me to believe that when you're standing there saying you don't want to see me again."

He groaned. "I'm doing this all wrong. I'm sorry. I never wanted you to think this had anything to do with you. You're the most beautiful woman I've ever known." He stepped toward her. "You have your whole future ahead of you."

She moved back. "Save the pep talk. I've heard lines like yours before. I don't need to hear it again. I was so wrong about you."

"What's that supposed to mean?"

"It means I thought you were different from the other guys I've known. I thought that I could trust you, but obviously I was wrong."

Her words were like spears that slammed into his chest. He didn't know it was possible to feel this low. He deserved every painful word she spewed at him. And more...

To keep from reaching out to her, he stuffed his hands in his pockets. "Don't you get it? I don't do well with long-term commitments."

She waved off his words. "Save it. I don't need to hear this. I have packing to do."

There was still the surprise party to deal with and Lizzie was in charge. But after the accident, he couldn't imagine that she'd be up for any part of it. Still, he couldn't just disinvite her. "What about Massimo's party?"

Her gaze lifted to meet his. "Are you serious? You really expect me to go and pretend that everything is okay between you and me?" She shook her head, her long blond hair swishing over her shoulder. "That party is for your family—something I'll never be."

His gaze dropped to the black plush rug with a white swirl pattern. He choked down the lump in his throat. "What should I tell everyone?"

She gave him a hard, cold stare. "This one is all on you. I'm sure you'll figure something out." She strode off down the hallway. Without even bothering to turn around, she called out, "Don't worry. I'll be gone before you return to the city."

Her back was ramrod-stiff and her shoulders were rigid. He tried to console himself with the knowledge that she'd be better off without him. The fate of women who fell in love with a DeFiore was not good. Not good at all.

CHAPTER TWENTY-ONE

HE COULDN'T BRING himself to celebrate.

Dante worked his way to a corner on the patio. There was no quiet place to hide. The musicians his father hired didn't know how to keep the volume down. And the cacophony of voices and laughter grated on Dante's taut nerves.

It didn't matter who he ran into, they asked about Lizzie. It was as though he and Lizzie were expected to head for the nearest altar as soon as possible. When he explained that Lizzie was returning to the States, they all sent him an accusing look.

He should be relieved. He had his utter freedom back. No chance that he could get hurt and grow old, miserable and alone like his grandfather, father and Stefano. No taking part in the DeFiore legacy. So why did he feel so miserable?

Dante could barely hear his own thoughts. There was nothing quiet about the DeFiore family. Everyone spoke over everyone else, hands gestured for emphasis and laughter reigned supreme. Lizzie would have loved being part of such a big gathering. And she'd have fit right in.

"How's the *ristorante*?"

Dante turned to find his father standing behind him, puffing on a cigar. Dante hadn't even heard him approach.

"It's good." Now that the decision had been made, he decided to let his father in on it. "There was an offer to buy the *ristorante*. It was made by some outfit looking to expand their portfolio."

"Are you going to accept?"

It was good to talk with someone about something other than Lizzie and his failed relationship. "I thought about it. I considered selling and moving home to help with the vineyard."

His father's bushy brows rose. "You'd want to come back after you fought so hard to get out of here?"

Dante shrugged. "I thought it'd make things easier for you."

"I don't need you to make things easier for me." His father's tone was resilient. "I take it you came to your senses and turned down the offer."

Dante considered telling him that they wanted the family recipes as part of the deal but that he just couldn't go through with it. No amount of money could compensate for giving away those family secrets. Some things weren't meant to be shared. But that wasn't the real reason he'd ended up turning down the offer.

Dante nodded his head. "I almost went through with it. But in the end, I couldn't do it."

"What changed your mind?"

"Lizzie." Her name slipped quietly over his lips as the pain of loss overwhelmed him.

"You were planning to run the place with her by your side? Like your grandparents had done?"

Dante didn't trust his voice at that moment. He merely nodded.

"Then why are you here alone? Why did you let her get away?"

His father always thought he failed at things. Well, this time his father was wrong. "I didn't let her get away. I pushed her away."

"What? But why would you do that?" His father put out

his cigar in a nearby ashtray before approaching Dante. "Let's walk."

Dante really didn't want a lecture from his father, but what did it matter? He couldn't be more miserable. His father led him off toward the vines. When people wanted to be alone, the vines always offered solace.

"Son, I know you never had a chance to know your mother, but she was an amazing woman. You remind me a lot of her. I know if she were here she'd insist that I give you some advice—"

"Papa, I don't need advice. I know what I'm doing. I won't end up like you." He realized too late that he'd said too much.

"You sent Lizzie away so you wouldn't end up miserable and alone like your old man, is that it?"

Dante couldn't deny it, so he didn't say anything. He kept his head low and concentrated on the path between the vines, which was barely wide enough for them to walk side by side.

"I'll admit it," his father said. "I didn't handle your mother's death well. I never expected to be alone with two young boys to raise. I…I was scared. And…I took my anger and frustration out on you. I'm sorry. You didn't deserve it. Not at all."

What did Dante say to that? *You're right* didn't seem appropriate. *No big deal* wouldn't work either because it was a big deal—a huge deal.

"If you had to do it over again—falling in love with Mama—would you?"

"Even knowing how things would end, I'd still have pursued your mother. She was amazing. When she smiled the whole world glowed. Loving your mother was one of the best parts of my life."

"But you…you always look so sad when anyone mentions her."

"And that's where I messed up. I closed myself off

from life. I dwelled so much on my loss—my pain—that I couldn't see clearly. I missed seeing what I was doing to my family."

"Is that why you never married again?"

Papa nodded. "I was too consumed with what I'd lost to see anything in front of me." He ran a hand over his face. "I can't go back and change any of it. My only hope is that you boys don't make the same mistakes. Love is like life—it's a gift not to be squandered."

Dante studied his father's face, trying to decide if his father was being on the level with him. "Are you serious? You'd be willing to give love another try?"

"If the right woman came along. What about you? Do you love Lizzie?"

Dante's heart pounded out the answer before he could find the words. He nodded. "But how do I live knowing that something might happen to her? That someday I might be alone?"

His father gripped his shoulder. "You don't. You just have to cherish the time you have together. No one knows the future. But by running from love, you're going to end up old and alone anyway."

Dante hadn't thought of it that way. In fact, if it weren't for Lizzie, he wouldn't be having this conversation with his father. Somehow Lizzie had worked her magic and reconnected him with his family.

His father cleared his throat. "Here's something else for you to consider. You've always known you're different from me and your brother. It's your mother's genes coming out in you. I know sometimes that drove a wedge between us. But that doesn't mean that I love you any less. Sometimes being different is a good thing."

Really? And here he'd been punishing himself for being so different from his father and brother. But if he differed from them in his choice of professions, why couldn't he be different when it came to love? Maybe there was a chance his story would end differently than theirs.

"Now, what are you doing standing here talking to me?" His father gave him a pointed stare, like when he was a boy and had forgotten to do his chores. "Go after the woman you love."

Dante turned to the villa when he realized that he didn't have his car. And the next train was hours away. He didn't have time to waste if he was going to catch Lizzie and beg her forgiveness.

"Hey, Papa, can I borrow the truck?"

His father reached into his pants pocket and pulled out a key ring. "You know it's not fancy like that sports car of yours."

"That's okay. I've learned that sort of stuff isn't what makes a person happy."

Lizzie had taught him that lesson.

Now he had to track her down, even if it meant flying to New York. He'd beg her forgiveness. Whatever it took, he'd do it.

Maybe he and his father weren't all that different after all.

CHAPTER TWENTY-TWO

How could she have let herself get caught up in a dream?

That was what this whole trip had been—one amazing dream. And now Lizzie had awakened to the harsh glare of reality. The truth was no matter how much she wanted to believe that Dante was changing, he was never going to be willing to let his guard down enough to let her in—even if she'd foolishly let him into her heart.

After Dante had left, she'd spent the night lying in the dark reliving her memories of Dante—memories that she'd treasure for a lifetime. Because no matter how the fairy tale ended, it'd still been a dream come true—falling in love under the Italian sky and kissing the man of her dreams in a breathtaking vineyard.

Tears streamed down her cheeks as she called the taxi service to take her to the airport. She took one last look around the apartment, but she couldn't bring herself to walk down the hallway to the master suite. Some memories were still too raw for her to delve into.

With the front door secure, she made her way down to the restaurant. With it being Sunday, it was closed. Maybe she had time to slip inside and—what? Remember the time she'd spent there with Dante? No, that wasn't a good idea. There was only so much pain she could take.

Would that taxi ever show up?

At the sound of an approaching vehicle, she turned. She frowned when all she saw was an old truck ambling down the road. Needing something to distract her, she reached into her purse and pulled out her cell phone. She'd been putting off calling Jules for as long as possible. Her foster sister would be full of questions as soon as she learned that Lizzie was catching an earlier flight than was planned.

Her fingers hovered over the keypad. How was she going to explain this?

"Hey, are you here for the hostess position?" came a familiar voice from behind her.

Lizzie spun around to find Dante leaning against an old truck. "What are you doing here? I mean, what are you doing back so soon? Is the party over already? You did have the party, didn't you?"

She was nervously rambling and he was smiling. Smiling? Why was he smiling? The last time she saw him, he'd looked miserable.

"The party is probably still in full swing. Once my family gets started, it goes on and on."

"That's good." She didn't want to think that anything she did would ruin this special day for Massimo. "I…I'll be out of your way in just a minute."

"Don't go."

"What?" Surely she hadn't heard him correctly.

Before Dante could repeat himself, a taxi pulled over to the curb. She should feel relieved, but she didn't. Whatever Dante's reason was for returning early, it was none of her business. He'd made that abundantly clear before he left yesterday.

Lizzie turned and slung her purse over one shoulder and her carry-on over the other shoulder. She grabbed the handle of her suitcase and turned in time to see Dante leaning in the window of the taxi, handing over a wad of cash. What in the world?

As she approached them, Dante straightened and the taxi pulled out.

"Hey! Wait!" She was going to miss her flight. The last

one for the day. She turned on Dante. "What did you go and do that for?"

"We need to talk."

She frowned. She wasn't up for another battle of words. She was bruised and wounded from their last go-round. All she wanted was to be alone to lick her wounds. "There's nothing left to say."

"I'm sorry."

His words caused the breath to catch in her throat. This time she was certain about what she heard. But whether he was talking about how he'd dumped her or whether he was referring to dismissing the taxi, she wasn't sure.

"About what?"

"Let's go inside and talk." He moved to the restaurant door and unlocked it. When he held it open for her, she didn't move. "I promise that if you hear me out and you don't like what I have to say that I'll drive you to the airport myself."

She glanced at her wristwatch. "You've got five minutes."

"Fair enough."

She must be losing her grip on reality. What other reason would there be for her to agree to put herself through more heartache and pain?

Her feet felt as though they were weighed down as she walked inside the oh-so-familiar restaurant. She really was going to miss this place and the amazing people that she'd gotten to know here—most of all, she'd miss Dante.

She stopped by the hostess desk and turned to him. "What is it you want?"

"You."

"What?" Her lack of sleep was not helping her make sense of what he was telling her.

"I want you, Lizzie. I love you."

Her heart tripped over itself. She'd been waiting for so long to hear those words, but before she went flying into his arms, she needed to understand. "But what about yesterday?"

"I panicked. When I got a phone call telling me that you'd been in an accident, I overreacted. It seems like the DeFiore men are destined to grow old alone and I thought—Well, it doesn't matter. All I could think about is that if I lost you I'd be devastated and unable to go on."

Really? No one had ever cared about her that much.

"But if you felt that way, how were you able to just dump me?"

"I thought that by protecting myself that I wouldn't be hurt. But my father pointed out the fallacy of my logic—"

"Your father? You two were discussing me?" She wasn't so sure how she felt about that detail.

"Thanks to you, we had a talk that was long overdue." He looked around at the restaurant and then back at her. "You opened my eyes to a lot of things including how much I love this place…especially with you by my side."

Her heart tap-danced in her chest. "Do you really mean that?"

He peered deep into her eyes. "I love you with all my heart. And I would be honored if you'd consider staying here and running Massimo's with me."

"I couldn't think of anything I'd like more."

He stepped closer and wrapped his arms around her. "I promise no more panic attacks as long as you promise not to take up skydiving."

"Now that's a promise I can readily make." She smiled up at him as she slipped her arms up over his shoulders. "I'm scared of heights."

"So we're partners?"

She nodded. "But I think we should kiss to make it official."

"I think you're right."

His head dipped. Their lips met and the rest of the world slipped away.

At last Lizzie was home.

EPILOGUE

A month later

THE CLINK OF champagne flutes sounded in the empty dining room.

"To the most amazing man." Lizzie stared into the eyes of the only man she'd ever loved. "I love you."

"I love you, too." Dante pressed a kiss to her lips that promised more to follow. And soon.

"Can you believe we were on television? Our grand premiere." Lizzie couldn't keep a silly grin from her face.

"And you were amazing."

She waved off his over-the-top compliment. "I think those bubbles are going to your head."

"Nope. It's just you."

"Can you be serious for just a minute?"

The truth was that she had never been this deliriously happy in her entire life. Even the evenings she'd spent sitting next to Dante on the couch watching soccer...erm, football made her smile. And she never thought she'd ever appreciate sports, but Dante was opening her eyes to football and so much more.

"I can be serious. As long as it doesn't take too long." His gaze dipped to her lips.

When he started to lean forward, Lizzie held out her hands. "Dante, do you think of anything else?"

A lazy smile pulled at his lips. "Not if I can help it."

"Well, try for just a second."

His tempting lips pursed together. "What's on your mind?"

"What do you think about the television studio's offer to give us our own show?" They'd just received the call and Lizzie was too excited to trust her own reactions.

"I can think of something I'd like better."

She searched his face to see if his mind was still in the bedroom, but his expression was totally serious. "What is it?"

"How about you become my partner?"

"Well, of course I'll be your partner. That's what the studio is interested in. You and me working together—"

"No, I don't mean that." He took her hand in his and looked deep into her eyes, making her heart skip a beat. Then he dropped to his knee. "I mean I want you to be my family."

The breath hitched in her throat as tears of joy obscured the view of the man she loved with all of her heart. She blinked and the tears splashed onto her cheeks. With effort she swallowed the lump of giddy emotion in her throat.

"I can't think of anything I'd like better."

He got to his feet and encased her face in his palms. "I'm sorry I'm unprepared but I hadn't been planning to propose tonight. I've been playing it over and over in my mind. And I just couldn't wait any longer."

She stood up on her tiptoes and pressed her lips to his. Her heart thumped with excitement. She didn't know how it was possible but she'd swear with every kiss it just kept getting better and better.

When Dante pulled away, she pouted. He smiled and shook his head. "I take it that was a yes?"

"Most definitely."

"I have one more serious question."

"Well, ask it so we can get back to the good stuff."

He laughed and she grinned.

"I have an idea and I don't know how you'll feel about it, but what about having the wedding at the vineyard?"

She couldn't think of a more romantic spot on the entire earth. "I love it but…"

"But what?"

"What about Jules?" The thought of being permanently separated from her foster sister dimmed her excitement. "She's my only family—"

"Not anymore—I'll be your family, too. And Jules is always welcome here."

"But she has grad school. I won't let her give up. She's worked too hard for this. I want her to reach for her dreams."

"And she will. We'll make sure of it."

"But how?"

Dante pressed a finger to her lips. "Shh… Nonno always says, *Where there's a will, there's a way.*"

Lizzie's mind and heart were racing. The two people she loved most in this world were divided by an ocean. "I don't know."

"Look at me." Dante's gaze caught and held hers. "Do you love me?"

Without any hesitation she uttered, "With all of my heart."

"Then believe in us—in the power of our love. Believe that the future will work out for all of us. Maybe not in the way we'd expect, but sometimes the unexpected is just what people need. There's a way to make this work with Jules and we'll find it. Do you believe me?"

"I do."

He pressed his lips to hers and the worries faded away. Together, they could do anything.

* * * * *

Don't miss the second in Jennifer Faye's
fabulous THE DEFIORE BROTHERS *duet,*
BEST MAN FOR THE BRIDESMAID,
coming April 2015.

"If you apologize again, I'll slug you." Zora glared at Lucky.

He laughed, an unexpected rumble that rolled right into her heart. "That's my Zora." A bout of hard breathing reawakened the hope he might finally kiss her, but instead he sucked in a gulp of air and held it. "Okay. Better."

"Better than what?"

He ignored the question. "Since I inveigled you into working today, let me buy you lunch to celebrate."

"You're on." The heat in her body hadn't exactly dissipated, but it had faded into her normal pregnancy-enhanced high temperature. As for Lucky, clearly he didn't, couldn't and never would accept Andrew's babies as his own.

As common sense reasserted itself, Zora was suddenly glad nothing had happened. Going any further would have been yet another in a long line of mistakes she'd made with men. Gathering her possessions, she waited until Lucky locked up, and they sauntered out together. Friends again, nothing more.

Which was obviously how they both preferred it.

THE BABY BONANZA

BY

JACQUELINE DIAMOND

Published in Great Britain 2015
by Mills & Boon, an imprint of Harlequin (UK) Limited,
Eton House, 18-24 Paradise Road, Richmond, Surrey, TW9 1SR

ISBN: 978-0-263-25118-0

23-0315

Harlequin (UK) Limited's policy is to use papers that are natural, renewable and recyclable products and made from wood grown in sustainable forests. The logging and manufacturing processes conform to the legal environmental regulations of the country of origin.

Printed and bound in Spain
by CPI, Barcelona

The daughter of a doctor and an artist, **Jacqueline Diamond** has been drawn to medical themes for many of her more than ninety-five published novels, including her Safe Harbor Medical series for Mills & Boon. She developed an interest in fertility issues after successfully undergoing treatment to have her two sons, now in their twenties. A former Associated Press reporter and columnist, Jackie lives with her husband of thirty-five years in Orange County, California, where she's active in Romance Writers of America. You can learn more about her books at www.jacquelinediamond.com/books and say hello to Jackie on her Facebook page, JacquelineDiamondAuthor.

Chapter One

It was the first time Zora could recall agreeing with Lucky Mendez about anything. Although their truce surely wouldn't last long, she appreciated his good judgment this once.

"No way are you letting that creep move into our house," the male nurse told their landlady and housemate, Karen Wiggins. With his striking dark hair, muscular build and flamboyant tattoos, Lucky made an odd contrast to the pink streamers festooning their den.

"Everybody hates Laird Maclaine," Zora added as she arranged baby shower prizes on a side table. Being seven months pregnant with twins, she had to avoid any strenuous activity. In fact, as one of the shower's honorees—along with two of their former housemates—she could have dodged setup duty, but she refused to take the easy way out.

Ever.

"He's the only one who responded to the notice I posted on the bulletin board." Atop a step stool, Karen tied a bunch of balloons to a hook. In shades of pink and purple, each balloon proclaimed: Baby!

"We have a vacant room and the rent's almost due," she continued. "It's either Laird, or I post on the internet and we fend off the loonies. Unless you guys can produce another candidate, fast."

Lucky hadn't finished castigating the topic of the conversation. "One drink and Laird's telling raunchy jokes. Two drinks and he's leering at any lady who walks by." His lip curled. "Three drinks and we call the police."

"For a staff psychologist, he doesn't have a clue about how decent people act," Zora threw in.

"I don't care for him, either, but there are bills to pay." Karen, a financial counselor at Safe Harbor Medical Center, where they all worked, had inherited the five-bedroom home from her mother the previous December. Forced to take out a loan to repair the run-down property, she'd advertised for roommates. The arrangement had worked well despite the diverse personalities who'd signed on.

So far, three of the women had become pregnant, but the other two had married and moved out, unlike Zora. There was little chance she would marry the father of her babies, because he was already married. He was also her ex-husband, with whom she'd foolishly and, just before finalizing their divorce, trustingly had sex in the belief that her on-again, off-again high school sweetheart still loved her.

Zora rested her palm on her bulge, feeling the babies kick. How ironic that she'd gotten pregnant by accident at the worst possible time, after she and Andrew had tried for more than a year to conceive. They'd been on the point of seeking fertility treatments when she'd discovered he was cheating on her.

"We have plenty of other colleagues," Lucky persisted. "You guys are in a better position to meet them than me, since my office is out in the boonies." Lucky worked in the medical office building adjacent to the hospital.

"I've tried, but... Oh, yuck!" Karen broke off as a breeze through the rear screen door carried a fetid whiff of decomposing vegetation and fish from the estuary behind the property.

Zora nearly gagged, too. Karen praised the marsh ad

nauseum because it provided critical habitat for plants and small animals, as well as for California's migratory birds. However, despite the cooling weather at the end of September, it stank. "Who left the door open?"

"I must have forgotten to close it after I swept the patio." Lucky shut the glass slider with a thump. "How about renting to that receptionist in your office?"

"She declined." Descending from the stool, Karen stood back to assess the position of the balloons. "She prefers to save money by living with her parents. Speaking of money, if we don't find anyone by next month, I'll have to divide the room rent among you guys and Rod."

Their fourth and newest housemate, anesthesiologist Rod Vintner, had gone to pick up the party cake. He'd also gone, in Zora's opinion, to avoid anything approaching hard labor, although he *had* promised to clean up afterward.

"We could use the spare room as a nursery." Lucky cast a meaningful gaze at Zora's large belly. "If someone would inform her ex-husband that he's about to be a father and owes child support, she could afford the extra space."

"Don't start on her," Karen warned, saving Zora the trouble. "Go set up the chairs in the living room."

"Yes, ma'am." With a salute, Lucky strolled off. Zora tried to ignore the muscles rippling beneath his T-shirt and the tight fit of his jeans. The man was a self-righteous pain in the neck, no matter how good he looked.

Surprisingly, he hadn't brought home any dates since they'd moved into the house last February. Or none that she'd observed, Zora amended. Since Lucky occupied the downstairs suite, he could easily slip someone in late and out early without the others noticing. Men did things like that.

"You can stop staring at his butt now," Karen said dryly.

"I wasn't!"

"You can lie to anyone else, including yourself, but

spare me." The older woman—forty-two to Zora's twenty-nine—tightened the ponytail holder around her hair, which she'd dyed black this month. "Was that the kitchen timer?"

"I didn't hear anything." Zora adjusted a gift-wrapped box with a slot for envelopes. The front read: Nanny Fund. They planned to share the services of a specialist nanny among the three new moms and their collective total of six infants. Well, they *did* work at a hospital noted for its fertility treatments, although only one of the pregnancies had high-tech origins.

The timer buzzed. "There!" Karen said with satisfaction. "I knew it would sound any second."

"You must be psychic." Zora waddled behind her past a table displaying shower-themed paper plates and napkins.

"I have a well-developed sense of when food is done. Call it experience." In the kitchen, Karen snatched pot holders from a hook and opened the oven, filling the air with the scents of orange and lemon, almonds and balsamic vinegar.

Karen set the tins of Mediterranean muffins on the stove to cool. "I'd better start on the finger sandwiches. Only two hours before the guests are due, and I have to dress." She tied an apron over her blouse and long, casual skirt.

"I'll finish the vegetables." From the refrigerator, Zora removed the containers of celery, carrots and jicama that she'd cut up earlier, along with sour cream to mix for the dip and peanut butter to fill some of the celery sticks. "Would you get the olives and an onion soup packet from the pantry? I'm too big to squeeze in there."

"Gladly." Karen angled her slender shape around the narrow bend that led to the storage area. "Just black olives, or green ones, too?"

"Both." Zora lowered herself onto a chair, grateful she could still reach the table around her abdomen. A railing underneath allowed her to prop up her swollen ankles, but nothing alleviated the strain on her lower back. It ached more each day.

She hid her discomforts, determined to continue working as long as possible. Being an ultrasound tech meant standing on her feet all day and angling her midsection so she could scan the patients, but she was saving her paid maternity leave for after the twins' birth. Two months left—if they didn't arrive early.

After retrieving the requested items, Karen spread out her sandwich fixings on the counter. Through the kitchen's far door, Zora heard the scrape of folding chairs being opened and placed around the front room. She respected Lucky's work ethic; he always pitched in with an upbeat attitude. If he could only master the art of minding his own business, he'd be...well, tolerable.

Footsteps thudded on the carpet, announcing Lucky's return. His short, military-style haircut emphasized the strong planes of his face, which reflected his Hispanic heritage. "Where are the chair covers hidden? Someone else stored them after Anya and Jack's wedding."

"Upstairs in the linen closet," Karen said.

"Can I ride the stair lift or is that only for mommies?" Lucky teased. Both women narrowed their eyes at him, and he lifted his hands in a yielding gesture. "Just asking."

"Go play somewhere else," Zora muttered.

"Alone? That's no fun." With a rakish grin, he dodged out.

"You two should swap rooms so you could be downstairs," Karen observed from the counter. "Let him ride the stair lift if it gives him a thrill."

"I can't afford the extra rent." Lucky's large room commanded a correspondingly larger price. While Zora didn't care about having a personal patio exit, she did envy him the private bath. Karen had one, too, upstairs in the master suite, while Zora shared a bathroom with Rod and Melissa.

Or, rather, with Rod and whoever moved into the room Melissa had vacated when she'd remarried her ex-husband.

Some people have all the luck. A sigh escaped Zora. Too late, she tried to cover with a cough.

"A pickle chip for your thoughts," Karen said.

"No, thanks." Zora popped a black olive into her mouth.

"You really are entitled to support," Karen observed. "I wonder whether you'd have faced your ex by now if Lucky weren't such a nag."

"He has nothing to do with it."

"You're stubborn," was the reply. "Seriously, Zora, how long can you keep this secret? I'm amazed Andrew's mother hasn't spilled the beans."

"Betsy doesn't know." Zora's former mother-in-law was the nursing supervisor at the hospital. The kind-hearted lady had suffered through the loss of two beloved daughters-in-law, thanks to her son's faithlessness.

Zora wondered whether Betsy was being more cautious about bonding with Andrew's third wife, a Hong Kong native he'd met on a business trip while he was married to Zora. Unexpectedly, tears blurred her vision. *How could he cheat on me? And then, just when I was ready to let him go, trick me into believing he still loved me?*

"Betsy sees you in the cafeteria every day," Karen reminded her.

"She's aware that I'm pregnant," Zora agreed. "But she has no idea who the father is."

Karen stuck a hank of black hair behind her ear. "She isn't stupid."

"But I doubt she believes Andrew is capable of…of being such a grade-A jerk." Damn those tears stinging her eyes again. "Aside from my closest friends, most people accept my explanation that I made a mistake after my divorce. I let them assume I picked up a guy in a bar."

"And that's better than admitting you slept with Andrew?"

"It's better than admitting I'm a complete chump."

More footsteps, and Lucky reappeared. "They aren't there. Let's skip the seat covers."

"I refuse to have guests in my house sitting on ugly folding chairs," Karen said.

The man tilted his head skeptically. "What's the big deal? People have been sitting on folding chairs without covers since the dawn of time."

"No, they haven't." Hastily, Zora shielded the relish tray from his attempt to grab a carrot. "Hands off!"

"Evidence found in caves throughout northern Europe indicates that Neanderthals shunned folding chair covers as a sign of weakness," Lucky said. "And why so stingy with the veggies?"

"I'm still arranging these. Go eat a corn chip." Zora indicated a bag set out to be transferred into a large bowl.

"I'm a vegetarian."

"Corn is a vegetable."

"Corn chips do not occur in nature," he responded. "Just one carrot. Pretty please."

She flipped it toward him. He caught it in midair.

"Try the closet in my bathroom for the covers," Karen suggested to Lucky. "Top shelf."

"I have permission to enter the inner sanctum?" he asked.

"It expires in sixty seconds."

"Okay, okay." He paused. "Before I run off, there's one little thing I should mention about today's guest list."

Zora released an impatient breath. "What?"

"I invited Betsy."

"You didn't!" Keeping her ex-mother-in-law in the dark at work was one thing, but around here the babies' paternity was no secret.

Karen turned toward Lucky, knife in hand. "Tell me you're joking."

He grimaced. "Sorry. Spur-of-the-moment thing. But

your motto *is* the more the merrier, and besides, Betsy's a widow. If she's interested in renting a room, that would solve all our problems." With a carroty crunch, off he went.

"Unbelievable," Karen said.

If she hadn't been so huge, Zora might have given chase. She could easily have strangled Lucky at that moment. But then they'd have to find *two* new housemates.

"I'd say the cat's about to claw its way out of the bag," Karen observed. "Might as well seize the bull by the horns, or is that too many animal metaphors?"

"Considering the size of the rat we live with, I guess not," Zora growled.

Karen smiled. "Speaking of rats, if you'd rather not confront Andrew-the-rodent yourself, don't forget you can hire Edmond to do it." Edmond Everhart, their former roommate, Melissa's husband, had been Zora's divorce attorney.

"That'll only create more trouble." Zora scraped the onion dip from the mixing bowl into a container on the relish tray. "Andrew'll put me through the wringer."

"If that's your only reason for not telling him about the babies, I'd rate its validity at about a three on a scale of ten." Karen trimmed the crust from a sandwich.

Zora dropped the spoon into the mixing bowl with a clunk. "He's the only man I ever loved. I want to give him the benefit of the doubt."

"Zora, what benefit of what doubt?" Karen retorted. "He dumped you in high school, married someone else, then cheated on *her* with you after he ran into you at your class reunion. Let's not forget that he then cheated on *you* with what's-her-name from Hong Kong. Why on earth would you entertain the fantastical notion that Andrew will ever transform into a loving husband and father?"

With a pang, Zora conceded that that was exactly what she *did* wish for. While her rational mind sided with Karen, the infants stirring inside her with a series of kicks and squirms obviously missed their father. So did Zora.

"It can happen," she said. "Look at Melissa and Edmond. Three years after their divorce, they fell in love again."

"They'd quarreled about having children. Neither of them cheated on the other," Karen persisted. "Andrew can't be trusted, ever."

She spoke with the ferocity of a divorcée who'd survived an abusive marriage. It had taken more than a decade for Karen to trust a man again. She and their housemate, Rod, were still easing into their relationship.

"People can change." Despite a reluctance to bring up her family, Zora wanted Karen to understand. "Did I mention I have a twin?"

"Really?" Leaning against the counter, Karen folded her arms. "Identical or fraternal?"

"Identical." Zora wasn't about to reveal the whole story, just the important part. "But we quarreled, and we aren't in touch anymore. All I know of her is what Mom passes along." Their mother, who lived in Oregon, loved sharing news.

"Go on." After a glance at the clock, Karen resumed her food preparation.

"Nearly ten years ago, Zady ran off with a married man." Zora inhaled as deeply as she could, considering the pressure on her lungs from the pregnancy. "They live in Santa Barbara. He split with his wife and now he's devoted to Zady. They have a beautiful house and a couple of kids."

"Was there a wedding in there?" Karen asked dubiously.

"I'm sure there was, although she didn't invite me." The rift had been bitter, and there'd been no move toward reconciliation on either side. In fact, her mother said Zady had chuckled when she'd learned about Zora's divorce.

"So the guy married her, and you believe that if lightning struck your twin, it can strike you, too?" Karen murmured.

Zora's throat tightened. "Why not?"

"Because Betsy's about to arrive with her antennae on high alert. If I'm any judge, that woman's dying to be a grandmother."

"And she'll be a terrific one." The elder Mrs. Raditch did all the right grandmotherly things, such as baking and crocheting, a skill she'd taught Zora. "But…"

"You're running out of *buts*," Karen warned. "Unless you count Lucky's."

"I don't!"

"The way you guys battle, you're almost like an old married couple."

"We're *nothing* like a married couple, old or otherwise." Zora could never be interested in a man with so little class. Outside work, he flaunted his muscles in sleeveless T-shirts and cutoffs. While she didn't object if someone had a small tattoo, his body resembled a billboard for video games. On the right arm, a colorful dragon snaked and writhed, while on the left, he displayed a buxom babe wearing skimpy armor and wielding a sword.

Whenever she pictured Andrew, she saw him in the suit and tie he always wore as an international business consultant. He had tousled blond hair, a laser-sharp mind, sky-blue eyes, and when he trained his headlight smile on her, Zora understood why some poor fools became addicted to drugs, because the euphoria was irresistible.

At the image, vague intentions coalesced into a firm decision. "Andrew's the man I married. This…this *liaison* with what's-her-name is an aberration. Once the kids are born and he holds them in his arms, what man wouldn't love his own son and daughter?" *And their mother.*

Even Zora's own father, a troubled man who'd cheated on her mom, had stuck around while his kids had grown up. Well, mostly—there'd been separations and emotional outbursts that left painful memories. But there'd been tender times, too, including a laughter-filled fishing trip, and one Christmas when her father had dressed up as Santa Claus and showered them with gifts.

She longed for her children to experience a father like that. With Andrew's charm, he could easily provide such unforgettable moments.

For a minute, the only sound was the chopping of a knife against a cutting board as Karen trimmed crusts. Finally she said, "So you plan to hold it together until then, alone?"

"I have you guys, my friends." Zora struggled for a light tone. "All I have to do is stay on an even keel."

"Like a juggler tossing hand grenades on the deck of a sinking ship?" On a platter, Karen positioned sandwiches in a pyramid. "Well, it's your decision."

"Yes, and I've made it." Zora studied the relish tray through a sheen of moisture. Andrew would come around eventually. He had a good heart, despite his weak will.

"I'm happy to report that I found the chair covers and they look fine." Lucky's deep voice sounded almost in her ear, making her jump. "What do Neanderthals know, anyway?"

"Speaking of Neanderthals, how dare you sneak up on me?" she snapped. "I could go into labor."

"No, you won't." The corners of his mouth quirked.

"How would you know?"

"I'm a nurse, remember?" he said.

"Not that kind of nurse." He worked with a urologist.

"Pregnancy care is part of every nurse's basic medical training." His expression sobered. "Speaking of medicine, you're sure Cole's coming today?"

Dr. Cole Rattigan, the renowned men's fertility expert Lucky assisted, had been away this past week, speaking at a conference in New York.

"He and his wife RSVP'd," Karen assured him. "What's the big deal?"

"I can't discuss it. It concerns a patient."

"Why would you confer about a patient on your day off?" Zora asked.

"That's confidential, too." Grabbing the tray of sandwiches, Lucky whisked out of the room so fast it was a miracle the sandwich pyramid didn't topple.

"That's odd," Karen said. "I wonder what's going on."

As did Zora, but Cole, and in particular his wife, a popular nurse, were a touchy subject for her. As the first Mrs. Andrew Raditch, Stacy hadn't hidden her resentment toward Zora-the-husband-stealer, and most staffers had sided with her.

Among them, no one had been more hostile than Lucky. He'd eased up since he and Zora had started sharing this house, but in a showdown there was no question that his loyalty lay with Cole and his spouse.

Zora wished that didn't bother her. Well, she had more important things to deal with, anyway…such as facing the grandmother of her children in less than two hours.

Chapter Two

Lucky wove between clusters of chattering people in the living room, removing soiled paper plates and cups. Although he was enjoying the party, he wished he and his housemates had kept a tighter lid on the guest list. Only half an hour into it, the place was filling up—and not all the choices had been wise.

Inviting Betsy Raditch had seemed a clever trick to prod Zora into finally accepting the help she needed. Instead, the younger woman kept dodging her ex-mother-in-law, who sneaked longing gazes at Zora's belly but maintained a respectful distance. The would-be grandmother's wistful expression sent a guilty pang through Lucky.

And he hadn't counted on Karen inviting Laird, but here he was, fawning over Zora. The psychologist's colorless eyes—okay, they were gray, but a very *light* gray—lit up whenever she so much as flinched, providing an excuse for him to offer her a chair or a drink. Was the man flirting or just trying to charm his way into the house? Either way, he had a very strange notion of what women found appealing.

When Zora winced, the guy reached out to rub her bulge. Stuck in a knot of people across the room, Lucky barely refrained from shouting, "Hands off!" To his relief, Keely Randolph, a dour older nurse Lucky had never much liked until now, smacked Laird's arm and loudly proclaimed that people shouldn't shed their germs all over pregnant women.

After scowling at her, Laird gazed around, targeted Karen and approached her with a smarmy expression. Lucky caught the words *exquisite house* and *can't wait to move in.*

Rod Vintner came to Karen's rescue, his wiry frame and short graying beard bristling with indignation. "Who's moving in where?" he growled with a ferocity that indicated he'd willingly stick one of his anesthesiology needles into Laird's veins and pump it to the max.

Satisfied that the jerk was batting zero, Lucky glanced toward the front window. He never tired of the soul-renewing view across the narrow lane and past the coastal bluffs to the cozy harbor from which the town took its name. You couldn't beat the beauty of this spot.

Yet he might have to leave. And that had nothing to do with Laird or any other roommate.

Lucky had worked hard to earn a master's degree in nursing administration, which he'd completed earlier this year. Now he sought a suitable post for his management skills, but there were no openings at Safe Harbor Medical. Which meant he'd have to move away from the people he cared about.

They included Zora, who over the past few months had needed his protection as she struggled to deal with an unplanned pregnancy and a broken heart. They hadn't intended to grow closer; he wasn't even sure either would openly acknowledge it. Which was just as well. Because having once failed in a big way to be there for the people he loved, Lucky had vowed never, ever to take on such responsibility. Because he'd only fail again.

Still, he couldn't imagine moving away. His best hope for staying in the area would be the expansion of the men's fertility program in which he worked. Any minute now, its director, Cole Rattigan, would arrive. Most of the staff thought Cole had just been in New York to deliver a speech, but Lucky was more interested in hearing about his boss's private meeting with the designer of a new device.

It offered a slim possibility of helping one particular patient, a volatile billionaire named Vince Adams who was considering a major endowment to expand the hospital's urology program. If that happened, it might create a nursing-administration position for Lucky. Also, it would realize his doctor's dream of building a world-class program.

If not for Cole, Lucky might not be working for Safe Harbor Med at all, he reflected as he carried empty plates and cups to the kitchen. Two and a half years ago, when the newly arrived urologist had interviewed for office nurses, Lucky hadn't believed he had a chance of being hired. After his previous doctor retired, Lucky's tattoos had repeatedly knocked him out of the running for jobs. He'd been considering expensive and painful treatment to remove the evidence of his youthful foolishness.

But the tats hadn't bothered Cole. He'd asked a few questions, appeared pleased with the responses and offered the job on the spot. After that, Lucky would have battled demons if they'd threatened his doctor.

In the den, he poured himself a glass of fruit juice and noted that the sandwiches, chips and veggies were holding their own despite modest depletions. No one had cut the sheet cake yet, leaving intact the six cartoon babies, five with pink hair ribbons and one with blue.

"Aren't they adorable?" The soft voice at his elbow drew his attention to Betsy.

Lucky shifted uneasily. Despite his conviction that Zora ought to be honest with her children's grandmother, he had no intention of snitching. Still, he *had* invited the woman. "We ordered it from the Cake Castle."

She indicated the Nanny Fund box bordered by a few wrapped packages. "I didn't realize most people would be contributing money as their gift. I hope it's all right that I crocheted baby blankets."

"All right?" Lucky repeated in surprise. "The kids will treasure those keepsakes forever."

Betsy's squarish face, softened by caramel-brown hair and wire-rimmed glasses, brightened at the compliment. Why didn't Zora level with the woman? A doting grandma could provide the support a young single mother needed. Considering that Zora's own mother lived in Oregon, she'd be wise to take advantage of Betsy's yearning for grandkids.

"I'm glad to hear it," she said. "Also, much as I approve of the nanny idea, I suspect new mothers could use furnishings and toys."

"Oh, there's plenty of that." Lucky had been forced to park in the driveway for weeks due to the overflow in the garage. "Practically the entire staff has donated their baby gear. Anya and Jack got first pick, since she's already delivered, but they only have a singleton. There's plenty left."

"They're a lovely couple. So are Melissa and Edmond." Betsy indicated the long-legged blonde woman ensconced on the sofa, flanked by her doting husband and seven-year-old niece, Dawn, who lived with them. This was a rare outing for Melissa, who in her sixth month with triplets looked almost as wide as she was tall. "I'm thrilled that they remarried. They obviously belong together."

Was that a hint? Surely the woman didn't believe her son might reconcile with Zora. Aside from the fact that he had a new wife, the guy was the world's worst candidate for family man. "I'd bet in most divorces the odds of a happy reconciliation would be on par with winning the lottery."

"If that was for my benefit, don't bother," Betsy told him.

"Sorry." Lucky ducked his head. "I tend to be a mother hen to my friends. Or a father hen, if there is such a thing."

"At least you aren't a rooster like my son," she replied sharply.

"No comment."

"Wise man."

On the far side of the room, Zora circled past the staircase and halted, her eyes widening at the sight of Lucky standing beside Betsy. Lucky nearly spread his hands in a do-you-honestly-think-I'd-tell-her? gesture, but decided against it, since Betsy didn't miss much. She must be suspicious enough already about the twins' paternity.

While he was seeking another topic of conversation, his landlady bounced into the den from the kitchen. "Who's ready for a game?" Karen called. "We have prizes." She indicated a side table where baskets displayed bath soaps and lotions, while a large stuffed panda held out a gift card to the Bear and Doll Boutique.

"What kind of game?" Dawn asked from the couch.

"I'm afraid the first one might be too hard for a child," Karen said. "It's a diaper-the-baby contest."

"I can do that," the little girl proclaimed.

"Yes, she can," Melissa confirmed. "Dawn has more experience with diapering than Edmond or me."

"I used to help our neighbor," the child said.

"Then please join in!" Karen beamed as guests from the living room crowded into the den. "Ah, more players. Great!"

Among the group was their former roommate Anya, her arms around the daughter she'd delivered a few weeks earlier. "Nobody's diapering Rachel for a game."

"Certainly not," Karen agreed.

"However, volunteers are welcome to stop by our apartment any night around two a.m.," put in Anya's husband, Dr. Jack Ryder.

Rachel gurgled. A sigh ran through the onlookers, accompanied by murmurs of "What an angel!" and "How darling!"

"I'd be happy to hold her for you," Betsy said. "You can both relax and enjoy the food."

"Thank you." Anya cheerfully shifted her daughter into the arms of the nursing supervisor.

When Zora hugged herself protectively, Lucky felt a twinge of sympathy. She'd refused to consider adoption, declaring that this might be her only chance to have children, but the sight of little Rachel must underscore the reality of what she faced.

Children required all your resources and all your strength. How did this woman with slim shoulders and defiant ginger hair expect to cope by herself?

He reminded himself not to get too involved. Lucky didn't mind changing a few diapers, but he might not be here long, unless Dr. Rattigan brought good news. Now where was the doctor?

Waving a newborn-size doll along with a package of clean diapers, Karen detailed the rules of the game. "You have to remove and replace the diaper. I'll be timing you. Fastest diaper change wins."

"That doesn't sound hard," Laird scoffed.

"Did I mention you have to do it one-handed?" Karen replied, to widespread groans. "If you drop the baby on the floor, you're automatically disqualified."

"For round two, contestants have to diaper the doll blindfolded," Rod added mischievously. A few people laughed, while Dawn's jaw set with determination. That kid would do it upside down and sideways to win, Lucky thought. With that attitude, she'd go far in life.

Then he caught the sound he'd been waiting for—the doorbell. His pulse sped up. "I'll get it."

Someone else reached the door first, however, and friends rushed to greet the Rattigans. Despite his impatience, Lucky hung back.

With her friendly manner and elfin face, Stacy had a kind word for everyone. Her mild-mannered husband said little; Cole's reticence, Lucky knew, stemmed partly from the urologist's discomfort in social situations. It was also partly the result of having a brain so brilliant that he was probably carrying on half a dozen internal conversations with himself at any given moment.

Lucky could barely contain his eagerness to speak with the great man privately and find out if the device lived up to its promise. However, he drew the line at elbowing guests aside.

Stacy oohed over Anya's newborn and hugged Betsy, her former mother-in-law. The room quieted as the first Mrs. Andrew Raditch came face-to-face with the woman who had cheated with him before being discarded in turn. Most of the staff had cheered at Zora's misfortune, believing she was receiving her just deserts. Lucky was ashamed to admit he'd been among them. Now he wished he could spare her this awkwardness.

"Wow! Look at you." Stacy patted Zora's belly. "Have you chosen names yet?"

"Still searching," she said with a tentative smile. "For now, Tweedledee and Tweedledum."

This light exchange broke the tension. With her new marriage, Stacy had clearly moved on, and with her courtesy toward Zora, she'd brought her old nemesis in from the cold.

Silently, Lucky thanked her. Cole had chosen a worthy wife.

The game began, with guests lining up to participate. Seizing his chance, Lucky approached his boss, who spoke without prompting.

"I know you're anxious for news, Luke." Cole used Lucky's formal name. "Let's talk."

"We'll have more privacy in here." Lucky led the way into the now-empty living room.

ZORA HAD NO interest in diapering a baby. She'd be doing more than her share of that soon.

Stacy's display of friendliness left her both relieved and

oddly shaky. Having been treated as a pariah by much of the hospital staff for several years, Zora still felt vulnerable as well as guilty.

Also, Stacy's question about the names reminded Zora of her idea to leave the decision until they were born. She'd figured that if Andrew had a chance to choose the names, it might help bond him with the little ones. Today, however, the prospect of what lay ahead was sinking in.

For starters, what was she planning to do, call him from the delivery room and break the news of his paternity over the phone while writhing in agony? This kind of information should be presented in person, and she ought to get it over with now. Yet being around Andrew brought out Zora's weakness for him; the ease with which he'd seduced her when she dropped by with their divorce papers proved that.

If only Lucky would stop poking at her, she'd be able to think clearly. It might be unfair to focus her anger on her housemate, but this was none of his business. And why had he, one of the party's hosts, hustled Dr. Rattigan off in such a hurry?

Hungry as usual these days, Zora munched on a peanut butter–filled celery stick from the snack table. Keely drifted alongside, following her gaze as Lucky vanished. "Nice build," the older nurse observed in her nasal voice.

Amused, Zora said, "I don't believe he's dating anyone. Interested?"

Keely snorted. "Not my type."

Zora didn't dare ask what that was.

A hint of beer breath alerted her to Laird Maclaine's approach. The psychologist must have downed a brew before arriving, because they weren't serving alcohol.

"We're discussing Mendez?" He addressed his question to Zora, ignoring Keely. "If he snags a better job with that new master's degree of his, I'd love to rent *his* room. I hear it has an en suite bathroom."

"En suite?" Keely repeated. "What a pretentious term."

Laird rolled his eyes.

"He isn't leaving." While Zora understood Lucky's desire for advancement, she couldn't imagine him abandoning his friends.

The psychologist shrugged. "Either way, this is a fantastic party house. I'm expecting to move in next weekend."

Astonished, Zora slanted an assessing gaze at the psychologist. From an objective viewpoint, Laird wasn't bad-looking, although bland compared to Lucky, and she respected him for initiating and leading patient support groups. But it would be annoying to have to run into this conceited guy every morning over breakfast and every night at dinner.

Impulsively, she addressed Keely. "We have an empty room that used to be Melissa's. Any chance you're interested?"

"It's taken, by me," Laird rapped out.

"Nothing's settled," Zora said.

"Don't you already have two men living here?" Keely inquired. "You and Karen should bring in another woman. I'd join you, but I couldn't do that to my roommate."

"You wouldn't fit in, anyway," Laird growled.

That remark didn't deserve a response. "Who's your roommate?" Zora asked Keely. "Do I know her?"

"Oh, she doesn't work at the medical complex," the nurse responded. "She's a housekeeper."

"I admire your loyalty to her."

"Anyone would do the same."

A stir across the den drew their attention. It was Dawn Everhart's turn at the game. Deftly, the little girl rolled the doll with an elbow, tugged on one diaper tab with her fingers and caught the other in her mouth, all while onlookers captured the moment with their cell phones.

"Unsanitary," Laird protested.

"But clever," Rod responded from his post beside Karen. "Besides, it's a doll."

"And she's beating the pants off everyone else's time," Edmond observed, beaming at his niece. "Literally."

Her feet having swollen to the size of melons, Zora wandered into the kitchen and sat down. Through the far door, she detected the low rumble of masculine voices in the living room.

What were Lucky and his boss discussing so intently? Had Cole made job inquiries at the conference for his nurse's sake? Although she'd instinctively dismissed Laird's comment about Lucky moving, the man couldn't be expected to waste his master's degree.

If Lucky departed, who would run out for ice cream when she had a craving? Lucky had promised to haul two bassinets and a changing table to the second floor as soon as she was ready for them. Without him around, who would cart her stuff up and down the stairs? She certainly couldn't count on Laird pitching in.

Well, she'd survive. In fact, she shouldn't be relying on Lucky so much, anyway. Zora hated to depend on others, especially someone so controlling and critical and arrogant and judgmental. She might not have the world's best taste in men, but she knew what she *didn't* like, and Lucky epitomized it. Now what were he and Dr. Rattigan talking about so intently?

No matter how hard she strained, she couldn't follow the thread of conversation from the living room. Just when she caught a couple of words, a burst of cheering from the den obliterated the rest of the doctor's comments.

Judging by the clamor, Dawn had edged out Anya's husband, Jack, by two seconds. "I can visualize the headline now—Seven-year-old Defeats Obstetrician in Diapering Contest!" roared Rod, who, as Jack's uncle, had the privilege of ragging him mercilessly. "I'm posting the pictures on the internet."

"You do that and you'll never see your great-niece again," Jack retorted. He spoiled the effect by adding, "Will he, cutie?" apparently addressing the newborn.

Zora lumbered to her feet. She was missing all the fun and worrying for nothing.

Probably.

Chapter Three

Feeling miles from the festivities in the den, Lucky struggled to concentrate on Cole's account. He kept wishing that, if he focused hard enough, the results would be more encouraging.

"The new stent won't fix what's wrong with Vince Adams." The slightly built doctor ran a hand through his rumpled brown hair.

"Are you certain?" Lucky pressed.

Cole nodded. "It won't do anything for a patient who has that much scar tissue."

During the summer, Cole had used the latest microsurgical techniques in an unsuccessful attempt to open the billionaire's blocked sperm ducts. As the office nurse, Lucky hadn't assisted at the operation, but he'd read the follow-up report. The procedure hadn't been able to reverse the extensive damage left by a long-ago infection.

However, Vince continued to press them for options. Cole had told him about a new dissolvable, medicine-infused stent, and Vince had been excited that Cole would get an advance preview of the device. "We have the world's top urologist right here," the millionaire had trumpeted. "And I'll be the first guy he cures."

The higher the hopes, the harder the fall.

"Do you think his interest in Safe Harbor is entirely based on restoring his fertility?" Lucky asked.

"It's hard to say," Cole replied. "His intentions tend to shift with his emotional state."

A private equity investor, Vince Adams was powerful and rich. But wealth hadn't compensated for his inability to sire children. Over the years, he'd paid dearly for treatments without success, and others had paid dearly for his desire for fatherhood.

After several turbulent and childless marriages, Vince had wed a woman with two young daughters. Determined to adopt them, he had used his financial clout to overwhelm Portia's first husband in court.

The man he'd gleefully trounced was Lucky's housemate, Rod Vintner, who'd faced a doubly devastating loss. First, during his divorce, he'd learned that his daughters were actually the genetic offspring of his unfaithful wife's previous lover, now out of the picture. Second, Rod had been outspent and outmaneuvered fighting for joint custody.

For years, he'd been forbidden to talk or even write to his daughters, who lived a ninety-minute drive away, in San Diego. Then, earlier this year, the older girl had run away from home. The twelve-year-old had contacted Rod, who'd enlisted the aid of the girls' maternal grandmother here in Safe Harbor.

Although officially Rod was still banned, Grandma Helen had arranged for Tiffany—now thirteen—and her younger sister to visit her more often. Whenever possible, she let them meet with Rod, and, faced with Tiffany's threats to run away again, the Adamses pretended not to notice.

Vince's search for fertility, however, provided him with another avenue for keeping Rod in line. While Vince's interest in the hospital stemmed in large part from his discovery that one of the world's foremost urologists had joined the staff, it also ensured that Rod didn't dare become too much of an annoyance. An anesthesiologist would be a lot easier for the hospital to replace than a billionaire donor.

Lucky hated that the staff had to curry favor with Vince. Still, he felt compassion for a man desperate to produce a baby. The billionaire's motives might be self-serving, but his comments had made it clear that he would treasure his child. As long as parents offered a loving, secure home, it wasn't anyone else's right to pass judgment.

However, if Cole couldn't help him, it seemed likely Vince wouldn't follow through on his major donation. "Suppose he drops us," Lucky said. "Surely there are others we could approach."

"The world is full of rich people, but Safe Harbor tends to lose out to more prestigious institutions," Cole responded. "I admit, Luke, being at the conference whetted my appetite for better research facilities, more lab space and money for fellowships. In fact, I received three excellent offers to relocate."

Lucky's heart nearly skipped a beat. "You'd take another position?"

Alarm flitted across the doctor's face. "I shouldn't have said that."

Nevertheless, he *had* said it. "If you go, the program will never recover." *Neither will I. On many levels.*

At a burst of laughter from the other room, Lucky flinched. His friends had no idea that he was standing here with the ground crumbling beneath his feet.

Cole's brow furrowed. "I joined Safe Harbor with the intention of building a standout program. Although I'm no longer sure that will be possible, this is my wife's home, and mine, too. I haven't given up yet." But there was no mistaking his distress.

"Nothing else at the conference might be useful?"

"I'm afraid not. Perhaps we should suggest Mr. Adams cancel next Saturday's appointment and save himself a trip." The billionaire tended to arrive with plenty of pomp and circumstance by private plane or helicopter. On other occasions, Vince roared up the coast in a high-performance car that cost as much as many houses.

If only Lucky could find a solution, for his sake and for his doctor's. It would also be important to the medical center to achieve its goal of becoming a major player in the fertility field. Major gifts attracted additional donors; a lack of progress might, by contrast, eventually consign Safe Harbor to secondary status. And this place had been good to Lucky when he'd needed help the most.

"Don't cancel," he said. "That's a week from now. Things could change."

"I suppose you're right." Cole stretched his shoulders. "In any event, my patient deserves to hear the news from me in person."

To Lucky, it was a reprieve. He had a week to figure out the next move.

ZORA HAD NEVER seen Lucky abandon a party before. After talking to Dr. Rattigan, he'd spent the next hour in a corner of the living room, fiddling with his phone. Searching the internet or texting people? But why?

In view of the doctor's wistful expression, it didn't take a genius to recognize that they'd suffered a blow. They must have been counting on the New York conference for some reason.

Zora tried to shrug off Lucky's absence while she and her fellow moms-to-be opened gifts. Most people had contributed money, but Betsy's gifts were special.

Zora's throat constricted as she held up the soft pink and blue blankets. Her former mother-in-law had created these precious heirlooms even without being sure of her relationship to the twins.

Zora was glad now that Lucky had invited Betsy. To learn she'd been excluded from the baby shower would have been an undeserved slap in the face.

Catching Betsy's eye, Zora said, "These mean more than I can say."

"I'm glad." Wedged among the other guests, the older woman added, "If you need anything, please call me."

"You're a sweetheart." But Zora wouldn't ask for the other woman's help, not until after the babies were born and she revealed the truth to Andrew. When she did, she hoped Betsy wouldn't resent having been kept in the dark.

Her gaze drifted to the diamond-and-emerald ring on her ex-mother-in-law's right hand. Zora had worn the family heirloom during her marriage, treasuring both its beauty and its significance. After the divorce, she'd returned it, with regret. Neither of Andrew's other wives had worn it; there'd been a special bond between Betsy and Zora that had begun in her high school days.

Now, its glitter reminded Zora of how much she'd lost. Not only her husband, but a woman who'd been as close to her as family. Well, perhaps someday she and Betsy could be close again.

She hoped her children would meet her twin sister, too. That depended on whether Zora was ever secure enough to handle Zady's inevitable gloating at her downfall. For now, distance was best. Nobody could inflict as much pain as the people nearest your heart.

After the last guest departed, the adrenaline that had powered Zora all afternoon faded. She collapsed on the living room couch while, inside her, the babies tussled.

What a blessing it would be when they were born and her body returned to normal. And what a joy to hold them and see their sweet faces.

At this point, Lucky should have arrived to offer her refreshments. She missed his coddling, even though it was often seasoned with criticism.

Instead, he bustled about collecting trash as if she weren't there. From the kitchen, Zora heard Karen opening and closing the fridge to put away food, while in the den, Rod ran the vacuum cleaner. Zora would have pitched in if she'd had the energy.

As Lucky removed the white linen covers from the folding chairs, his dark eyebrows drew together like storm clouds. The dragon protruding from beneath one sleeve appeared to be lashing its tail.

Zora broke the silence. "Won't you tell me what happened?"

He tossed a cover onto a pile of laundry. "What do you mean?"

"You've been upset since you talked to Dr. Rattigan."

Lucky snapped a chair shut. "Doesn't concern you."

Zora tried a different tack. "Laird speculated you might move out of town to take a better job. He's angling to get your suite." She deliberately baited Lucky with that reference to the obnoxious psychologist.

Lucky grimaced. "I'd rather not discuss that lowlife."

"Then let's discuss what's eating you."

"Like I said, it's none of your business."

Any second, flames were going to shoot out her ears. "Oh, yes, it is!"

"How so?" he growled, wielding a chair as if he was prepared to thrust it at her.

The guy sure was prickly. "It's obvious Cole brought bad news from the conference."

Lucky set the chair down. "I can't discuss anything involving a patient."

He was right to safeguard the man's privacy, Zora conceded. Medical personnel were required to do that, by law and by hospital policy as well as by simple decency. Still, he'd dropped a clue. Now, why would a patient's condition bother Lucky so much?

From the kitchen, Karen's voice drifted to her. "I'm looking forward to having your girls in town next Saturday. Should we invite them and Helen for lunch?"

"I doubt there'll be time," Rod replied dourly. "They're

only being dropped off at their grandma's for an hour or two while Vince sees his doctor."

"Is he having problems?" Karen asked. "I don't usually wish anyone ill, but he's an exception."

"You can wish that jerk as much ill as you like." Rod's voice rose in anger. "Tiff and Amber loathe the man. He may not physically abuse them, but he's a bully, and emotional scars can be the worst kind."

As the rumble of the garbage disposal cut off further eavesdropping, Zora put two and two together. Everyone knew—because the billionaire had discussed it openly—that Dr. Rattigan was treating him. And the men's program counted on his support.

"It's Vince Adams," she said. "No, don't answer. I realize you can't confirm it."

Lucky stacked the chairs to one side. "Are you still mad at me for inviting Betsy? Is that why you're harassing me?"

Zora tried to hug her knees, but her bulge was in the way. "I'm glad you invited her."

"So we're good?" His fierce brown eyes raked over her.

"No. What if you leave?" she burst out, surprised by her rush of emotion. "We're having enough trouble finding one roommate, let alone two. We'll *have* to take Laird."

A knot in her chest warned that she was less concerned about Laird than she was about Lucky staying until the babies were born. Until Andrew hopefully came to his senses and fell in love with his children. *Until hell freezes over.* No, but if hell did freeze over, she'd counted on Lucky to be there with a warming blanket.

As a friend, of course. He'd been just as helpful to Anya—maybe more so—when they'd moved into this house. It was in his nature.

Lucky stopped fiddling around. "You shouldn't upset yourself. It might shoot up your blood pressure."

"Then talk to me."

He plopped his butt on the arm of the couch. "About what?"

"You've been delving into your phone all afternoon, trying to find a solution, right? But if Dr. Rattigan can't fix Vince—I mean, Patient X—neither can you."

"So?" Lucky folded his arms. They were muscular arms, and he folded them across a broad, powerful chest. Too bad the movement also flexed the shapely legs of a cartoon woman, which rather spoiled the effect for Zora.

"We have to figure out another way to keep the Adamses involved with Safe Harbor," she blurted.

"We?" Lucky was addicted to monosyllables today.

She'd surprised herself by saying that. But didn't she owe Lucky a favor, considering how much support he'd given her?

"Yes, *we*," Zora retorted, and, to cut off any argument, she added, "Some people have a ridiculously hard time accepting help, to quote a person I know."

That produced a tight smile. "What do you imagine you, or we, can do regarding this alleged situation?"

"I have an idea." Fortunately, a possibility had hit her. "I'll share it on one condition." She might as well benefit from this.

"Which is?"

"You stop nagging me about my personal choices, however stupid you may consider them."

Lucky didn't answer. Then, abruptly, he burst out laughing. "Sometimes I actually like you."

"Why?" she asked suspiciously.

"Because you're a tough little cookie. If only you would apply that quality to he-who-shall-remain-nameless."

"That's breaking the rules," Zora retorted. "No nagging and no smart-aleck remarks, either. Well?"

"You're draining all the fun out of our relationship." Lucky raised his hands in mock surrender. "I agree. Now, what's the suggestion?"

The sight of him leaning close, intent on her, sent a thrill across her nervous system. Must be the maternal hormones running amok. "Remember when Edmond gave that speech about trends in family law?"

Melissa's husband served as a consultant for staff and patients on the legal aspects of fertility issues.

"Sure." Another one-syllable response.

"Afterward, Vince approached him for advice." Zora had heard the story from Melissa. Quickly, she added, "It was in a public place. No attorney-client privilege."

"Advice about what?"

"About persuading Mrs. Adams to agree to in vitro." If Vince produced even a small amount of sperm, it could be extracted and injected into an egg, bypassing the need to fix his blocked ducts. "She refuses to undergo in vitro, however."

"He can afford to hire a surrogate," Lucky pointed out.

"He objects to bringing in a stranger while his wife is presumably still fertile." Although Zora detested Portia for Rod's sake, she understood why a woman approaching forty wouldn't be eager to undergo a process involving hormone shots as well as uncomfortable procedures to harvest her eggs and implant the embryos. There were also potential health risks from a pregnancy complicated by multiple babies.

"What does this have to do with us?" Lucky asked.

"Talking to Edmond renewed Vince's enthusiasm for Safe Harbor." According to Melissa, the hospital administrator had phoned later to congratulate Edmond on saving the day.

"Renewed his enthusiasm how?" Lucky persisted. "His wife still hasn't agreed, as far as I know."

"I'm not sure, but judging by what Rod says about him, he enjoys power trips," Zora observed. "He hates to lose. If we figure out how he can win in this situation, it might keep him engaged with Safe Harbor."

"Any suggestions?"

"Ask Edmond what *he* advised."

Lucky considered this in silence. At close range, Zora noticed an end-of-day dark beard shadowing his rough cheeks. Although she preferred men with a smooth, sophisticated look, she had to admit there was something appealing about Lucky's male hormones proclaiming themselves loud and clear.

What was wrong with her? At this stage of pregnancy, she ought to have zero interest in sex. Or men. Or sexy men. Or… *Stop that.*

"Any idea which days Edmond's at the hospital?" Lucky asked.

"Afraid not."

In the adjacent dining room, Karen rose after stowing a tray in the sideboard. "Monday mornings and Thursday afternoons. Why the interest in Edmond?"

"It's private," Zora and Lucky said simultaneously.

Descending the few steps to the living room, their landlady gathered the pile of chair covers. "That's unusual, you guys being on the same page."

They both returned her gaze wordlessly until she sighed and departed. Zora chuckled. That had been fun.

Lucky held out his hand. As her fingers brushed his, a quiver of pleasure ran through her. On her feet, she lingered close to him for a moment, enjoying the citrus smell of his cologne underscored by masculine pheromones. Then in the recesses of her mind, she remembered something he often said: *it's Andrew who should be helping you, not me.*

Even without speaking, he projected criticism. Glowering, and ignoring Lucky's puzzled reaction, Zora headed for the stair lift.

Chapter Four

On Monday mornings while Cole performed surgeries at the hospital, Lucky replenished supplies, scheduled follow-up appointments with patients and prepared for office procedures in the afternoon.

He'd hoped to slip out to talk to Edmond, but the attorney was fully booked and could only spare a few minutes at lunch. It would have to do. But the morning turned out to be busier than expected, due to a special request from the fertility program director, Dr. Owen Tartikoff. A new urologist, a specialist in men's reconstructive surgery, would soon be joining the staff and Dr. Tartikoff needed someone to review the applications for his office nurse. Due to Lucky's administrative degree, Cole had recommended him.

Pleased at the responsibility, Lucky sifted through digital résumés to select the best candidates. The final choice would be left to the new physician, since the relationship between a doctor and his nurse was crucial. The right person eased the doctor's job, increased efficiency and decreased errors.

The wrong person could cause all sorts of unwanted drama. Hospital lore included a by-now-legendary clash between Keely Randolph and Dr. Tartikoff shortly after his arrival a few years ago. There'd been a spectacular scene when the abrasive Dr. T had dressed her down for an error and she'd blown up, calling him arrogant and egotistical before stalking out.

In view of her long history at Safe Harbor, she'd received a second chance with another obstetrician, Paige Brennan. Miraculously, the chemistry between them had proved stable rather than explosive. Keely spoke of her doctor in glowing terms, which in Lucky's view was how a nurse should behave.

He smiled, remembering how Keely had stood up for Zora at the party, staving off Laird's attempt to touch her. While his attentions hadn't necessarily been sexual, Lucky wouldn't put it past the man.

An image of Zora filled his mind as he recalled her unexpected offer to aid in his quest to expand the men's program. Her teasing grin was irresistible, and who would have imagined a mother-to-be could radiate such sexy vibes? True, she'd been cute before she got pregnant, but Lucky had been too caught up in resenting her for Stacy's and Cole's sakes to take more than a passing notice.

Not that there was any risk of a romance developing between him and Zora. He would never fall for anyone who led such a messy life, and he didn't appear to be her type, either. Judging by Andrew, she went for slick and manipulative, hardly adjectives that applied to a tattooed guy from a rough part of LA.

A guy who'd committed his share of mistakes and was determined not to repeat them, especially if a wife and children were at stake. If he were ever so blessed, Lucky vowed to be sure his family's circumstances were as close to perfect as humanly possible. He'd give them a financial buffer. A protective circle of love, commitment and security. If he couldn't be sure he could provide those things, he'd rather not risk marrying at all.

Lucky focused on the résumés on the computer screen. There were a number of nurses eager to work in such a prestigious environment with regular hours and benefits.

He struggled to view them through the perspective of an employer instead of as a fellow nurse who'd spent a year on his own job search. More than ever, he appreciated Cole's willingness to bring him on board.

Clicking open a new résumé, Lucky frowned in confusion. Was this a joke? Someone had inserted a slightly altered photo of Zora. Her face was narrower, but he'd recognize her anywhere.

Only the name on the file was Zady Moore. *Zady, huh?* He read on, prepared for humorous remarks, but the data seemed straightforward. This so-called Zady had grown up near Safe Harbor, just like Zora. Same age, too. In fact, same birth date.

She claimed to have a nursing degree and to work for a urologist in Santa Barbara, a couple of hours' drive north of here. Switching to the internet, Lucky confirmed that there was indeed a Zady Moore listed in connection with that urologist's office. If this was a hoax, someone had gone to great lengths.

The name Moore struck him as familiar. Oh, right. He'd seen mail addressed to Zora Moore Raditch.

Could Zora have a twin she'd never told him about? Or did she have a cousin with an eerily similar appearance and the same birth date?

The alarm on his watch shrilled, a reminder of his meeting with Edmond. Lucky set aside the résumé with several others marked for further consideration.

From the fourth floor, he took the stairs to the medical building lobby and strode out past the pharmacy into the late September sunshine. A salty breeze wafted from the ocean a mile to the south, while seagulls wheeled overhead.

Next door, the six-story hospital rose in front of him, a lovely sight with its curved wings. Remodeled half a dozen years earlier to specialize in fertility and maternity services, it had established a national reputation by hiring distinguished doctors such as Cole and Dr. T, and by adding state-of-the-art laboratories, surgical suites and equipment. As a result, the side-by-side buildings were bursting at the seams with staff and patients.

Lucky glanced across the circular drive at the vacant dental building that had been mired in bankruptcy proceedings. Once the bankruptcy judge allowed a sale, it would be snapped up fast. The corporation that owned Safe Harbor Medical Center had expressed interest in buying it, but had balked at the high price.

When Vince Adams had expressed interest in funding the growth of the men's program, he'd seemed a gift from fate. Since then, Vince had demonstrated mood swings and a knack for throwing everyone off balance, but his donation remained the hospital's best chance of acquiring the building and boosting the men's fertility program to the next level.

Lucky entered the hospital via the staff door. Instantly, his senses registered tempting aromas from the cafeteria. Also nearby, the chatter of childish voices drifted from the day care center, to which he presumed Zora would soon be entrusting her babies.

As he shoved open the door to the stairs—Lucky seized any chance at exercise—he wondered how long he could go without nagging her. *Somebody* had to advocate for those kids, who deserved their father's financial support even if he was incapable of acting like a real dad.

What about this Zady character? If she was a family member, Zora could sure use the help.

On the fifth floor, Lucky passed the executive offices and entered a smaller suite. The receptionist had apparently gone to lunch, and an inner door stood ajar. The placard read, Edmond Everhart, Family Law Consultant.

Lucky listened in case a client remained inside. Hearing no one, he rapped on the frame.

"Come in." From behind the desk, Edmond rose to greet

him. In his early thirties, like Lucky, and also about five-ten, the guy was impeccably dressed in a suit and tie. Only his rumpled brown hair revealed that he'd had a busy morning. All the same, there was nothing glib or calculating about him.

After shaking hands and taking a seat, Lucky went straight to the point. "I understand Vince Adams was souring on Safe Harbor until he talked to you. You spoke with him in public, so I presume client confidentiality doesn't apply."

"That's true." Leaning back, the attorney removed his glasses, plucked a microfiber cloth from the drawer and polished the lenses.

"I'm curious how you won him over, because—" Lucky couldn't go into detail, since it involved Vince's treatment "—just in case he changes his mind again. What upset him in the first place?"

"He felt disrespected because the whole hospital is aware that he has fertility issues," Edmond said.

"A fact that he's publicized with his own…statements." Lucky had nearly said *big mouth*.

"Be that as it may, he believed people looked down on him because he can't father children."

"How'd you reassure him?"

"I shared a few personal details that put us on a par." After a hesitation, Edmond continued, "I explained that I'd had a vasectomy and later regretted it." His wife, Melissa, was carrying embryos donated by another couple. "I also asked his advice as a stepfather about parenting my niece while her mom's in prison. I'm not sure why, but the conversation eased his mind."

"My guess is that he felt you respected him," Lucky mused. "Did he bring up anything else?"

Edmond reflected. "Yes. He's frustrated with his wife's refusal to consider in vitro. She wasn't present, so I have no idea how she views the matter."

Lucky recalled Zora's comments. "And he rejects hiring a surrogate?" The hospital maintained a roster of screened candidates.

"That's right."

Wheels spun in Lucky's head. "If we persuaded Mrs. Adams to change her mind, that ought to solve the problem."

"It might," Edmond said. "But is it wise to try to manipulate a woman into having a child she might not want?"

"I believe she's worried more about the medical risk than about having another child." At a previous office visit, a successfully treated patient had arrived to show Cole his newborn son. In the waiting room, Portia Adams had reached out to touch the baby's cheek and studied the child wistfully. Catching Lucky's eye, she'd murmured something about missing those days now that her girls were growing up.

"Perhaps there's a compromise position that might satisfy them both," Edmond said. "What if his wife provided the eggs but didn't carry the pregnancy?"

Lucky hadn't thought about separating the two aspects of in vitro. "It's worth a try."

"Good," Edmond said. "Any other questions?"

"Yes, although it's unrelated." While Lucky had promised not to pressure Zora, he hadn't promised not to encourage others to do so. "Zora hasn't broken the news to her ex about the twins. You're her attorney. How about pointing out that the man has legal obligations?"

The attorney laced his fingers atop the desk. "I assure you, I already have."

"You may have to get in her face, so she can't brush you off."

Edmond tilted his head. "May I share something with you that I've discovered about relationships?"

"Sure." Lucky admired how much Edmond had grown and changed while reconciling with Melissa. "Lay it on me."

"It's important to respect her choices," Edmond said.

"Even if you disagree with them?"

"Especially if you disagree with them." Thoughtfully, the lawyer added, "And especially when she's the person who has to deal with the consequences."

"But Zora keeps repeating the same boneheaded mistakes," Lucky protested.

"I suspect she understands her ex-husband better than either of us," Edmond said. "Legally, she'll have to inform him about the babies once they're born, but until then, she might have reason to be cautious."

Lucky only knew Andrew by reputation. "I suppose it's hard to predict how a guy will react to that kind of news."

"Exactly."

The circumstances might not be perfect, but this was a situation of Andrew's own making. Any decent guy would accept responsibility. However, the man had proven repeatedly that he didn't care about honor *or* decency. "Thanks for the words of wisdom."

"You're welcome."

"Oh, one more thing," Lucky said as they both rose. "Does Zora have a sister named Zady?"

"I believe that's her twin," Edmond said.

"Thanks." A twin. Damn! By applying for the job, Zady had put Lucky in a delicate position. He felt as if he ought to alert Zora, but her sister's application was confidential.

He set off for the cafeteria, anxious to arrive before Zora finished eating so he could get her opinion about his discussion with Edmond. As for her mysterious twin, he'd better leave that hot potato alone.

BEING AROUND PERFECT people filled Zora with a sense of inadequacy. It was balanced by a fervent desire to figure out how they did it.

Take her obstetrician. Six feet tall with dramatic red

hair and green eyes, Paige Brennan was a doctor, mother to an eighteen-month-old daughter and wife of the head of a detective agency. Everyone admired and adored her, including her nurse, Keely, who could barely stand most people.

Busy as she was, Dr. Brennan had fit in Zora's exam during her lunch break. The woman was a step from sainthood.

As she sat on the examining table, Zora doubted she could ever develop such an air of confidence. As for inspiring others, she'd settle for earning their good-natured tolerance.

"Surely you have *some* questions," the doctor said after listening to the babies' heartbeats and reviewing Zora's weight gain and test results. They were fine considering her stage of pregnancy. "You never mention any problems."

"Am I supposed to?" Zora had been raised to consider complaining a sign of weakness.

"Frankly, yes." The tall woman draped her frame over a stool. "At thirty-two weeks with a multiple pregnancy, you must be having trouble sleeping, and your ankles are swollen. As I've suggested before, you should be on bed rest."

"I can't afford it," Zora said. "I don't have a husband to wait on me."

"What about the rest of your family?" the doctor asked.

"My mom and stepfather live in Oregon." She'd rather not have either of them around. And there was no sense bringing up her twin, perfect Zady with her ideal husband and kids, whom their mother never failed to mention when she talked with Zora.

The doctor's forehead creased. "Is your mom flying down for the birth?"

"Not if I have anything to say about it." Her mother would expect to be catered to, regardless of the circumstances. She'd be no help with a baby. At home, Mom waited on Zora's surly, demanding stepfather, but her attitude toward her daughters—toward Zora, at least—was just the opposite.

Dr. Brennan regarded her with concern. "Have you chosen a labor partner?" At every visit, she'd recommended Zora sign up for a birthing class.

"I won't need one for a C-section." Although twins didn't always have to be delivered surgically, Zora preferred to play it safe.

"If that's what you want, okay." The physician nodded. "But remember that what we call bed rest doesn't necessarily require staying in bed. You can relax at home and perform routine tasks as you feel capable."

"I feel capable of working." To forestall further objections, Zora added, "And providing ultrasounds doesn't harm the babies. It's not like X-rays or mammograms."

"But it does require standing on your feet all day. And for safety's sake, you should stop driving." Paige raised her eyebrows commandingly.

Zora *was* having trouble reaching the pedals in her car. "I could ride to work with my housemates." Rod, whose car frequently broke down, cadged rides from others, so why shouldn't she?

Keely chose that moment to step in from the hall. "I can drive her."

"Excuse me?" Paige blinked at the unexpected comment.

"If I rent a room in their house, Zora can ride with me." The nurse mustered a faint smile.

"I thought you had a roommate," Zora said.

"So did I. Can we talk at lunch?"

"Sure."

The obstetrician cleared her throat. "Keely, would you provide Zora with an after-visit summary and schedule an appointment for her in two weeks?"

"Yes, Doctor."

The doctor typed a note into the computer. "Zora, call

me if you have any problems, such as spotting or contractions, even if they don't hurt. Okay?"

"Will do." Zora accepted the nurse's assistance in rising from the table.

Once she was dressed, she tucked the printed summary into her purse and walked to the elevator with Keely. With her neck thrust forward, the woman's aggressive stance reinforced the impression of her as a difficult personality. Zora hoped she hadn't erred by suggesting Keely move in with them.

"What's the situation with your roommate?" she asked as they descended. The office was only one flight up, but in Zora's condition, that might as well be ten stories.

"She's in Iowa taking care of her mother," Keely said. "She only planned to stay a week but that's changed. Last night she emailed and asked me to ship all her stuff to her."

"That was short notice. Your rent must be due next week." It was the first of the month.

"That's right. I'm glad you mentioned the vacancy."

"Everything's subject to Karen's approval," Zora warned.

"I'll stop by her office later."

It sounded like a done deal. At least Keely would be an improvement on Laird.

In the cafeteria, the blend of voices and aromas filled Zora with eagerness to share this new development with Lucky. Where was he? Her gaze swept past the food serving bays and across the crowded room.

She spotted him sharing a table with a thin and most unwelcome companion: Laird. The psychologist was talking a mile a minute, oblivious to Lucky's irritated expression.

Zora would rather not discuss Keely in front of the competition. "Hold on," she said, turning.

Too late. Keely was stomping right over to the table. Judging by the set of her shoulders, she didn't plan to be subtle, either.

Chapter Five

Lucky had often heard the flow of gossip referred to as a grapevine, but in a hospital, a more appropriate comparison would be the circulatory system, with its arteries and veins. And its heart, the pump through which all rumors flowed, was the cafeteria.

As a rule, he enjoyed the hum of conversations, among which his ears caught intriguing snatches of news— about hirings and firings, love affairs and broken hearts. Once in a while the drama expanded to include the doctors.

Until today, however, Lucky hadn't understood the embarrassment of landing in the middle of a scene that drew all eyes. It started when Keely announced, without preamble, "I lost my roommate. I've decided to move into your house!"

People peered toward them. The story of Karen's home, its assorted occupants and the resulting pregnancies and marriages had already set many a tongue wagging.

Laird choked, although Lucky couldn't figure out on what. The psychologist hadn't stopped yammering long enough to eat anything. Instead, he'd plopped his butt into a chair at Lucky's table and begun citing his plans for throwing parties.

He'd also proclaimed that his huge TV screen would transform their outdated living room into game central.

Not that Lucky would mind, but the guy apparently didn't consider it necessary to solicit *Karen's* opinion.

"Like hell you're moving in!" Laird finally blurted in a voice that rose to a squeal. "Whatever gave you that idea?"

"I cleared it with Zora." Keely indicated that red-haired person, who gazed warily from the hot food line before ducking out of sight.

Lucky nearly bellowed, "Get over here!" but more heads were swiveling. Not his doctor, mercifully. Through the glass doors, he spotted Dr. Rattigan out of earshot on the patio.

"It's a party house!" Laird, his usually pale face reddening with anger, didn't appear to care who heard him roar. "You're the last person in Safe Harbor anyone would invite to a party."

Silence fell save for the clink of tableware and glasses. The chatter of a man talking on a cell phone sounded abnormally loud, and then that too ceased.

"Let's skip the insults, shall we?" Lucky deliberately employed a soft tone in the hope the others would follow suit.

The effort fell flat. "Oh, really?" Keely boomed. "I was invited to the baby shower, in case you forgot. As for you, Laird, you can take your grabby hands and go live in a brothel."

Lucky wouldn't show cowardice by retreating from the scene. But he could remove himself from the line of fire on the pretext of assisting the pregnant lady.

"Excuse me." Springing up, he narrowly restrained the temptation to break into a run.

Behind him, Laird snarled something about Keely being jealous because nobody made passes at her. Whatever the nurse responded, Lucky shut it out.

"Let me help with that," he told Zora, who had set down her tray as she paid for her lunch. He seized the tray without waiting for permission.

She stepped away from the register. "People are staring."

"Can you blame them?" Lucky halted as a tableful of volunteers arose, blocking their path. Grateful for the delay, he smiled encouragingly at an elderly lady, a gift shop regular who creaked to her feet at glacial speed. To Zora, he asked, "How'd you hook up with Keely?"

"She glommed on to me at Dr. Brennan's office," she explained.

"You had to see the doctor? You aren't having problems, are you?"

"Routine checkup."

"You sure?" He searched her face for signs of pain. She had a bad habit of toughing things out, but she looked well enough today.

What a sweet face, he thought, with a full mouth and a youthful sprinkling of freckles. Standing this close to Zora was having a weird effect on him. In light of their new pact, he wasn't sure how to respond to her. It had been easier when he could drop a comment about Andrew into any conversation and receive a predictably angry retort.

"Did you promise Keely she could move in?" That ought to stir a response.

"Yes, but I warned her Karen has the final say." Biting her lip, Zora peered toward Keely and Laird, who were continuing to insult each other. They'd lowered their voices a notch, but at this stage it only meant other diners leaned forward in their seats to hear them. One orderly went so far as to cup his hands around his ears. "She'd be a zillion percent better than Laird," Zora said.

"For once—twice, actually—we agree on something. Let's not make it a habit."

"Certainly not," Zora replied. "Life would get boring."

"I'm sure we'll find plenty to squabble about." Lucky dodged away as the elderly volunteer snapped her cane to the floor inches from his foot. "Hey!"

She ambled out, not hearing him. Another volunteer responded with a quiet, “Sorry.”

“Excellent reaction time,” Zora observed.

“Thanks.”

They resumed their journey toward the table, where Laird and Keely stood with arms folded, as if whoever was victorious in their staring contest would win the privilege of moving into the house. Around them, conversations slowly resumed.

“Isn’t Keely eating lunch?” Lucky murmured. “She didn’t stop to pick up anything.”

“Look on the bright side,” Zora said. “They can’t have a food fight.”

“I’d enjoy a food fight,” he teased.

“Of course you would.”

“I didn’t say I’d participate.” He lowered her tray onto the table beside his. “Guys, how about easing off?”

“Not till we settle this,” Keely said.

“We can’t do that without…” He broke off at the approach of their landlady, who projected authority despite being no taller than Zora. Maybe it was this month’s black hair or the distinctive long skirts she favored, but more likely it was the quelling expression she wore. “Hey, Karen,” he ventured.

Her frosty gaze swept the four of them. “Have a seat, everyone, and stop creating a spectacle.”

They obeyed. “Now, what is this about?” Raising a hand to stop a barrage of words, Karen said, “Starting with Keely.”

As the nurse explained about her roommate departing on short notice, Lucky watched Zora tuck into her food and thought about her twin. How could there be a carbon copy of her anywhere in the world? Surely no one had the same fiery temperament, or the same gift for frustrating the hell out of him while appealing to his masculine instincts. And why was Zady seeking to work near her sister, when the two appeared to be estranged?

Still, twins were supposed to have a special bond, in contrast to Lucky and his older brother. He didn't even know where Matthew lived now or whether he was still serving in the navy, and he didn't care.

Best friends during their teens, they hadn't spoken in sixteen years. Their last fight, after their parents' deaths, had been too bitter for either of them to forgive. Lucky deeply regretted his mistakes, but that didn't give his brother the right to make vicious, unfair accusations and repeat them to other family members. As a result, Lucky had distanced himself not only from Matthew but also from his aunts, uncles and cousins.

When Keely paused for breath, Laird jumped in. He insisted he had a prior claim and that the household needed him to liven things up.

"I wasn't aware we were dull," Karen snapped. "Frankly, after the behavior I just witnessed, I'd drop you both from consideration, but for financial reasons, I need someone to move in next weekend."

Laird lifted his chin. "Considering my position as staff psychologist, I outrank this woman."

Didn't the jerk realize he'd insulted Lucky, who was an RN on a par with Keely? And Karen herself held the middle-level post of financial counselor.

"This isn't a promotional position," she said. "No offense, Laird, but I think having a nurse across the hall from a pregnant woman would be the most sensible choice. However, I won't approve anyone without the consent of my other renters. Lucky? Zora?"

Nobody wished to become Laird's enemy. Nevertheless, Lucky tilted his head toward Keely, as did Zora. Turning, Karen pinpointed Rod. The anesthesiologist, who was sitting with his nephew and several other doctors, mouthed, "Kee-lee."

If Lucky imagined they'd fallen below everyone else's radar, a rustle of movement proved otherwise as people shifted to observe Rod, then moved their attention back to his table.

"I'm sorry," Karen told the psychologist. "The group agrees with my rationale."

Laird scrambled to his feet. "I hope you'll keep me in mind if there's another opening. Keely might not fit in as well as you assume."

"You're the one who doesn't fit in," the nurse sneered.

"You'll regret this." Noticing everyone's reaction to this threat, Laird added, "I mean, it wouldn't surprise me if they threw you out in a few months."

He stalked off, leaving his dirty dishes. Nostrils flaring, Keely watched him go before excusing herself to buy food.

"Alone at last," Lucky teased after Karen, too, departed.

Zora swallowed a mouthful of milk and wasted no time changing the subject. "Did you talk to Edmond?"

He sketched what he'd learned about Vince and Portia Adams. "My plan is to encourage her to donate eggs and him to hire a gestational surrogate."

"Splitting the difference? Excellent," Zora said. "I suspect you're right about Portia's maternal instincts. During Tiffany's last visit, she mentioned that her mom's developed a fascination with her friends' babies."

"Any suggestions how to nudge her further in that direction?"

"Talk to Rod," she advised.

First she'd recommended he consult Edmond, now Rod. "Why?"

"He used to be married to Portia. If anyone can comprehend how her mind works, it's him." Having polished off her entrée, Zora tackled her custard.

He should have thought of that, Lucky mused. But a marriage that had ended bitterly half a dozen years ago hardly qualified the anesthesiologist as an expert. "You're a mom, or soon will be. Put me into her perspective about this pregnancy business."

"She's a fashion plate who I'm sure injects stuff into her wrinkles and suctions her flab," Zora said. "It's partly ego but I also think she feels she has to compete for her husband's affection. How's she going to fend off gold diggers ten years younger when she has a big round pregnant body?"

"But donating eggs might be okay?"

"Better, although those hormone shots and the mood swings aren't fun," Zora said.

Lucky sighed. "Well, thanks for bouncing ideas around with me."

"Glad to do it." Abruptly, Zora set down her fork. "Something just hit me."

If it would help bring the Adamses together, he was eager to hear it. "Yes?"

"I—" She broke off as a ringtone sounded and she took out her phone. "This is Zora."

Lucky could happily have smashed the device for interrupting them. "Don't lose that thought!"

Frowning, Zora answered. "Yes? Now? Okay. I'll be right there." She clicked off. "It's radiology."

How frustrating. "Before you go, tell me what occurred to you."

"No time. We can discuss it tonight." Hands on the table, Zora hoisted herself upright. "Will you dispose of my dishes? I'd hate to be a slob like Laird."

"Of course," he said. "But—"

"It's a patient of Dr. Tartikoff's," she explained. "The tech went home sick, and he's waiting with her."

Nobody wished to cross the imperious head of the fertility program. "I understand."

"Thanks, Lucky," she said. "I can always count on you."

It was on the tip of his tongue to note that she ought to be able to rely on the father of her children, but he'd promised to lay off that subject. And Lucky found it rather gratifying that he and no one else was the person she counted on.

Talking to Lucky was more fun now that he no longer poked at her sore spot, Zora reflected as she lumbered along the sidewalk to the medical office building. And even though she hadn't planned it, she'd rather enjoyed needling him by withholding information.

On the third floor, she entered Dr. T's medical suite and headed for the room set up for the ultrasound. Nurse Ned Norwalk, a surfer type with a deep tan, appeared around a corner. "You?" he demanded.

"Me, what?" Zora asked. Although she and Ned moved in different circles, she'd never had any problems with him.

"There wasn't any other tech available?" He obviously didn't expect an answer. "Never mind. Fair warning—Dr. T hasn't eaten lunch."

Great—he'd be crankier than ever. "I'll tiptoe around. Where's the patient's chart?"

"The doctor has it. The patient has a mass on her right ovary. You'll be doing a transvaginal ultrasound."

"Okay." Sonograms to examine ovarian cysts—fluid-filled pockets in or on the surface of an ovary—as well as other growths were commonplace. While most cysts vanished on their own, some caused pain, and there was the scary possibility that an ovarian growth could be cancerous. The best view of the ovaries was obtained by inserting a probe into the patient's vagina. "Is she pregnant?"

"No. But—you're sure there wasn't anyone else available?"

"If you doubt me, call radiology."

"Never mind."

Zora had often assisted Dr. T's patients. She didn't understand why Ned was making a big deal of this, but she didn't intend to question him and keep the great physician waiting.

Ned opened the door and retreated. Near the small ultrasound machine paced a scowling Dr. Owen Tartikoff. Even his russet hair seemed to be sizzling with impatience. "Finally," he growled.

"Sorry for the delay. The scheduled tech went home sick." Zora's gaze shifted to the dark-haired woman lying on the examining table, her lower half covered with a paper sheet.

When almond-shaped brown eyes met hers with a jolt, Zora struggled to catch her breath. The patient was Lin Lee Raditch, Andrew's third wife.

Although they'd never been introduced, she'd seen the woman with him around town, and judging by the other woman's reaction, Lin recognized Zora, as well. That explained Ned's attitude. Either the scheduler hadn't noticed that they shared a last name, or had no other options.

"Is there a problem?" The doctor's cross tone slapped at her. He didn't seem aware of their connection.

Zora darted a glance at Lin. The patient had the right to object to an inappropriate care provider. And for the sake of her own emotional state, Zora wasn't sure she ought to go through with this.

Lin's lips pressed tightly. Was she reluctant to offend the celebrated doctor? Then Zora noticed tears glittering in the patient's eyes. *She's frightened.*

In that instant, Lin transformed from the jezebel for whom Andrew had abandoned Zora into a scared woman who might face a terrifying diagnosis.

"This won't hurt," she assured the patient, and went to work.

Chapter Six

"These appear to be fluid-filled cysts," Dr. Tartikoff told the patient as Zora finished her scan. "However, before recommending a treatment plan, I'll have the radiologist review the images."

"It isn't cancer?" Lin's body had gone nearly rigid, although Zora had encouraged her to relax during the procedure.

"I doubt it." The obstetrician continued studying the screen. "If these were solid, or partially solid, I'd be more concerned."

The patient swallowed, evidently still worried. "Will you have to remove my ovaries?"

"It may be possible to perform a cystectomy, excising only the largest cyst." Dr. T patted Lin's shoulder reassuringly. "Or we might remove one ovary, leaving the other in place."

"I can still have children?" Lin's slightly accented voice trembled.

"Yes, but first let's deal with the discomfort you've been suffering."

"Thank you, Doctor." She regarded him gratefully.

How ironic, Zora thought, that Andrew's wife was concerned about being able to bear his children, while Zora herself stood there with his babies thumping inside her.

Nevertheless, her heart went out to the anxious young woman.

Did life have to be so complicated? It would be easier if Zora could simply blame Andrew's faithlessness on his new wife. Instead, she related to Lin's pain. Carrying twins was hard, but being unable to bear children would be worse.

"The radiologist's report should reach me within a few days. I'll review it immediately," Dr. T advised. "Please set up an appointment for next week. Your husband should accompany you."

Lin's smile vanished. "He travels and is very busy."

"You're his wife. There's nothing more important than your health." In his intensity, Zora heard the conviction of a man devoted to his wife and children. "Would you like me to explain the situation to him?"

"No, no, Doctor, that isn't necessary." Lin sounded anxious.

"You're sure?"

When she again declined, Dr. T excused himself and left.

"I'll be out of here in a minute so you can dress," Zora said. She shifted the equipment cart away from the examining table.

Lin touched her arm. "Thank you for being gentle."

Astonished, Zora wondered what the woman had expected. "You're welcome."

"I am wondering…" She indicated Zora's expanded midsection.

Was she asking about the father? Zora pretended not to pick up the hint. "Twins," she said. "Due in late November."

"You are fortunate to be fertile." The patient sat up. "I am desperate for children to bind my husband to me and prove my family is wrong."

"Wrong about what?" Zora asked.

"They believe I married a man who will treat me badly." She sniffled. "And they're angry that I moved to another country after they sacrificed to send me to college. My mother will not talk to me on the phone."

On the verge of inquiring why Lin was sharing this with her of all people, Zora realized how isolated the woman was. "That must be difficult." She handed over a tissue.

Lin wiped her eyes. "Pardon me, but also, I wonder why you are pregnant when you did not want children."

A weird sense of déjà vu swept over Zora. During her marriage, Andrew had claimed his first wife had refused to have kids. Only later had she learned that the opposite was true: Stacy had longed for children but delayed pregnancy at Andrew's request.

Same lies, same manipulations. Pain knifed inside Zora. *Lucky's right. I must be the most gullible person on earth.*

"What is wrong?" Gathering the paper covering her, Lin eased off the table. "The babies are hurting you?"

This show of compassion undid her. Suddenly Zora couldn't hold her secret inside for another instant. "Andrew lied to you. These are his children, except he doesn't know that yet."

Lin stood frozen with her bare feet on the linoleum. "That is impossible. He had a vasectomy. You insisted on it."

"No, I didn't. When…?" Zora gave a start at a tap on the door.

Ned Norwalk entered, holding a sheet of paper. "How's everything in here?" The nurse halted at the sight of them obviously engaged in a discussion. "Are you okay, Mrs. Raditch?"

"I'm fine," both women said.

"The current Mrs. Raditch."

They glared at him.

He blinked, registering the unexpected collusion, and,

to his credit, decided to respect their privacy. "I'll be at the nurses' station if anyone wants me."

After Ned beat a strategic retreat, Zora refocused on her companion. "If Andrew had a vasectomy, it wasn't at my request. And these *are* his children."

"You are wrong," Lin insisted. "He showed me the scar."

Zora preferred not to think about the location of that scar or the intimate circumstances under which he'd displayed it. "When was that?"

The other woman, a few inches shorter than her, considered briefly before saying, "Eight months ago, while we were engaged. Before you became pregnant, if you are in the seventh month."

Could he have faked the scar? Then a better explanation occurred to Zora.

"After a vasectomy, a man's sperm count doesn't immediately drop to zero. It can take a month or more before the sperm is completely gone." She absorbed a lot of medical information in her work. "We were still married—barely. He must have been fertile, because I haven't slept with anyone else."

Lin steadied herself on the edge of the examining table. "These babies, they really are his?"

"I'm afraid so. It all makes more sense now. No wonder he didn't insist on contraception—he'd had a vasectomy." Zora had assumed that, at some level, Andrew had wished to father a baby with her. Instead, he'd believed he was safe.

Lin hugged herself and shivered. "You will take away my husband."

That was precisely what Zora had fantasized. Now, witnessing the other woman's distress, she faced the fact that Andrew had coldheartedly plucked Lin from her family and country, then lied to her and manipulated her. He'd also played on Zora's love for him, using and discarding her yet again. Why? For ego's sake?

The man had no heart and could never be trusted. Zora was truly alone in this pregnancy. Except for Lucky. And her other friends, of course.

To her astonishment, the primary emotion pumping through her was relief. She didn't have to pretend any more. She could tell the truth, to herself most of all.

"I don't want him back," Zora said.

The dark-haired woman studied her in confusion. "But you carry his babies."

The man isn't capable of loving anyone except himself. A burden lifted from her shoulders, filling her with unaccustomed lightness despite the weight in her womb. "You can keep him with my blessing."

A couple of quick steps and Lin flung her arms around Zora. "You are my sister in spirit. I shall try to be strong like you."

Zora hesitated only a second before returning the hug. When she and Andrew broke up, she'd been utterly friendless. That experience intensified her empathy with this woman whose world was collapsing. "What will you do?"

Lin breathed deeply before replying, "I will think hard."

"If you need a divorce attorney, I recommend Edmond Everhart," Zora said. "He's a consultant on staff at the hospital."

"That is good advice," Lin said.

"Best of luck."

As Zora exited, she ignored a questioning look from Ned in the hall. Struggling to sort through what she'd learned, she wished she didn't have to endure Lucky's comments when he heard about this encounter.

And yet, she felt liberated. "Sorry, babies," Zora whispered. "We're all better off without your dad."

Then fear quivered through her. How could she raise

these kids without a father? Her own might have been flawed, but she'd always sensed that he loved her and Zady.

Unlike her dad, Andrew lacked the capacity to care about others. Zora had to accept that and move on, no matter how badly it hurt.

She hoped she wouldn't have to put up with any I-told-you-so taunts tonight from Lucky, who would no doubt hear about this entire scene via the gossip mill. With her heart aching and her mood unsettled, she was in no mood to tolerate his sniping.

WITH EVERYONE EAGER to chat about Keely's pending arrival, Lucky and his three housemates gathered at the dining room table earlier than usual on Monday night. While they ate, they relived the scene in the cafeteria and speculated about Laird's not-so-veiled threat.

Would he try to intimidate Keely to keep her from joining them? Did he honestly believe they'd accept him if he did?

Karen related that Keely had paid a deposit and arranged to move in Saturday afternoon. Her only question had been whether the nearness to the estuary caused illness among the residents. Karen had assured her that, despite the smell, they all stayed remarkably healthy.

Questions and comments flew, but the usually talkative Zora didn't join in, Lucky noted. Instead, she downed her soup and salad while avoiding his gaze. Was she annoyed at him?

Perhaps she'd found out about her twin applying for a job. After reviewing the remaining résumés, he'd confirmed that Zady's qualifications merited a spot among the top half dozen contenders and had scheduled her for an interview next week, when the new urologist would be visiting. But if that was the problem, why wasn't Zora interrogating him?

During a lull in the conversation, she slanted a glare

at him. He'd done nothing to deserve that, Lucky was almost certain. "What?" he demanded.

"What do you mean, what?"

"I mean, why are you scowling at me? I haven't done anything." *Recently.*

"You will," she muttered.

"Suit yourself." Lucky let the subject drop. If he'd offended Zora, it was her responsibility to be frank about it.

Rod and Karen finished eating and carried their dishes into the kitchen. As Zora started to rise, Lucky recalled her hasty departure from lunch and the idea she'd mentioned. "Hold on a sec."

She grimaced. "We might as well get this over with."

"Get what over with?"

Still not meeting his gaze, she said, "I refuse to make it easier for you."

He was growing more confused by the minute. She'd been friendly at lunch, and Lucky had been too busy during the afternoon to ruffle anyone's feathers. To compensate for his absence at the convention, Dr. Rattigan had squeezed in so many patients that Lucky had skipped his coffee break and stayed at the office late.

"Is this about your—" He nearly said *sister*, but caught himself. Besides, there was another thing he'd been waiting to discuss. "Idea about the Adamses?" he finished.

"What idea about the Adamses?"

"In the cafeteria, you said something hit you, and then you took off to see a patient," Lucky reminded her.

"Did I?" Zora rested her chin in her palm. Pregnancy had darkened her cute freckles and rounded her cheeks. Her hair had thickened and taken on a shine, as well.

"Please don't tell me you forgot the idea."

She frowned so hard that Lucky feared she'd get a headache. Then she brightened. "I remember!"

"Shoot."

"Portia has mixed feelings about pregnancy because

she fears it will turn Vince away from her, but she might change her mind if she realizes it could save her marriage," Zora said.

"Why is she so afraid of losing him?" Lucky countered. "In a divorce, she could take her husband to the cleaners."

"There's always the possibility that she loves the guy. Besides, from what I've read, Vince's previous two wives didn't fare very well," she replied.

Lucky recalled news reports about the man's insistence on prenuptial agreements. Nevertheless, the women had been left financially comfortable by ordinary standards. "A few million apiece might not be much compared to his billions, but it ain't too shabby."

"It's not only the money." Rod joined the conversation from the kitchen entrance. "Portia loves having a ringside seat at New York Fashion Week, being invited to A-list parties and hobnobbing with celebrities. A couple of million dollars doesn't do that. Being married to Vince Adams does."

Lucky supposed Rod knew her better than any of them. "Wouldn't having a baby interfere with all that partying?"

"Not when you can afford live-in nannies," he growled.

"You can be a devoted mom and still hire a nanny," Zora said. "Don't forget, she has lots of free time during the day, since she doesn't work."

"Portia will do whatever she believes is in her best interest, and to hell with anyone else," Rod snarled, and ducked out of sight.

While Lucky had a less jaundiced view of Mrs. Adams than Rod, he did agree that she'd fight to save her marriage. "Interesting point," he told Zora. "It's worth bearing in mind."

Silence descended, aside from random noises in the kitchen. Zora poked at the remaining bits of lettuce on her salad plate. "Stop torturing me."

He might as well take the bull by the horns, Lucky decided. "Is this about your sister?"

"My sister?" Her blank expression indicated he'd missed the mark.

He had to cover his mistake, fast. "I heard you have a twin sister."

"From who?"

He couldn't cite the job application and he'd rather avoid implicating Edmond, who'd merely confirmed what Lucky had already stumbled across. "Informed sources."

"She's none of your business," Zora snapped. "We aren't in touch. Stop changing the subject."

Rod stuck his head through the door again. "Oh, seriously, Lucky, quit acting coy. Everyone's dying to find out what happened between the two Mrs. Raditches."

That was what had gone down today? And he hadn't heard a word.

Lucky threw up his hands. "I skip my coffee break for one afternoon and miss the gossip of the century. You went mano a mano with the new Mrs. Raditch?"

"She's a patient. I can't discuss..." To his dismay, Zora's face crumpled, and tears rolled down her cheeks.

Lucky scooted over and put his arms around her, enjoying the warmth of her pregnancy-enhanced body. "You discovered she's no more a demon than you are, and Andrew's an even bigger rat than you realized. Am I close?"

"I feel bad for her." Zora scrubbed her cheek with the back of her hand. "Her family rejected her when she married him. She's alone in a foreign country. And he lied about me, like he lied about Stacy. As if we're interchangeable."

To Lucky, there was nothing interchangeable about Zora and any other woman on the planet, including her twin. That was irrelevant, however. "You're crying for her sake?"

"And because what I learned means he'll never love

these babies. Before today, I believed that deep down, he wanted them." Her gray eyes darkened with sorrow. "Ever since I've been steeling myself for you to say, *I told you so*. Go ahead and get it over with."

Cradling her against him, Lucky said, "Okay. I told you so."

A painful whack in the ankle sent him jolting backward, nearly overturning his chair. "Ow! How'd you do that from this angle?" Releasing her, he rubbed the spot where she'd kicked him.

"Public opinion agrees that you deserved it," noted Rod, who'd resumed snooping from the doorway.

"Beat it," Zora ordered him.

"Me?" Rod feigned innocence.

"This is between me and this pain in the neck," she retorted.

"Pain in the ankle," Lucky corrected.

From behind Rod, a feminine hand gripped his shirt collar and tugged him out of sight. Lucky wafted a mental thanks in Karen's direction.

"If my shin is black-and-blue tomorrow, I'll sue for assault." He moved to a chair at a safer distance.

"Felled by a pregnant midget?" Zora wisecracked. "What a wimp."

Footsteps moved through the den and around to the front. The stairs creaked as their housemates ascended, leaving them in privacy.

Once Lucky heard Karen's door close upstairs, he felt safe to ask, "What's your next move?"

Zora stretched her legs under the table. "I talked to Edmond. He says Andrew has to pay half of the uninsured costs for my pregnancy and half the child-care expenses."

"You'll let the attorney deal with him?" That seemed wise.

Zora nodded. "I'm still not sure how I'd react to Andrew in the flesh."

"More importantly, how would he react to *you*?" Lucky's hands formed fists at the idea of the man bullying Zora.

"I hate being weak." She dabbed her eyes with her napkin.

"There's nothing weak about using good judgment," he said. "You don't have to prove how tough you are."

"That's not what I mean." She indicated her enlarged abdomen. "When I'm alone with Andrew, he slips past my defenses. Here's the living proof."

"You can seize control if you're determined." Surely she could resist the man after everything he'd put her through. "Zora, you're strength personified with everyone else."

"Am I?" She gazed into space. "My dad used to swing between being a jerk and being the most loving father in the world. No matter how hard I resolved to stay angry, I couldn't."

"Did he drink?" In Lucky's observation, alcoholism was often associated with that sort of behavior.

"Yes, sometimes." Zora inhaled deeply. "I used to long for a family I could rely on, where people were actually happy. That's still my dream, I guess."

It was Lucky's, too, he reflected with a lump in his throat. Money had been tight for his family when he'd been young, and his parents had struggled to keep their store profitable. There'd always been love, but there'd been stress and long work hours, too.

While nothing could excuse the way Lucky had let them down, the pressure to help support the family had been difficult for him to handle as an immature teen. Before he risked establishing a family of his own, he'd make sure their finances were on a secure footing and find a wife who shared his values. Those included careful planning, postponing having kids and communicating honestly.

"What happened to your dad?" Lucky knew Zora's mom was a widow, but had never heard any details.

"When I was twenty-two, they had a big fight and he moved out." She paused, and then the words spilled out. "Mom claimed he'd cheated on her, which to me was such a betrayal of the whole family that I refused to speak to him. A few months later, he dropped dead of a heart attack. We never said goodbye."

"I'm sorry." What a burden of guilt that must place on her. "It wasn't your fault."

"If you love somebody, shouldn't you keep trying to rescue the relationship?"

"But past a certain point, you're only enabling him." Lucky eased farther away in case she tried kicking him again.

Instead, Zora lurched to her feet. "Well, I'm done enabling Andrew. Edmond can handle him from now on."

"I agree in principle." Reaching over, Lucky collected her dishes and piled them with his. "You can't avoid him forever, though."

"I can try." A pounding on the front door sent Zora's hand flying to her throat. "Oh, my gosh, you don't suppose that's him, do you?"

The thuds grew louder. "Stay there. I'll get it." After depositing the dishes in the kitchen, Lucky went to answer.

On the porch, hand raised for renewed hammering, stood a man of about thirty, a tailored suit jacket failing to disguise his pudgy gut. Blond hair, blue eyes, sneering expression. "Andrew Raditch?" Lucky guessed.

"Where is she?" The man stomped in. Had Lucky not dodged him, they'd have collided. "I insist on talking to my wife."

"Which wife would that be?" Finally, here was the man who'd created endless trouble—and, Lucky conceded, a measure of entertainment—over the past few months. Andrew was shorter than he'd imagined, and not nearly handsome enough to explain his appeal to women.

"Don't mess with me, mister." Feet planted in the entry, Andrew bellowed, "Zora, where the hell are you?"

How could this rude oaf be the son of Betsy Raditch? But then, he had alcohol on his breath.

From around the corner of the staircase, Zora regarded her ex-husband coolly. "What's your problem, Andrew?"

"What did you say to Lin?" the man demanded. "She admitted to my face that she talked to you."

As if that were a crime, Lucky thought.

"So?" Still half in the living room as if prepared to dodge away, Zora watched him guardedly.

"She packed a bag and walked out on me," Andrew said. "She was crying. Did you enjoy hurting her?"

"I'm not the one who hurt her." Zora remained admirably calm, in Lucky's opinion.

"You must have filled her head with lies!" Andrew smacked his hand against the wall.

"You accuse *me* of lying?" Zora stood her ground. "You should study the definition of truth. It seems to be an alien concept to you."

"Cut the crap." Andrew prowled toward her. "You call Lin right now and apologize."

"For what?"

"For whatever you…" As Zora stepped into full view, big belly and all, Andrew's jaw worked without producing another sound.

Lucky enjoyed the man's shock. Finally, Andrew had discovered he was going to be a father.

Chapter Seven

To Zora, Andrew seemed different tonight. Was it the extra height of the ceiling that dwarfed him or the contrast between him and Lucky? Andrew's muscles from playing high school football were running to fat—in contrast to Lucky's well-toned build—and his once-thick blond hair had begun receding at the temples.

As for his blustering manner, usually it yielded to calculated charm as soon as he saw that he'd intimidated her. Tonight, though, with Lucky on hand and the memory of the afternoon's anguished scene still raw, she remained in control of her emotions. No intimidation, and hence no charm to obscure his true reaction.

For a revealing moment, she watched Andrew's expression shift from disbelief to anger to disdain as he weighed his response to her pregnancy. Before today, while Zora had recognized the self-serving motives that rippled below the man's slick surface, she'd soon been sucked under by his charisma. Tonight, the curl of his lip and the flare of his nostrils might have belonged to a stranger. A stranger she disliked.

"Now I understand what you dropped on Lin." With a wave of his arm, he indicated—and dismissed—her pregnancy. "You persuaded her it was mine, didn't you? I can't imagine how you fooled her. She knows I had a vasectomy."

Behind him, Zora caught Lucky's startled blink. Funny how keenly she registered her housemate's responses, and how grateful she was for his protective stance.

"Your doctor did warn you that a vasectomy doesn't instantly render you sterile, I presume," she said.

"It takes a few weeks," her ex responded confidently. "I gave it a month."

He'd calculated the timing, or so he believed. "I have two words for you," Zora told Andrew. "Paternity test."

"You went out and slept with someone else," he sneered. "No doubt right after I signed the divorce papers."

"Did your doctor confirm that your sperm count had dropped to zero?" Lucky asked. In response to Andrew's who-the-hell-are-you? scowl, he added, "I work in a urologist's office. It takes ten to twenty ejaculations to completely clear the sperm."

Andrew paled. "The baby *can't* be mine."

"Babies, plural," Zora corrected.

"Beg pardon?"

"I'm carrying twins," she said. "And in California, a paternity test isn't necessary for you to owe child support. According to my attorney, if the parents are married, by law the husband is automatically the father. And we *were* still married that night."

At the memory, pain threatened her detachment. She'd dropped by Andrew's apartment to urge him to sign the divorce papers after weeks of him playing games. Instead, he'd sworn that he regretted cheating on her, declared that she was his true love and drawn her into his bed. A few nights later, while she nursed the hope that he planned to cast off his fiancée and stay with her, he'd dropped the signed divorce papers on her porch and fled.

"You waited, what, seven months to inform me?" His other tactics having failed, Andrew assumed the mantle of outrage. "Any man would doubt these children are his. I refuse to pay for what isn't mine."

"If you insist, I'll arrange for a test." Might as well seal the deal.

That didn't appear to be the answer he'd expected. "You'd risk your babies' safety by sticking a needle in there?"

"You're out-of-date, man," Lucky announced. "It doesn't take an invasive test to establish paternity anymore. They can extract the baby's DNA from the mother's blood with ninety-nine-point-nine percent accuracy."

Andrew grimaced. "Fine. Whatever."

Zora seized on his apparent consent. "The test's expensive and insurance won't cover it. Since you're insisting on it, you can pay."

He shifted on the balls of his feet. "Half."

She supposed arguing the point would be futile. Instead, she added, "Okay, but legally you also owe half of my other maternity-related expenses." Oh, drat, her voice was trembling. Did the man feel absolutely nothing after learning that he'd fathered two children-to-be? He hadn't asked their genders, or Zora's due date, or whether she'd selected names.

Names. She'd planned to let him choose those in the absurd belief that doing so would strengthen his connection to the twins. After tonight, though, Zora resolved that he'd have nothing to do with selecting the names if she could help it.

"Let's run that test before you start counting my money," Andrew snarled. He turned abruptly, sidestepped Lucky and stalked out of the house.

Zora struggled to catch her breath. Since learning of her pregnancy, she'd imagined this scene repeatedly, in a thousand variations. Anger and awe, apology and acceptance—she'd credited Andrew with those feelings. Well, he'd shown the anger. Aside from that, however, the only other thing he'd displayed was utter indifference to his own kids.

"High five or knuckle bump?" Grinning, Lucky raised his hand for her response.

She burst into sobs.

"What's wrong?" The man looked flummoxed. "Zora, you were magnificent. You stood up to every trick he threw at you. Didn't you hear me silently cheering you?"

She struggled for control. "How could I hear something silent?"

"It was written all over my face." His dark eyes glowed. "Tonight, I witnessed a miraculous transformation. Right here in our living room, you became a kick-ass superhero."

His praise felt wonderful. It also filled her with wariness, because she didn't deserve it. "I forced him to agree to a blood test, that's all."

"And hit him up for half your expenses."

"He hasn't paid yet."

"Zora!" Lucky gripped her gently under her arms. "I'd swing you around to celebrate, only I doubt the twins would appreciate it."

"You're right." The duo were squirming. At this stage, she'd read, their auditory functions had developed enough for them to hear the argument. How sad that on their first exposure to their father's voice, it had been filled with rage.

Already, the babies might be forming lifelong impressions of masculine and feminine behavior. She hoped that Lucky's gentler tones offset Andrew's harshness. "He didn't ask a single question about his children. Maybe it hasn't sunk in yet."

"And maybe he's a self-centered prick. If I accidentally fathered babies, I'd be determined to give them the best," Lucky assured her.

"You'd take care of their mother, wouldn't you? You'd never let her down." Zora caught her breath, unsure why his answer mattered so much.

"I certainly wouldn't whine and try to weasel out of

my obligations," Lucky responded. "But I'm doing everything in my power to avoid running that kind of risk. I won't be ready for a family till I pay off my education loans and save a down payment for a house. My kids deserve a happy childhood with two parents who're mature enough to provide them with stability."

Zora's spirits plummeted. During the confrontation with Andrew, she'd drawn strength from Lucky's nearness, from having a man care about her without making demands. Well, of course he didn't make demands, because he didn't want anything from her, as he'd just indicated. He wanted the perfect wife, the perfect family, and she was far from perfect.

Why can't he love me, messy life and all?

What was wrong with her? She didn't love Lucky. Or if she did, it was the casual, friendship kind of love. He wasn't her type. Too rough around the edges and too judgmental. Still, the way he'd stood by her these past months had been more than kind. It had been...fatherly. And maybe more.

He was still holding her. Still gazing at her fondly. "I wish my children had a father like you," Zora blurted.

Lucky stared down at her for a moment. Then he released her. "I appreciate the compliment, but these are Andrew's kids."

She was on the verge of pointing out the obvious, that her ex-husband didn't want them, when it struck her what Lucky really meant—that he couldn't or wouldn't be their father, either.

The discovery chilled Zora. How naive she'd been, to believe even for an instant that Lucky could fill the void in her heart. How utterly unrealistic. *Typical of me, I guess.*

"I'd better lie down," she said.

"I didn't mean to upset you," he responded. "I only meant..."

Zora waved away the explanation. "Don't bother. I'm a total idiot when it comes to relationships."

"Did I miss something?" Lucky asked.

How adorably clueless he was. "I'm tired. It's been a long day."

"It's only eight thirty."

Zora struggled to ignore his worried gaze. "That's late, for a pregnant woman." A pregnant woman whose last lingering illusions had been shattered.

Until tonight, her bond to Andrew—imaginary though it had been—had shielded her from any other man like a brick wall. Now, vulnerable and hurt, she seemed to be stumbling over a bunch of loose bricks. "Good night."

"If you're sure."

"I am." Zora hurried away, although she wasn't sure about anything. Okay, about the no-more-Andrew part, yes. But as for Lucky, somewhere along the line, love had mushroomed in the dark. What defense did she have against her best friend?

In her bedroom, she dropped onto the floral bedspread, grabbed a dainty pink pillow and began punching the stuffing out of it.

TOO BAD STANDING up to her loathsome ex-husband had exhausted Zora when she ought to be celebrating, Lucky thought. And how typical that Andrew hadn't bothered to consider how his actions might affect a woman coping with a multiple pregnancy.

What a joy to witness Zora bravely tackling that creep. How frustrating it had been these past months, watching such a smart, feisty woman repeatedly yielding to foolish delusions.

Yet, unfortunately, she might still forgive the jerk. If Lucky had learned anything about Zora, it was that her emotions regarding her ex-husband seesawed like crazy.

Once the babies were born, if Andrew showed any paternal instincts at all, her resistance would probably crumble.

That remark about wishing her kids had a dad like Lucky…for a split second, he'd wished the same thing. Then he'd faced reality. To her, the twins would always belong to Andrew.

Lucky sighed and clicked on the lamp in his bedroom, which was spacious enough for his video games and exercise equipment. During the day, when he opened the curtains, the sliding glass doors revealed a splendid view of the gray-and-green wetlands with their ever-changing tableau of wildlife. Tonight, by contrast, the lamp—on a ceramic base enlivened by a turquoise-and-black geometric pattern—bathed the room in a cozy radiance.

When he'd moved in here, Lucky had purchased several Hispanic-inspired accents, including the rainbow-striped serape draped across a chair as well as a ceramic Aztec calendar plaque that hung on the wall, its buff background covered with red-and-black designs. Although his family was three generations removed from its Mexican-Indian roots, Lucky valued his connection to ancient traditions. He'd worked hard to master Spanish both because of his heritage and to assist patients.

Overhead, the floor creaked, a reminder that Karen and Rod were awake. Lucky tried not to speculate about what they might be doing in Karen's suite. Whatever it was, he appreciated that they'd remained out of sight during the verbal fireworks with Andrew.

If only Zora had more energy, Lucky would have enjoyed sharing a late snack with her, teasing her across the table. It had been fun earlier tonight, figuring out how to persuade Vince to stay involved with Safe Harbor.

How sharp of Zora to note that Portia would do whatever was necessary to preserve her marriage. Especially since, in Lucky's observation, the woman's longing for a baby might tip the scales in favor of undergoing fertility treatments.

Whatever happened at Saturday's appointment, his involvement, if any, had to be discreet. Unhappily, he acknowledged that all this head scratching and cogitating might be for naught. It was possible that, upon receiving Cole's bad news, Vince would simply haul his wife out of there and bid Safe Harbor adios.

It would help to have a second set of eyes and ears. Zora had proven perceptive, and if she were around…

Why not? In addition to working weekdays, Zora filled in occasional evenings and weekends. Cole hadn't scheduled a full roster of patients for Saturday morning. Lucky could identify a few men due for ultrasounds who might be glad to move up their appointments. He'd request that Zora be assigned.

Satisfied with that plan, he changed into exercise clothes and switched on his elliptical machine.

WHILE GROWING UP, Zora had never had a close girlfriend. Her twin, who should have been her dearest pal, had become a rival because their mother had constantly pitted them against each other with criticism and shifting favoritism. By high school, Zora had transferred that competition to other girls as well, a view reinforced by Andrew's flirtations while they were dating.

Then she'd started working at Safe Harbor and, during the lowest period of her life, met Anya. She'd never understood why bubbly, popular Anya had defied the staff's general hostility to Zora and invited her to share an apartment, but she'd been deeply appreciative.

Sharing confidences and movie nights with a friend had been a revelation. A year later, after their rent increased and they moved into Karen's house, they'd continued to be best friends. Zora had been the first to learn that Anya was carrying Jack's baby, and it had been Anya who accompanied Zora to buy a pregnancy kit and discover her own impending motherhood.

Anya's marriage a few months ago, followed by the birth of her daughter, meant that Jack and little Rachel came first. Lonely again, Zora had drifted into Lucky's company, despite his irritating attempts to run her life. But now that her feelings toward him had changed, being around him was dangerous.

Zora needed a friend. And although Keely was far from the warm, cuddly type, she had a kind side. Late Tuesday afternoon, when Zora stopped into Dr. Brennan's office to inquire about paternity testing, the nurse immediately arranged for the doctor to order the lab test. She requested Andrew's email address and promised to send him the information, as well.

"The results take eight working days after you both provide blood." The older woman refastened the pink barrette in her hair. "Say, are you driving home with Karen today? I saw you arrive together. In case she has to stay late, I'd be glad to take you."

A hint of anxiety in the nurse's expression, as if the response really mattered, touched Zora. Not only did she need a friend, but Keely did, too. Also, Karen had texted that she'd be delayed about an hour and hoped Zora didn't mind waiting. The alternative—calling on Lucky—went against Zora's resolve to steer clear of him.

Dr. Brennan's warning about safety had resonated with her on the drive home yesterday, when she'd found that she could no longer reach the pedals without her baby bulge pressing against the steering wheel.

Thank goodness her housemates had volunteered to pick up the slack, and now Keely was joining in. "Actually, I *could* use a ride, if it's not too much trouble."

The lines in Keely's face softened. "Let's do it!" They arranged to meet in the medical building lobby in fifteen minutes, after Keely got off work. Zora had finished her shift an hour earlier.

At the lab, she had blood drawn. Thank goodness for the newer technique, which extracted fetal DNA from her blood plasma and compared it to the father's DNA. All the same, she'd be willing to bet that Andrew would complain about it. Too bad he didn't have to endure the doctor's poking, the morning sickness, the sleepless nights and the labor pains.

As she rose to leave with a small bandage on her arm, Zora supposed that women from the dawn of time had resented men for escaping the painful consequences of pregnancy. She wouldn't resent Lucky, who took care of her, though. But as he'd pointed out, these weren't his babies.

Recalling that she ought to alert Karen to the change in plans, Zora sent the other woman a text. When she reached the meeting place, Keely was already there, pacing. "Am I late?" Zora asked.

"No. I wasn't sure you'd be here."

"Why not?" Stupid question. Keely's low self-esteem spoke for itself. "I mean, you're doing me a favor. Of course I'm here."

"I'm parked in the main garage," the nurse said. "Is that too far? I could pull around."

"The exercise is good for me. And it's not far." As they set out at a slow pace, Zora asked, "Are you ready for the move this weekend? Did your landlord hassle you about the short notice?"

"Not after I explained the circumstances with my roommate." Keely brushed a speck of dust off her navy uniform. "And told him it was my birthday."

"It's your birthday?" Zora wondered about her new friend's age. It seemed rude to ask, though.

"Last Sunday."

"You should have mentioned it earlier! We'd have celebrated."

"Why?" Keely's eyebrows drew into a dark, straight line. "Turning fifty isn't anything to cheer about."

Well, she'd answered *that* question. "Every birthday is precious," Zora said as they passed a flower bed crowded with red, white and purple petunias. "Considering the alternative."

"What alternative?"

"Dying young."

Keely snorted, which appeared to be her manner of laughing. "Never thought of that." Halting at the garage's elevator, she pressed the button. "I can't afford to get old and sick, without a family to lean on." She punched the button again, although it was already lit.

"Fifty isn't old," Zora ventured.

"My mom was fifty when she had to go on disability." Keely's forehead creased. "I moved in with her after Dad died. She was forever consulting one doctor or another. Aches and pains, high blood pressure, swollen ankles. They ordered her to exercise and quit drinking. She insisted the booze was medicinal and that it hurt to move around."

"To move around at all?" Zora asked. "What did she do, spend the whole day on the couch?"

"Pretty much. I did the shopping and cleaning, while working full-time."

No wonder the nurse had a grumpy attitude. "Is she living?"

A shudder ran through Keely. "I'd rather not talk about it."

"I didn't mean to pry."

The elevator arrived and they rode up in silence. Had she offended Keely? Zora wondered. The woman had a reputation for being touchy.

At last the nurse spoke again. "I take it back. It's better for you to hear the truth."

"About what?"

They exited onto the third level. "About what happened to my mom," Keely answered. "I got arrested and lost my last job because of it."

That sounded shocking. Zora struggled to contain her reaction as they strolled between rows of vehicles. Behind them, an SUV pulled out cautiously. Ahead, a woman beeped open her sedan. Although there was a faint smell of exhaust, the garage's open-air design dissipated the fumes.

"What happened?" Quickly, Zora added, "Obviously, the police made a mistake." *Or did we agree to share our house with an ax murderer?*

"One morning Mom claimed she sensed a heart attack coming on." Keely's voice echoed off the hard surfaces around them. "She was constantly saying such things and complaining to the neighbors about how I neglected her. I'd missed too much work already, running Mom to doctors for no reason. I told her to call nine-one-one if her symptoms worsened."

"Oh, dear." Having grown up with a mother who insisted on being the center of attention at any cost, Zora empathized.

Keely's eyes glittered with tears. "After work, I found her stone cold in her favorite chair. A neighbor told the police I'd been abusing her."

"You must have been devastated." If Zora had ignored her mother's complaints and then she'd ended up passing away, she'd be overwhelmed by guilt.

"The clinic fired me as soon as they heard I'd been arrested." Keely paused at a bend in the row. "There I was, out on bail, handling my mother's funeral arrangements and terrified of being sent to prison."

"That's horrible." Zora's heart went out to the woman. "What did you do?"

The nurse sucked in a long breath before continuing. "Mom's doctors explained to the investigators that I was always bringing her in for one symptom or another. The district attorney decided not to prosecute."

"What about your job? Surely they offered to hire you back."

"I wouldn't work for those doctors again. They were cruel and unfair." Lifting her chin, Keely resumed walking. "I got a job at Safe Harbor. It was a community hospital in those days, before the remodeling. If the top brass now had any idea I'd been arrested for elder abuse, I doubt they'd put up with me."

"But the DA cleared you," Zora responded.

"Dr. Tartikoff hates me. If it weren't for Dr. Brennan…" Keely broke off. "Oh, no!"

She was staring at a boxy brown sedan with bumper stickers that read, Ask Your Doctor—Not Your TV Commercial, Cancer Cures Smoking, and Get Off Your Phone and Drive. The car also sported four flat tires.

"That's yours?"

Keely nodded grimly.

Four flat tires couldn't be a coincidence, Zora thought. "This is vandalism. We should call the police."

Keely shifted for a closer inspection. "They aren't slashed." Her jaw tightened. "Somebody let the air out. It's a nasty prank kids used to do to me in high school."

Keely had been bullied as a teenager, and someone was bullying her again. That aroused Zora's fury, along with her sympathy. "We should at least tell security."

"I'll call the auto club. They'll handle it." Keely swung toward her. "Please don't hold it against me that you have to wait."

"I wouldn't hold it against *you*!" Zora protested. "You're the victim here."

"I appreciate that."

Near the curve where they'd stood talking a moment ago, a motor started and a blue hybrid with a bike rack on top pulled out. It occurred to Zora that the perpetrator of this so-called prank might have lingered to observe—and enjoy—the consequences. "Do you recognize that car?"

"Afraid not."

In the dim light, Zora could see only enough of the driver to be fairly sure it was a man. Then, as the car drove off, she noticed that Keely wasn't the only staff member to display bumper stickers.

The one on the hybrid read, Psychologists Do It on the Couch.

Chapter Eight

"Thanks for calling me," Lucky told Keely after parking his car across from hers in the garage. She'd phoned to alert him to what had happened and asked if he could drive Zora home.

Reclining in Keely's rear seat with the door open, Zora eyed him askance. "You're both very kind, but I'm not a fragile doll."

Not a doll, but more fragile than she was willing to admit, Lucky thought, assessing her swollen calves and the weariness in her gaze. He was tempted to stroke a damp strand of hair from her temple, but her stubborn expression warned him against fussing over her.

"The auto club could take half an hour," Keely responded tartly to Zora. "Meanwhile you're breathing auto fumes. It's bad for the baby."

"She doesn't always exercise the best judgment," Lucky agreed.

"I'm right here! Please refrain from talking about me in the third person," Zora snapped.

Ignoring the complaint, he continued addressing Keely. "I notified security. A guard should be here soon to take a report."

Keely shrugged. "Fine. I have nothing else to do till the auto club arrives, but we can't prove Laird did this."

"Motive plus bumper sticker equals Laird," Lucky replied.

"*We* know that," Zora said. "But who else will believe a psychologist would stoop to such juvenile tricks over being bumped from a room rental?"

"Anyone who heard him squabbling with Keely in the cafeteria." Realizing that his comment might seem insulting, Lucky added, "No offense. I meant that he was the one squabbling."

Keely waved off the apology. "Don't bother softpedaling, Lucky. I'm tough. I butted heads with Dr. Tartikoff and survived, in case you forgot."

"How could anyone forget?" he teased. "You're a hero."

"Heroine," Zora corrected.

"You planning to argue with everything I say?" Lucky didn't mind, though, as long as she was safe. No sooner had he clicked off the call than frightening scenarios had rampaged through his head. What if the vandal had tampered with Keely's brakes and they'd crashed? "Keely, as a precaution, have the auto club tow your car to Phil's Garage to check the brakes and engine. I think they're open till seven."

"And spend my hard-earned money for nothing?" She shook her head. "I doubt the louse would go that far."

"I recommend playing it safe, but it's your decision." Reaching out, Lucky helped Zora rise.

He was glad he'd replaced his old low-slung coupe with a practical black sedan he could drive for years. And which didn't force a pregnant woman to pretzel herself into the front seat.

"All set?" He leaned inside to adjust Zora's seat belt.

A slap on the wrist knocked his arm away. "No touching the merchandise!"

"The seat belts can be tricky." He didn't attempt to assist again, however.

As a rule, Lucky preferred mild-mannered women, but

Zora's peppery manner had its pluses. Never boring, for one thing. Also, no stored-up complaints to be unleashed later. One ex-girlfriend had unloaded on him out of the blue, calling him an arrogant muscle head before breaking off their relationship. Until that evening, Lucky had believed they were doing fine.

Zora didn't hesitate to lob insults at him on the spot. In fact, *arrogant muscle head* was mild by comparison to some of her descriptive phrases. But at least he knew what she thought of him.

Yet despite her feisty spirit, she had a knack for landing in scrapes that begged for a rescue. If he had to move elsewhere for a job, who would show up on a moment's notice? *Somebody* had to take care of her.

As he navigated the curving ramp, Lucky glanced at the resolute mommy-to-be beside him. The full lips, the curving line of her lashes—spicy and sweet, like hot chocolate with a dash of cayenne pepper.

It occurred to him that he hadn't yet updated her on the latest twist to his plan. "Did you hear from the radiology scheduler about working Saturday morning?"

"No. Will I?"

He explained that he'd requested her. "You'll be nearby when the Adamses are here."

"To do what?" Zora demanded. "I doubt I'll get anywhere near them."

"I'd like your insight." Belatedly, he asked, "Do you mind?"

"I suppose not, but next time, ask me first." She flinched as, ahead, a car shot back into the aisle, blocking their path.

Lucky tapped the brake. "I saw it."

"Of course you did."

"You doubt me?"

"Always."

He chuckled. "About the Adamses, you might observe something I miss."

"Seriously?" When they emerged from the garage, lingering daylight glinted off the coppery highlights in her hair. "I thought you considered me a borderline drooling idiot."

"That's a wild exaggeration," he said.

"Which part—the drooling or the idiot?"

"The borderline."

She laughed. "I should have figured."

Heading south on Safe Harbor Boulevard, they crested a coastal bluff. Before them spread the shimmering harbor and adjacent stretch of sand. The arrival of October's cooler weather meant less traffic and smaller beach crowds, a situation Lucky relished.

Growing up, he'd been accustomed to his family's flat, landlocked neighborhood in LA. But after living in Safe Harbor, he'd never be satisfied being far from the expanse of the ocean.

Zora lowered her window. "That sea air smells wonderful."

"Better than exhaust?"

"Thank you for picking me up, if that was a hint." She stretched her shoulders. At this stage of her pregnancy, she ought to have regular massages to ease her discomforts. Lucky nearly volunteered, but the notion of running his hands over her body struck him as dangerously intimate, especially since she was sexy as hell.

"I'll drive you to and from work the rest of the week." He swung left onto Pacific Coast Highway. "Karen can alternate with me, but your hours are more in line with mine. Next week, after Keely moves in, I'll coordinate my schedule with her."

"You sure are bossy," Zora joked.

"Save your grousing for the Sunday meet-up." The residents of Casa Wiggins, as they referred to Karen's house, assembled once a week to review plans and problems.

"Keely will be there, which means I'll have an ally," she said.

"I'm used to you and Anya ganging up on me," Lucky replied calmly. "I can handle it."

"Handle it? You enjoy having women around even if they aren't bowled over by your tats," Zora said.

"That's true. Women share ideas and support each other more than most men do." Living in Casa Wiggins had taught him the value of friendships with the opposite sex. He'd grown up in a predominantly male household, with a strong-minded father and brother. His mom had been quiet by comparison, with a steady, low-key temperament. Lucky wished he'd had a chance to know her as an adult, but he'd lost her, a painful memory he'd rather not dwell on. "So, have you set up the paternity test?"

"None of your business."

He grinned. It felt normal to bicker with Zora. And he was glad she'd agreed to be at Dr. Rattigan's office on Saturday. Whether or not her input proved helpful, he was glad she'd be there.

THROUGHOUT HER SHIFT on Saturday morning, Zora stayed attuned to the activities in the rest of the office. Usually she only paid attention to her patients, but today she noted Lucky's familiar footsteps, registered the steady tone of his voice, and picked up the fact that Vince Adams was late. Very late.

Perhaps he and his wife had abandoned the possibility of a pregnancy under any circumstances, or decided to use a surrogate in San Diego. All of Lucky's planning could be for nothing.

He might have to leave. How would she handle that?

The sight of him at the garage on Tuesday had been far more welcome than Zora had expected. Since then, riding beside him to and from work, she'd been keenly aware of his powerful thigh close to hers and his muscular arms controlling the steering wheel. Fortunately, their habit of verbally poking at each other made it easy to hide her reactions.

Today, they'd arrived together but then separated to attend to their duties. The schedule kept Zora busy with a series of male patients.

During Zora's training, performing scrotal ultrasounds had required considerable getting used to. She had to adjust the patient's penis and scrotum, apply gel and move the paddle to obtain varied views.

During the procedure, the man often stared at the ceiling, responding to her requests as if commanded by a robot. Others cracked jokes to cover their embarrassment during the twenty- to thirty-minute procedure. Occasionally, she encountered a man whose sexual innuendos crept toward harassment. Her crisply professional manner and request for a nurse to observe had always sufficed to dampen the patient's ardor.

Zora preferred it when the wife accompanied her husband, which was the case with her fourth patient of the morning. A thin fellow in his late fifties, he gripped his wife's hand as Dr. Rattigan checked him before departing.

During the sonogram, a booming voice from the hall alerted Zora that Vince had arrived. Why did he trumpet every word? The man behaved as if everyone else, except a select few such as Cole, was not only invisible but also deaf.

Then a door closed and silence fell. Ominous silence. Scary silence.

Suddenly Lucky's faith in her powers of observation seemed ridiculously misplaced. His future and the expansion of the men's fertility program at Safe Harbor might be crashing and burning, and unable to see or hear what was happening, Zora had nothing to contribute. If only she could do *something*.

"How does it look to you?" The patient's question broke into her thoughts.

Instead of dwelling on the obvious fact that she wasn't a doctor, Zora tried diplomacy. "Dr. Rattigan will review the results with you personally. He takes great care with his patients."

"Yes, but..." The man broke off as his wife patted his shoulder. "I can't help worrying."

"We're almost finished," she told him. "Am I hurting you?" The procedure was painless unless the man was especially sensitive. However, asking the question ought to distract him from further inquiries.

"No, no. Thank you."

While she did observe some anomalies in the man's images, Zora wasn't qualified to interpret what they meant. Entering the medical field, she'd dreamed of helping others rather than simply clocking in to a routine job each day. And often, she *did* help them. She hoped that whatever was wrong with this patient could be put right.

The early loss of both her grandparents had inspired her interest in health care. She cherished memories of her mother's parents, who'd adored her and Zady. Unfortunately, they'd smoked, avoided exercise and ignored symptoms of heart and lung disease until it was too late for lifesaving treatments.

Zora didn't hold an exalted position like a surgeon, but she was part of a team that improved people's lives. She wouldn't trade her career for anything.

Once she'd finished the exam, she gently wiped off the conductive gel. "You can resume normal activities immediately."

"I think a leisurely lunch at Salads and More is in order," the wife said. "Don't you, honey?"

"How about Waffle Heaven?"

Their gazes locked. "Papa Giovanni's?" she countered.

"Done," he said.

Zora envied their easy rapport. How wonderful to have a spouse with whom you communicated in shorthand and who stood by you through life's ups and downs. The way Lucky did with her…but that was temporary.

"You may get dressed," she told the patient. "I'll be out of here in a minute."

"No hurry."

As she bent to retrieve a cord, her babies squirmed. Did they sense she was hungry? Pushing the cart out of the room, Zora smiled at the idea that her growling stomach had awakened them.

In the hall, she nearly ran into a bulldog of a man. His powerful frame corded with tension, Vince Adams scowled at the elegant woman beside him. Model thin, Portia Adams wore a svelte pink suit and to-die-for designer shoes. She struck Zora as determined and apprehensive.

Apparently the couple had finished their meeting with the doctor. Most patients avoided private discussions in the hallways, but not these two.

"You call that a compromise?" Vince demanded of his spouse. "I've told you I won't tolerate a surrogate! No stranger will be carrying my children. That's what I have a wife for."

In Portia's smooth face, only her eyes betrayed her fury. "I agreed to hormone injections and egg retrieval," she said in a low voice. "And I want a baby, well, almost as much as you do. But at my age, to take on a possible multiple pregnancy…" She shook her head and let the sentence drift off.

Spotting Zora, the billionaire maintained his glare for an instant before his expression softened. "Excuse me," Zora said, and eased the cart to the side to clear a path.

Instead of picking up the hint to exit, Vince bathed her in a smile. "What a beautiful sight you are, miss. Frankly, I find a pregnant woman's body irresistible."

"Thanks." Zora gritted her teeth, eager to escape.

Vince advanced toward her. "Your husband must be thrilled."

His wife glowered. Her twisting mouth conveyed resentment, but there was also a trace of fear in her eyes. Was she really that afraid of losing her husband?

"I don't..." Zora cleared her throat.

"She isn't married. She lives in that house with Rod," Portia snapped. She and Vince had attended Anya and Jack's wedding there when their daughters—Jack's cousins—had served as flower girls.

"You're not married?" Touching his thumb to Zora's chin, Vince tipped her face up. "The men around here must be blind."

Okay, that's enough taunting of your wife. She stepped back. "I'll remove this cart so you can get past."

"You do that," Portia snarled.

Before Zora could squirm farther away, however, Vince laid a meaty hand on her abdomen. "Boy or girl?"

"One of each." She wished she dared smack his arm.

To her dismay, he caressed her bulge with relish. Enjoying his wife's discomfort, or Zora's? Or both? "They're active little rascals, aren't they?"

Behind him, Lucky appeared. Mercifully, the interruption allowed Zora to break free and dodge behind the ultrasound equipment.

Unfazed, Vince addressed his wife. "Well, honey?"

The threat was unmistakable. If Portia didn't yield to his demands, he'd find a woman who would.

A long breath shuddered out of the socialite. "You don't care about the risk to me? Never mind, I already know the answer."

"You're exaggerating the dangers," her husband retorted. "You're only thirty-nine. Lots of women in their forties have babies."

Lucky intervened politely. "There is an increased risk, Mrs. Adams, but if there are no underlying health issues, it ought to be manageable with careful monitoring. You should discuss that with your doctor."

Her nose wrinkled. "What does a man know? He doesn't have to carry a baby."

Lucky didn't miss a beat. "We have excellent female obstetricians on staff."

Portia gripped her purse. "Do any of them perform in vitro?"

"Several," he said.

Vince faced Zora again. "Who's your doctor, honey?"

"Paige Brennan," she said.

"Dr. Brennan often works with in vitro patients," Lucky added. "You'd find her sympathetic, Mrs. Adams. She underwent fertility treatment herself in order to have her daughter."

That was none of their business, Zora thought. However, Dr. Brennan *had* spoken publicly about that aspect of her medical history.

"And she's married?" This appeared important to Portia. Did she think her husband so lecherous that he'd chase her obstetrician? Of course, he *had* just groped an ultrasound tech.

"Quite happily," Lucky assured her.

Portia gave a reluctant shrug. "I suppose she's acceptable."

Triumphantly, Vince draped an arm over his wife's shoulders. "Well done. Why don't we stay an extra day and attend that charity event you mentioned? I'll buy you a new outfit at South Coast Plaza."

"Not that I'll fit into it for long," his wife muttered, but quickly rallied. "Thank you. I suppose this might work out okay. A baby really will be a lot of fun."

To Lucky, her husband said, "Set up an appointment with Dr. Brennan. My wife can send you her schedule."

"Glad to." Judging by the light in Lucky's eyes, he was barely keeping a lid on his excitement.

While he escorted the wealthy couple to the front, Zora stowed the cart in its closet. On her return, she found Lucky performing a victory dance around the nurses' station. Fortunately for his reputation, there was no one else present.

He beamed at her. "I have no idea how you persuaded them, but you were brilliant."

"I didn't do anything." *Except let him grope my baby bump.* However, Zora supposed that Vince's behavior fell within what many might view as acceptable limits. A lot of people assumed—wrongly—that it was okay to touch a pregnant woman's belly.

"Too bad it's illegal to shoot off fireworks in a doctor's office." With a whoop, Lucky caught her. "We did it!"

Zora's discomfort evaporated. Close to him, she felt safe and sheltered. How easily she could forget everything and everyone, except… "Isn't Dr. Rattigan around?"

"He had to perform emergency surgery." Lucky rubbed his cheek over her hair. "He left right after talking to the Adamses."

"An emergency in urology?" Unlike obstetrics, the specialty rarely dealt with life-or-death situations.

"A patient suffered injuries in a car crash." Lucky mentioned a nearby hospital that handled trauma patients. "The lead surgeon called Dr. Rattigan to assist. Would you stop fidgeting and let me hug you?"

"That's nearly impossible in my shape." But Zora yielded happily as he wedged her against him. How strong he was, yet he held her with a tenderness that almost overwhelmed her.

Zora became acutely aware of his quick breathing. The discovery that she excited him spurred her passion. She floated in the heady scent of his citrus cologne, her nerve endings coming alive.

When Lucky's mouth brushed Zora's, her lips parted.

The flick of his tongue sent rivulets of desire streaming through her, and an answering moan burst from him.

She grabbed his shoulders and lightly rubbed her breasts over his hard chest. The sensations flaring through her were almost painfully intense. Lucky angled her tighter, his hands closing over her derriere.

The urge to bring him inside her, to merge with him, proved irresistible. "Let's find a place to be alone," she began, and then, shifting position, he stumbled.

"Oh, hell!" Lucky caught his balance against the counter, anchoring her against his hip. "Are you all right?"

"Delirious," she murmured.

Drawing in a ragged breath, he studied her in confusion. "We shouldn't be doing this."

"You're right. It's a terrible idea." Clinging to him, Zora didn't mean a word of it. "But as long as we've gone this far…"

"I never expected to get carried away." His thoughts seemed to turn inward. "What's wrong with me?"

"Wrong?" Zora bristled.

"I never lose control this way," Lucky said. "Considering your condition and our situations, I apologize."

"For what?" Oh, why was she torturing herself by prolonging this conversation? Zora wondered. She'd acted impulsively, and clearly Lucky didn't like the way he'd reacted. What a control freak! "Never mind. Forget the whole thing."

"That's a good idea." He sounded as if he was struggling for composure. "That wasn't how a gentleman behaves."

"If you apologize again, I'll slug you."

He laughed, an unexpected rumble that rolled right into her heart. "That's my Zora." A bout of hard breathing reawakened her hope, but he sucked in a lungful of air and held it. "Okay. Better."

"Than what?"

He ignored the question. "Since I inveigled you into working today, let me buy you lunch to celebrate."

Was that his interpretation of what they'd been doing—celebrating? Slapping him would have been totally satisfying. Still, she was starving. Why reject a good meal? "Where did you have in mind?"

"There's a new vegetarian Chinese restaurant I've been meaning to check out."

Zora loved Chinese food. "Do they serve anything besides tofu?"

"Kung pao mushrooms, according to the online menu. Deep fried, with a tangy sauce. And more, I'm sure."

"You're on." The heat in her body hadn't exactly dissipated, but it had faded to her normal pregnancy-enhanced high temperature. As for Lucky, he'd evidently banished whatever desire he'd experienced.

I guess I'm nowhere near close enough to perfection to suit him.

As common sense reasserted itself, Zora recalled his previous comment about her babies. Never mind Lucky's withdrawal from her—he didn't, couldn't and never would accept these babies as his own.

She was glad they'd stopped. Going any further would have been yet another in a long line of mistakes she'd made with men.

Gathering her possessions, she waited until Lucky locked up, and they sauntered out together. Friends again, nothing more.

Which was obviously how they both preferred it.

Chapter Nine

Lucky enjoyed the Sunday meet-ups at Casa Wiggins. He'd learned from his parents, who'd run a small business, that organization was the key to controlling your destiny. In the eight months since the household had formed, the gatherings had enabled the group to stay on track through changes in occupants and in individual situations.

This afternoon, despite his awareness that the future was more of a meandering path with speed bumps than a superhighway, he felt optimistic about his plans. Thanks to whatever diplomacy Zora had exercised toward the Adamses yesterday, all systems appeared to be a go.

Relaxing in his favorite armchair in the den, he sipped white grape juice from a glass. As usual, Rod and Karen had chosen the couch, with their sock-covered feet propped on the worn coffee table. Zora preferred the straight chair, which was easier for a pregnant woman to get in and out of. That left newcomer Keely, who clomped down the staircase to join them.

"Am I late?" she asked. "I had trouble finding the laundry room."

"It's the narrow door next to the garage," Zora said.

"I thought that was a closet."

"Everybody assumes that," Karen assured her. "Don't hesitate to ask where things are."

"You're running laundry already?" Rod fingered his short, graying beard. "You just moved in."

Karen nudged him. "Not our business, dear."

"It's a harmless question."

"I'm a strong believer in hygiene." Crossing the den, Keely lowered her sturdy frame onto the remaining armchair. "How often do we clean and who does what? With a pregnant woman on the premises, we must be vigilant about germs."

Don't tell me she's a germophobe. Lucky rolled his eyes, then caught Zora's stern gaze and subsided.

"We have a rotating schedule. I'll give you a copy," Karen promised. "Feel free to swap chores with anyone who's willing."

"Surely Zora doesn't have to handle chemicals or do heavy work." Keely slid to the edge of her seat, no doubt having discovered that otherwise she sank into the depths of the chair. Lucky decided to ask Karen about replacing the cushion. They maintained a household fund for that sort of thing.

"We have a great system," Rod said. "We chain pregnant women to a wheel in the basement so they generate electrical power."

Keely's jaw dropped.

Zora, who was seated closest to her, murmured, "There is no basement. I handle dusting and other light chores."

Their newest housemate nodded. "I forgot that Dr. Vintner is famous for joking."

"Dr. Vintner? Anytime you see me with my shoes off, you can call me by my first name." Rod wiggled his sock-clad toes on the coffee table.

Karen presented a few more house rules, such as putting snack plates and cups in the dishwasher rather than accumulating them in the sink. "And no sticking them in the oven because you're in a hurry," she tossed in Zora's direction.

"Anya and I only did that once," she replied cheerfully. "It's not our fault someone turned on the oven without checking if there was anything inside."

"Oh, dear." Keely clutched her hands together. "What if I do things wrong?"

"We'll toss you out," Rod replied.

"Where would I go?" To Lucky's astonishment, Keely regarded Rod in dismay. The woman needed to develop a sense of humor.

Zora reached over to pat the newcomer's hand. "You'll get used to our silliness. Are you still upset about what happened on Tuesday? That must have thrown you off balance."

The older nurse's head bobbed. What had happened on Tuesday? Lucky had to search his memory before he dredged it up. "You mean that nasty prank with your tires? What's the connection?"

"She was bullied in school," Zora said fiercely. "I understand what it's like to be an outsider. Keely, nobody will bully you in this house. If they do, we'll toss *them* out."

"You bet," Karen affirmed.

"I'll cheer while Lucky does the physical tossing," Rod said.

"No problem." Lucky was pleased when Keely responded with a smile.

What a spirited defense Zora had mounted, he thought. As for that outsider business, he bore a share of the responsibility for being tough on Zora. When she first arrived at the house, he'd considered her a heartless predator who'd hurt Stacy. Gradually, he'd forgiven her, and since she'd stood up to Andrew, he'd come to respect her. As for her empathy toward Keely, that demonstrated her kind heart.

The doorbell rang. "I'll get it." With unaccustomed speed, Rod hurried to the door. Lucky heard low voices and then caught a heavenly whiff of garlic, tomato sauce and cheese.

Rod returned toting three large pizzas. "My treat. This will be my atonement for cracking jokes at Keely's expense."

"Three pizzas?" the nurse replied in astonishment. "That's too much for five people."

"Don't you like leftovers?" Lucky asked.

"And it *is* Sunday," Karen said. "People might drop by."

"I'll set out the paper plates and stuff." Rod was definitely acting out of character today—for a reason, as Lucky knew.

To distract Keely, and also because he cared about the answer, Lucky said, "I've been wondering about the timetable for the in vitro process. It's not a situation Dr. Rattigan and I usually deal with. We have a patient who might be affected."

"I'm happy to answer, but are we finished discussing house rules?" The dark-haired woman glanced from him to Zora to Karen.

"Yes, unless you have more questions," Karen said. "Don't let Lucky rush you."

"I'm fine. Is everyone interested in hearing about in vitro?"

"I am," Zora said. She, too, was probably wondering how long it might take before Portia and Vince saw results.

Keely launched into a spiel that she must have heard Dr. Brennan deliver to patients a hundred times. "Depending on the phase of the woman's cycle when you begin, the whole process can take about a month."

"Fantastic." Noting her puzzled reaction, Lucky quickly added, "Go on."

With increasing confidence, she complied.

ZORA LISTENED ATTENTIVELY, though that was partly for Keely's sake—the other woman obviously craved reassurance that she belonged here. The subject matter was familiar to her, but she wanted a clearer picture of how things might progress for the Adamses.

The first stage, Keely noted, was the administration of medication to stimulate the ovaries, almond-size glands that flanked the uterus. Normally, only one or two eggs matured each month, but drugs could produce the simultaneous maturing of multiple eggs. This improved the chances of harvesting and fertilizing enough viable eggs.

Keely was explaining step two, harvesting, when the doorbell rang again. From the table at the farthest part of the den, Rod plummeted toward the front door. No one attempted to rise; if they had, he'd have bowled them over.

A creak of the door, and excited, girlish voices filled the air.

"Daddy!"

"Grandma Helen, give Daddy the cake before you drop it."

"I'm not that decrepit," responded the dry voice of their grandmother.

"I'll get it." Lucky, who'd ordered the cake, went to join the new arrivals.

Until yesterday, the plan had been for the Adamses to return to San Diego that same day. However, Portia had been lobbying to stay over at a hotel so she and Vince could attend an exclusive charity concert and reception tonight, and in his expansive mood, he'd agreed. Helen Pepper had promptly called her former son-in-law to inform Rod that she and the girls could join the household for dinner tonight.

As long as they were having guests, Lucky had decided this was a good chance to show their new roommate what a great group she'd joined. Zora couldn't wait to see her reaction to the cake honoring Keely's birthday.

"I smell pizza!" cried thirteen-year-old Tiffany Adams, her red braids bouncing on her shoulders. "Ooh, where are my manners? Hi, everybody. Zora, you're *huge*!"

"The twins have grown since August." Last summer,

Rod's daughters had visited often, since their parents had rented a beach house nearby while Vince underwent surgery.

Eleven-year-old Amber followed shyly. "Have you picked names?" she asked Zora.

"Not yet."

"Gee, they brought dessert." Grinning, Lucky carried in a castle-shaped pink box bearing the logo of the Cake Castle. "Is somebody having a birthday?" No one responded. "Or did someone have a birthday last weekend?" he asked with feigned innocence.

Keely shook her head. "You don't mean me, do you?"

"Hmm. Let's check."

As Lucky passed Zora, she studied his physique appreciatively. His tattoos and muscular build used to remind her of her stepfather, a foul-mouthed ex-gangbanger. Now, she knew that Lucky was nothing like that loser. In fact, as yesterday's encounter had proved, she found him tantalizingly attractive.

Last night, she'd lain awake, her brain defiantly replaying the incident. What if he hadn't stumbled? How far would they have gone? At this stage of pregnancy, making love wasn't wise. Just as importantly, if he'd repeated his insistence afterward on holding out for Ms. Perfect, she'd never have forgiven him.

It was fortunate for Zora's sanity and their friendship that they'd stopped. If only her dreams would quit defying her common sense. But then, where a man was concerned, this was familiar territory.

Carefully, Lucky opened the box to reveal the cake. "It says, 'Happy 50th Birthday, Kelly.' Doggone it! I spelled 'Keely' for them twice!"

The amazement on Keely's face touched Zora's heart. "It's for me?" She approached the table and stared at the icing inscription. "But being fifty isn't worth celebrating. I'm over the hill."

"You consider fifty old?" The girls' grandmother patted Keely's shoulder with an arthritic hand. "My fifties were my best years. Still, I don't mind growing older, not when it means watching these darling girls grow up."

When Zora reached fifty, she reflected, she'd have twenty-year-old twins. For a second, she visualized them with dark hair and smooth olive skin, like Lucky. But of course, they'd either have her reddish hair or Andrew's blond coloring.

Amber joined the small group around the cake. "It's beautiful. I want a rainbow on my next birthday cake, too."

Tiffany took out her cell phone. "I'll snap a picture so we don't forget."

"Hang on, honey." Rod caught his daughter's wrist. "You said Vince snoops through your stuff, right?"

"Oh, rats." The girl scowled. "He'll demand the details of who it was for and where we saw it."

"He's mean." Amber's frown mirrored her sister's.

Keely looked puzzled. "I don't understand."

"I'll explain while we eat," Rod said.

Over pizza, they filled in the story of how Vince had wrested his stepdaughters from the man who'd raised them and attempted to banish Rod from their lives.

"Surely the Adamses must suspect that they visit Dr. Vintner." Keely had chosen a tight spot at the table's corner, declining the place of honor toward which the others had tried to direct her.

"They sort of know but pretend they don't," Amber said. "I'm sure Mom has an idea."

"It's like a game," Tiffany put in.

"Despite the satisfaction of flipping them the bird, we shouldn't be forced to sneak around." Rod spoke from the head of the table, the seat Keely had bypassed. "I spent my life's savings fighting that man in court."

"If you run into Mr. or Mrs. Adams, please don't mention that you met their daughters," Karen told Keely.

The nurse swallowed a bite of food. "I won't. I promise."

Lucky met Zora's gaze. They were both thinking the same thing, she gathered: that it was fortunate Karen had issued the warning before Portia became Paige Brennan's patient. Keely would be running into her often.

"The girls might be in town more often now that my daughter's trying for another baby," Helen observed.

"Mom and Vince plan to rent a beach cottage again, closer to the medical center," Tiffany filled in.

"What about your education?" Rod asked. "You'll have to switch schools."

"I don't mind," Amber answered. "The kids at my school are snotty."

"Besides, private schools bend over backward to accommodate you if your parents give a big donation." Tiffany's cynical attitude bothered Zora until the girl said, "Oh, yeah, and Mom and Vince promised a gift to the animal shelter here, because it's our pet project."

"Pet project?" Rod waggled an eyebrow.

"Tiffany made a pun!" Amber giggled.

"And you volunteer there, Dad," his older daughter said. "It'll be cool for Vince to be funding *your* favorite charity without realizing it."

Zora wondered how Vince would treat his future genetic child or children. And how would he behave toward his stepdaughters? Perhaps he'd mellow out. She doubted it, though.

After wiping her hands on a napkin, Zora rested them on her bulge. Thinking about daddies reminded her that Andrew had had his blood drawn on Wednesday. The results might arrive by the end of the week, not that she had any doubts about them.

"Let's cut the cake." Tiffany jumped up to clear the table.

They'd polished off the better part of two pizzas, with leftovers to stock the fridge. Karen, with her usual efficiency, would jot on the cardboard box the number of slices allocated to each resident. Despite occasional carping in the early days—accustomed to living with other guys, Lucky had pushed for the first-come-first-served approach—they'd found that this method maintained the peace.

Karen produced birthday candles, which Lucky lit using a strand of spaghetti in lieu of the fireplace torch they'd misplaced. Then they sang, lustily if raggedly, a round of "Happy Birthday."

Keely stood with hands clasped and eyes sparkling. As they finished amid cheers, she sniffed. "I can't believe you guys did this."

"You're part of the family now," Karen said.

"Hurray for Keely!" added Tiffany, who hadn't had a clue to the woman's identity until today.

Amber sidled up to the newcomer and took her hand. "Being fifty sounds good. I bet nobody bosses you around."

Too choked up to speak, Keely nodded.

Rod did the honors, at Karen's request. "This is as close as I get to performing surgery," the anesthesiologist said as he divided the cake. "Keely, which piece do you prefer?"

"Take the one with the rainbow roses on it," Amber advised.

The nurse bestowed a quavering smile on the youngster. "If you recommend it."

"I do."

Across from her, Zora watched Lucky beam at the cozy tableau. He was deriving as much joy from the situation as if they'd thrown *him* a surprise birthday party. What a natural father he'd make.

Whenever he found the perfect time and the perfect woman.

THAT WEEK, KEELY, Karen and Lucky alternated providing rides for Zora. Since Rod's unreliable car was in the shop, he tagged along, too. That led to hilariously nonsensical discussions, and kept Zora from feeling that she was imposing too heavily on her friends.

On Friday, the radiology scheduler assigned her to the same-day surgery unit on the fourth floor of the hospital. Busy with clients, Zora only glanced at her phone in rare free moments in case of urgent voice messages or texts. There was one asking her to call Keely, which she presumed meant a change in whoever was driving home from work.

During her break that afternoon, Zora headed for the fourth-floor staff lounge, eager to put her feet up and answer messages. Waddling around a corner, she nearly collided with her ex-mother-in-law. Her hand shot out to the wall for support.

"Sorry." Betsy braced as if preparing to catch her. "Are you okay?"

"Sure." Zora removed her hand. "I, uh, don't usually see you here." The nursing supervisor's office was on the fifth floor, although Betsy's duties might take her anywhere in the building.

"I was looking for you." The older woman walked with her toward the lounge. "Radiology said you were on this floor today. Can we talk?"

Zora occasionally chatted with Betsy about crocheting or mutual acquaintances when they ran into each other, but the older woman didn't usually single her out this way. "Is there a problem?"

"Hold on." Opening the lounge door, Betsy scanned the interior. It was empty, Zora saw. The vending machines and kitchenette appeared in pristine condition, no doubt tidied since lunch. "Good. We're alone."

Why was that good?

Zora settled on a couch. Without asking, the older woman brought her a cup of herbal tea from a machine.

"You ought to stay hydrated," Betsy said from an adjacent chair. "In fact, you should be on maternity leave."

"I'm saving as much of my time as possible for after the twins are born." Zora hoped she could hold out another few weeks.

"You don't have to go through this alone." Betsy's green eyes, augmented by her spectacles, zeroed in on her. "I wish you'd felt comfortable confiding in me, although I understand your reluctance."

"Andrew told you that he's the father?" He must have received the lab results of the paternity test today.

"Yes, he did." Worry lines deepened in Betsy's square face. "That's why I wanted to talk with you. I believe you ought to hear his plans."

He was up to something already? With a sinking sensation, Zora conceded that she should have expected this. She sighed. "Hit me with it."

Chapter Ten

Trying not to panic while Betsy gathered her thoughts, Zora stretched out along the couch. As usual, she'd been floating on what Lucky had once termed the river of denial. She hadn't bothered to consult her attorney to prepare for Andrew's stratagems, such as ducking child support payments. She'd let matters drift, while he'd apparently prepared a trap.

Betsy spread her hands in dismay. "There's no way to soften this. He might sue for custody."

"What?" Zora would have bolted to her feet except that she was long past the ability to bolt anywhere. "How ridiculous! He doesn't want the kids." More objections tumbled through her mind. "And since Lin walked out, who does he think would care for them on the wildly improbable chance that he won the court battle?"

"Me," her ex-mother-in-law said. "He asked me to raise the babies. I guess he assumed I'd leap at the chance, because he knows how much I would love grandchildren."

Zora stared at her, stunned. Never in her most bizarre dreams could she have concocted such a scheme. Finally she found her voice. "You told him no, right?"

"Without a moment's hesitation."

"Can you please explain what he was thinking?"

Betsy rolled her eyes. Zora didn't recall ever seeing her ex-mother-in-law do that before. "I long ago gave up on understanding my son. Sadly, he takes after his father. In case you don't remember Rory very well, my ex is a total narcissist."

"He seemed distant." As a teenager, Zora didn't recall exchanging more than superficial greetings with Andrew's father. When she and her old flame reconnected ten years later, his parents had divorced.

Rory hadn't attended their wedding, a lovely ceremony followed by a reception she'd rather forget. Zora's mother had drunk too much, waxed maudlin about her baby girl, then vomited on the buffet table.

"I asked Andrew why the hell—excuse me, heck—he'd sue for custody," Betsy said. "He claimed you'd tricked him into fathering kids just so you could hit him up for support, and he doesn't plan to let you win. His words, not mine."

The man had incredible nerve. "He lied to me about reconciling so he could seduce me. That's how I got pregnant." Embarrassment heated Zora's cheeks. "I was naive. The fact that he didn't bother with protection struck me as a sign that he was serious, because we'd been trying to have kids. I had no idea until later that he'd had a vasectomy and believed he was sterile." Then she realized what she'd revealed. "I'm sorry to drop that on you."

"Oh, my son already did," Betsy said wryly. "He was almost gleeful as he informed me these are the only grandchildren I'll ever have. He failed to grasp that I can be their grandmother without depriving them of their mom."

Betsy was running a risk by bringing Zora the truth—she might offend her son and she had no guarantee Zora would grant her access to the kids. "Of course you're their grandmother. I'd love for you to be part of my children's lives, and mine, too."

The other woman glowed with relief. "I've always felt as if you were my daughter."

"Me, too." In high school, Zora had often relied on

Betsy for comfort and advice, since she couldn't trust her own mom. A rush of happiness ran through her, to be on intimate terms with Betsy again.

"I doubt any court in California would hand my son sole custody," Betsy added. "If you need me to testify about how unfit he is, just say the word."

Zora swallowed hard. "You're a saint."

"Oh, I have my faults." With a quirk of the eyebrow, the grandmother-to-be inquired, "To change the subject, I've been wondering—have you picked names?"

Suddenly, Zora had an answer. Half of one, anyway. "The girl will be Elizabeth."

Betsy's eyes widened. "For me?"

"Absolutely." Also, Zora liked that name.

"Count on me as your number one babysitter." The nursing supervisor appeared about to explode with joy. "Do me a favor, would you?"

"Sure. What?"

"Don't name the boy Andrew." Quickly, Betsy added, "Not to deprive my son. It's because being a junior can cause confusion."

"Understood." The reason scarcely mattered; Zora wouldn't name her little boy Andrew for a million dollars. Well, maybe a million. And then she'd use a nickname.

Outside in the hall, she heard light footsteps approaching. In midafternoon, there hadn't been much traffic in this wing. Same-day surgeries were conducted early enough for patients to recover by late afternoon, and most were still recuperating at this hour.

Zora glanced at her watch. "Sounds like we're about to have company, and I'm due to see a patient."

"If you need help arranging for leave, let me know."

"Thanks, but..."

The door opened and a woman peered in, reddish-brown hair rioting around her head. "Excuse me. I'm supposed to be interviewing with Dr. Davis on the fourth floor but I can't find his..."

Utter and total silence fell over the lounge. Because the face looking back at Zora was her own.

FOR LUCKY, FRIDAY afternoons could be crammed with last-minute patients or, like today, extremely light. Cole had accepted several extra surgeries and ordered him to reschedule office appointments.

Since Keely had to work late, Lucky was happy to switch their arrangement and drive Zora home, but she wasn't answering her phone. Not unusual—she might be with patients. After determining that she'd been assigned to the same-day surgery unit, he decided to grab a snack at the cafeteria and stop by the fourth floor to try to catch her in a free moment.

Emerging from the stairs, he had a moment of disorientation when he spotted her down the hall. Why was Zora wearing street clothes, and— Wait a minute—what had happened to her pregnancy?

Then he remembered that Dr. Davis was in town to interview nurse candidates and find a place to live. He'd be joining the staff at the beginning of November, a few weeks from now. Zady, one of the nurses slated for an interview, must have been confused about which fourth floor was involved—she'd gone to the hospital instead of the office next door.

"Miss Moore?" Lucky didn't like to shout, but she failed to hear him. Instead, with no nurses' station in sight, she headed for the next best thing, the staff lounge.

After opening the door, she stood frozen, her shoulders rigid. A warning bell rang in Lucky's head.

Standing behind the slender figure with hair a shade lighter than Zora's, he peered inside. Sure enough, staring at Zady with her mouth open was the shocked face of his housemate.

From the recesses of his suddenly sluggish brain, Lucky dredged up the words, "I can explain." But before they reached his vocal cords, a third woman spoke from the side.

"What a pleasure to run into you, Zady." Betsy Raditch, he realized, must have met Zora's twin when the girls were teens.

While she and Zady exchanged greetings, Lucky tried wafting apologetic vibes in Zora's direction, but she ignored him. It hadn't occurred to him the sisters might come face-to-face today. In the event that Zady landed the job, he'd assumed there'd be plenty of time for him to break the news once it was no longer a matter of confidence.

He wondered what issues had separated the sisters. If someone unexpectedly threw him together with his brother, there'd be hell to pay. But their split had occurred under unusually traumatic circumstances.

He snapped to attention, hearing Zady say she was in search of Dr. Davis's office. "That's on the fourth floor of the building next door," he said.

"Dr. Davis?" Betsy's forehead wrinkled. "Oh, the new urologist. I heard you were vetting the nurse candidates, Lucky."

Two pairs of large gray eyes fixed on him. "You must be Mr. Mendez," Zady said.

Zora mouthed the formal name—*Mr. Mendez?*—and grimaced.

He'd have to wait until later to provide the details of his involvement. "I'll escort you," he told Zady, adding for Zora's benefit, "I'm driving you home today. Keely has to stay late."

"Fine," she growled. Since he'd brought her in this morning, she knew where he'd parked his car.

The twins regarded each other hesitantly. "I don't understand why—" Zady began.

"What're you doing—" Zora started.

They paused, radiating mistrust. But something else too, Lucky thought. Hope, perhaps?

"You ladies should talk," Betsy said. "But right now, I gather there are people waiting. Do you have each other's phone numbers?"

Both heads shook. While they input the numbers in their mobiles, Zady said, "I'm staying at the Harbor Suites. Let's meet when you finish work." She provided her room number.

"I don't mind driving you over there," Lucky put in, although he didn't expect to receive any thanks.

"Okay." To her twin, Zora said, "Good luck with the interview, I guess."

"Yeah, thanks. I guess."

Lucky accompanied Zady to the elevator. In answer to her query, he said he was one of Zora's housemates, which seemed to puzzle her even more.

She had a lot of questions, including why Zora was renting a room in a house instead of living with her husband. Lucky told her he'd leave that for her sister to answer.

How strange that Zady didn't know her twin was divorced. But then, he had no idea whether his brother was married or had kids, or what Matthew had been doing these past sixteen years. The only cousin with whom Lucky kept in touch diplomatically avoided the subject.

Occasionally, Lucky had considered searching online to scope out Matthew's status, but that risked arousing old fury and resentment. Better to let sleeping dogs lie. He'd fought hard to regain his equilibrium after his brother lined up the rest of the family against him. Now that he'd found a second home among friends, why revisit the past?

Unlike Lucky, these sisters had a mother with whom Zora was in contact, and Zady probably was, too. Why hadn't she passed along vital information such as Zora's marital status?

Lucky expected to learn more in due time. Although he might catch a scolding from Zora during the drive, it would be worth it.

AFTER ZADY DEPARTED, Zora struggled with a wave of bewilderment and regret. Had it really been nine years since they'd fought? Her outrage had long ago dissipated. But according to Mom, Zady did nothing but boast about her happy marriage and loving children while dropping snide remarks about Zora. Yet if Zady was content, why did she want to leave Santa Barbara? And why apply for a job at the medical center where Zora worked?

Betsy broke the silence. "I know you two are estranged, but I've never heard why. Granted, it's none of my business. Still, I noticed during high school that whenever I saw the two of you laughing and having fun together, the next thing I heard, you were fighting. I hope you've outgrown that."

Zady used to play nasty tricks on Zora, after which she not only feigned innocence but leveled accusations at *her*. It would be childish to dredge that up, however. "A lot of siblings fight."

"I can't speak from experience. My brother was much older, more like an uncle, and I only had one child." Betsy arose. "You have a patient scheduled?"

"Oh, that's right!" She'd forgotten to watch the clock.

"I hope you'll talk to your attorney about Andrew," Betsy added.

"I will." After a quick hug, Zora departed, her mind buzzing with the latest developments.

Good thing she'd have Lucky to review them with after work. Right after she read him the riot act.

ON THE SECOND level of the garage, Zora approached the familiar black sedan where Lucky was comfortably ensconced, apparently listening to music. On the sloped ramp, she paused to observe him.

With his dark coloring and dramatic cheekbones, Lucky had drawn her attention as soon as he'd started working at Safe Harbor, about a year after she had. While she'd considered him handsome, he wasn't her type, and she'd been married to Andrew.

Later, when Cole fell in love with Stacy, loyalty to his doctor—although Cole had never indicated any animosity toward Zora—had turned Lucky into her fiercest critic. She'd refused to let him scare her out of moving into Karen's house, however, and over the past months, he'd changed.

When he'd reviewed the nurses' applications for Dr. Davis, why had he chosen her twin as a finalist—to create trouble? Surely he hadn't eliminated more qualified applicants for Zady's sake, though. Perhaps she simply deserved to be considered.

"Oh, good, I caught you." Rod's voice yanked her from her reflections. "My transmission's on the fritz again. Blast that car. I'm definitely trading it in."

"Hi, Rod." He must have received Lucky's permission to join them—how else would he know the car's location? Zora mused as they strolled side by side to the car. "We have a stop en route," she informed the anesthesiologist. "My sister and I are having a, well, touchy reunion."

"Fine with me." He opened the rear door for her. Inside, the blare of country music cut off. "I'd offer to sit in the back but it's safer for you to be there."

"Thanks." Zora hefted her body inside.

"I'll drop you at the Harbor Suites," Lucky said from the front. The one-bedroom suites rented by the day or week. "I'll pick you up again after I take Rod home."

"That's a lot of driving," Zora said.

"It's ten minutes in each direction." Rod closed her door

and hopped into the front, adjusting his fedora to avoid it bumping the roof.

Lucky put the car into reverse. Although tempted to ask why he'd approved her sister as a potential colleague, Zora wasn't keen on reviewing the whole business in front of Rod.

Fortunately, he was preoccupied with the latest developments concerning his daughters. Helen had reported that the girls were starting at their new school next week, and that Vince had insisted both of them play soccer, which Tiffany hated.

When the youngster begged to study dance instead, her stepfather had said he was tired of her complaints. He planned to send her to boarding school in Switzerland when she entered high school the following autumn.

"Her mother doesn't bother to defend her," Rod said angrily. "If the girls are too much trouble to have around, they should let me raise them."

"Not much chance of that, is there?" Lucky observed.

"I wish there were. Karen would welcome them. They can have my room." Rod and Karen had begun spending nights together in her master suite.

Vince would never let go of anything he considered his, Zora reflected. The thought of the billionaire sent a shiver through her. The memory of him groping her abdomen repulsed her. Well, he'd accomplished his goal of arousing his wife's jealousy, and hopefully that was the end of that.

They pulled into the parking lot in front of the Harbor Suites. Among the vehicles, she spotted license plates from neighboring states: Arizona, Oregon, Utah, Nevada. Patients undergoing fertility treatments often rented rooms here.

Lucky halted in front of the office. "You want me to stay? If you're worried, I will."

What a sweet offer. "I'll be fine."

"If we hear screaming, we'll turn around," Rod joked.

After Zora got out, Lucky lowered his window. "I'll pick up food on my way back."

Why was he acting so nice? In self-defense, Zora supposed. "Chinese would be good. Or Italian."

"Okay."

Despite her brave words, dread filled Zora as the car drove off. Years of silence between her and Zady loomed in front of her like an abyss.

Still, she was curious about her sister's situation, she conceded as she followed a sidewalk between the one-story buildings. And if Zady ended up at Safe Harbor, they'd have to reach an accord sooner or later.

Halfway across the grassy courtyard, past a few squatty palm trees, Zora spotted the room number Zady had given her earlier. Taking a deep breath, she knocked on her sister's door.

Chapter Eleven

Inside, footsteps rushed across the carpet. Zora's pulse sped up as the door opened and she stared into a face at the same height as hers, a face that mirrored hers, from the freckles to the wary expression.

A memory sprang up. For their senior prom, they'd accidentally bought the same dress and, after a horrified moment, they'd dissolved into laughter. Rather than quibble about who should return the gown, they'd coordinated the rest of their outfits, as well. Their classmates had assumed they'd deliberately picked matching dresses and shoes, while they'd confounded their mother. It had been rare fun.

"Hi." Zady moved aside, admitting her to an austere living room furnished with a nondescript sofa and reproductions of seascapes on the walls.

Zora noted a can of soup in the kitchenette next to the microwave. If that was her sister's idea of dinner, Zady was either on a diet or short of money. Well, according to their mother, her sister had three children, enough to strain any budget.

"Let's get one thing straight." Zady's words sounded rehearsed.

"What's that?"

"If Dr. Davis offers the job, I'm accepting it."

It hadn't occurred to Zora to suggest otherwise. "That's fine. I won't beat around the bush, either."

"Okay." Hands clenched, Zady waited by the couch.

Ignoring the sofa, Zora chose a hard chair. "Regardless of what Mom may have claimed, here are the facts. Right before Andrew and I finalized our divorce, I slept with him because I believed he still loved me. Then he married his new girlfriend. Now I'm pregnant with twins, which I plan to keep."

Zady dropped onto the couch, eyes wide. "You're divorced? Mom said your husband dotes on you. Takes you on luxury cruises, showers you with jewelry—I'll admit, it didn't sound like the Andrew I remember from high school, but—you're carrying twins? Are they identical?"

"No. A boy and a girl."

"That's good. Maybe they won't hate each other."

The remark brought an unexpected pang. "Do you hate me?" Zora asked.

"No, I assumed…" Zady broke off.

Although Zora was dying to learn more about her sister's feelings, first things first. "Why did you apply to Safe Harbor? What about your husband and kids—are they moving here?"

"Dwayne and I never married." Zady kicked off her low-heeled pumps. "And I don't have kids, unless you count his three obnoxious children who treat me as their personal maid."

The world was shifting on its axis. "Are you still living with him?"

"No." Her twin didn't look up, apparently fascinated by her stocking-clad feet. "He's like Dad, forever cheating."

"So is Andrew!"

"And I was too stubborn and proud to admit it until he forced my hand."

"Me, too."

They regarded each other across the coffee table. Zora could almost have laughed, except the situation was pathetic.

"You didn't finish your story," Zady said. "Since Mom obviously lied about everything, I'd like to hear the truth. She said Andrew sought you out during his first marriage because he'd never stopped loving you. Is that right?"

"No. We bumped into each other at our high school reunion. Wish you'd been there."

"Are you kidding? I was too embarrassed about my situation with Dwayne. Go on."

Zora poured out the tale of how Andrew had dumped Stacy, then cheated on Zora. "In high school, you told me he sneaked around with other girls," she recalled. "I'm sorry I accused you of being jealous."

"And I'm sorry I didn't listen when you warned me that Dwayne was a jerk."

"I guess I did." With all that had happened since, Zora had forgotten that she'd tried to steer her sister away from him. She'd had more sense about Zady's choices than her own.

"You were right not to trust him." Zady waved her hands in a gesture Zora recognized, because she did it herself when agitated. "Not only didn't he marry me, Dwayne refused to have kids. He stuck me with his unholy brood during their vacations, claiming I should learn to love my 'stepchildren.' He used the free time to play around. I closed my eyes to it, until his new girlfriend got pregnant."

"How did he react to that?"

"Oh, he's excited about being a proud papa again." Bitterness laced Zady's voice. "I wouldn't count on it lasting, if I were her."

"Andrew didn't refuse to have children with me," Zora said. "We were trying for a pregnancy before he met, well, *her*. I stopped taking birth control pills during our last year together, but nothing happened until after we separated."

"Hmm…that timing is weird." Zady frowned.

"I agree, but it's not as if he tricked me while we were married. I'd have noticed if he was wearing a condom."

"If I've learned anything, it's that a manipulative jerk will do stuff you'd never dream of."

"Maybe, but I can't imagine how..." Zora stopped. "Oh, Lord, you're right. I may have just figured it out."

"What?" Her sister leaned forward.

Zora smacked herself in the forehead. "After I stopped taking the birth control pills, he claimed he threw them out. I was touched. But what if he crushed them into my food?"

"For an entire year?"

"There was a three-month supply in the drawer." He'd become solicitous about her diet, preparing breakfast to be sure she ate properly for their future children. "As my husband, he'd have had no problem refilling the prescription."

"But a year's a long time." Zady appeared both disgusted and fascinated.

"He went out of town on occasion," Zora conceded. "But we weren't having sex during his absences, either. And I marked our wall calendar with what I assumed were my most fertile days. I was frustrated when he always claimed to be exhausted after he got back from a trip right when we should have been making love. I should have suspected something."

"What a lot of trouble. He could have sneaked off and had a vasectomy without telling you," Zady said. "The scar's usually very small."

Zora threw up her hands—just as her sister had done moments earlier, she realized. "Why be straightforward when you can be manipulative? Andrew enjoyed playing games and tricking people. Or I could be wrong about this."

"I'm sure it must be illegal to dose a person with prescription medication without her consent," Zady added.

"That wouldn't bother Andrew." Nothing could be proven now, Zora supposed, even though the scenario explained a lot about Andrew's behavior. "Well, eventually he did have a vasectomy, but he assumed his sperm count was zero after a month. Now he's attempting to punish me for demanding child support."

"How?"

She described the plot to sue for custody and persuade his mother to raise the kids. "Betsy gave me all the details earlier today."

"That's what you were discussing in the lounge?" Zady slapped the coffee table. "How could we have fallen for such jerks? Why didn't we tell them to go to hell a whole lot sooner?"

"Gullibility. Love," Zora assessed. "And pride. Mom kept bragging about how perfect your life was."

"I cried on her shoulder practically every week. And she regaled me with stories of how happy you were." Zady blushed. "I couldn't give up on Dwayne because I refused to let you win."

"I felt the same way." Zora winced at how easily they'd been maneuvered. "How long do you think she's been lying to us?"

"Since we were born?"

Zora recalled Betsy's observation. "You're right. Whenever we had fun together, you could count on something happening to mess it up."

"Such as you borrowing my new sweater and ruining it." That incident had triggered their final blowup while they were in college. The squabble over a minor transgression had deteriorated into cross accusations and name calling. Soon afterward, Zady had left town with Dwayne.

"I didn't touch your sweater," Zora said. Had their mother really stooped that low? Obviously, yes. "You didn't borrow my earrings and lose one, either, did you?"

"No." Zady buried her face in her hands, then peeked between her fingers. "How sick, that she was jealous of her own children being close."

"Mom destroyed your sweater and my earrings so we'd fight." Zora struggled to grasp how cruel that had been.

"She always had to be the center of attention," Zady noted.

"That's why we were sitting ducks for Andrew and Dwayne," Zady said. "We grew up being manipulated."

"Imagine how she'll react when she learns we're on good terms again." Zady blew out a long breath. "She'll do anything to split us up."

"Let's not tell her." As she spoke, Zora could almost hear Lucky coaching her in the background, urging her to avoid her old traps by changing her behavior.

"How can we avoid it?"

"If we confront her, she'll start scheming," Zora pointed out. "We should say as little as possible to her."

A smile lit Zady's face. "That'll drive her crazy."

"Exactly."

"But if I land the job at Safe Harbor, she'll realize we must be talking," Zady said.

"We can say we only see each other around the building. End of story."

"She'll interrogate her old friends who live here."

"If she has any, they won't know anything." Zora's only contact from her mother's generation was Betsy, who was too smart to play those games.

"Wow." Zady regarded her in admiration. "That's both simple and diabolical."

"Let's function as a team. Full disclosure about everything."

"Done!"

Across the coffee table, they high-fived each other. For nearly ten years, Zora had been missing part of herself. "I'm only sorry it took us this long to come together. I'm glad my kids will have an aunt."

"Me, too." Zady regarded Zora's bulge wistfully. "How

will you raise them alone? If I'm living here, I'll pitch in, but I'll be working all day, too."

"There's day care at the hospital. And I have friends." Zora would be lost without her supportive household. "They've already raised money for a part-time nanny." Her phone buzzed with a text. Glancing down, she saw Lucky's message. "And there's my ride, waiting out front."

"Is that Mr. Mendez?" Longing shaded Zady's expression. "He's very kind. And he admires you, I can tell."

This was interesting news. "Did he say so?"

Her sister shook her head. "Not specifically. It's the way he looks at you, and how he avoided revealing too much about your situation while he walked me to the office building. He was protecting you."

"As a friend." Yet what if it meant more? Was it possible Lucky was falling in love with her, too? But he'd never abandon his ideal scenario, let alone agree to raise Andrew's children. "I shouldn't keep him waiting."

"Of course not."

Rising, Zady held out her hand to boost Zora. Then they flung their arms around each other.

"We're back," Zady crowed. "Twins forever!"

No more allowing others to separate them. "I hope, hope, hope you get the job."

"Me, too."

Amazement filled Zora as she eased out of the suite and along the path. How wonderful it would be to have family in town, especially the person who ought to be closest to her.

She couldn't wait to share their conversation with Lucky.

AS THE OCTOBER darkness gathered, Lucky drummed his fingers on the steering wheel. He had no idea what to expect from Zora—complaints? Fury? But his tension also derived from another matter.

Rod's complaints on the drive home had reminded him that Vince and Portia were barreling ahead on their pregnancy project. Once his wife had yielded, the billionaire hadn't wasted a moment. Since his treatment needed to be coordinated with hers, Lucky was able to follow their efforts.

After reviewing Portia's up-to-date medical records and confirming that she was in excellent health, Dr. Brennan had started her on medication to adjust her cycle. Once her eggs ripened, Dr. Rattigan would remove sperm from Vince's testes. Then her eggs would be harvested and injected with her husband's sperm.

Despite the most advanced treatments available, there were no guarantees. The average pregnancy rate per cycle was in the 20 to 35 percent range, but Portia's age lowered her chances. It was likely to take more than one cycle for the implantation to be successful.

But the men's program had to win Vince's support sooner than that. Cole had informed Lucky yesterday that the bankruptcy court was expected to approve the vacant dental building going on sale by mid-November. Several doctors' groups had expressed interest in the space.

Without that building, expansion of Lucky's program would be difficult. No comparable facility with offices and labs existed in Safe Harbor. As for constructing a new one, the logistics of acquiring land and receiving government approvals made that option prohibitive.

So if Vince delayed too long, Lucky might have to choose between using the degree he'd worked so hard for and leaving his friends. Friends who, as he'd become keenly aware, filled the lonely places in his soul.

The creak of the car door jerked Lucky from his reverie. Zora swung onto the seat beside him. "Have you met Dr. Davis? Is he a nice guy? Do you think he'll hire Zady?"

She sounded excited rather than angry, thankfully.

"You're in favor of her landing the job?" Lucky switched on the ignition.

"Yes!" She drew the seat belt across her body. "It would be fantastic to have my sister here. My kids could grow up with their aunt, and besides, we belong together."

Things had gone well, then. Lucky smiled. "I was afraid you'd take my head off."

"For keeping her interview a secret?" Zora issued a growly noise. "You deserve it! But no."

"Her application was private." Moot point, now that Zady had revealed the facts to her sister. "I only met Dr. Davis briefly, but I like him. As for who he'll choose, the other candidates are also excellent. Tell me, what did you and Zady discuss?"

"Everything! It's incredible." Any concern that she'd keep Lucky in the dark vanished as she described Zady's selfish boyfriend and the similarities in their romantic experiences. The revelation about Andrew's possible abuse of her birth control pills was outrageous, but, unfortunately, in character for the louse.

Navigating along Coast Highway toward their house, Lucky maintained a leisurely speed to prolong the conversation. Beside him, Zora radiated an almost sexual intensity. The curve of her cheek invited his hand to stroke it, but he gripped the wheel tightly.

It wasn't safe to get distracted while driving. And once he touched her, he might not be able to stop there. He'd recognized his susceptibility to her that day in the office, when they'd nearly gone too far.

If it were only a question of the two of them, maybe... but he refused to risk giving his whole heart to a family that he couldn't be sure he could provide for. And what if Andrew decided he wanted to be a father to the twins? How he could be sure he'd never let Zora or the children down when, ultimately, control could be snatched out of his hands?

He'd made a workable plan for the future, one he could live with and sustain, and right now that plan did not allow for a wife and kids. No matter how he felt about Zora, ultimately he'd have to move past it.

"I understand better now why we fell for Mom's crap." She adjusted the seat belt, which tended to creep up on her abdomen. "Our mother pulled stunts to pit us against each other, and we bought it. She's been lying to us for years, convincing each of us that we were in competition."

She'd never told him that before, only that her mother was an alcoholic and her stepfather a bully. Lucky hadn't pressed for details, partly because he and Zora hadn't been close until recently, and partly because he resented it when people probed his own past. "I had no idea she was fomenting trouble for you."

"Neither did I. It's because of her that Zady and I had our last big blowup." She outlined how their mother had destroyed their property and tricked them into blaming each other. "It was cruel. We've lost nearly a decade. Our mother must be a— Who was that Greek guy that fell in love with his own reflection?"

"Narcissus."

"That's it! She's a narcissist."

"You should cut her off," Lucky said. "It's what she deserves."

"We're putting up a united front," Zora responded. "Keeping her at arm's length will drive her nuts."

"Don't play games." Zora's assertiveness was new and likely fragile. She could easily be sucked back into self-defeating behavioral patterns if she continued to speak to her mother. "You should have nothing further to do with her."

In the faint light as they passed a streetlamp, he saw frown lines pucker her forehead. "She's our mother."

"To feed her ego, she groomed you to be patsies," he retorted. "Don't let Zady persuade you to stay involved with your mother. It's great that you've reconnected with your twin, but not if she's a bad influence."

"My sister isn't a bad influence!" Zora's shoulders stiffened. "And how we handle our mother is none of your business."

"It is if you spiral back into codependency," he said. "Because I have to live with you."

She appeared about to argue, but curiosity won. "What's codependency?"

"Codependents try to save loved ones from the consequences of their own actions because of a misguided sense of loyalty." After reading about the subject in a class on substance abusers and their families, Lucky had been astonished at how often he spotted the behavior in acquaintances and patients. "They feel guilty and trapped and blame themselves for the other person's faults, as you did with Andrew. You're a raging codependent, Zora."

"Now you're claiming I have a mental defect?"

"I'm helping you keep your life on track." To him, it seemed obvious.

"Wow, and I thought you'd changed." Far from heeding his warning, she was working up a head of steam. "Mr. Judgmental."

"It's for your own good." Lucky winced at the banality of his words. "That may be a cliché but in this instance, it's true."

"You expect me to abandon my mother and my sister because that's what you did with your brother when he crossed you."

Anger flared. Her situation didn't remotely compare to Lucky's. "You have no idea what separated Matthew and me."

"I know you're estranged from your entire family," Zora snapped. "He offended you, so Mr. High and Mighty Luke Mendez rejected him and everyone who stood by him."

"I had very valid reasons."

"What reasons?"

"He said vicious things no one could forgive, and obviously he doesn't regret it, since he never apologized."

"What did he say that was so terrible?"

"I have no intention of repeating it." Although Lucky had been only eighteen, his older brother's cruel words remained seared into his brain. *It's your fault our parents are dead, and you cheated me of my inheritance. You should be in prison.*

Matthew had repeated the lies to their aunts and uncles, who had barred Lucky from family gatherings. After several attempts to reason with them, he'd decided to cut himself off from them entirely.

True, he'd messed up, badly. He'd never forgive himself for the mistakes that had hurt their parents. But he hadn't caused their deaths and he would never, ever cheat anyone.

"Maybe he's changed," Zora suggested.

"I've led a fulfilling life without my brother's destructive influence," Lucky replied tautly. "You should do the same with your mother."

"I'm not you." As they entered the driveway, Zora said, "Thank heaven."

"I agree."

"You do?"

"If you were like me, you'd be the first pregnant man in history."

She didn't laugh. Too bad. Lucky had been aiming to lighten the mood.

He supposed she believed that his promise not to nag her over Andrew also applied to the rest of her behavior. But to him, she'd come so far in the last couple of weeks, he didn't want to see her lose her newfound confidence and self-esteem.

If he'd annoyed her, it was worth it.

Chapter Twelve

Angered by Lucky's arrogance, Zora avoided him over the weekend. She kept busy exchanging photos and messages with Zady, and went grocery shopping with Keely, although the nurse's insistence that she buy organic foods ran up the bill.

It was more than Lucky's haughty attitude that disturbed her, she realized after a second night of troubled sleep. In her dreams, her angry father raged at her, Zady and their mom. After his sudden death from a heart attack when she was twenty-two, Zora had pushed those ugly memories aside, preferring to dwell on her father's kinder, more loving moments. But the discovery of this rigid, unforgiving side of Lucky's nature had reawakened them.

Not that she hadn't expected this, at some level. After all, he insisted on the perfect family situation, including, presumably, a wife who arrived without baggage. No messy old relationships, and no children.

Yet, foolishly, she'd allowed herself to count on Lucky, to venture close to loving him, as if he might find it in his heart to change.

Why do I keep falling for the wrong guy?

If she entered another intimate relationship, Zora vowed to do it with her eyes open. Until then, once she discovered a man's fatal flaw, she'd distance herself from him, no matter how much her heart ached. And Lucky's fatal flaw was his intolerance for other people's flaws.

On Monday, she consulted Edmond regarding child support. He promised to file for half of Zora's unreimbursed medical and other maternity expenses.

"Once the babies are born, their father will be entitled to visitation and possibly shared custody," Edmond advised from behind the desk in his fifth-floor office. "That doesn't necessarily mean he gets physical custody half the time, but he will have an equal say in decisions about their care."

Much as she would hate sharing the children with their unworthy father, Zora supposed that she could hardly refuse contact. "He can't take them away from me, though, can he?"

"That would be extremely unusual," Edmond assured her. "He would have to prove that being around you endangers the children, such as if you were using drugs."

"I'd have to prove that for him, too, to block shared custody?"

"That's right." He adjusted his glasses. "In a case like this, it's tempting to try to cut him out. However, the courts have ruled that it's in a child's best interest for him or her to have a relationship with both parents."

Privately, Zora doubted it. However, she understood that laws and legal rulings had to apply to a wide range of cases.

When Lucky drove her home that evening, she suppressed the instinct to spill out what she'd learned from Edmond. She hadn't shared Betsy's confidence about Andrew's latest ploy, either.

He's judgmental and pitiless. The words played through her mind on a repeating loop, warning her to maintain a distance.

So when the silence weighed too heavily, she broached the merits of organic foods, a topic that interested him.

Lucky explained that he was vegetarian more for health reasons than for philosophical ones, although sparing animals' lives was a bonus. The man didn't appear to notice that she was withholding any information of a personal nature.

On Tuesday morning, Zora was assigned to perform sonograms at Dr. Brennan's office. Her obstetrician urged her to stay off her feet as much as possible, and Keely brought enough cups of tea to double her already frequent trips to the restroom.

While every patient was important and required her focus, Zora sensed an undercurrent of excitement building among the staff in the late morning. The reason became clear when she wheeled her cart into an exam room where Portia Adams lay on the table. Her auburn hair highlighted with chestnut and gold strands, she wore a hot-pink hospital gown that she must have brought with her. The only other person present was the doctor.

Lips pressed into a thin line, Portia watched Zora with a flare of the nostrils. Was the woman still jealous? *How sad*, Zora thought as she readied her equipment.

She was thankful for Dr. Brennan's narrative during the sonogram. "Everything's right on target." Seated on a stool, the doctor crossed her long legs. "We may be ready to harvest your eggs by the end of next week. Are you experiencing mood swings?"

"No more than usual," Portia said tartly. "How soon will my pregnancy start to show? I'm on the committee of a Christmas charity ball for the animal shelter and I must be sure my dress will fit."

Dr. Brennan blinked. She must have heard a lot of odd questions, Zora mused as she removed the probe, but this one evidently caught her by surprise.

"If you become pregnant on the first try, you'd still only be a few months along by Christmas," she said. "Maternity clothes probably won't be necessary. However, for comfort, I recommend a loose-fitting style."

"That's what I meant," Portia said. "I just want to buy the right style."

When Keely entered the room, Zora started to wheel her equipment out. As she opened the door, she heard the nurse say to Dr. Brennan, "Mr. Adams has arrived. Shall I send him in?"

"Wait till I straighten my gown," Portia responded. "How's my hair?"

It was too late for her to retreat, Zora realized as the door closed behind her, leaving her alone in the hallway. And there he was, his large frame nearly filling the corridor and forcing her to halt.

"Well, well." Despite the expensive cologne and expertly cut hair, Vince had a sleazy air. "If it isn't the lady with the earth-goddess body."

"Your wife's waiting for you, Mr. Adams." Zora peered past him, hoping to spot another staff member. No such luck.

"Has anybody told you lately how sexy you are?" The man's low voice might not carry into the closed examining room, but Zora wished it would. Then surely Dr. Brennan or Keely would respond.

"Thank you." She rattled the cart. "Excuse me."

Vince's expression hardened. "I'm an important man around here. You should consider the advantages of keeping me happy."

What nerve! "That's hardly appropriate for a woman in my condition." *Or any woman in any condition.*

"There are other ways of pleasing a man," he muttered close to her ear.

Zora's stomach churned. "I have a patient waiting." Not true, but she didn't care. And neither, she gathered from Vince's unmoving stance, did he.

Mercifully, noises from inside the examining room finally penetrated his awareness. From his pocket, he produced a business card and scribbled a phone number on the reverse. “My cell.” He stepped aside. “Call me.”

Zora stuck the card in her pocket and hurried away. As she stored her equipment, her hands were trembling.

What was she going to do? The only way to be sure of avoiding the man in the future was to complain about his disgusting behavior. Sexual harassment violated hospital policy, but it was his word against hers.

No, not entirely. She’d attended a talk by the hospital’s staff attorney, Tony Franco, highlighting the seriousness with which such claims were regarded.

But if the hospital hassled Vince, that ended any chance of a donation. His wife could transfer to a doctor in San Diego. Was it worth it? The man hadn’t tried to *force* Zora to do anything against her will. He’d merely been unpleasant.

Still shaky, she headed for the elevators. In her pocket, she imagined the card covered with slime. Best to discard it immediately. Except, what if she needed to prove that he’d propositioned her? Zora resolved to let her emotions settle before reaching a decision.

After washing her hands—it was impractical to take a shower, despite the icky emotional residue left by her encounter—she went to the cafeteria. In her present mood, she’d rather avoid Lucky, and was glad to see no sign of him. Instead, she spotted Betsy at a table with Lin. The third Mrs. Raditch must have had her follow-up appointment with Dr. T this morning.

With her tray of food, Zora joined them. At nearby tables, heads swiveled and voices murmured. Didn’t these people have anything more substantial on their minds?

Betsy pulled out a chair. “I’m glad you’re here.”

“Me, too, Grandma,” Zora said lightly. “Lin, how are you?”

"Dr. Tartikoff found nothing suspicious," the young woman replied.

"That's wonderful." Zora hesitated to raise another sensitive topic. Lin's next comment spared her that.

"I have talked to the attorney you recommended." Lin placed her dirty tableware neatly atop her empty plate. "He suggests an annulment on the grounds that Andrew defrauded me."

"By pretending to be a human being?" Embarrassed at her bluntness, Zora glanced apologetically at Betsy. "Sorry."

"No offense taken." Her ex-mother-in-law's mouth quirked.

"He lied about the vasectomy," Lin answered. "He claimed he had it during your marriage and promised to reverse it for me."

"Instead, he had the vasectomy *after* you got engaged." Which meant he didn't intend to reverse it, in Zora's opinion.

"Mr. Everhart called me after he contacted Andrew's attorney. It appears he will agree to the annulment," Lin said. "It will be as if the marriage never occurred."

How strange that, a month ago, this was what Zora had dreamed of, she mused as she ate. No more third wife. Instead, her sympathies now lay with Lin. "Will you stay in America?"

The other woman sighed. "I called my parents and they are eager for me to return."

"I wish you all the best," Betsy told her. "I hope you meet a man who deserves you."

"I doubt I will have as nice a mother-in-law," Lin said.

"How sweet." Betsy gazed at her pensively before turning to Zora. "If I may ask, what's the latest on your sister?"

Zora sketched the situation to her rapt audience. When she finished, she spotted Lucky standing with his tray, gazing around. A tremor ran through her at the reminder of the difficult choice she faced about Vince.

If she told him what Vince had done, how would he respond? Was it possible he'd think Zora had invited the other man's attention? Or, with his rigid insistence on propriety, would he pressure her to report Vince's harassment?

"You look pained," Betsy said. "Are you okay?"

"It's heartburn." Zora didn't dare reveal the truth. As nursing supervisor, Betsy would be obligated to inform the administrator.

"I must go." Lin stood, and Betsy, who'd finished her meal, did the same. "It is good to meet you again, Zora."

"Congratulations on your annulment." Zora almost regretted that Lin was returning to Hong Kong. She'd grown fond of her fellow sufferer.

How had Andrew managed to trick three intelligent women into loving him? Zora recalled Lucky describing her as a raging codependent. It must be a common condition.

He strode over, nodding to Betsy as she departed. Keely headed in their direction as well, her strong-boned face alight.

As the housemates settled, Keely spoke first. "I have great news! Mr. Adams plans to announce his donation soon."

Lucky gave a start. "He told *you*?"

"Dr. Brennan and me." The nurse transferred her dishes from the tray to the table. "He said the hospital is arranging a press conference. They're rushing the announcement because the dental building is going on sale."

Lucky slapped his thighs. "Fantastic!"

"He won't be able to jerk us around anymore," Zora burst out.

"Absolutely." Lucky's dark eyes sparkled. "Once he donates the money, we can stop worrying."

"That's right." This development reinforced Zora's resolve to keep quiet. Losing the billionaire's support at this point would be devastating, and unnecessary. But what a relief that she only had to hold out for a little while longer.

"He and his wife were joking about whose name will go on the building," Keely added. "Just his, or both of theirs."

"I can guess which side Vince was on." It wouldn't surprise Zora if the man's monstrous ego required the hospital to paint an enormous portrait of him covering the front of the structure as well. She wondered how hard it would be to sneak out and ornament it with a large mustache, blackened tooth and eye patch.

"They can put their daughters' names on it, too, as far as I'm concerned." Lucky popped open his carton of milk. "We can call it the Everybody Who's Ever Been Named Adams Medical Building."

Zora tucked into her tapioca pudding, relishing the creamy texture and vanilla flavoring. The rest of her meal had gone down almost untasted.

Idly, she wondered why a number of other diners were sneaking glances at them. Betsy and Lin had left, and Keely hadn't spoken loudly enough for her disclosure to carry above the general chatter. Lucky's enthusiastic reaction might have drawn attention briefly, but the staring seemed to be increasing.

"What do you suppose Laird's up to?" Lucky indicated a compact male figure perched triumphantly on a chair while the listeners at his table leaned toward him attentively.

Keely stiffened. "He keeps smirking at me."

"That's the third table he's bestowed his noxious presence on." Lucky didn't miss much. "The man already took his petty revenge on you for beating him to the rental. What more does he expect to gain?"

A lull fell across the room as a group of prominent physicians—Dr. Tartikoff, Cole Rattigan and hospital administrator Mark Rayburn—entered from the patio dining area. Into the quiet, Laird's words—*her own mother*—jangled like an old-fashioned telephone. The administrator frowned at him before glancing in Keely's direction with a troubled look.

The nurse paled. "Oh, my gosh! How did Laird find out?"

"Find out what?" Lucky asked.

As Zora tracked the path of the doctors toward the exit, the answer hit her. "He must have heard Keely and me talking in the garage. He was lurking in his car to watch her discover the flat tires."

"What were you discussing?" Lucky queried.

"It's...personal." Keely closed her eyes, her face a study in anguish. Fury rose in Zora at the jerk who'd inflicted this on her.

Or could she be mistaken? "That was two weeks ago. I don't understand why Laird would wait till now to attack you."

Keely's shoulders slumped. "I do."

"Would somebody please enlighten me?" Lucky said, clearly growing frustrated.

"I'll start at the beginning." Keely described her mother's death and the false allegation of elder abuse made against her that she'd eventually been able to disprove. "On Monday, Dr. Brennan asked if I was involved in any legal proceedings. I told her I wasn't. She apologized for jumping to a conclusion."

"I don't follow." What did Dr. Brennan have to do with Keely *or* Laird?

"Neither did I, but it worried me," Keely admitted. "When I pressed her, she said her husband had asked if I was still her nurse. That's all, but it reminded me that he's a private detective."

"Laird must have hired him to dig into your background." Unbelievable. To go that far, the psychologist had to be deadly serious about driving Keely away.

"I'm sure the detective informed him that the charges had been dropped." Lucky scowled in Laird's direction.

"People already dislike me." Keely shuddered. "Did you notice Dr. Rayburn's expression? Laird must have gone to him."

"You haven't done anything wrong," Lucky insisted.

"When the old community hospital was sold, we all went through a rehiring process and background check." Keely's thick eyebrows formed an almost straight line. "They asked if we'd ever been charged with a crime. I put down 'No.'"

"Well, you weren't," Zora protested.

"But I was arrested," the older nurse said. "Some people assume that's the same thing."

"Let's call an emergency house meeting tonight," Zora said. "We'll help you deal with this. Okay?"

Keely nodded. Lucky tilted his head in agreement, but in view of his judgmental tendencies, Zora was prepared to stand up to him tonight. She might not be able to take on Vince Adams, but Lucky Mendez was another story.

Chapter Thirteen

Due to schedules and commitments, it was nine o'clock before the household assembled in the den. Lucky had filled in Karen and Rod, who were ready for action.

"I'll chip in for an attorney." As usual, Rod shared the couch with Karen. "Legal costs can grind you under. That might be part of Laird's agenda."

Lucky assumed the anesthesiologist's view was colored by his own experience with the legal system.

In her chair beside Zora, Keely twisted her hands. "Do I *have* to get a lawyer?"

"It might be premature. Has anyone from Human Resources spoken to you about this?" Karen asked.

Keely's straight dark hair slashed the air as she shook her head.

"Edmond offers a free consultation." Lucky studied Zora's reaction, and was disappointed that she gave no sign of how she felt. He'd been hoping to learn that she'd met with Edmond herself to set the wheels rolling against Andrew.

How frustrating that she'd barely spoken to him since their disagreement on Friday. When Lucky had urged her to shut out her mother and, if necessary, her sister, he'd never expected her to shut *him* out instead. He had to admit, he might have gone overboard where her sister was concerned. Although he didn't entirely trust Zady's influence, she meant a lot to Zora. And family was precious—unless they performed a demolition act on your happiness.

But he hadn't had a chance to soften his position in the face of Zora's stonewalling. Talk about driving a person crazy.

Talk to me. Not this instant, of course, but he wished she'd stop avoiding his gaze.

This afternoon, he'd confirmed that the hospital had scheduled a press conference for a week from Thursday to announce a major donation. Lucky should have been exultant, but his emotions refused to cooperate because he couldn't share his happiness with Zora. After all, expanding the program would allow him to stay in Safe Harbor. It angered him that she seemed willing to forgive Andrew almost anything, and him nothing.

However, they had a more immediate matter on the floor. Lucky seized the initiative. "We should advise Dr. Rayburn about Laird's behavior. Don't forget he let the air out of Keely's tires—"

"We can't prove that," Zora interrupted.

"You saw his car at the scene." Lucky had checked, and her description, including the bumper sticker, fit Laird's vehicle. "He also hired a private detective to snoop into a staff member's background for revenge."

"We can't prove that, either," Rod observed. "And if there was a hospital policy forbidding nosiness, we'd all be out of a job."

Keely hunkered down, arms crossed protectively. Zora scooted her chair closer to Keely's as an indication of solidarity.

"Laird's an embarrassment to the hospital." Lucky had developed a disgust for the man since witnessing his drunken, lecherous behavior more than a year earlier during Elvis Presley night at the Suncrest Saloon. "I'm willing to march into Dr. Rayburn's office and demand he put a stop to this bullying. Who's with me?"

Zora laid a hand on her bulge, which was rippling beneath her maternity top. "Before we start painting protest signs, let's hear Keely's opinion."

"Fine." From his easy chair, Lucky fixed his attention on the older nurse.

She cleared her throat. "I'd like to run this by Dr. Brennan."

"Tomorrow?" Lucky urged.

"She's busy on Thursdays," Keely said. "She has surgeries scheduled."

"She can spare five minutes." The doctor had already showed concern for her nurse when she mentioned her husband's question, hadn't she? "Get her on your side."

"I don't want to drag her into my personal business."

"Don't let Laird intimidate you." With adrenaline pumping through his system, Lucky felt the urge to jump to his feet and pace.

"Oh, quit pressuring her," Zora snapped. "Keely has a right to handle this however she chooses."

"You mean through avoidance?"

Karen raised her hands. "Peace, everybody. As Zora said, this is Keely's decision. We're the backup team."

"Yeah, okay." How had this conversation become an argument between him and Zora, anyway?

Keely released a breath. "I'll talk to my doctor tomorrow."

"Good for you," Zora said.

How come she didn't give Lucky any credit? He'd pushed Keely to do exactly that.

"Are we finished?" Rod asked. Everyone nodded. "Before we break up, you'll all be pleased to hear that I plan to replace my broken-down junkmobile. Any suggestions?"

"A hybrid," Zora said. "You'll save a fortune on gas."

"Consult the online ratings," Keely contributed.

"I'm considering a sports car," Rod added. "Possibly red."

"Watch out. The cops will ticket you every time you edge a few miles over the speed limit." Lucky had heard that from officers who'd chatted with him during his stint as an ambulance driver.

"I should drive a gray SUV instead?" Rod demanded. *"Boring."*

"Buy a car that seats five or six," Karen recommended. "So you can transport the girls and their friends."

"If only."

"Speaking of guests, that brings us to the topic of Thanksgiving," their landlady said, deftly seizing control of the discussion. "How about cooking our dinner a day or two after the holiday? There'll be more chance your daughters can join us."

They speculated on how next week's announcement might affect Vince and Portia's holiday plans but weren't able to reach a conclusion. As for the dinner, scheduling it on a Saturday was fine with Lucky. He usually volunteered to serve food at a homeless shelter on the holiday.

Amid yawns—they were an early-rising bunch—the meeting dispersed. Aware that Zora customarily drank a glass of milk before bed, Lucky watched for his chance and slipped into the kitchen when she was alone.

He noted her cute freckled nose, red hair that frizzed by day's end and legs propped up on a nearby chair. Choosing a chair around the corner of the small table, he reached for her nearest foot.

"Hey!" Zora attempted a glare that bore a strong resemblance to a squint.

"Tired?" Lucky drew his thumb along her instep.

"It's been a busy day." She patted her belly for emphasis.

She should go on maternity leave before she collapsed and delivered in a hall. However, Lucky was trying to reconnect with her, not irritate her. "How're things with Betsy and the third Mrs. Raditch?" he ventured.

"Fine."

He gritted his teeth. As he lifted her other foot and massaged it, her body relaxed. Progress! "Any word from your sister about the job?"

"No." She sank lower in her chair, eyelids drooping.

As Lucky stroked her feet, he noted they were puffy. It must be agony for her to stand all day. *None of your business.* Great—he didn't have to speak any longer; her responses sprang up automatically in his thoughts.

"It must be interesting, working in a different department each day," he said.

"Oh, there are a lot of repeats," she murmured, and fell silent.

"Doggone it!" Oops, he hadn't meant to speak out loud.

Her eyes flew open and her muscles tightened. "What's your problem?"

"You never talk to me anymore." Had he really said that? He sounded like an old married woman. *Or man. Don't be sexist.*

"Why should I? So you can critique my behavior and complain about how stupid I am?" she demanded.

"Of course not." Resentment flared at this unfair description of his statements. "I'd merely advise and counsel you."

"Same difference." Her feet vanished from his hands. Lucky felt like the prince, caught on his knees, rejected by Cinderella.

"What happened to our truce?" He realized he'd entered dangerous territory, since their pact had required him to refrain from criticizing her. But their agreement had been specifically about Andrew. It was unreasonable of her to extend that to a blanket ban on all helpful comments.

"Don't pretend we're teammates," Zora grumped. "We agreed to collaborate to secure the Adamses' donation, and apparently we succeeded."

"There's still a week to go." Lucky was grasping at straws. But surely they could resume their camaraderie.

"I promise not to screw things up before then. Satisfied?" An unfamiliar tightness transformed her into a woman he scarcely recognized, older and more guarded.

This was what he'd been trying to prevent by steering Zora past her poor choices. Before he could assess what it meant or frame another question, the tension vanished and she was once again his peppery little friend.

"I'm off to bed." She handed him her empty glass. "Do something useful. Put this in the dishwasher."

"Not the oven?"

"Whatever." Thrusting her feet into her slippers, she padded off.

Well, at least she'd addressed him directly, Lucky mused as he carried the glass to its destination. He'd count that as a victory.

HOW FORTUNATE THAT LUCKY had the male clueless gene, Zora reflected tartly while she prepared for bed. He'd mentioned nothing was certain for another week, and at the prospect of facing another week in which she might be exposed to Vince's obnoxious behavior, she'd suffered a wave of revulsion. She'd schooled her features quickly, though, and was fairly sure Lucky hadn't noticed.

She was unclear about the precise mechanism of the donation, but she assumed the billionaire would hand over a check or sign a document when he announced his gift. After that, she doubted he'd withdraw it merely because an ultrasound tech refused to service his needs.

Wrenching her mind away from the whole awful situation, Zora climbed into bed for the night. Mercifully, maternal hormones zapped her into an instant deep sleep.

Over the next few days, the housemates did everything in their power to counter the spread of the rumors about Keely. They told others the true circumstances, including that the charges had been dropped. They pointed to examples of the older woman's kindness, which were often overlooked due to her downbeat personality. They also cited Laird's unscrupulous motives, although by now he must realize they'd never let him move into their house.

It was an uphill battle. Gossip spread madly and either distorted Laird's account even further, or else he embellished it himself. According to one version that reached Zora, Keely had gotten off murder charges on a technicality. By another, she'd been suspected in the deaths of several elderly patients. Many workers, having consulted Laird about their personal problems in the past, were inclined to trust him implicitly.

Keely declined to mount a defense. "I should have stayed home with my mom that day," she told Zora. "I deserve my share of blame."

"Stop acting like a codependent," Zora replied, and, for clarification, displayed the definition on her cell phone. Keely just shrugged.

As they'd expected, Dr. Brennan supported her nurse. Although a few of her patients who were staffers at the medical center claimed to feel uncomfortable around Keely due to her history, no one requested a change of doctors.

But rather than fading, the opposition was growing. In the corridors, people avoided Keely. Zora had been ostracized to an extent for stealing Stacy's husband, but it had never sunk to this level.

Human Resources had contacted Keely and reviewed her history, but there'd been no attempt to fire her. Nevertheless, on Thursday she informed her housemates that she was tired of being a pariah and planned to search for another job. Shoulders hunched, she brushed off their objections.

"She feels guilty," Karen observed after Keely left the room. "The hardest person to forgive is yourself."

"That's ridiculous," Lucky growled. "The past is the past and we should leave it there."

Zora didn't bother to point out that he ought to leave his quarrel with his brother in the past. She was too worried about Keely to waste her energy bickering.

On Friday at lunch, a lab technician deliberately bumped Keely as she walked to their table. Fortunately, Keely kept a tight grip on her tray. Her stoic air didn't fool Zora, though. She knew her friend was close to tears.

"Don't you dare leave without eating," she told the nurse, and walked beside her to their seats. Karen, Rod and Lucky closed ranks with them.

Once they were settled, Zora dared to hope they could eat in peace. Then a tall woman of about fifty, with short brown hair and weathered skin, stalked over and stood over Keely, scowling until the chatter quieted.

"What's on your mind, Orla?" Rod demanded.

The name prodded Zora's memory. Orla Baker was a circulating nurse, which explained how Rod knew her—circulating nurses set up the operating room and checked the stock of instruments and disposable items, which they refreshed during the procedure. They played a key role in protecting patients from mistakes by verifying their identities and reviewing the site and nature of the operation with the surgeon.

"It's disgusting that she left her mother to die." She spat out the words as if it had been *her* mother who'd perished. "The DA may not have charged her, but what kind of person does that? She should be ashamed."

In the stillness, Zora spotted Laird leaning against a wall, arms folded and a smile playing around his mouth. If she'd had a rubber band, she'd have shot it at him to wipe the smirk off his face.

Rising, Lucky pointed at the psychologist. "Orla, *you* should be ashamed for allowing that man to manipulate you into bullying her. He's trying to drive her away because of petty resentment."

Zora had never admired anyone more in her life. Awkwardly, she rose, too. "Laird Maclaine played a mean prank on Keely by letting the air out of her tires. What is this, high school?" Her voice rang out with a touch of shrillness. "He also hired a detective to dig up dirt that he then distorted for his smear campaign. How can any decent person be a party to that?"

Karen sprang up. "Keely may not be slick and persuasive, but she has a kind heart and I'm with her one hundred percent."

Rod stood beside her. "That goes double for me, Orla."

The circulating nurse wavered. "My mother has Alzheimer's. I understand the stresses involved, but there's no excuse for abandoning her mother."

Keely sat silent, unwilling to speak on her own behalf. Zora feared others would take that as an indication of guilt.

Across the cafeteria, a six-foot-tall woman with a commanding air uncoiled. All attention fixed on Dr. Paige Brennan, whose eyes flashed with anger.

"This situation has been discussed at the highest levels and the case is closed," she declared. "If anyone continues creating a hostile work environment for my nurse, I will ensure that disciplinary measures are taken against them. And that is the last I or any of us had better hear about this."

The other obstetricians at her table burst into applause. With a spurt of amusement, Zora registered that the loudest clapping came from Dr. Tartikoff. Apparently he'd forgiven Keely for their long-ago dispute, or else he had zero tolerance for bullying.

Orla spoke directly to Keely. "I apologize. I shouldn't have listened to gossip."

"Have a seat." Karen waved her over. "I'm sorry about your mom, Orla. How're you holding up?"

After a brief hesitation, the circulating nurse sank into a chair. "Some days are better than others."

As the conversation flowed, Zora noted that Dr. Brennan's declaration had restored the color to Keely's face. Orla's apology appeared to have helped, too.

But best of all was watching Laird slink from the cafeteria. Paige Brennan's scorching setdown must have impressed on him that his campaign against Keely had not only failed, it had also damaged his own reputation with the top staff.

A wise person would take a long, hard look in the mirror. She didn't credit Laird with wisdom, however.

That night, Casa Wiggins celebrated the victory with meatless burgers and fizzy apple juice. There was no more talk of Keely changing jobs.

Still, it was too soon to let all her anxiety go. In less than a week, the future of the men's program would be secure, Zora hoped, and prayed silently for nothing to go wrong.

Chapter Fourteen

"I produced fifteen eggs?" From the examining table, Portia stared in dismay at Dr. Brennan. "You must be kidding!"

"That's an excellent number to ripen," the doctor assured her as Zora carefully adjusted the position of her ultrasound wand. "We'll select those in the best condition, fertilize them and choose the healthiest embryos to implant. If we have more than three, we can freeze the rest for later."

"Three? Surely two is plenty!" Portia's fingers curled, as if she longed for someone to hold her hand. Vince, who'd positioned himself in front of the ultrasound monitor, didn't appear to notice.

He'd barely glanced at Zora, either. She'd been disturbed on discovering she'd been assigned to Portia, but the scheduler had insisted.

"I'd prefer four," Vince announced. His wife gasped. Zora might not like her, but she empathized with the woman.

"That would violate hospital policy," Dr. Brennan said. "Portia, if you don't want more than two, we'll respect your wishes."

After a tense pause, the patient said, "Three will be fine."

"You're sure?"

Vince blew out an impatient breath.

Tautly, Portia said, "Yes."

Dr. Brennan jotted a note in the computer. To Zora, the doctor appeared concerned, but didn't press the point. "Now that the eggs are mature, timing is crucial. As I explained, you'll need an injection of HCG—human chorionic gonadotropin—to prepare for ovulation. Harvesting should take place thirty-six hours later."

As Zora finished her work, she half listened to the details. Normally, the patient's husband, after being shown how to give the shots, would have injected her with hormones for the past week or so, and would administer HCG at ten o'clock tonight. Instead, the Adamses had hired a visiting nurse.

"We'll set the egg retrieval for Wednesday morning," Dr. Brennan continued. "Mr. Adams, we'll coordinate with Dr. Rattigan to be sure he collects your sperm before then."

"I can attend the egg harvesting, I presume." The billionaire shifted from one foot to the other as if cramped by the confines of the examining room.

"Absolutely," the doctor said.

"We'll use the same sonographer, as per my instructions?"

Zora's stomach tightened. Today's assignment hadn't been by chance. Did the billionaire simply enjoy throwing his weight around or was there more to it?

Dr. Brennan looked startled. "The egg retrieval is a specialized procedure. We'll have a team in place."

"It's good luck to have a pregnant woman nearby. Maternal hormones and all that." Vince gestured toward Zora. "The process has gone smoothly so far with her present, hasn't it, Doctor?"

If Portia had had a death ray, Zora didn't doubt she'd have used it. *On me.*

"That's true." Dr. Brennan smiled. "However, I'm not sure we can credit Zora's maternal hormones." Without further comment about the sonographer request, she provided them directions to the hospital's retrieval room on the second floor, where the procedure would take place. "Don't eat or drink anything after midnight Tuesday, Mrs. Adams, and be sure to arrive an hour early."

"I'll be asleep for it, I hope," Portia grumbled as she sat up, finally receiving her husband's hand in assistance.

"You'll be sedated, and in recovery for two to three hours afterward," the doctor said. "We'll let you know later the same day how many eggs were retrieved. They'll be examined by an embryologist, and by Thursday we'll inform you of how many we were able to fertilize."

Thursday was the day of the press conference. Of course, the embryos wouldn't be implanted into Portia's womb for a few more days to give them time to grow in the lab. Was Vince also going to demand that Zora be present for the implantation?

He wasn't likely to succeed; as Dr. Brennan had indicated, the fertility team worked with its own techs. However, to be sure of preventing any further contact with the man, Zora could schedule her maternity leave. She had to admit that, with her ankles swollen and her abdomen sore, she was overdue.

When Keely entered the room, Zora rolled out her cart. Her knees weak with relief at having weathered the encounter with Vince, she headed around a corner toward the storage closet.

She'd just stowed the equipment when heavy male footsteps jolted her pulse into high gear. Turning, she spotted Vince Adams at a bend in the hall.

This late in the afternoon, there was no one else in view. Before she could exit, the heavyset man blocked her escape.

"What're you doing?" Zora demanded.

"You should have called me." He reached for the nearest door and shoved it open to reveal an empty examining room. "Let's talk inside."

"I'm fine right here." The words emerged breathlessly.

"This is a private conversation."

"Forget it." Zora tried to dodge past, lost her balance and stumbled. He caught her arm as if to assist, but instead pulled her into the room.

"Listen, I'm donating twenty million dollars to this hospital. And I'll spend money on you, too, if you make it worth my while." This close, she caught the scent of alcohol on his breath. Zora knew all too well what effect that had on the wrong kind of man.

"Leave me alone." She pressed her palms against his chest, but that only seemed to amuse him.

"Be nice to me, honey," he slurred.

She flashed on stories she'd heard about Vince's past: that he'd gotten his start through gang connections in a rough part of Phoenix and that a former business rival had disappeared under mysterious circumstances. Yet she'd never imagined he'd dare to assault her.

The door flew open. There stood Keely, aghast. "What is this?"

Vince glanced over his shoulder. "If you know what's good for you, Nurse, you'll keep your mouth shut."

Instead, Keely commanded, "Get your hands off her!"

"Shut up, you…"

While he was distracted, Zora grabbed a pair of scissors from a drawer. "Let go of me!"

Startled, the hulking man released her. "Neither of you says a word to anyone or you're both out of a job."

Angry breathing filled the room. No one spoke, and finally, he left. Heart pounding, Zora clutched the scissors, ready to fight if he returned.

"Are you all right?" Keely asked.

The adrenaline seeping out of her, Zora set the instrument on the counter. "Thank goodness you showed up." How far would that monster have gone?

"Has he done anything like this before?"

It was on the tip of her tongue to deny it. *Keep the secret, don't cause problems.* But Zora had kept his secret once, and this was where it had led. "Yes, although it wasn't this bad."

"We have to report him."

Despite her outrage, Zora hesitated. "If we raise a fuss, there goes the donation. Think what that will do to the hospital, and to Lucky."

"Men like Vince Adams depend on their victims keeping silent," Keely growled. "That's how they get away with it."

"I don't want to involve the police." Zora had no idea how this situation would appear to an officer.

"You might have to," Keely said. "But you can start with Dr. Rayburn if you prefer. I'll come with you."

How brave of her, and what a great friend. Tearfully, Zora nodded. "Okay."

"First, let's settle your nerves," the nurse advised. "How about tea and peanut-butter crackers?"

"Thanks."

Twenty minutes later, after a snack in the lounge, Zora could speak without trembling. Her brain still skipped from objection to objection, however. What if her complaint smashed Lucky's dreams? What if the administrators believed she'd encouraged Vince? But she had to do this, for other potential victims as much as for herself.

It was nearly five o'clock when they reached the hospital's fifth floor. What if Dr. Rayburn had left for the day? If Zora had to wait until tomorrow, she wouldn't be able to sleep.

As they approached the executive suite, she heard movement inside. Then the last two people on earth she'd expected to see emerged into the corridor.

Vince and Portia Adams. He regarded Zora with a superior smirk. His wife gave a start, her face pale.

With the sensation of falling into an abyss, Zora realized that her tormenter had performed an end run around her. Whatever story he'd concocted, it would make her sound like a liar—and possibly end her career.

LUCKY KNEW SOMETHING was wrong when Keely texted that she'd drive Zora home instead of him. Why the last-minute change? Keely had added that she was calling a house meeting as soon as everyone arrived.

When he tried to call Zora, her phone went to voice mail. Was she in labor? But if she was, why would Keely be bringing her home?

Perhaps Laird had pulled another stunt and the women wanted to talk about it in private. Or maybe Dr. Brennan had discovered something worrisome about Zora's pregnancy.

Adrenaline pounded through Lucky's system. If Zora was in danger, he should be there to protect her.

In the garage, he cruised up along the ramp in search of Keely's car. With most of the staff gone and few outpatients or visitors on hand, he should have been able to spot it, but no luck.

Cursing himself for wasting time, Lucky headed home. He had to fight the tendency to stomp on the gas pedal.

Why was he reacting so strongly? It was silly and useless. But he kept imagining Zora's emotions in turmoil and longing to reassure her.

At the house, he was glad when he spotted Keely's car in the driveway. Just ahead of him, Karen pulled into the remaining open spot, with Rod beside her.

Lucky parked at the curb and broke into a lope. "What gives?" he asked when he came within earshot.

"No idea." Karen straightened her blazer. "I haven't heard any gossip from our receptionist." That young woman, Caroline Carter, reputedly had the keenest radar in the hospital.

Rod's fedora shadowed his face as the three of them followed the walkway. "I haven't picked up anything in the doctors' lounge, either."

Inside, Lucky barreled into the den, grateful that neither Karen nor Rod objected when he bypassed them. He felt a spurt of relief when he saw Zora in her usual chair, sipping a cup of juice. Keely paced nearby, unable to contain her restlessness.

Just like me. "Are you okay?" Lucky demanded.

Zora didn't answer.

"Sit down." No sign of Keely's customary reticence. "Everyone."

He took his favorite chair, while Karen and Rod slid onto the couch, not bothering to remove their shoes or hats or jackets. "Don't keep us in suspense," Rod said.

"This afternoon, I walked in on Vince Adams assaulting Zora." Disgust emphasized the deep lines in Keely's face.

"He did what?" Lucky sprang up, prepared to find the man and pummel him. "Were you hurt? You should go to the police."

"Let us finish, please." When he subsided, Keely described the scene she'd interrupted in an examining room. Thank goodness she'd arrived when she had, although Lucky would have paid a fair amount of money to watch Zora stab that jerk with scissors.

But before they could take the matter to Dr. Rayburn, Vince had beaten them to the punch, claiming Zora had tried to extort money by threatening to accuse him of harassing her.

"Mark can't believe that," Karen protested when Keely paused for breath. "It's ridiculous."

"Still, I'm glad to have Keely as a witness." Zora's voice trembled. "And I showed Dr. Rayburn the business card

Vince gave me with his private number scrawled on the back. He pressed it on me the last time he cornered me."

"He's done this before?" The revelation sickened Lucky. "Why didn't you report it?"

"It didn't go this far," she told him. "And I was worried it might have an impact on the men's program."

"The program isn't your responsibility," Karen said.

"But I care about—about the rest of the staff," Zora replied.

"You were protecting me?" Lucky would never allow her to put her safety at risk. "I didn't ask you to do that."

"You were happy enough when Portia agreed to in vitro," Zora shot back. "He all but said he'd leave her for some 'earth mother,' as he described me, if she didn't agree to in vitro instead of insisting on surrogacy."

Stunned, Lucky recalled the scene outside Dr. Rattigan's examining room. He'd never known the details of how Portia had made her decision. And all this while, she'd kept Vince's mistreatment a secret?

Once, long ago, Lucky had vowed never again to let down anyone he loved the way he'd let down his parents. Yet now he had. Worse, by scheduling Zora to work that first morning because he valued her insight, he'd put her in harm's way.

Wordlessly, he listened as the conversation moved on around him. In the administrator's office, Mark had been accompanied by attorney Tony Franco. They'd assured Zora that her job was safe and that she had every right to contact the police.

"Great idea." Lucky would love to see Vince hauled off in handcuffs.

"As if I'd have any chance against a billionaire and his legal team," Zora said miserably.

"We have honest cops in Safe Harbor," Karen responded. "Tony Franco's brother is a police detective."

"Vince will just repeat his claim that I tried to extort

money from him," Zora said. "How can I prove I didn't? And if he sues me for slander, I can't afford to fight."

It was unfair that his wealth enabled a man like Vince to crush people, as he'd already done with Rod. If only Lucky had been the one to discover that scene today, he'd have taught the bastard a lesson on the spot.

And probably lost his job, not to mention being locked up for assault. But it would have felt good to smash his fists into the man's oily face.

"Dr. Rayburn seemed worried about the emotional and physical effects on Zora," Keely put in. "He offered her an extra two months of paid maternity leave, not in lieu of anything else, just for health reasons."

"He suggested I go on leave immediately while he sorts this out," Zora added. "I refuse to slink away as if I did anything wrong, but I am going to start my leave on Monday, because I already had that in mind."

"Extra paid leave—that's a positive thing, anyway," Karen said.

"How does Dr. Rayburn intend to sort this out?" Lucky persisted. Zora had been attacked at work, and other staffers could be at risk, too. If only Vince weren't so rich, and the hospital staff so eager for his donation.

Including me. It revolted Lucky to think of how hard he'd worked to keep Vince involved with Safe Harbor.

"Dr. Rayburn said there are complicating issues." Having practically worn a path in the carpet with her pacing, Keely plopped into an armchair.

"Like what? Vince's money?" Rod grumbled.

"He and Portia are patients, so disrupting their care would be unethical if no wrongdoing is proved." Zora clasped her hands atop her baby bump. "It's a crucial week for them."

"The hospital should cancel that damn press conference." No matter what the donation meant for Lucky or his doctor, he'd never sacrifice an innocent person's well-being. Especially Zora's.

"Dr. Rayburn has to discuss it with the hospital corporation," Keely said. "They'll make the final decision. Except he was very clear that he will not allow any repercussions against Zora or me."

"Dr. Brennan would be up in arms if he did, I'm sure," Karen said.

"Along with the rest of the medical staff," Rod added. "No one would believe Vince's story."

Zora set her empty cup on the table. "Keely and I aren't exactly the most popular members of the staff."

"You've seen what our household can do," Lucky reminded her. "If you need us, we're here."

Both women nodded. "Oh, we aren't supposed to discuss this," Zora added. "Please don't tell anyone else."

Despite an eagerness to rally the troops behind Zora, Lucky supposed he had to respect her decision. "All right." *For now.*

"How about dinner?" Karen got to her feet. "I'll bet the mommy-to-be is starving."

Rod stood also. "My cooking skills may be notoriously bad, but Jack taught me how to cook angel-hair pasta with wine and onions. It doesn't take long. And the alcohol in the wine evaporates."

"I'll fix a salad," Lucky volunteered.

The dinner went well, but he continued to be frustrated for the rest of the evening. He should be the person Zora turned to, but instead she remained glued to Keely's side. Lucky tried in vain to catch her alone so he could massage her tense little shoulders. Or fetch her ice cream—why didn't she send him on errands anymore?

How ironic that he'd criticized her for leading a messy life. Now she'd landed in her biggest crisis yet, and the person most to blame—after Vince, of course—was Lucky himself.

Yet again, he'd been responsible for causing pain to someone he cared about. And yet again, there didn't seem to be any way to make up for his mistakes.

Chapter Fifteen

Catching sweet, sympathetic glances from Lucky all evening, Zora yearned to fly to him. Temporary though the respite might be, she longed to curl up in his arms and enjoy the illusion of safety.

But it *was* an illusion. She understood Lucky too well. Their relationship could only progress to a certain point before he'd slam the door on her. She and her babies would never fit his requirements for a perfect family.

How ironic that, while she failed to measure up to Lucky's standards, his influence had helped her shake free of her old codependent habits. She'd told off Andrew, stood up to Vince Adams and marched into Dr. Rayburn's office when her instincts screamed at her to flee.

It had been terrifying to confront two such powerful men in the meeting. Dr. Rayburn had towered over her dauntingly when they'd shaken hands. As for Tony Franco, beneath his reserved manner lurked a brain capable of raising who-knew-what legal complications against which an ordinary mortal was defenseless.

Zora had been grateful that Keely was there, and for the strength that she was beginning to realize had been within her all along. She'd managed not to break down in tears when the administrator repeated the lie Vince had told them. She'd stuck doggedly to the facts, painful as they were. There'd been two previous incidents, and she had the business card to prove it. Not much evidence, but it helped, as did Keely's testimony.

Tossing and turning in bed that night, she searched without success for a solution. If the Adamses canceled their planned donation, the whole hospital would suffer and Lucky might have to go elsewhere to build his career. But if the grant went forward, how could Zora stay? The vengeful billionaire would find a way to destroy her.

In the morning, she received a message from her sister: Got the job! Start in 3 weeks!

Under other circumstances, that would have been fantastic news. Now, Zora worried that if Vince saw her identical twin, he'd target Zady, too.

She arrived at the medical center on Tuesday with her senses on high alert. As the day progressed, no one mentioned Vince's accusations, but the news spread about Zora starting maternity leave on Monday. The hospital's public relations director, Jennifer Serra Martin, presented Zora with a pair of adorable teddy bears that played lullabies. Dr. T's nurse, Ned Norwalk, slipped Zora a gift card to Kitchens, Cooks and Linens.

"I'm not sure whether you're short of pots and pans, but you can always use more knives." He whisked off before she could ask what he meant. Had that been a veiled reference to her scissors wielding?

By Tuesday's end, the press conference hadn't been canceled, nor, apparently, had the next day's egg retrieval. And she learned that Vince had undergone the procedure to collect his sperm. The only change Zora observed was that the billionaire was now accompanied everywhere by a male patient care coordinator, supposedly to ensure his comfort.

And to protect me and the other women on staff?

On Wednesday morning, Zora was again assigned to Dr. Brennan's patients. No danger of running into the Adamses, whose egg retrieval was taking place in the hospital. Dr. Brennan, Zora discovered, had arranged for Dr. Zack Sargent to perform the procedure on the grounds that he performed more of them.

The moment she spotted Zora, Dr. Brennan zeroed in on her. "I'm sorry that you were assaulted."

"I'm fine."

"It was an unforgivable act, and I'm furious that it took place on my watch," the tall woman said. "If you need me to go to bat for you, just say the word."

Zora thanked her, pleased to have another person on her side.

At lunch, aware of prying ears, Zora and her housemates were careful not to discuss what was foremost on everyone's minds. She had almost finished eating when a call came from Dr. Rayburn's assistant, asking Zora to meet with him.

"I'll go with you," Keely announced.

"You have patients," Lucky reminded her.

"You can't let them down," Zora echoed. Despite her words, Zora shivered to think of what lay ahead. What if the corporation insisted on firing her? What if… Her brain wouldn't stretch further than that.

"Dr. Rattigan's in surgery for another hour, so I'll go with you." Lucky piled her dishes onto his tray. "No arguments."

"I didn't plan to raise any."

On the elevator ride to the fifth floor, Zora held Lucky's hand. Tension rippled across the muscles in his neck and arms, with the ironic effect that the dragon protruding from beneath his navy blue sleeve appeared to be winking at her.

"I hope I don't break down." She released her grip as they stepped into the empty hallway. "I've always been terrified that someday everything would fall apart and I'd be alone."

He touched her shoulder gently. "You aren't alone."

Zora blinked back tears. Impulsively, she asked, "What's *your* biggest fear?"

"Failing the people I love," Lucky said without hesitation. "And I'm not about to do that again."

Did he include her among the people he loved? Zora cautioned herself against leaping to conclusions. She had a bad habit of hearing only what she wished to hear.

"Don't go out on a limb for my sake," she told him.

"My integrity isn't for sale," Lucky answered. "Cole's isn't, either. He has opportunities elsewhere, although before he leaves Safe Harbor, I'm sure he'll consider the impact on Stacy."

"Oh, great." Zora hadn't considered how wide the fallout might be from the loss of Vince's donation. "As if I haven't done Stacy enough harm already."

"You did her a favor, taking Andrew away," Lucky returned. "I should have realized that sooner."

In the administrative suite, the assistant regarded Lucky in surprise. "I'm here for moral support," he said.

"Hold on." She picked up her phone.

From one of several inner rooms, Tony Franco appeared, his rust-brown hair rumpled as if he'd been running his fingers through it. After introducing himself to Lucky, he shook hands with them both. "Dr. Rayburn and I would like to speak to Mrs. Raditch alone."

"Without her lawyer?" Lucky demanded.

Tony gave a start. "If she wishes…"

"Lucky, that isn't necessary." How could she afford it? Also, since Edmond worked as a consultant for the hospital, he had a conflict of interest. Where would she find another lawyer on short notice?

"Then I'm sitting in," Lucky responded firmly. "I'll keep quiet, I promise."

To Zora's surprise, the attorney acquiesced. "Very well."

Tony's expression remained opaque. Did they learn

how to do that in law school? she wondered, and pictured a classroom full of law students training their features to remain flat.

When they entered Dr. Rayburn's office, the administrator rose to shake their hands, and it was obvious he hadn't mastered the same art. In his face, she read unease, a touch of surprise at Lucky's presence and regret.

Oh, damn.

True to his statement, Lucky took a seat in a corner of the large office. Dr. Rayburn, whom she'd expected to retreat behind the desk, instead positioned himself in a chair beside hers. "I'll get straight to the point. The corporation insists we accept the Adamses' sponsorship of the men's program and move forward with tomorrow's press conference."

Zora swallowed. She hadn't seriously expected the hospital to reject millions of dollars simply to spare the feelings of one ultrasound tech, had she?

"They would have preferred that I not talk to you directly about this, but that's bull," he continued.

"Mark," the attorney warned.

"Hey, Tony, you're the guy who recommends our doctors apologize to patients when they've made a mistake." Dr. Rayburn's thick eyebrows rose in emphasis. "Isn't it your opinion that honesty and contrition cut the risk of lawsuits?"

"Mark!" Tony said more forcefully. The reference to lawsuits must have set off alarm bells in the man's head.

Dr. Rayburn returned his attention to Zora. "I disagree with this decision, but I've done all I can. I've negotiated for you to receive six months of paid parental leave." Normally, staffers received two months. "Afterward, you can resume your job if you wish, with a guarantee that you won't be assigned to attend to either of the Adamses."

Relief warred with an awareness of how touchy the

situation would be, in numerous respects. "What about my sister?"

"Your sister?" Dr. Rayburn asked blankly.

"My identical twin sister is joining the staff." *Please don't let this mess things up for Zady.* "She'll be assisting the new urologist, Dr. Davis."

The administrator regarded the attorney, who fielded the question. "That's tricky, since Mr. Adams is a patient in the men's program. However, we can take precautions so she won't be put at risk."

But what about other women who might be subjected to Vince? Then Zora remembered the patient care coordinator shadowing the billionaire. Apparently, safeguards were already in place. "Okay."

"To bring you up to date, the corporate vice president will be flying in for tomorrow's events," Dr. Rayburn said. "There'll be a gala reception beforehand at the yacht club. The press conference will be at 5:00 p.m. in the auditorium. The staff is invited."

"I plan to skip it." Zora had no interest in watching the billionaire gloat.

"That's your choice." Dr. Rayburn still sounded dissatisfied. "You've undergone a traumatic experience. The hospital will be happy to provide sessions with a therapist."

With Laird? Zora's fists clenched. "No, thanks."

"We can arrange outside counseling with a woman." Tony must have noticed her reaction.

"I don't think that will be necessary. But I'll let you know if I change my mind." Despite her anxiety, Zora hadn't suffered nightmares about the incident. Still, she respected the value of professional help. If she'd received it during her divorce, she might not have clung to her foolish delusions for so long.

Neither she nor Lucky had any more questions, and the meeting ended. She still disliked the situation, but not enough to consider leaving Safe Harbor.

In the hall, Lucky kept pace with her. "Are you okay? I'm glad you mentioned Zady. I was wondering whether to bring her up, but you beat me to it."

"I appreciate the backup," she said. "Having someone who was in my corner there was important."

How had she failed for so long to realize what a strong, kind man he was? Of course, his previous antagonism toward her might have had something to do with that, Zora reflected.

And now? Circumstances had thrown them onto the same team, their loyalties more or less aligned. But was she really destined to remain nothing more than friends with him?

Now that she'd summoned the courage to confront her problems, maybe she ought to call Lucky to task for ignoring how much they meant to each other. But standing up for herself at work was one thing. Relationships were an entirely different matter. Where men were concerned, Zora still didn't trust her instincts.

That afternoon, the gossip mill at the hospital focused on possible developments at tomorrow's press conference, and she heard no mention of Vince's misconduct. On the drive home, Lucky agreed with Zora's observations.

"Dr. Rattigan doesn't seem to have any idea what happened between you and that jerk or that there was any question about accepting the donation," he told her as they headed south. "He was singing to himself in French this afternoon, which means he's excited."

"Why in French?" Zora asked.

"His father's French," Lucky said. "They aren't close, but Cole has an affinity for the language."

"At least he's happy." She sighed. "And this means he and Stacy won't have to consider moving." *Nor you, either.*

"I only wish the circumstances were different." Stopped at a red light, Lucky drummed his hands on the wheel.

"When I threw myself into winning Vince's support for the program, I had no idea he'd harm someone I care about."

"Even me?" Zora teased.

"Especially you!" But his next words disappointed her. "Or anyone." The light changed and he tapped the gas pedal. "If the men's program does expand and I land a management post, I'll stand by my nurses. That man better leave them alone."

"After he donates the money, surely he won't continue meddling." Zora assumed that was the case. "If he and Portia have children, there'll be no reason for further treatment."

"I suspect he'll find a way to keep us dancing on his strings." Lucky's jaw tightened.

Reluctantly, Zora agreed. Then she decided not to worry about matters beyond her control. For once, her practice in denial stood her in good stead.

A LOT OF stomping shook the two-story house that night. Rod stomped to and from the kitchen, complaining about the upbeat conversations he'd overheard in the operating room. "Everyone thinks Vince's generosity is fantastic. Don't they realize they're bringing in a monster?"

Lucky did his share of stomping as he carted a pair of cribs upstairs and assembled them in Zora's oversize closet-turned-nursery, which had a small window. To accommodate her displaced clothes, he also hauled a rack to the second-floor alcove.

While he was happy to help, he mused that Andrew ought to be chipping in so the new mom could afford the larger downstairs suite. Fond as Lucky was of his quarters, he would willingly swap.

Did Zora plan to let her ex continue to ignore his financial obligations? Surely she didn't maintain the fantasy that he'd return to her after the babies' birth. Yet in spite of everything, she might.

Lucky feared that in her mind, the twins would always be Andrew's babies. And with his current marriage dissolving, the man might decide to toy with her emotions again, just to feed his ego. Until he found another wide-eyed young woman to fall for his manipulations, and broke Zora's heart all over again.

Lucky went downstairs for a snack. "You going to the press conference tomorrow?" he asked Rod, who'd taken the next-to-last slice of apple pie left over from dinner.

"You bet. I never miss a chance to see my girls." The slender man tugged at his short beard, which, like his hair, was going gray. Rod was only in his early forties, but stress from his long custody battle might have played a role in giving him more gray hairs. "I'm sure he'll require Tiff and Amber to show up, since it's scheduled after school hours."

"I'm not sure I should attend," Lucky admitted. "My opinion of Vince might show on my face."

"I doubt he'll care," Rod said.

In the den, a phone rang. Lucky heard Karen answer. "Edmond? What…?" Then her tone grew urgent. "Of course. I'll meet you at the hospital. No problem!"

Lucky's brain leaped to the likeliest conclusion: Melissa was having her triplets. In their haste to talk to Karen, he and Rod collided in the doorway. "Sorry!"

"Ow, damn it!" Rod snapped. "I mean, I'm sorry, too."

"Anyone need medical attention?" Karen inquired dryly. "No? Great. Rod, want to ride with me to pick up Dawn? She's spending the night with us." Karen occasionally babysat the seven-year-old, who always proved good company.

"Sure." Rod plucked his fedora from a coat rack. "Melissa's in labor?"

"Her water broke. She's at thirty weeks, earlier than they were hoping for but not bad for a multiple birth. They're assembling a team."

"I'll notify Zora and Keely." There were others who should be informed, too, Lucky thought. "Also Anya and Jack. Should I make up one of the couches for Dawn?"

"She can sleep with me," Karen assured him.

Rod sighed. "Guess I'm alone in my bed tonight."

She punched his arm. "Discretion!"

He grinned.

"Please tell Melissa and Edmond I'm rooting for them," Lucky said. Despite the skill of the hospital's doctors and nurses, the birth of triplets would pose a challenge.

"I will." Karen headed out with Rod behind her.

If all went well, this would be a joyous event, Lucky reflected on his way upstairs to spread the news. What a timely reminder of the miracles wrought at Safe Harbor.

Although his gut churned at the prospect of tomorrow's press conference, the donation would enable the staff to perform even more miracles. Too bad the price tag included putting up with a preening, triumphant Vince Adams. At Zora's expense.

Chapter Sixteen

"We had a devil of a time agreeing on names for three girls," Edmond remarked to Zora at midday as they viewed the triplets in the intermediate care nursery.

Weighing over three pounds and with mature lungs, little Simone, Jamie and Lily were in excellent shape. Nevertheless, they had to be observed for signs of infection or other potential problems.

Wrapped in pink and attached to monitors, the trio were adorable. Zora's arms ached to reach through the viewing window and hold them. A tiny yawn from one—was that Jamie?—was almost too cute to be real.

"I still don't have a name for my son." Zora rested her hand on her by-now enormous bulge. "My daughter's name will be Elizabeth."

"After her grandmother?" The attorney knew Betsy, of course.

She nodded. "I read that the first Queen Elizabeth was named after *her* grandmother."

"Here's a bit of trivia—both her grandmothers were called Elizabeth." Edmond adjusted his glasses.

"I'm impressed that you know that."

"History fascinates me. Melissa and I used to travel and tour historic sites as often as we could." He gazed dreamily at the babies. "Someday we'll take the kids abroad."

"I'm envious." Since there was no one else nearby, Zora added, "Any further word from my charming ex?"

"His attorney indicated he'll comply with the law," Edmond said. "I did forward your list of expenses, but I've heard nothing since."

"Thanks, and I'm sorry to bring this up when you must be exhausted." Zora had spoken without thinking.

"I took a nap this morning." The new father grinned. "I went home and crashed after dropping Dawn at school." The excited seven-year-old had visited the hospital early to meet her new cousins, after spending the night with Karen.

"You've adjusted well to fatherhood." As Melissa's former housemate, Zora recalled that her friend's marriage had broken up over Edmond's refusal to have children.

"I'm grateful for the second chance. I had no idea what I was missing." Joy shone from his face.

A lot of events had changed Edmond, from accepting custody of his niece after his sister went to prison for robbery to the discovery that Melissa had "adopted" three embryos. Parenting Dawn had awakened Edmond's suppressed instincts, and his renewed love for his once and future wife had filled in the rest.

Once, Zora had believed Andrew might undergo a similar change of heart. Witnessing his cruelty to Lin had erased the last of her delusions, however. That, and being around Lucky. He demonstrated how a man ought to behave, in contrast to her father, her stepfather and her ex-husband.

A touch of heartburn roused Zora with a reminder that she ought to eat. "I'm going to the cafeteria," she told Edmond. "Please assure Melissa I'll visit her later."

"I'll do that," he said. "And soon she'll be visiting you in the maternity ward, too."

"That's true, isn't it?" When Lucky installed the cribs last night, it had emphasized to Zora that soon her babies would emerge into the world. Despite an eagerness to lighten her physical load, she wasn't sure she was ready to cope. But then, what single mother *was* ready to cope with twins?

On the ground floor, receptionist Caroline Carter waved her to a halt. "I have something for you. Can you hang on a minute?"

"Sure."

The young woman darted into her nearby office, returning with a children's book. "Sorry it's not wrapped, but I wanted to catch you before your leave starts."

"How beautiful!" Zora traced a finger over the stunning cover photograph of a butterfly. The book described how to study nature in your backyard, a topic she found especially relevant in view of the fact that her home was located next to an estuary.

"Nurse Harper Gladstone took the photos," Caroline said. "And her husband wrote the text."

Harper, a widow with a young daughter, had married a biology teacher. "It's perfect. Thank you."

"Enjoy your lunch. Oh!" With a confidential air, Caroline leaned closer, her brown eyes alight with her favorite subject: gossip. "Did you hear that Vince Adams assaulted a woman?"

Zora couldn't breathe. Apparently, the news had spread. Yet Caroline didn't seem to realize she was addressing the target of that assault. "Who told you that?"

"Laird," the receptionist said.

Since he had an office near Dr. Rayburn's, he must have caught wind of the confidential discussions. What a creep to shoot his mouth off! "He isn't always truthful." That was the best Zora could do.

"Yes, but he usually has reliable sources." Caroline shrugged. "Do you suppose it will spoil the press conference?"

"The less we talk about it, the better." Zora hoped the other woman would heed her warning.

"You're right." Caroline wrinkled her nose. "I keep swearing I'm going to stop spreading rumors. It's addictive, though."

"Thanks for the book. I'm sure the twins and I will enjoy it." On that note, Zora beelined for the cafeteria.

If word of what Vince had done reached the media, how would that affect the billionaire's donation? And if her name became attached to the rumor, there was no predicting what the reporters would say. The notion of the press camping out on Karen's lawn horrified her. Whiffs of swamp gas might discourage them, but she doubted it.

Zora decided not to mention the story to her friends. As she'd said to Caroline, the more discreet they were, the less risk the press conference would be disrupted.

THE STAFF, REPORTERS and VIPs filled the auditorium, leaving Lucky and a scattering of press to line the edges. Standing in the back above the steeply raked rows, he studied the scene uneasily.

Seated on the stage with the administrator, the public relations director, the corporate vice president and the Adamses, Cole appeared relaxed and cheerful. He evidently didn't notice what Lucky considered warning signs that something was going to go wrong.

Vince's ruddy complexion was flushed and, judging by his gait when mounting the steps, he'd imbibed more than he should have at the reception. While he sprawled on his chair with his legs apart, Portia's shoulders were painfully stiff beneath her ivory suit jacket. Her gaze traveled frequently to her daughters, who fidgeted in the front row beside their grandmother.

Around Lucky, more members of the press squeezed in, with cameras bearing the logos of LA news teams and a couple of national networks. He hadn't seen this much media since Cole presented a speech on men's declining sperm rates, sparking a furor that had blown the matter wildly out of proportion. Surely Dr. Rattigan's involvement couldn't account for this much interest, but what did?

Next to him, a reporter murmured to a photographer, "Wonder if Adams can keep his hands to himself on stage? That PR lady's awfully pretty."

"And he's well oiled," the other man responded. "Hey, it's a slow news day. We can always hope."

Anxiety churned in Lucky's stomach. What had these guys heard? He was grateful that Keely had driven Zora home earlier, sparing her any immediate fallout.

On the stage, Jennifer Martin took the microphone. After a brief greeting, she introduced Medical Center Management Vice President Chandra Yashimoto.

The dark-haired executive, whose striking black-and-white suit rivaled Portia's for elegance, glided to center stage. With a practiced smile, she sketched the history of the medical center's transformation from a community hospital to a national center for fertility and maternity care.

When she cited the importance of Dr. Cole Rattigan, Lucky braced for an audience reaction. If reporters planned to revive their silly stories terming him Dr. Baby Crisis, they'd start lobbing questions now. But no one reacted.

They seemed to be waiting. For what?

Ms. Yashimoto didn't call on Dr. Rayburn, whose furrowed brow reflected a less than enthusiastic attitude, nor did she ask Cole to speak. Instead, she cut to the announcement: Safe Harbor was poised to become an international center for the treatment of and research into men's fertility, thanks to a twenty-million-dollar gift from San Diego financier Vincent Adams and his wife, both of whom were—according to Chandra—well-known philanthropists.

Lights flashed and lenses clicked as Vince strode to the front and shook hands with the vice president. A staff photographer captured the moment, but to Lucky it seemed that others snapped only perfunctory shots.

"Thank you, Chandra." Vince beamed, in his element as the center of attention. "This program means more to me than merely putting my name on a building. It means leaving a legacy of children, mine and other men's, that will last until the end of time."

"There's modesty for you," the nearby reporter observed in a low tone.

"This week, my wife and I moved forward in our quest to expand our family," Vince continued. "My wife prefers that I not go into detail, but thanks to Dr. Rattigan, we expect to have a blessed event of our own by next year."

Portia's eyes narrowed. No doubt she'd asked him to keep that private, too, especially since they hadn't implanted the embryos yet.

The reporter murmured, "I wonder if she'll be the only woman popping out his offspring."

Was the man referring to Zora? Lucky wouldn't put it past the more irresponsible members of the press to imply that her pregnancy was the result of a liaison with Vince. Never mind facts or her DNA test—they'd drag her name through the mud.

When Vince paused for breath, a man in a central row scrambled to his feet. "Mr. Adams, this morning your former personal assistant Geneva Gabriel filed a five-million-dollar lawsuit against you in San Diego Superior Court, alleging sexual assault. We understand the district attorney is investigating. Care to comment?"

That explained the reporters' snide exchanges! Lucky experienced a spurt of relief, then immediately regretted it. He was sorry that Ms. Gabriel had suffered, too.

"She's just out for my money." Vince spluttered with fury. "I fired that witch because she's stupid and incompetent."

Chandra Yashimoto stood frozen. Cole's face registered his confusion, while Lucky could have sworn Mark Rayburn was barely suppressing a smile.

Jennifer rose to the occasion, literally. Crossing the stage to seize the microphone again, she said, "I'm sure Mr. Adams will have his attorney respond to your questions. My assistant is handing out a press release with the details of Mr. and Mrs. Adams' generous gift. Thank you for joining us."

After a few inaudible words to Vince, she steered him and Portia toward a side door. Shaking with anger, the billionaire gestured at the front row, summoning his daughters. Tiffany might have stood her ground, but when Amber raced up the steps, the older girl followed.

Cole and the others left the stage via a second exit. Unable to reach them as the crowd filled the aisles, Lucky shuffled out with the rest of the audience.

In the corridor, he passed Laird, who'd shanghaied a couple of puzzled reporters. "I'm embarrassed to be associated with a hospital that would accept money from a man like Vince Adams," the man announced. "That's why I'm handing in my notice and joining a private practice in Newport Beach. My name is Laird Maclaine."

A listener thrust out a small mic. "Are you a doctor in the men's fertility program?"

"I'm the staff psychologist."

"You're the staff opportunist," Lucky called, and dodged away. He wove through the milling assemblage, in case his doctor had been hemmed in by the press. He'd learned from experience that a show of muscle could prove handy.

Rounding a corner, he spotted a small group bunched near the staff entrance—the Adamses and the public relations director. All Lucky could see of the man blocking their escape was his fedora.

"You're in no condition to drive." Rod's voice was shrill with emotion. "The girls stay here."

"Get out of my way, Vintner." The bigger man towered over his opponent.

"Rod, you're making things worse." That was Portia, hovering beside her daughters. Jennifer, the only non-family member of the group, regarded the scene with uncertainty.

Where was Mark? The administrator, a former football player, was a physical match for Vince, but he must be occupied whisking Cole and Chandra out of harm's way.

"You're drunk," Rod persisted. "I'll take the girls to their grandmother." They'd left Helen behind in their rush, Lucky saw.

"Out of our way!" Vince shoved Rod, hard. The girls gasped as the smaller man staggered and fell against the wall. When blood spurted from his nose, Vince raised his fists in a victory gesture.

Rage surged in Lucky at the man's brutality. His fury mounted when the billionaire clamped onto Amber's wrist. "Let's go."

His younger daughter wriggled fruitlessly. "We're not supposed to get in a car with a drunk driver."

"Shut up." Vince yanked the girl toward the exit.

"Leave her alone!" Tiffany screamed.

As their stepfather wrenched open the door, Lucky barreled forward. The others parted, leaving him a clear shot at the distracted billionaire, who half turned to gape at him.

Lucky's kick hit its target: Vince's knee. With a cry of pain, the big man released Amber and stumbled out into the parking area reserved for administrators.

"Let's get out of here." Tiffany gestured to her sister. "Dad needs a doctor." Clearly, she meant Rod.

"Never mind him. You're both coming with us," their mother snapped.

"No." Tiffany slid an arm around the dazed Rod, who had a tissue pressed to his nose. "Thank you, Lucky."

"My pleasure."

Portia flinched as, outside, her husband bellowed for her. "He's too impaired to drive," Lucky warned, following her through the door. "Please stop him before he injures someone."

She glared. "Mind your own business."

"Where are the girls?" Vince roared, standing between his high-performance sports coupe and Dr. Rayburn's sedan.

"They're staying," Lucky retorted.

"I'll have you fired for this," the billionaire snarled.

"You planning to push me around, too?" Lucky demanded. "Or do you only attack people smaller than you?"

He could see Vince weighing the urge to punch him out. The man might have tried, but a shift of position put too much weight on his injured knee and he stumbled and then produced a deep groan. Regaining his balance with a hand on the sedan, the man snarled at his wife, "In the car. Now!"

"Let her drive," Lucky said. "For both your sakes."

"Shut up, you punk."

Mouth pressed into a thin line, Portia slid into the passenger seat while Vince got behind the wheel. How sad that she'd thrown in her lot with her husband, willing to sacrifice her safety to maintain her wealth and status. Worse, she'd been ready to risk her daughters' safety, too.

A hand on Lucky's arm alerted him to Jennifer's presence. Holding her phone in the other hand, she said, "Thanks for intervening. I arranged with Mark to make sure Rod gets medical treatment and the girls stay with their grandmother."

"Watch out!"

They beat a quick retreat as the sports car shot in reverse. After scraping the bumper of another car, Vince twisted the wheel, hit the gas and zoomed forward. He and Portia disappeared around the building.

"I'm calling the cops." Lucky took out his cell. "That's a hit-and-run. Also, he shouldn't be driving in his condition."

"Good." Jennifer straightened her spine. "I'd better corral the press. I don't want them harassing the staff."

Lucky thought of Laird. "Nor do we want the staff taking advantage of this mess."

Despite a puzzled glance, she didn't request an explanation. Duty was calling, and she hurried inside.

He dialed 911 and explained the situation to the dispatcher. Although Lucky hadn't observed which direction Vince took, the Adamses' beach cottage lay south of here. The most direct route would be along Pacific Coast Highway.

The dispatcher thanked him and said she'd alert patrol officers to be on the lookout. One would stop by to take a report about the hit-and-run, as well.

Bathed in October sunlight, Lucky eased his breathing. He'd never imagined such a devastating outcome of today's announcement. There was nothing anyone could have done to prevent this, he supposed. The lawsuit filing had changed everything.

Damn Vince and his arrogance. But at least the girls were safe. As for Rod's injury, the man had every right to report the assault and to sue for damages. However, he'd learned a hard lesson about the difficulties of fighting Vince in court.

Checking his phone, Lucky saw he'd missed a call from Zora. He returned it, and after two rings, her excited voice said, "Lucky! Keely's driving me to the hospital."

"Why?"

"I'm in labor!" she said happily.

"Everything's okay?"

"Yes—the pains aren't bad yet," she said. "I called ahead and they're setting up a C-section. Honestly, I was surprised what a relief it is. And the day after Melissa! Must be fate."

He gave a low chuckle. "Well, if that doesn't put the cap on an already over-the-top day."

"What happened?" She must not have been following the news. He presumed that radio reporters were already describing the brouhaha on the air.

"Vince's former assistant is suing him for sexual assault," Lucky told her. "He stalked out in a huff. Guess you're not the only one he's victimized."

"I hope she nails him to the wall."

"Five million dollars' worth of wall," he agreed.

"Yay for her." Then Zora gasped, "Watch out!"

"What…?"

The call went dead.

Inside Lucky, fear tightened into a knot. Had there been an accident? Surely not, yet…

The shortest route from Karen's house to the hospital was via Pacific Coast Highway—directly in Vince's path. His heart nearly stopped.

Don't be ridiculous.

On his phone, Lucky pressed Zora's number. He listened, struggling for calm, as it rang and rang, then went to voice mail.

He heard a siren in the distance. Then another. They sounded as if they were heading for Coast Highway.

Lucky began to pray.

Chapter Seventeen

The sports car appeared out of nowhere, weaving madly across lanes, and only Keely's swift veer to the right prevented a crash. Overcorrecting, the other car swerved, hit the curb and went airborne.

With a horrifying crunch, it landed on its roof. Shaken, Zora realized that she'd recognized the occupants as they sped past: Vince and Portia.

A siren shrilled almost instantly. Within seconds, a patrol cruiser and a fire truck swarmed in, followed by paramedics. An officer stopped behind Keely's brown sedan, which was parked on the right shoulder.

The police had been watching for Vince's car, he explained while examining Keely's license. After asking whether the two women were injured—neither was—he prepared to take their statements.

Zora cried out as another pain gripped her. "She's in labor," Keely explained.

"I'll call for another ambulance."

"We're only two miles from the hospital. It'll be faster if I drive," Keely said. "Don't worry. I'm a nurse."

After radioing the dispatcher, the officer offered to follow them in case they required aid, and they accepted. As they drove, Zora and Keely listened to a news station's account of billionaire Vince Adams facing a harassment lawsuit. There was no mention of the crash yet.

As the initial shock wore off, Zora recalled Vince's puffy face behind the windshield and Portia's terrified expression. How weird that the Adamses had nearly hit them. Since she hadn't observed any reporters in pursuit, Vince had no one but his arrogance to blame for his speeding.

However, he was probably in no condition to blame anyone. And what about Portia?

Zora regarded Keely, who'd remained stoic throughout the incident. "That was awful. Do you suppose they're…?"

"Badly injured or worse, unless they had their seat belts fastened." Swinging onto Hospital Way ahead of the cruiser, the nurse said, "I don't believe there was anyone else in the car."

The girls. How could Zora have forgotten them? "I sure hope not."

They stopped at the maternity entrance. Staffers rushed out with a gurney to assist them.

Keely checked a message on her phone. "Dr. Brennan's on site. She'll do the surgery."

"Fantastic." That was reassuring.

"They have the pediatricians prepping, too." There'd be one for each twin, the doctor had said earlier.

"Okay." After the near miss on the road, Zora had no strength left. Fortunately, she could simply lie back and entrust her care to the experts.

Her thoughts returned to the Adamses. Vince might be a repulsive man, but she'd never wished him dead. And certainly not Portia. How badly were they hurt? How would this affect their daughters?

As Zora was transferred onto the gurney, Lucky raced to her, breathing hard. "Is she okay? Zora?"

"I'm fine. Sorry I left you dangling." In the heat of the moment, she'd forgotten their interrupted conversation. Later, she'd been vaguely aware of her cell ringing, but had been too overwrought to answer.

He stared down, desperately drinking in the sight of her. She'd never seen him so shaken.

"The Adamses nearly hit us." Zora stroked his arm, yearning to take away his tormented expression. "Keely steered out of their path."

"What about Vince and Portia?"

"We saw their car flip over," Keely said, joining them after conferring with the officer. "Beyond that, I have no idea."

Lucky swept the older nurse into a hug. "Bless you!"

"I didn't sneeze," she said tartly.

"You kept a cool head, from what I hear," Lucky responded.

Keely extricated herself from the hug. "Anyone else would have done the same."

"Not necessarily." Lucky turned to Zora. "How's my sweetheart?"

"Still trembling." Lying on the gurney, Zora was glad when he took her hand, his strength flowing into her. She wished *he* was the babies' father. Then he could stay with her, comfort her and share her joy.

An orderly moved the gurney forward, toward the entrance. "I'll stay with her after I answer a few questions for the police," Keely told Lucky.

"So will I."

"If you wish, but how is Dr. Rattigan handling all this?" the older woman asked.

"I have no idea."

Reminded that their plans for the future might have been crushed today, Zora felt a twinge of concern. "You should check on him."

"I'll text you when she goes into surgery," Keely volunteered. "They won't let you in, anyway."

Another spasm seized Zora. "Ow!" A curse word slipped out. How did women bear this for hours and hours?

She was very glad she was having a C-section and the doctor would give her something to stop the labor.

As the contraction eased, she wished Lucky would stay. But when he excused himself to attend to his doctor, Zora merely nodded.

"Later," she whispered into the air.

ZORA WAS SAFE. Yes, there were risks in surgery and childbirth, but nothing like what Lucky had feared: a head-on smashup at high speed, pieces of car scattered across the highway, horrifying injuries to the occupants.

He'd witnessed the aftermath of such tragedies as an ambulance driver and a paramedic. The fact that Safe Harbor Medical didn't have an emergency room had added to its appeal when he'd joined the staff, because he didn't have to witness the arrival of trauma patients and relive those terrible memories. But today they'd hit him full force.

I love her, Lucky acknowledged as the gurney vanished into admitting. It was foolish and irrational and inescapable. He had no idea when he'd fallen in love with Zora, or what to do about it.

He'd clung to his ideals of perfection since his parents' deaths. If they had a family at the ideal time and in the ideal circumstances, money problems didn't force parents to neglect their children's internal struggles and teenagers didn't have to work such long hours that they rebelled—or so he'd rationalized.

He'd been trying to control the future, to prevent a repeat of his family's tragedies. But danger could strike without warning, as it had today. How stubbornly blind he'd been to his own flaws, criticizing Zora's illusions while harboring his own.

Yet she was still having another man's babies. Even a slug like Andrew would surely visit them, and there remained a possibility—remote, but real—that she would reconcile with her ex. Lucky might love her so hard and deep that his entire soul throbbed with it, only to have her torn away from him.

He could do nothing about it while she was in surgery. Frustrated, he decided to make himself useful elsewhere.

Since people gathered in a central location in a crisis, Lucky set out for the cafeteria. En route, he passed the elevators, one of which opened to reveal a welcome pair: Karen, her expression worried, and Rod, holding a cold pack to his nose.

Lucky halted. "I hope it's not broken."

"No, fortunately," Karen said. "They X-rayed him and gave him pain pills."

"Hurts to talk," Rod muttered.

Lucky didn't doubt that. "Zora's having the twins. Keely's with her." He filled them in on the details.

"I'm so glad they're okay," Karen said.

"The girls." Rod peered down the hall. "Where are they?"

"Helen said she was going to get them something to eat. Let's try the cafeteria."

Sure enough, they spotted Tiffany and Amber huddled with their grandmother at a table. Doctors, nurses and other staffers were sprinkled around the large room. Although some were eating dinner, most appeared to be waiting for news. Cole looked tense but composed, drinking coffee alongside Dr. Tartikoff.

From the food service area, Jennifer greeted them and asked Rod how he was feeling. Her dark hair was rumpled and her mascara had smeared. Today's events must be a PR director's nightmare.

"Thank you," she said after her questions had been answered. "Now I'm sure you're eager to join your daughters."

Rod agreed, and off he went with Karen. Lucky lingered, unsure where he could help the most.

"Any word about the Adamses?" he asked.

"So far, only that the police are on the scene."

"Well, I have a little more info than that."

She listened intently to the account of Zora and Keely's close call. "Thank heaven they escaped," she said, then raised a hand for silence. "Hang on. I'm monitoring news reports." She listened on her earpiece before saying, "No updates."

"Where's the press?" Lucky had expected to find them crowding the hallways.

"They went haring off to the crash scene," she said. "The police public information officer is handling them, although I'm also receiving calls for our reaction."

"What kind of reaction?" How could anyone respond to such a complex situation?

"Our official position is that our thoughts and prayers are with their family," Jennifer said.

"That sounds right." Lucky admired the publicist more than ever.

"Keep on the alert for stray reporters, will you?" she asked. "We can't let them eavesdrop or hassle people."

"Agreed." While he respected the job of the media, this was a traumatic enough situation without the press breaching people's privacy.

"There should be a counselor on hand. For some reason, I can't reach Laird," Jennifer fretted.

"He's leaving for private practice." Lucky repeated what he'd heard the psychologist announce.

She groaned. "Great timing. I'll arrange for an outside crisis counselor."

A murmur ran through the room. Tony and Mark had just entered. The attorney strode over to the girls' table and spoke in a low voice. The group, including Rod and Karen, got up and accompanied him out.

Lucky's chest clenched. This couldn't be good.

Once the girls and their entourage had departed and

Jennifer gave the all clear from the hall, Mark took a position in full view of everyone. Thanks to his height and deep baritone, he had no trouble commanding attention.

"I'm sure you've heard that Mr. and Mrs. Adams were involved in a single-car crash on Coast Highway," he said. "I've just received word from the police chief that both of them died at the scene."

Gasps and a few sobs rose from the crowd. Even Lucky, angry as he'd been at Vince, was shocked by their deaths. Yet this could have been worse, much worse. Tiff and Amber might have died, too, if he and Rod hadn't prevented the girls' parents from forcing them into the car.

Mark resumed addressing the staff. "For those of you wondering how this will affect the men's fertility program, I'm afraid we don't have an answer on that yet. Any other questions?"

There were a few, which the director fielded with complete frankness. Then a buzz of conversation broke out as staffers shared their grief with each other.

At a tap on his arm, Lucky swung around to meet Betsy Raditch's solemn gaze. "I heard Zora's having her babies," she said. "Have you talked to her?"

"Yes. Did you know she and Keely had a near miss on the road?"

"What do you mean?"

He repeated the story. The nursing supervisor clamped her hand over her mouth. "That was close!"

"She should be in surgery now," Lucky added.

"I'll tell Andrew," Betsy said. "And, Lucky, I heard what you did, keeping Rod's daughters safe. That was heroic."

"Thanks, but I don't deserve that," Lucky responded. "Heroes are people who risk their safety, like Rod. I knew I was a match for that—" in view of Vince's demise, he decided against using a harsh term "—that man."

"You and Rod both deserve credit," the nursing supervisor said. "Well, I'd better get moving. Some of my nurses are in shock, and we have a hospital to run."

"Absolutely right." If Lucky had a supervisory position like hers, he'd be eager to support his nurses, too.

Outside the cafeteria, Cole caught up with him. "We're holding a strategy session in Dr. Tartikoff's office. You should be part of it."

"I'd like that." Lucky joined his doctor and a handful of others. To be included with this prestigious group was an honor, and his future might depend on what they devised.

All the same, en route to the fifth floor, his thoughts were mostly on Zora. She'd been his collaborator this past month, as invested as he was in trying to ensure the billionaire's gift. All she'd requested was for him to stop nagging her.

She'd kept Vince's hateful harassment a secret, no doubt to prevent this type of blowup. What had she gained by it? Her position and her advancement didn't depend on the program's expansion.

She did it for me. From simple generosity, or because she hadn't been able to bear the prospect of Lucky leaving? Had Zora started loving him, too, perhaps without realizing it?

If Andrew reached her first, would she still fail to recognize that her heart belonged to Lucky?

Suddenly he couldn't wait to be with her. But Dr. Rattigan was counting on Lucky's input.

He steeled himself to have patience. In view of Andrew's track record, there was no reason to assume he'd show up promptly.

The distinguished group of top staffers, including several whom Owen Tartikoff had brought with him from his Boston practice, gathered around the conference table in the fertility director's office. They included Alec Denny, the director of laboratories, and Jan Garcia Sargent, head of the egg donor program.

For the next hour, they brainstormed, tossing out the names of distinguished foundations, government grant programs and Silicon Valley billionaires. Could or would any of them respond—let alone quickly enough to purchase the dental building?

Just as they were about to call it a night, the administrator entered. Dr. Rayburn's dark eyes were rimmed with red.

"Have a seat." Lucky vacated his chair, since all the others were taken.

The big man accepted the offer. "Considering you're a hero, I shouldn't, but I've had a rough day. As we all have."

Lucky decided not to bother arguing about the hero designation. No one questioned it, so apparently they'd all heard the tale.

"On such a terrible day, I'm pleased to bring good news." When Mark coughed, Lucky fetched him a glass of water from the sideboard. The administrator swallowed a few gulps before continuing. "Portia's mother, Helen Pepper, is a very kind woman. In the midst of her grief, she informed me that her daughter and son-in-law placed their estate in a living trust. They designated her as the successor trustee on behalf of the couple's children."

Lucky had assumed Vince's money would be tied up for a year or more as the estate was settled. Without a living trust, probate in California could be a lengthy, expensive and complicated process.

"She and her granddaughters intend to carry out the Adamses' wishes to donate twenty million dollars to our program." A smile broke through Mark's weariness. "And a million dollars to the Oahu Lane Animal Shelter, which appears to be a favorite of the girls."

Around the table, the others expressed relief and gratitude. "I hate to raise the question, but how soon can this happen?" Cole asked. "That building will be snapped up quickly."

"Helen plans to talk to an attorney tomorrow." Mark downed more water. "She's agreed to let Jennifer Martin and Ms. Yashimoto arrange the funeral while she looks into setting up a foundation to underwrite the men's program. She said that having her daughter and son-in-law's names on the building will be a fitting tribute."

Lucky was pleased that they'd include Portia's name. She deserved it.

The news buoyed the exhausted participants, though no one was happy about the circumstances. The impact of today's events would play out in everyone's emotions for a long time, including Lucky's.

A glance at his watch sent his heart speeding off. Several hours had passed since he'd last seen Zora. He'd received texts from Keely, indicating the C-section had gone well. By now, the new mom should be out of the recovery room, which meant he'd finally be able to visit.

After excusing himself, he hurried down to the third floor. Despite his eagerness to reach Zora, the window of the intermediate care nursery drew him irresistibly.

He spotted Melissa and Edmond's triplets—had it really been only two nights since their birth?—and a sprinkling of other newborns. Among the half dozen babies in clear isolettes, he wasn't sure which were Zora's, but if he had to bet, he'd put his money on a red-haired little girl and the blond boy beside her. Both appeared alert and healthy.

At the nurses' station, Lucky obtained Zora's room number. "Mr. Raditch is with her," a nurse advised him.

A lump stuck in Lucky's throat. He hadn't thought Andrew would arrive so fast.

Why was he here? To stake his claim? He *was* the babies' father. But it was his claim on *Zora* that worried Lucky most.

It was up to her whether she would reconcile with Andrew, but Lucky didn't intend to let her go without a fight. He'd waited too long already to realize that she was the perfect woman for him.

Chapter Eighteen

The first thing that occurred to Zora when her ex-husband entered was, *You're the wrong man.*

She longed for Lucky's honest, caring presence. Why hadn't she told him she wanted him to stay with her, that he was the most important person in her life? Sure, it meant taking a big emotional risk. Maybe he'd never accept her, flaws and all, but something about the way he gazed at her said otherwise. She'd taken leaps of faith, over and over, with the unworthy Andrew. Now she'd let Lucky go off without asking for what meant the most to her—keeping him close.

He must be busy, though, with the hospital in an uproar. Keely had brought news of Vince and Portia's deaths, and the two women had shared their turbulent reactions. Zora supposed the aftermath would affect her for a long while. Her heart went out to Tiffany and Amber on the loss of their mother, but mostly she was thankful she and Keely had escaped injury.

After Keely left for dinner, Edmond had peeked in. He'd been visiting his wife and triplets, and stayed just long enough to express his best wishes and present a gorgeous bouquet that perfumed the room.

And now here was her ex-husband. "So you had the babies." Andrew hovered near the exit as if fearing a giant clamp might drop from the ceiling to hold him in place, forcing him to—what?—take responsibility? "They look, uh, cute."

That was the sum of his reaction? When Zora had cradled the babies after their delivery, their delicate scent and wonder-filled faces had instantly become engraved on her heart. Elizabeth had a tumble of reddish-brown hair and inquisitive gray eyes, while the boy was blond with bright blue eyes. As she crooned to each of them, she'd been rewarded with a gaze of pure devotion.

She'd have died for them. Their father thought they were, *uh, cute.*

Andrew shifted from one foot to the other. "Have you picked names?"

"The girl's Elizabeth."

"Like my mother."

"That's right." She waited, wondering if he had ideas about the boy's name. What a silly fantasy she'd harbored, that he would leap at the chance, yet the moment had played through her mind so often that it almost seemed real: Andrew declaring that he'd always loved the name something-or-other, or that he couldn't wait to take Elizabeth and what's-his-name to the zoo. When he didn't speak, she blurted, "I might call the boy Luke." That ought to get his attention.

"Okay." Obviously, Andrew hadn't connected the name to Lucky. Maybe he was too busy preparing his next revelation, which was: "I'm transferring to New York."

He was moving out of state? That seemed sudden. "When?"

"Next month."

"Permanently?"

"That's the idea."

Once, this news would have arrowed pain deep into Zora's gut. Now, she experienced relief tinged with sadness for this self-absorbed man. He would never do anything more important than fathering these children, yet clearly he didn't intend to play much of a role in their upbringing. As she'd suspected, his bid for custody had been merely an attempt to one-up her.

"Good luck with that." She didn't bother to point out that states enforced each other's child-support requirements. Her lawyer could take care of the details.

"Do me a favor, would you?" Andrew muttered.

Warily, she asked, "What?"

"Let my mom play with the kids once in a while. She's into this grandmother thing."

He'd been around Zora since they were teenagers, yet he believed she might exclude Betsy? "You don't know me at all," she said.

"Is that a yes?" He sounded like a sales agent impatient to conclude a deal.

Zora lifted her head from the pillow for a better view of the man who used to dominate her world. Yep, he'd definitely shrunk. "Okay," she said. "Thanks for stopping by."

Andrew regarded her with a shade of disappointment. "That's it?"

He must have expected her to plead for him to stay in Safe Harbor. After Lin's rejection, his ego was hungry to be fed. "That's it. Sayonara."

He glared at her. "Whatever," he said, and stalked out.

The air smelled suddenly fresher, and the colors of the flowers intensified. Then the best thing of all happened.

Lucky peered in. Although his face could use a splash of water and his navy blue uniform had picked up bits of lint, he was the handsomest man in the world.

THE DISMAY ON Andrew's face as he stomped down the hall thrilled Lucky. "You knocked him down to size," he told Zora admiringly as he entered her room. "You're such a tiny thing but wow, you pack a punch."

She lifted an eyebrow. "You're just figuring that out?"

Careful to avoid jostling her, Lucky sat on the edge of the bed. "Among other things. A lot of them."

Including that his image of a perfect wife and kids had been nothing more than a defense mechanism to protect against the kind of devastation that had torn his family apart. That his delusion about controlling the future was as self-defeating as anything he'd accused her of. That he didn't see how he could go through life without this delightful, maddening woman.

"Did you figure out yet that you're in love with me?" As soon as the words flew out, blood rushed to her cheeks. "Oops. I didn't mean to say that aloud."

Lucky nearly bounced off the bed in glee. "Yes, I'm in love with you. Now tell me you're in love with me, too."

"Um…I have to think about it."

"Zora!" He could barely tolerate the delay.

She folded her arms. "What other things did you figure out today, smart guy?"

"That you have the most precious children in the world." Lucky visualized the babies again. "Your twins are the red-headed girl and the blond boy, right? I couldn't read the names on the isolettes."

Her face remained adorably flushed, this time with pride rather than embarrassment, he guessed. "Elizabeth and Luke."

Lucky couldn't have heard correctly. "You're giving him my name?"

"I'm trying it on for size." Zora shifted against the pillow.

Much as Lucky cherished the idea, it wouldn't be fair to the boy. "He should have his own name," he said. "How about Orlando?"

"Like the city in Florida?"

"Like my father." He'd meant to reserve that honor for his firstborn son. Well, this little guy had taken over that spot in Lucky's heart.

"I might go for that," Zora responded. "But if you name him, you might have to claim him."

"I'm claiming both of them." Lucky smiled at the dear, freckled person studying him expectantly.

"You don't still consider them Andrew's children?"

Her question startled him. "I consider them *your* children. I meant that *you* considered them Andrew's children."

"Really?"

"I believed you might forgive him for past sins if he, shall we say, embraced the miracle of fatherhood."

Zora's nose wrinkled. "I was an idiot. I believed love could conquer all, but it can't conquer heartlessness. Or a weak character. Or—should I go on abusing him, or is that enough?"

"For now, because I have something important to say." Lucky gathered his courage. "Let's get back to the part where I confess I'm in love with you."

Why didn't she respond in kind? But perhaps she was waiting for him to lay out the whole picture. Well, he'd better start by being cautious. Although it appeared Lucky might be able to stay in Safe Harbor, there was no guarantee he'd be hired in the new program. He might not be as hung up on financial security as before, but he couldn't ask for a commitment from Zora without pointing out that his situation was still unsettled.

"Another thing I discovered today was that I couldn't bear to leave Safe Harbor unless you go with me," he blurted. "Will you?"

"You have to go?" Her joy dimmed. "But…that means leaving our friends."

"I'll make it worth your while."

"I'd go with you in a heartbeat," Zora answered. "Except…"

"What?" His breath caught.

"My sister did that and ended up unmarried and unloved." She stared down at her hands.

"Such trust," he murmured.

She folded her arms and hunkered down.

His impatience nearly exploded. But what did he expect, reassurance before he popped the question? *Put it out there, fella. Quit stalling.*

From the zipper compartment in his wallet, Lucky produced a gold ring set with diamonds and emeralds. Then he slid off the bed and onto one knee. "Zora, will you marry me?"

She stared at him in astonishment. "What about your perfect family?"

He pushed past the lump in his throat. "You are my perfect family. You, Elizabeth and Orlando."

"But your plans…saving for a house…"

"I nearly lost you today," he said. "That put everything into perspective. I want you today, and tomorrow, and forever. Marry me, Zora."

"Yes."

"Yes?" He couldn't quite believe she'd said it so simply and plainly. "No ifs, ands or buts?"

"Don't be silly. I love you."

"I love you, too!" Hoisting himself onto the bed again, he showered kisses on her forehead and cheeks and mouth.

Chuckling, she held up the ring. "Let me put this on."

He straightened. "Of course."

As she angled it toward her finger, her forehead creased. "Where did you… This looks familiar."

"I borrowed it from Betsy." Lucky had run into the nursing supervisor in the hall and shared his plans. When he mentioned that he wished he had a token ring to present until he had a chance to buy a new one, Betsy had removed the heirloom from her finger and loaned it to him.

"Did she mention that I wore this ring during my marriage to Andrew?" Zora asked, laughing.

"She left out that part." Lucky sighed, sorry that he'd screwed up such an important detail. "I was planning for us to choose our rings together later."

Zora studied it fondly. "It's beautiful and it means a lot to Betsy. How sweet of her to loan it to us."

"This doesn't change your answer, does it? We *are* engaged, right?"

"You bet."

Sliding his arms around Zora, he leaned down for a long, tender kiss. She smelled of babies and happiness. Lucky's heart swelled as her arms closed around him and the two of them hung there, happily suspended in a private world.

A world they would share with their little guys. A world that would be full of bumps and twists and imperfections, exactly as it ought to be.

"For the record, I came to the conclusion that we loved each other long before you did," she whispered in his ear. "It didn't occur to you until today? Slow, slow."

Lucky grinned. "Guess I am. By the way, there's an excellent chance we won't have to leave Safe Harbor." Releasing her, he explained about Helen's proposal to fund the expansion.

"That's fantastic." Zora tapped her fingers together restlessly.

"What?" he asked.

"Maybe I shouldn't bring this up now."

"Let it out," Lucky told her. "If you have reservations, now's your chance to air them."

"It's not exactly a reservation."

"What is it?" He stroked her hair. Whatever the problem was, they'd deal with it.

"Your brother," Zora said.

Lucky blinked. He hadn't been expecting *that*. "What about him?"

"Do you still reject him for whatever he did?" she said earnestly. "Are you still so rigid?"

Despite an urge to protest that he could never forgive what Matthew had done, Lucky paused to reflect. This past month, he'd learned a lot from Zora's generous nature. While her weakness for Andrew had infuriated him, she'd also befriended Lin Lee, mended fences with Zady and regained her closeness with Betsy. He could use some of her grace.

"I'd like to tell you what happened," he said.

Zora gripped his hands. "Please do."

As Lucky began, the hospital faded around him and he was once more in his parents' convenience store in LA. He could hear the street traffic and smell the salty temptation of potato chips. When he looked up, a security mirror revealed a bulging image of shelves crammed with the odds and ends of a neighborhood market.

"My brother Matthew joined the navy at eighteen," he said. "I was proud of him, but that left me to juggle attending high school and helping my folks keep the store afloat." He'd unloaded supplies, stocked shelves, carried receipts to the bank and fetched change. He'd also operated the cash register many evenings late into the night.

"It must have been hard, missing school activities," Zora said.

"Yes, and I longed for the occasional evening to hang out with my friends." Lucky felt a twinge of his old resentment. "I rebelled in small ways. Sneaking a cigarette, showing up late or leaving early. Mom used to scowl and Dad complained that I was letting down the family while my brother risked his life for his country."

"How did you feel about that?" she asked.

"Guilty, but angry, too." In retrospect, his selfishness haunted him. Still, he owed her the whole truth. "One evening, we were supposed to close at nine, but my mother insisted on staying open late because customers kept drifting in. While she worked the register, she sent me into the storage room to open boxes of supplies we'd received that day and catalog the contents. I was furious."

"Where was your father?"

"He'd put in twelve hours and gone home exhausted." Lucky's gut twisted. "If I smoked on the premises, my mom would smell it. So I sneaked out the rear door into the alley."

Strange—he'd relived that night repeatedly in nightmares, yet now he had trouble dredging up the details. *Get it over with.*

"While I was outside, a junkie entered the store and demanded cash from my mother," he said. "The store surveillance tape showed he had a bulge in his jacket, but not whether it was a gun."

"How terrifying." Zora's gaze never strayed from Lucky's face. "What happened?"

"My mom collapsed." Lucky swallowed. "Later, the coroner said she died from stress cardiomyopathy, which is a response to overwhelming fear. A huge jolt of adrenaline can cause the heart to develop ventricular fibrillation—abnormal rhythms. She literally dropped dead."

Zora shivered. "I'm sorry. But you weren't at fault."

"If I'd been inside, I might have heard the robbery, rushed in and scared the creep away," Lucky said. "Maybe before Mom succumbed."

"If he did have a gun, he'd have killed you," she countered.

"I doubt he did." Lucky refused to let himself off that easily. "Anyway, he snatched a handful of cash and ran."

"Did they catch him?"

"More or less." His jaw tightened. "He was a meth addict—a couple of days later the police found him dead of an overdose, probably with drugs he bought at my mother's expense."

"And that didn't bring her back," she observed sympathetically.

"No, it didn't." The discovery of his mother lying on the floor, the sirens, the arrival of police and paramedics had blurred into a montage of pain. Worst of all had been accompanying the police to inform his sleepy, disbelieving father.

Lucky had feared his father might collapse, too. Instead, Orlando Mendez had thrown himself into his work. "He gave his all to that store. I offered to postpone college and put in longer hours, but he refused. Instead, he hired an assistant. Nearly a year later, we discovered the assistant was embezzling from us."

"That's terrible." Zora stroked his arm.

Lucky had had trouble believing anyone could take advantagc of pcoplc who were already suffering. Sadly, he and his father had learned otherwise.

"The guy fled to South America and we never recovered the money. A month after that, Dad died of an aneurysm," Lucky said grimly. "Literally, of a broken heart. I had to sell the store. There was barely enough to cover the debts and the funeral expenses."

That brought him to the bitter quarrel with Matthew. When his brother had attended their mother's funeral, he'd scarcely spoken. After their father's death, Matthew had blown up at Lucky.

"He accused me of contributing to our parents' deaths." Although the years had lessened his outrage, the memory stung. "He claimed I cheated him of his inheritance, that I'd used the profits from the sale of the store to pay for college. He even filed a theft report with the police. After they cleared me, Matthew informed our relatives I'd hidden the money and gotten away with it."

"Wow," Zora said. "That puts my quarrel with Zady in the shade."

As she spoke, guilt and regret flooded through Lucky.

"If I hadn't been such an immature jerk, we might have avoided the argument. In a way, he was right. I let everyone down with my irresponsible actions the night my mother died. And I vowed that I'd never do that again to anyone I cared about, yet I let you down with Vince."

"What?" Astonishment filled Zora's face.

To his dismay, a sob shook Lucky. He never cried. He was the strong one, the tough guy. But the idea that Zora had put up with that man's groping in order to protect Lucky's career was intolerable. "I'm glad he's dead. I'm sorry about his wife, but…" His hands formed fists. "I messed up. And I had the nerve to rag on you about *your* mistakes."

"Yeah, that was the worst thing. I mean, death and destruction and being estranged from your brother hardly count compared to your nagging."

Her mischievous tone had the desired effect of banishing his self-pity. "You little goof."

Zora reached out to cup his cheek. "You're a wonderful man, Lucky. You've carried this burden for too long. I don't think you need to forgive your brother as much as you need to forgive yourself."

"I let everyone down. I can't undo that." Her touch soothed him, though.

"How many people did you save as a paramedic?" she asked. "And according to what I heard, if not for you, Rod's daughters might have died today. You were a kid when you sneaked out for a smoke. I don't know if you can mend the rift with Matthew, but as for the rest, let it go, Lucky."

Relief spread through him, a healing balm. "When did you get so smart?"

"When I fell in love with the right man," she said.

Lucky hugged her again, careful of her surgical wound. "You don't mind sharing a house with Karen and Rod? We could rent an apartment."

"I'd rather stay there, if it's okay with you," she said. "It's like having a big family."

"I agree." While it might not be possible for that family to include his brother, Lucky intended to try.

They were starting fresh, a man and woman who'd stumbled and screwed up plenty. Yet the future gleamed ahead of them in rainbow colors, because together they were stronger and wiser than separately.

They'd have a lot more fun, too.

Chapter Nineteen

The adobe house had neatly trimmed bushes and a red tile roof, with striped woven curtains tied back at the windows. Mounting the porch steps, Lucky rubbed his damp palms on his jeans.

In response to his inquiry, a cousin had emailed that Matthew was stationed here in Point Hueneme, a few hours' drive to the north of Safe Harbor. Lucky hadn't even been sure how to say the town's name, which he'd learned on the internet was pronounced WY-nee-mee.

When he'd phoned, Matthew had cautiously agreed to meet with him. He'd suggested meeting at his house today while his wife and school-age children were attending a birthday party.

It might have been more sensible to choose a public place, Lucky mused. What if his brother threw a punch at him?

Well, he hadn't slammed down the phone or insulted Lucky. Although his tone had been wary, Lucky's mood was cautious, too.

Not finding a bell, he knocked, then wiped his palms on his pants again. Had Zora been this nervous when she'd prepared herself to see her sister? She must have waited like this, uncertain, anxious…

The door opened. Sixteen years had matured Matthew's olive face. He was, surprisingly, a couple of inches shorter than Lucky— *I must have grown.* Yet in every other respect, despite the passage of time, Matthew was incredibly familiar. In a rush, Lucky realized how much he'd missed the pal who'd taught him to play baseball when their dad was too busy and had advised him on which classes to choose in high school.

"Thanks for agreeing to meet me," Lucky said.

Matthew extended a strong, callused hand. They shook, and then his brother pulled him close and clapped his shoulder. "I'm glad you had the guts to make the first move."

"Damn," Lucky said. "If I start to cry, I'll be embarrassed."

"Nothing to be ashamed of." Releasing him, his brother moved aside to let him enter.

A couch and comfortable chairs, along with a bookshelf, TV and game system, filled the living room. On the wall hung a red, black and buff ceramic Aztec calendar almost identical to Lucky's. "Hey, we have the same interior decorator."

Matthew followed his gaze to the plaque. "It's like the one Grandpa and Grandma used to have."

"I'd forgotten."

"Aunt Maria and Uncle Carlos own it now. Man, I'm sorry." Matthew stood squarely balanced on both feet, his khaki T-shirt emphasizing the breadth of his chest and shoulders. "You should have been at those family gatherings all these years."

Their grandparents had died before their parents, so Lucky hadn't been denied the chance to say goodbye to them at least. As for the aunts and uncles, it had been their decision to exclude him without hearing his side. "I'm fine. Just got engaged, in fact."

"Fantastic!" Matt raised his hands to signal he had more to say. "Let me get this out. I nursed my anger at you for years, until gradually it dawned on me that I was angry about a lot of things that had nothing to do with you. At myself for not being there when our parents needed me. Also at leaving you to carry the burden. I worked such long hours that I ran off to join the navy to get away from the store."

Lucky had never suspected that his brother's motives in enlisting had included escape. Not that he blamed Matthew. "I resented working so hard, too. That's why I sneaked out for cigarettes, which was totally irresponsible. I should have been there with Mom that night."

"I wasn't there, either. Even though I'm proud to serve my country, I signed up partly for the wrong reasons." His brother shook his head. "The other day, looking at some new recruits, I noticed how young they were, and it hit me you were about that age when our parents died."

"Eighteen," Lucky recalled. "Grown-up."

Matt tilted his head. "A baby."

"So were you when you enlisted."

"That's no excuse for my behavior." A crooked smile brightened his brother's face. "Enough beating ourselves up. Can we put this in the past?"

"That's why I'm here," Lucky said.

"Tell me about this fiancée of yours," his brother said.

"I'll show you a picture." He took out his phone.

Soon they were lounging on the furniture, downing soft drinks and catching up on everything they'd missed.

"YOU'VE NEVER BEEN able to fix a pie crust as beautiful as mine." Playfully, Zady indicated the luscious apple pie on a side table reserved for Thanksgiving desserts. "I admit, your pecan pie looks yummy, but your crust isn't as shiny. The secret is to brush the unbaked crust with an egg mixed with a couple of tablespoons of cream."

Zora gave her sister a poke. They'd turned their old rivalry into friendly teasing since Zady had moved to town a few weeks earlier. "Insult it all you like. Lucky bought the pecan pie at the supermarket."

"You're kidding! You didn't bake your own pie?" Zady chuckled. "Mom would have a cow."

"Feel free to tell her."

"I doubt she's speaking to either of us since we informed her of your wedding after the fact."

At the reminder, Zora gazed happily down at the ring Lucky had placed there a week earlier. Although he'd offered to buy a more expensive one, she preferred this simple, classic design in gold. "I'm not sure which bothered her most, that I didn't invite her or that you served as my maid of honor."

She'd been a little saddened not to be able to include her mother. But after Mom's drunken behavior at Zora's first wedding and her cruel manipulations with Zady, Zora had stuck to her resolve to keep some distance between them. Afterward, she'd written her mother informing her of her marriage and asking for her blessing. There'd been no reply.

The wedding at the county's picturesque Old Courthouse had been modest but magical, thanks to the love flowing between the bride and groom. And they'd been surrounded by friends and family. While Betsy and Keely held the twins, Zady had served as maid of honor and Matthew as best man. Zora had immediately liked Matthew, as well as his dark-haired wife and children. They planned to hold another reunion at Christmas.

"Are you ladies squabbling?" Lucky's arm around Zora's waist restored her to the present. "You'll set a bad example for our children."

"It'll teach them to stick up for themselves," she countered, and rested her cheek on his shoulder. "Besides, Zady and I don't fight any more. Just a little sisterly competition."

"That's okay, then."

What a wonderful man she'd married, she thought, nestling against Lucky.

As for a honeymoon, that was on hold until the babies were old enough to wean and leave with others. When she and her husband took a trip, there'd be no interruptions, however cute.

"These little guys are ready for their nap." From the den, Betsy brought Orlando into the kitchen, yawning in his hand-crocheted blanket. On her finger glittered the ring that would always remind Zora of their close connection.

"Elizabeth's dozing, too." Keely cradled her precious charge.

"Much as I adore them, thank goodness they're asleep." Breast-feeding two babies consumed more energy than Zora had imagined, and she was grateful for the help. "I'm starving."

The aroma of roast turkey and stuffing had been wafting from the kitchen all afternoon. Tiffany and Amber had insisted on pitching in to help Karen cook, while Rod and Grandma Helen arranged the dining room.

"Upstairs we go," Betsy said. "Keely?"

The nurse gave a start. "Of course." Head lowered, she hurried after the older woman.

Keely had been acting distracted since the wedding. Guiltily, Zora reflected that she hadn't been paying much attention to her friend.

For a while, Keely had been upbeat, buoyed by the news of Laird's departure. As his replacement, the hospital had hired a family and child counselor named Franca Brightman, whom Edmond had recommended. Already, she was helping the Adams girls adjust to their loss.

But since the wedding, Keely had retreated into long silences. Now that Zora was on leave and no longer required rides to work, they had less chance to speak privately.

Today was hardly the occasion for a tête-à-tête, but Zora resolved to find a moment alone with Keely later. Perhaps she was suffering a posttraumatic reaction to their brush with death, or struggling to adjust to the many changes at the hospital.

With the purchase of the dental building, buzz filled the halls about the planned renovations and new staff to be hired. Exciting though it was, Zora remembered all the disruptions over the past few years as the hospital had been transformed. Perhaps that had contributed to Keely's downcast mood.

Her stomach growled as Tiffany and Amber paraded in and set hot dishes on the breakfast table, which would be used for serving. "I wish we lived here instead of at Grandma's," Amber said as she placed a casserole carefully on the tablecloth.

Tiffany glanced around. No sign of Helen. "I love Grandma, but honestly, we're underfoot in her house." Helen owned a two-bedroom cottage a few miles away.

"Especially with her arthritis," the younger girl added. "She's always cleaning up after us. I try to be neat but hey, I'm a kid."

Although newfound wealth had enabled Helen to hire a housekeeper to shop, cook and handle major cleaning, hosting a pair of active granddaughters was taking its toll, Zora had noted from the older woman's increasingly stiff movements. However, she respected that Helen chose not to buy a mansion or invest in more staff. She insisted on keeping the girls in touch with reality. In addition to sharing a bedroom, they would be transferring to public school next year.

Also, Tiff had enrolled in a dance class. Amber, who had loved to swim competitively until Vince turned every meet into a do-or-die situation, was easing into the sport again.

Partly to assist Helen, Rod had offered to relinquish his room to them and move in with Karen. The grandmother had replied firmly that she couldn't let the girls grow up in a home with a pair of unmarried adults sharing a bed.

Karen brought out a bowl of mashed potatoes, and Rod followed with a platter of sliced turkey. His daughters hurried into the kitchen to collect the salad and stuffing.

Helen joined them, along with Betsy and Keely. That was the whole group for today—Melissa, Edmond, Dawn and the triplets were dining with his parents, while Jack, Anya and their baby had flown to Colorado to share the holiday with her large family.

"I put the monitor by my place in the dining room," Keely told Zora. "That way, if the babies fuss, I can check on them. If you don't mind."

"Mind?" Zora repeated. "You're doing me a favor!"

"No problem." Keely avoided her eyes.

Before Zora could question her friend, she felt Lucky's hand on her spine, propelling her toward the food. "Serve yourself first. You're a nursing mommy."

Amid a chorus of agreement, she complied. Soon they were all seated, and after a prayer of gratitude for this special gathering, they dug into their heaped-high plates.

What a year it had been, Zora thought as she took in the beloved faces around the table. When a group of friends had moved into this house last February, they'd had no idea that by the end of November, there would be six babies born and three marriages.

"Have you found an apartment yet, Zady?" Betsy asked amid the chatter. Zora's sister was staying in a small unit at the Harbor Suites.

"Nothing I really love," Zady admitted.

Keely toyed with her food. In contrast to the others, she appeared to have little appetite for her meal.

Zora shot her a concerned glance. Keely ignored it.

"Can we have dessert?" Amber indicated the plate she'd cleaned at top speed.

"Where are your manners?" reproved her grandmother. "Not till everyone's finished."

"How about the pumpkin bread?" Amber persisted. "That isn't really dessert, is it, Grandma?"

"I suppose not." Seated between her granddaughters, Helen acquiesced fondly. "Why don't you bring in the plate for everyone?"

"I'll get it." To Zora's surprise, Rod sprang up. Usually the anesthesiologist moved at a slower pace than everyone else, and he'd milked his injured nose for sympathy until the bruising faded. He whisked out of the room, and Zora heard a cabinet open and shut in the kitchen.

"What's Dad doing?" Amber asked.

"I guess we'll find out," Tiffany said.

The slightly built man returned, jauntily hoisting the plate of pumpkin bread. When he set it in front of Karen, Zora saw a miniature van displayed in the center.

"What's this?" Their landlady lifted the little vehicle to inspect it.

"It's the first part of my surprise." Rod stood next to her, bouncing with anticipation. "That's a stand-in for the van I'm buying. I'll be taking delivery of it next week. It carries eight, so we can drive the girls and their friends. Helen, I made sure it was accessible for you to get in and out of."

"That's lovely." She sounded puzzled, though, and Zora suspected they all were. Why display this in the middle of Thanksgiving dinner?

"The doors and hood open," Rod prompted.

"It would be hard to drive it otherwise." Beside Zora, Lucky smirked at the other man.

Instead of riposting as he usually would, Rod cleared his throat. "I mean the miniature. Open the hood."

With a bemused expression, their landlady tipped it open and gasped. "Oh, Rod!"

"What is it? What is it?" The girls crowded around.

Karen held up a diamond engagement ring. "My gosh."

Rod dipped, suggestive of lowering himself to one knee, although he never quite touched the floor. "Will you make an honest man of me?"

Karen's mouth hung open. Then she gathered her wits. "Of course I will, you crazy man!" To the girls' cheers, she kissed him.

Zora could have sworn Helen's smile revealed a hint of relief. This meant the girls could move in with their father and new stepmother, while living only a few miles from their grandma.

"Congratulations." Betsy seemed as thrilled as the rest of them.

A soft sob on Zora's far side riveted her gaze to Keely. The woman appeared to be fighting tears.

"What's wrong?" Surely the nurse hadn't fallen in love with Rod. Zora had seen no sign of it.

"I don't mean to spoil the happy occasion." She sucked in air.

"Calm down and share what's bothering you," Zora urged. "Please."

Glumly, Keely answered. "You're all families now. Of course your sister should live here, too."

"Why?" Zady asked.

Keely didn't have to answer, because Zora understood. "You've been expecting us to ask you to leave?"

The older nurse nodded.

"No way," Lucky said.

"You belong here," Karen chimed in.

"She's your twin," Keely said doggedly. "It's only right."

Zora wished she'd addressed this issue long ago. It simply hadn't occurred to her. "You saved my life. The twins' lives, too."

Zady spoke up, too. "Keely, my sister and I have been feuding for years. Yeah, we love each other and we're friends again, but share a house? We'd be at each other's throats in five seconds."

"Blood on the floor," Lucky said calmly.

"No, you wouldn't." Keely refused to be comforted. "You're a member of her family, and I'm not."

"I can fix that," Zora said. "I hereby dub you the babies' honorary aunt. You are therefore a relative. And we love you."

There was a chorus of agreement. "Including me," Rod put in. "Don't tell anybody at work."

Keely joined in the ripple of laughter that greeted this remark. "Really?"

"Really," Zora said.

"Will you help me plan my wedding?" Karen asked. "Since my mother died last year, I've been wishing I had more family."

"You have?" Keely sniffled.

Their landlady gazed dreamily around the table. "Growing up, I wished I had a houseful of brothers and sisters, and other relatives to celebrate holidays. My wish has come true. Keely, you have a home here as long as you want it."

The nurse appeared too choked up to speak.

"Can we eat dessert now?" Amber asked.

"That's the best idea I've heard all day," Lucky said. "Aside from Rod and Karen getting married, and Keely becoming an honorary aunt to our children."

Zora couldn't have agreed more.

* * * * *

MILLS & BOON
Two superb collections!
40% OFF!
One Night with a REGENCY LORD
One Night with a TEMPTING PLAYBOY
ROBERTS FERRARELLA
ONE KISS IN... Paris
GRADY MACKENZIE MARTON
ONE KISS Miami
One Night with a SEDUCTIVE SHEIKH
GATES McARTHUR WEBBER
One Night with a GORGEOUS GREEK
MORGAN MONROE SHAW
HEWITT ELLIS
ONE KISS London
MARINELLI BROOKS STEELE